Sarah M. M. Turner has always loved writing and weaving fantastic stories filled with heroic characters and evil villains. As the third eldest of seven children, she took pleasure in reading bedtime stories to her young siblings – including numerous fanfictions she wrote herself. When not writing, she enjoys rereading a selection of stories by her favourite authors, singing opera and musical theatre, and dressing up in costume for a concert or Shakespeare Party.

Sarah loves to hear from her readers. You may contact her via her website or social media:

sarahmmturner.com
facebook.com/SarahMMTurner
instagram.com/sarah.m.m.turner

RHIANNON MCBRIDE AND THE DRAGON'S CUP

~A Fantasy Novel~

SARAH M. M. TURNER

Published by Sarah M.M. Turner
sarahmmturner.com

First published 2022

Copyright © Sarah M.M. Turner, 2022

 A catalogue record for this
book is available from the
National Library of Australia

ISBN 978 0 6456125 0 9 (pbk–YA)
ISBN 978 0 6456125 1 6 (ebk–YA)

Cover design by Joolz & Jarling—Julie Nicholls & Uwe Jarling
Map design by Sarah M.M. Turner and computerised by Peter Turner
Typeset by Helen Christie, Blue Wren Books

To my nieces and nephew,
Amariah, Naomi and Zachariah.
Thank you for bringing so much light
and joy into my life.

CONTENTS

KINGDOM OF ÁLNAIR

SEA OF DORLAND

Deadwater Cove

Mérosorc (Place of Exile)

Titus River

Enchanted Barrier

Ruined City of Glenwing

OLD ROAD OF VAROS

Forbidden Mountains

Pine Woods

White Rock Bay

SEA OF NILOR

Caves of The Fallen

To the ISLE OF FIRE

Wastelands

Farmland

Mt Perdus

Farmland

Town of Tolgor

Thaos Wood

Coral Bay

The Fell of Fiachra's Woe

City of Lothian

City of Ardara

Lake Tamesis

Gulf of Amdon

Finbar Forest

Farmland

ROAD

Langwell Hills

GRAYNOR ROAD

Valley of Dreams

Village of Wynoras

Shadow Pass

Idon River

Pool of Rememberance

Norgan Bight

Wildlands

Mt Solus

Del Enger Mountains

Underground city of the Rolvian Clan

Black Forest

Lumen Sea

Town of Belnight

ROAD

ROAD TO SHADOW PASS

Wildlands

Aidan Desert

SOLVANUIN OCEAN

Farmland

Ryegoth Academy

Réalta Lake

MAIN ROAD

Town of Salrock

Shaimar Forest

The High Wolds

Radamus Point

City of Cendillis

Cendillis Harbour

Dena River

ROAD

Heart of the Black Forest

Idon River

Farmland

ROAD TO ARDARA

Haldoron Bridge

Town of Kelmore

Valieoth Castle

Deer Park

ISLE OF CULHOS

Lagoon

Luwyneth Cove

Kinpar Rocks

Wildlands

Town of Melson

Boffin Bay

City of Graynor

Aureus Bay

N
NW NE
W E
SW SE
S

DAIRION OCEAN

MALPARS

To the uninhabitable REALM OF KHOSHEK

Author's Note

There are several names used in this book which are taken from various cultures in our world, along with many names and words from the ancient tongue of the dragons (Drakaron). The writer has done her best to provide to the reader a pronunciation guide for these words. However, she cannot guarantee they are 100% accurate. The reader should remember there may exist different versions of the spelling and pronunciation for the names from our world, and that Drakaron is a very old language, which is no longer spoken here.

Names

Aleda	*A-lee-da*	Izana	*ee-zah-na*
Arastar	*Ara-star*	Maiwen	*My-win*
Asaph	*A-saff*	Mórell	*More-el*
Baegolz	*Bay-golz*	Mórfran	*More-fran*
Cináed	*Kin-ahd*	Níall	*Ne-al*
Dairíon	*Die-re-on*	Nuallán	*Noo-al-ayne*
Daiki	*Die-key*	O'Faenart	*O-'Fay-Nart*
Edranel	*Ed-ra-nel*	Orthoríon	*Or-thor-re-on*
Elvanor	*EL-va-nor*	Raeden	*Ray-den*
Endrille	*En-'dril*	Ryegoth	*Rye-Goth*
Fendrel/Sados	*Fen-drel/Sar-dos*	Siana	*See-uh-na*
Fíachra	*Fee-ach-ra*	Sujan	*Sue-Juhn*
Fjenador	*Fee-en-a-dore*	Thandyl	*Th-an-dil*
Hikari	*Hee-kar-ee*	Valieoth	*VAL-e-oth*

Herbs/Plants

Entrose	*Ent-ross*	Erímos	*air-ih-mos*
Somlyne	*Som-lin*	Parvus	*Par-vus*
Thranlaire	*Thran-lair*	Síuld	*See-ul*

Dragon Breeds

Locations

Álnair	*Al-nar*	Ranos-kí-arda	*Ra-nos-kee-arda*
Cendillis	*Sen-del-es*	Rëalta	*Ray-al-ta*
Culhos	*Cul-hos*	Shaimar	*Shy-mar*
Dairíon	*Die-re-on*	Solus, (Mount)	*Sol-us*
Malpars	*Mal-pars*	Vetus svet	*Ve-tus sve-t*
Mérosorc	*Mare-os-orc*		

Charms

Afflictolapsis	*A-flik-toe-lap-sus*	Liborean	*Lib-or-e-an*
Aoratos	*ei-ora-tos*	Limarus	*Lim-ar-us*
Confanimo	*Con-fa-ni-mo*	Sepono	*Se-'po-no*
Dissoutentar	*Diss-outen-tar*	Solavit	*Sol-a-vit*
Eruptusilma	*E-rup-tus-il-ma*	Soporus	*So-por-us*
Exsusartus	*Ex-sus-ar-tus*	Tarmach filiste	*Tar-'mar fil-'Est*
Flacartus	*Flak-ar-tus*	Undolthgare	*Un-dol-th-gare*
Glaciocaptus	*Gla-si-o-'Kap-tus*	Varjocaptus	*Var-jo-cap-tus*
Horatos	*Hor-a-tos*	Varjolaxus	*Var-jo-lax-us*
Inhoudentar	*In-how-den-tar*	Vinaro	*Vin-a-ro*
Ketevos	*Kay-ter-vos*	Volverso	*Vol-ver-so*
Laeflamos	*Lay-flam-os*		

Other Terms

Drakaron	*Dra-ka-ron*	Pelatarrof	*Pel-a-tar-roff*
Foramens	*For-a-mens*	Praeterium	*Pray-ter-re-um*
Laedary	*Lay-dar-ee*	Snaffler	*Snaff-ler*
Míargstan	*Me-arg-stan*	Transonus	*Tran-so-nus*
Mórskarin	*More-ska-rin*	Trínondras	*Trin-on-dras*
Myrkroth	*Mere-kroth*	Tuagusts	*Tu-a-gus*
Neushallough	*New-shal-low*		

Phrase

Eiíos í fiondae na quelduil,	*eye-ih-os ih fee-On-day Na kwel-juel,*
san í lakínell o dharlow	*san ih la-kee-nell OH Dar-low*

PROLOGUE

In the underground passage all was silent. No chattering voices or heavy footsteps echoed off the walls of living stone. White torchlight shone down from two rows of sconces, the soft glow illuminating the sole occupant of the long tunnel.

Her slim form draped in a flowing white nightgown, and her wide emerald eyes unfocused in a pale face framed by a cloud of ebony curls, the girl walked slowly along the cold, smooth path of levelled rock. She approached a small door at the end of the tunnel. A dull shimmer of light radiated around the frame. The light faded, and the door slid open.

The girl stepped across the threshold and into a room glimmering with an unworldly brilliance. The wide space was bereft of any objects, save for several shelves filled with gold-bound tomes and a tall crystal stand with another gold book resting upon it. Embellished with precious stones, the book shone brightly, and engraved into its glistening cover was a line of runes.

The girl approached the stand. She raised her right arm, then reached out towards the book. As her hand hovered over it, the cover suddenly opened, the gilt-edged pages flickering until they stopped on a blank section.

Gently, the girl placed her hand at the bottom of the page. A faint whispering noise, like the murmur of dozens of voices, began to fill the room, the sound slowly increasing until individual words became clear. Then the girl watched, unmoved, as those same words began to form upon the page in indelible print.

Before the twelfth month dies the child will come,
in wind and with suffering shall the ancient line appear.
And the marked darkness shall stir,
and seek release from its sealed imprisonment.

~ *Chapter 1* ~

A STRANGE TURN
OF EVENTS

To many thirteen-year-olds, the prospect of spending the Christmas holidays alone would be truly horrifying.

However, to one student attending Brakenhurst High School in northern New South Wales, Australia, the idea of being left alone for Christmas considerably brightened her last week of the seventh grade.

Rhiannon McBride sat at her desk in the small, humid classroom, barely containing her impatience as she watched the ancient clock above the blackboard. Its hands were slowly ticking away the minutes until she could escape and begin to enjoy the next few weeks of freedom granted to her.

Another trickle of sweat slid down her face. Looking up, she glowered at the ceiling fans, which had decided to stop working during the sweltering summer. It also didn't help that the last lesson for the year was geography with Mr Lonsdale (the surly old grouch believed to have been inhabiting the school since it was built in 1925).

The little gremlin probably only continues teaching so he can enjoy terrorising us, thought Rhiannon, then jumped when an aged hand slapped a bundle of papers on her desk. She lifted her head to stare at the wrinkled old man glaring down at her.

'And some of you clearly need to improve your listening skills,' Mr Lonsdale snapped, his thick glasses glinting menacingly. He turned away and stalked back to his desk. 'The last announcement is that Mrs Clitherow wants all library books returned before you leave today. Anyone with a book still against their name after she finishes cataloguing tonight will be charged the replacement cost. Now, as I have no desire to waste my breath by speaking to any of you again in the last few minutes remaining, you're all to stay seated at your desk until you're dismissed.'

Clearly considering himself to have fulfilled his obligations, he sat down in his chair, lowered his eyes to the opened newspaper on his desk and proceeded to ignore his class.

Several students immediately scrambled to find any long-forgotten library book buried in their bags. The others began chatting among themselves, their loud voices failing to stir the interest of their indifferent teacher.

However, Rhiannon sat quietly, idly twirling a pen in her hand as she recalled her trip to the library at lunchtime. She mentally marked off each book she had returned, including one of her favourites: *A Treasury of Riddles & Verse* by E. Nig-Ma.

Satisfied she wouldn't be made to pay for any unreturned book, she glanced down at the papers Mr Lonsdale had slammed on her desk. Her cheerful mood melted as quickly as a block of ice on a hot tin roof. The official front page was emblazoned ostentatiously with the school's crest, and read,

Brakenhurst High School Report

of

Rhiannon Marie McBride

Rhiannon quelled the groan rising to her lips. She crossed her arms defiantly, refusing to touch the vile document in front of her. In her experience, school reports were just another source of grief she could do without. No matter what results she brought home, these were always overlooked and brushed aside. Meanwhile, her foster sister's efforts were applauded and praised effusively, despite the fact that Annabelle Rochester, Brakenhurst's celebrated piano virtuoso, cheated in every test, and persuaded one of her many followers to do all her assignments for her.

Rhiannon scowled at the report. Then she resolutely turned her head to stare out the window. The faint reflection of her pale, unremarkable face with its wide golden eyes and small nose stared back at her. Was it too much to ask for just one person to be genuinely interested in her? she asked herself. To have someone who cared enough to ask to see her report?

Rhiannon's mind began to weave a pleasant image of herself racing home with the report in hand, eager to devour the contents inside it over an after-school snack of biscuits and cold lemonade. Her hands itched with anticipation as she lost herself in the fantasy. Her desire to read the report increased so much that she unconsciously reached out and opened the booklet in front of her. Realising what she had done, she could not help opening her eyes to look down at the page. She stared at the neat but slightly slanted writing. Unexpectedly, she felt a tiny smile tug at her lips when she glimpsed the first teacher's comments.

Rhiannon has been an industrious and enthusiastic student of History and English. She shows a good appreciation of historical issues and a great love of literature. She makes wonderful use of knowledge in her assignments and is attentive during lessons. I wish her all the best for the new year and remind her not to be afraid to speak up in class.

Rhiannon's lips twitched in amusement at Mr Hutchinson's last suggestion. There was not much opportunity to speak up with his booming voice bombarding the class with information on Shakespeare and C.S. Lewis, plus all the finer points of the major events of the twentieth century. He also had a habit of answering most of his own questions before anyone had a chance to draw breath, let alone try and think of a reply.

Having fully abandoned her resolve not to look at the report, Rhiannon turned to the next page.

Personal Education & Fitness

Rhiannon's nose crinkled in distaste at her most hated subject. Then she read the terse comments made by Mrs Parker.

> Rhiannon has struggled significantly with this subject. Her physical performance skills in even the simplest sports are poor. I would suggest she learn to set aside her books and make an attempt to involve herself with her peers, as this may assist in raising her less than adequate result to at least an acceptable one in the new year.

Rhiannon scoffed in disbelief, then vehemently closed the report. Being physically targeted by nearly everyone in class didn't exactly help her performance skills!

And who wants to involve themselves with me? she thought bitterly. The Dashmont's 'untalented' foster child that everyone knew Annabelle treated like her own personal slave because of her precious hands!

Rhiannon slouched over the desk, her elbows resting on the hard, smooth surface.

It's all Mrs Dunstan's fault! she thought miserably, recalling the day Brakenhurst's best music teacher told her foster parents Annabelle should avoid doing anything that might damage her hands. She never has to do anything anymore! I get stuck with all her chores, and I can't believe they're going to insure her hands just because of an article about some hand model doing it! Now they're going to spend even more money on her, as if the Steinway piano and the cruise weren't enough! At least when she goes to the college in London, I might finally get a new uniform, or at least a new bag.

She looked down at the decrepit object at her feet. She doubted if it would last another year.

I might even ask if I can start having lessons again.

The thought summoned wistful memories of the piano classes she had given up several years ago. She had enjoyed them, until she realised her fairly average skill could not compare, in her foster parents' eyes, to Annabelle's natural flair. After her valiant effort at playing Beethoven's *Moonlight Sonata* had been completely overshadowed by Annabelle's flawless performance of Liszt's *Hungarian Rhapsody*, she had never played again. Instead, she had focused on her schoolwork – or she had, until Annabelle's hands became sacrosanct. Then she never had the time to study because of all her extra duties, having to rely only on what she did in school and her good memory to pass her exams.

BRRINNNNGG!

The shrill of the electronic bell brought Rhiannon's head up with a jerk. School was finally finished for the year!

She shoved the report in her bag as the classroom erupted around her, the other students swarming towards the exit in a mad rush.

'Tidy up the room, McBride, then you can go.'

Rhiannon gaped in disbelief, staring at her teacher's back as he disappeared through the doorway after the remaining students. It was one thing to be treated like a slave at home, but to have your own teacher do it as well?

Impatiently, she stood up and completed the tasks with perfunctory haste. Collecting her bag, she walked to the door, sighing in relief when a soft breeze blew through it, the cool wind gently stirring the damp tendrils clinging to her forehead.

Rhiannon wiped the perspiration away from her brow and stepped through the doorway, her eyes narrowing against the fierce glare of the afternoon sun.

At the school's entrance came the shout of laughter.

Rhiannon gazed longingly at the merry groups of students. How she wished there might come a day when she'd be accepted into one of them.

'Don't be stupid,' she rebuked herself after a moment. 'Nothing's going to suddenly change after all these years. There isn't a single person in this town who truly cares what happens to you.'

As though to prove her correct, a hard body crashed into her, sending her sprawling painfully on the hot cement. The rough surface tore open the skin on her knees and hands.

'Watch where you're going, McBrainless.'

Sniggering taunts broke out from the small group gathering around her.

A foot swung out, kicking her bag against the wall.

There was an unmistakeable crack.

Rhiannon winced. There goes my calculator, she thought, and felt a familiar tingling warmth surround her torn flesh. She looked down to see her skin fully repaired with only a faint residue of blood to mar its unblemished appearance.

'You unnatural freak!'

The insult was followed by a hand pulling at her long hair, revealing the small but peculiar reddish-brown mark at the corner of her left eye, curiously shaped like a seven-rayed star.

'You don't belong in our school. Why don't you take your marked face and disappear off the face of the planet?'

Rhiannon twisted and bit the hand. Hard.

A shrill scream of pain rang out.

'You'll pay for that, McBride!' a voice bellowed.

Rhiannon kicked out. Scrambling to her feet, she struggled against the hands pinning her against the wall.

A flutter of black and white wings against the blue sky caught her eye. Without hesitation, she called out, 'Help me!'

There was a terrifying chorus of harsh cries. Then, like a squadron of fighter jets, the magpies swooped on Rhiannon's tormentors.

Their arms waving frantically above their heads, the group retreated, screaming in terrified panic across the quadrangle with the birds pursuing them.

Rhiannon rubbed her head, still feeling the stinging pain of having her unruly chestnut curls almost yanked out by their roots. Not even bothering to check the contents of her bag, she picked it up and set off across the parched assembly area.

The sun scorched her back through her thin dress uniform, and her naturally sturdy build cast a long shadow on the yellowing grass.

She cast a quick look at the clock on the bell tower.

Three forty-five.

Rhiannon's face broke into a wide grin.

'They would've left by now.'

Her cheerful mood returning, she adjusted the bag over her shoulder and announced with satisfaction, 'Four whole weeks to myself, with no endless lists of chores to do, and no smirking Annabelle waiting around every corner. I might actually have some fun this Christmas.'

'Well, some fun this is going to be!'

Rhiannon tightened her grip on the sheaf of paper, creasing her foster mother's handwriting.

> Attached is a list of chores Gregory wants done, and Annabelle said she left a library book in her room that needs to be returned today. Her room's a bit messy, but I'm sure you'll be a good sister and clean it up for her.
>
> There's spare food in the freezer and pantry.
>
> Don't use the phone - unless it's an emergency.
>
> The Wilburys have said they'll be home for the holidays, so contact them if you have any problems.

Rhiannon slammed the note back on the table and stormed past the grand piano dominating the large drawing room of Gregory and Patricia Dashmont's double-storey house at 15 Dart Street. The collection of trophies in the enormous cabinet glinted at her mockingly as she made for the door, while in the plethora of photos immortalising Annabelle's numerous triumphs at national championships, the proud, smiling faces of her foster parents made the pain in her heart burn with a fierce intensity.

Stalking across the tiled foyer and up the staircase to her bedroom, she shoved open the door of the sparsely furnished room and threw her bag on the floor.

'I hate this place! I hate it!'

The tearful cry was accompanied by a fierce kick aimed at the wall.

Her sandal provided little protection against the impact, but the momentary physical pain helped to dull the ache in Rhiannon's chest.

She turned towards the wardrobe in the corner. Bending down, she withdrew a small envelope from beneath it with practised ease.

Carefully, she opened the envelope and slid out a torn scrap of newspaper stained yellow with age.

Rhiannon looked at it, her eyes lingering on the two faces smiling joyously out at the world from their black and white universe. The curling ringlets in her hair were a longer version of her father's, while her smile was a mirror image of her mother's. Then, with a desperate longing in her heart, she reread, for possibly the hundredth time, the article she had inadvertently discovered only three weeks ago during a history class excursion to the Brakenhurst Public Library.

Concerns as to Whereabouts of Missing Parents

By Tyrone Durrell

Monday, 4 January 1993

The search continues for two-year-old Rhiannon McBride's parents, who disappeared last Thursday night.

Patrick Ewan McBride (pictured above left, aged 25 years) and his wife, Claire Emmaline McBride (pictured above right, aged 24 years) placed their daughter in the care of their neighbour on Thursday afternoon of last week. Upon being questioned by police, Mrs Smith confirmed Mr and Mrs McBride were to attend a masquerade ball being held at a private residence in Baylon Street, in the township of Hanville. Further inquiries by the police have revealed the missing couple left the premises in Baylon Street at approximately 11:20 pm and set out on foot to the Town Square for the New Year Fireworks Display. No one attending the event has been able to confirm their attendance, and their vehicle remains unclaimed. Police have put out another plea seeking the public's assistance.

'Any information would be of enormous help,' Chief Inspector Phillip Doherty of the Hanville Police

Department said yesterday. 'There's a little girl who's missing her parents very much. I urge anyone who saw anything that night, or who knows the current location of Mr and Mrs McBride, to contact the station, or to call Crime Stoppers on 008 333 000.'

Speculation is rife within the community as to whether the missing couple could have been abducted, or if they simply abandoned their child and disappeared. Chief Inspector Doherty refused to comment on this issue, saying a full investigation needed to be completed before an official statement would be given.

Rhiannon touched the faded pictures of her parents with a gentle finger, while an overwhelming urge to scream at the unfairness in her life churned inside her. A few months after celebrating her second birthday, her world had been turned upside down when her parents' disappearance labelled her in the eyes of the world as either a penniless orphan with no family, or a pitiful castaway, solely reliant on the indifferent care of the foster parents she had been placed with.

Added to all this were the two unnatural abilities she possessed.

From her earliest memory, she had never received an injury that did not instantly heal, leaving no trace it had ever occurred. And when not only cats and dogs but all kinds of wild animals showed no fear in approaching her and seemed to understand every word she said, she wondered if there was some truth to Annabelle's taunts of her being a misbegotten freak.

'Would you know why I have these abilities? Did you have them too?' Rhiannon asked the still image of her smiling parents. 'Why did you disappear? Why did you leave me here alone?'

As always, no answer came.

Rhiannon sighed, then slid her most precious possession into the envelope and placed it back in its hiding place. Not bothering to change out of her uniform, she left her room and headed for Annabelle's.

The door to the room was already open.

Rhiannon took one step inside, then froze in shock.

The spacious and brightly lit room looked as though a clothes bomb had been detonated in it. A colourful array of material lay scattered across the floor, the unmade bed, in among the wide selection of cosmetics and jewellery on the wooden dressing table, and even on top of the tall wardrobe.

Rhiannon surveyed the room in dismay.

'"A bit messy"!' she exclaimed. 'Surely she's capable of folding up her own clothes! Why don't they just officially call me her slave and have done with it.' Then she made her way through the rainbow minefield to begin searching for the book.

'Little toad probably did this deliberately considering she's never borrowed a single book in her life,' she muttered.

She carefully checked inside the wardrobe but found nothing except Patricia's diamond ring that she had been accused of losing the week before.

A search of the cluttered desk resulted in a similar lack of success.

Rhiannon glanced at the unmade bed. She contemplated it briefly, then knelt down on one of Annabelle's favourite concert dresses of red satin to crawl underneath the bed frame. Pushing a large pile of fashion magazines out of the way, the discovery of a mouldy half-eaten sandwich made her nose wrinkle up in disgust.

She started to pull back.

Wait!

There, between the mattress and the wooden slats of the bed.

She shoved aside a pile of dirty clothes.

'Why that —!'

Rhiannon scrambled out from under the bed, leapt to her feet and pulled up the mattress to reveal *The Mysteries of Ancient Greece*

Uncovered, a textbook bearing the distinctive barcode from the school library.

Snatching up the book, Rhiannon stalked out of the room and headed back downstairs. She paused in the kitchen to grab a slice of bread, then left the house.

There was no one to see her devouring the bread as she walked across the pristine lawn and out the tall, ornate front gate.

The afternoon sun was still shining brightly, and the sweltering heat soon had Rhiannon considering taking a short rest under the large, shady oak tree at the corner of Dreyer Street. In its branches she could already hear a chorus of currawong and grey shrike-thrush warming up for their evening song.

Out of nowhere, a strong gust of wind swept across the area, nearly lifting her off the footpath. The trees in the street shook violently, the fierce sway of branches startling the birds from their sheltered abode. A collection of leaves and debris swirled into the air.

Rhiannon dropped the book to shield her eyes against the fierce onslaught. The wind plastered the thin material of her uniform to her body. Tendrils of hair whipped her face.

'What in blazes —?'

Rhiannon's startled exclamation broke off when the wind disappeared as suddenly as it had arrived.

Her hand dropped to her side.

She stood immobile in confusion.

However, she had only a second to ponder the unusual occurrence before another strange phenomenon arose.

The air began to swirl about her, the loose leaves at her feet spinning as though caught in a whirlwind.

The scene before her shimmered and blurred into a myriad of colours.

The dizzying kaleidoscope gathered speed.

Then, the world tilted on its axis.

Her body was twirling; or was it the images around her?

Rhiannon closed her eyes against the discombobulating sight.

A feeling of nausea struck her in response to the sharp pull she felt, as though she were being tugged upwards in a great vacuum.

Her arms flailed madly.

Her mouth opened in a silent scream of surprised terror.

Her body tumbled around and around, like a rag doll in a spin dryer.

A burst of warmth enveloped her.

Then she was falling. Falling at a great speed. Her hair was blown into an upward stream above her head, the wind rushing over her skin to leave it tingling and raw.

A sudden decrease in speed.

The feeling of a gentle force lowering her with precision.

A soft thud as she reconnected with solid ground.

Rhiannon's eyes flew open and she fought to remain upright as her feet sank into a blanket of icy softness.

The mysterious uprush of wind abruptly vanished without a trace, leaving her standing beneath a chilly dawn sky, surrounded by a thick forest and ankle-deep in freezing snow.

Chapter 2

A CARELESS ATTACK

Rhiannon swiftly discovered that her thin clothing and sandals offered little protection against the biting chill of a winter frost.

Frantically, she rubbed her hands over her cold flesh, desperate to prevent the blood from freezing solid in her veins.

Her eyes became like dry ice as she gazed in disbelief at her new surroundings.

A host of oak and beech trees stood among their snow-dusted evergreen neighbours, their skeletal appearance lending a haunted atmosphere to the scene.

'This is j-just weird.'

A puff of white accompanied the words through her chattering teeth.

Had she found the real-life Narnia? Or perhaps some mad scientist had just sent the world back to the Ice Age.

Rhiannon continued her bewildered musings as she stood shivering in the snow.

Then a dreadful thought came upon her.

'The b-bread! What was on t-the bread?'

But as swiftly as it came, she dismissed the thought of her

foster family trying to poison her. A free maid was hard to come by after all!

She glanced around once again. Then, she reached up and tightly pinched herself on the arm. Wincing at the pain, she soothed the reddened flesh with a firm rub.

'I g-guess that rules out h-hallucination or daydream.'

Rhiannon shivered violently when a cold breeze pierced the thin cloth of her uniform. Panic began to rise within her. She could feel her lips turning numb with cold.

Then her more pragmatic side surfaced.

She examined the view around her more closely. Surely there was somewhere she could shelter from the icy wind.

Trees. Snow. Shrub. Snow. More trees. More snow.

Great! she thought dismally. To seek refuge here, I'd have to be the size of a rodent. Even then I'd probably end up a frozen ferret popsicle, or the main course on some animal's dinner menu!

She clenched her teeth in an effort to quell their noisy chattering, then set her chin determinedly.

'I w-will get out of here.'

Spotting a clearer path on her right, she set out resolutely in its direction.

Above the trees the golden orb of the sun slowly continued to rise. The source of light, which only mere moments ago had been her enemy, was now a comforting presence. Its shimmering form was something familiar in a strange place, giving promise of future warmth with its gentle radiance.

The rough path continued ever onward.

Rhiannon's feet, numb with the wet and cold, had no chance to defrost as she followed the twisting trail.

Endless snowdrifts and thick forest loomed on every side.

Her optimism dwindled to a tiny spark.

She tripped over a rock and tumbled to the ground. Rhiannon picked it up and hurled it.

Grimacing, she stumbled on with sodden fabric now clinging to her legs.

'I w-wish I had my coat. Even if it's worn out at least it'd be better than just wearing this p-paper-thin rag.'

She plodded on, her thoughts a jumbled mess.

Where was she? *When* was she? Would a Saint Bernard soon come running out from between the trees?

She carefully stepped over a large gaping hole in the snowy path.

How long did a person have before they froze to death?

Rhiannon shook away the last thought.

Then a smidgen of hope!

The trees finally appeared to be thinning out.

Rhiannon quickened her steps.

Soon she approached a row of snow-flecked hedges guarding the edge of the trees.

Eagerly she moved to find a way through them when an excited shout broke across the early morning air.

Instinctively, she crouched to the ground.

Shivering, she inched forward to a thick section of the hedge. She peered through the tangled web of evergreen branches and snow, striving to find the source of the gleeful cry.

There was the muffled thud of running in the snow. A harried rustle.

Without warning, a large form flew over the hedge and landed within a foot of her startled form.

Rhiannon's eyes widened in panic.

A shocked gasp escaped her frozen lips.

But then, she beheld the majestic figure towering above her. Its rich, mahogany fur glistened healthily, and dark eyes met hers with a strange dignity that was almost regal.

Trepidation melted away and was replaced by relief.

Rhiannon smiled warmly. Her voice when she spoke was a confiding whisper.

'Somehow I get the f-feeling you don't want to be found either?'

The tall stag bowed its head, its twelve-pointed antlers missing her face by mere inches.

'Are you the one t-they're chasing?'

At Rhiannon's soft query the stag once again lowered his head.

'Well, you'd b-best get out of here, hadn't you?' Rhiannon smiled encouragingly when the stag didn't move. 'Don't worry 'bout me. That's why you s-stopped, isn't it?'

Solemn eyes held hers as the stag inclined his head.

The excited cries drew closer.

The stag still did not move.

'Y-You have to leave.' Rhiannon's voice was stern. 'I'll be fine. I'll s-stay here where they c-can't see me.'

For a moment it seemed the stag would ignore her words. Then he bowed his head and turned away. In a single powerful bound, he leapt forward and took off with swift grace, his body weaving between the trees before he vanished from sight.

Alone once more, Rhiannon's apprehension increased.

The voices were now quite close.

Her hands and feet were blue with cold. Everything felt dreadfully numb.

She peeked through the small gap in the hedge again, then blinked at what she saw.

A group of horsemen were rounding a small hill in the open field, their mounts approaching the forest at a furious gallop.

Rhiannon frowned when she finally made out the clothes of the riders.

What was this? Some sort of fancy-dress pageant!

All the riders wore a fine, long-sleeved tunic of white cloth with a gold insignia of twelve stars encircling a crown embossed upon the breast. Around each pair of shoulders was draped a long cloak of dark grey, with the exception of one who wore one of crimson red. Each rider wore a muffin cap adorned with a single feather perched upon their head. Their legs were encased in high leather boots and black riding breeches. Alarmingly, a sheathed sword was at each of their belts.

Rhiannon inched closer to the hedge.

The group continued in her direction.

She stiffened when a young male voice declared loudly, 'He must have gone through here!'

'If he did, then there's no use chasing him any farther, we would never find him,' a deeper voice answered. 'We'll have to inform Keeper Sujan he'll need to find another buck for his herd.'

They're not hunters?

Rhiannon shifted her balance, wondering if it was safe to approach the group.

Her foot slipped.

Rhiannon's hand shot out to grab the hedge in front of her. The force of her action shook the bush. Snow collected atop it fell to the ground with a dull *plomp*.

For an infinitesimal moment the world froze.

The breath caught in her lungs.

Her heartbeat stuttered to a halt.

No sound broke the sudden stillness.

Then, 'THERE!'

Rhiannon had only a second to dread the enthusiastic yell.

A flash of light blinded her.

Then there was only pain.

The fierce, burning sensation sprang to life in her heart, then spread to every inch of her being. Time ceased to hold any meaning as she felt her body collapse backwards into the snow. Her limbs were incapable of moving. Even her eyes remained still and unblinking.

Pure, unadulterated terror flooded her mind, distorting the annoyed voices approaching her into unintelligible static.

'Beetle-headed idiot ... that charm ... not supposed to ...'

But then, even the voices began to disappear. A dreadful darkness crept forward at the edges of her consciousness.

NO!

Her mind's voice took on an hysterical note of panic. She mentally fought the entity attempting to overpower her, the battle draining her last reserves of strength. She felt a pull on her eyelids. Then the sight of the early morning sky through the bare, snowclad branches of the towering trees disappeared.

~Chapter 3~

HEALING THROUGH PAIN

'AH! THERE HE GOES!'

The excited cry rang out across the open, snow-covered fields.

David reined in his fiery black stallion, his golden hair windswept and a heavy scowl between his dark eyebrows. He flung back his cloak, exposing the sword attached to his belt.

'At this rate, with him screeching like a banshee every time we spot that blasted stag, this'll take all day!' he informed his companion. 'Did anyone even tell Mister Zealous Idiot over there that the whole purpose of this outing was to capture the stag, not engage in a long-distance game of hide-and-seek!'

Under a mass of auburn curls, his companion's green eyes twinkled.

'Don't be so hard on him. It's his first time out. Besides, he's had to deal with Wyvern breathing down his neck for the past nine months.'

David snorted, his eyes, an unusual violet hue, flashing impatiently. 'Nine months?' he retorted, brushing a strand of hair off his face. 'I've had to put up with him almost daily since I was six years old, and I haven't seen anyone step forward to offer their sympathy for *my* plight over the last eight ... actually make that almost *nine years!'*

'Well, that's because you're a special case.'

'Yes, special in the head to ever have allowed myself to be roped into this farce of an expedition in the first place.' At yet another laugh from his companion, he demanded, 'Admit it, John. It's ridiculous! I can certainly think of better things we could be doing right now, rather than chasing after ...'

'... the one thing old Sujan wants above everything else,' John finished for him. He smiled, showing a set of white but slightly uneven teeth. 'Just remember how pleased he'll be to get his prize stag returned to him. And maybe it wouldn't hurt to keep in mind how many times he lets us bother him, showing us the latest newborns, or the injured creatures he's found.'

David ruefully rubbed the back of his neck, a guilty flush burning his fair cheeks at the reminder. 'I'm being an impossible brat, aren't I? I'm sorry, John. I really don't know why you put up with me sometimes. I'm surprised you've never requested to be released from your appointment to me.'

John grinned affectionately at David's woeful expression, then leant over in his saddle and lightly cuffed his shoulder. 'Now, how would I amuse myself if you weren't around to poke fun at?' he teased, then added thoughtfully, 'I suppose I could always torment Delia.'

Pulled out of his self-recriminations by his companion's comments, David stared at him for a moment, then shook his head in disbelief. 'I know your sister. You wouldn't last twenty minutes before she'd have you in a headlock.'

'But I'd get a good laugh out of it.'

'John, I think even if you were in the process of being devoured by a starving boar, you'd still find something in the situation to laugh about.'

'Only if it started chewing on my funny bone,' John retorted cheerfully.

An excited cry in front of them interrupted their light-hearted banter.

David looked in the direction of the sound, then gave a loud groan of irritation. The group of riders was galloping around the small hill in the distance.

'That sapskull just managed to chase Sujan's stag towards Shaimar Forest. And considering his stellar performance so far, I wouldn't be at all surprised if he tried to go in there after it.'

'You were complaining about getting bored only a minute ago,' John commented with pseudo innocence. 'Maybe this is what you need: a high-speed gallop through the forest to brighten you up.'

David glared at him.

'And face the wrath of Flavian when I return Cináed to the stables covered in scratches, and most likely a limp leg as well?' he said impatiently. 'No, thank you. I'd sooner face off alone against a whole army of irritable trolls.'

'Then we'd best catch Officer Exton before he does anything else too stupid.' John patted his horse's white neck proudly. 'No horse can match Asaph for speed, so that shouldn't be a problem for me.'

David huffed indignantly at the slight to his own mount's ability. 'You think so? I'll wager you fifteen pieces of silver Cináed can get to the edge of Shaimar Forest before you even make it to the hill,' he challenged.

'Done!'

John's shouted acceptance rang out. Then both horses were racing across the snow-covered ground at a furious pace.

David grinned. He urged his mount on with cries of encourage-ment and heard John doing the same. Their shouts drowned out the dull thud of their horses' hoofs connecting with the soft snow overlaying the ground.

'Come on, David, what's the matter? Put on a bit of extra weight, have you?'

David frowned at the other horse two lengths in front of his own.

He bent low over his saddle.

'Cináed, I have every faith in you,' he murmured. 'Now, show those two who they're dealing with!'

The black stallion shot forward in a burst of speed, overtaking their rivals in a matter of seconds.

'Hey!'

David chuckled at John's exclamation of surprise.

'See you at the forest, sluggard!' he called out.

'We'll see about that!'

'You want to double the wager?'

'Triple it! You'll never beat us!'

'HA! Just hang on to Cináed's tail – if you can catch it!'

David's stallion powered on at a full gallop, his dark colour contrasting brilliantly against the white snow.

Then they were approaching the hill.

David negotiated the hazardous turn with care. Then, Cináed surged forward again.

Adrenaline pumped through David's veins.

He saw the group nearing the edge of the forest.

'We've almost got 'em!' he heard John call out. 'Thunder an' turf, their horses must be slow!'

David opened his mouth to agree.

'THERE!'

The piercing yell thundered through his head.

A burst of pale blue light shot into the forest.

David's breath caught in his throat.

'Did he just ...?'

John's horrified voice trailed off.

'He did,' David said grimly, all thought of their wager instantly forgotten. His eyes blazing with fury, he swiftly led the way across the remaining distance.

'ARE YOU ALL ABOUT IN THE HEAD! You're not supposed to use that charm on *any* mammal! Do you have any idea what it does to them?'

David and John reined in and dismounted to the sound of Captain Morton's gravelly voice.

They ignored the argument brewing around them, quickly making their way over to the section of the forest where Exton's charm had been directed.

'*Sepono.*'

At David's quiet command a grey light shone briefly. Then the hedge slowly parted, creating a clear opening into the forest.

'At least let's hope the poor creature had a quick end,' John said in a low voice as they stepped through the gap. 'I hate to think what he would've gone through otherwise.'

David made a small sound of agreement. He took another step forward, then froze.

With a startled prayer on his lips and a hasty crossing of himself, he fell to one knee on the ground, his blue cloak billowing around him.

'David, what's wro –?' John's concerned question broke off into a sharp gasp. 'Great stars in the heavens! It's a girl!'

David nodded silently, staring at the pale face of the deathly still body. He removed his gloves and placed a gentle hand against the girl's neck. A vibrant hot warmth encompassed his fingers, as though he had just put his hand too close to an open flame.

'How –?' John's voice broke off. He paused, then started again. 'She looks like she was no more than twelve years old! For the love of Álnair, what were her parents thinking letting her come out here alone!'

'She's not dead.'

'What?'

'She's not dead,' David repeated in a louder voice.

The arguing group behind him suddenly fell silent.

He hurriedly removed his woollen cloak and carefully tucked it around the girl's body.

'Her skin is hot; her heart's still beating.' Then feeling a soft breeze faintly brush against his cheek as he leant over her face, he added, 'And she's breathing.'

'But, that's impossible!' John's tone was incredulous. 'It was definitely a Glaciocaptus Charm he shot at her. How could she possibly survive that?'

'I don't know,' David replied softly. 'But I do know she's not out of danger yet. Her heartbeat isn't steady. It keeps changing! One moment it's fast and the next it almost disappears.' He frowned, running a hand through his hair. 'It's almost as though she's fighting the charm, and we dare not try and use the counter to stop it. Who knows what that could do. It could end up killing her!'

Into the stunned silence came the crunching of several heavily clad feet approaching from behind.

David's anger returned. He barked out, 'Exton, if you believe in an afterlife you'd better start preparing yourself for it! Once Sir Raeden gets through with you, there's going to be a certain four-legged female who'd like to see you.'

One set of footsteps faltered at these words and there came a quiet whimper.

'Captain Morton.' David turned his attention on the most senior member of the group. 'I shall need you to watch over the girl with John. I believe we're going to need help with this.'

He did not wait for a reply. Standing up, he moved back out of the forest and past the group gathered at its edge. When he stood some distance away, he closed his eyes, his brow furrowed with intense concentration. Ignoring the shivers moving up his uncloaked body, he grasped what appeared to be thin air in front of his chest and breathed out in a voice barely audible to the group behind him, 'Endrille, Queen of all dragons and last of the ancient race, I, David, of the House of Valieoth, humbly request your urgent assistance. Hear my plea and answer.'

The last words had barely passed David's lips when he felt a large presence glide up beside him and land with only a whisper of sound. The air around him was infused with a warm scent, like that of heather fields on a fair summer's morning, and a gentle heat dispelled the winter chill rising from the snow-covered ground. He turned in relief to gaze up at the breathtaking form towering above him.

Last of the ancient race, and worthy of her dragon lineage, Endrille's enormous form was covered in rich mahogany scales, while her silver underbelly glistened in the early morning sunlight. The wisdom and knowledge of many ages of Men was engraved upon her kindly reptilian face, while the two rows of long, white teeth in her mouth (which looked capable of easily biting a full-grown man in two) were enough to inform any casual observer that she would be a fierce adversary when roused. At the end of her four powerful legs were five claws, and a thick mane of fiery red hair ran from the top of her elongated head, down her long neck and back to the end of her lengthy tail. The only blemish on her body was a jagged black scar under her left bat-like wing.

'You are fortunate we were already on our way to the forest; but honestly, what have you done this time, David?' said Endrille in a gently chiding voice with only a hint of exasperation. 'Only you could get into trouble this early in the morning,' she continued, her large brown eyes twinkling with amusement. 'Would you not agree, Sir Raeden?'

David grimaced at the name. He transferred his gaze from Endrille to the pale, stern face of the extremely tall man who stepped out from behind the dragon's body.

With his lean, muscular figure wrapped in a dark burgundy cloak, his legs clad in long black breeches and high boots of supple leather, a fine sword at his side, and his stormy blue eyes glaring from underneath an impressive set of eyebrows which matched the raven-black hair he wore shorn about his shoulders, Sir Raeden Wyvern made quite an imposing figure as he stalked forward.

'Indeed,' said the cold voice David was all too familiar with, 'it is a source of never-ending astonishment to me how someone lauded for his intelligence could possess the ability to cause havoc at every misbegotten opportunity.'

Infuriated at the immediate presumption that this disaster was somehow of his making, David retorted, 'For your information, *Sir*, I'm not the one who directed a dangerous capturing charm into an unfamiliar area, at an unidentified target, without first checking to see what it was! That would be one of *your* men!' He pointed a finger towards the forest and furiously announced, 'There's a girl in there! A girl who is slowly dying because some idiot couldn't be bothered remembering that you don't use Glaciocaptus without first checking there isn't a mammal nearby that could get hit by it.'

David's last words rang out in the wide clearing. He could not fail to see the incensed tightening of Sir Raeden's lips, or the infuriated glint flashing across Endrille's normally warm eyes.

'Glaciocaptus!' No one could mistake the fury in the dragon's voice, or the angry twitch of her long tail. 'That charm was specifically designed for dragon anatomy and is only to be used for the immobilisation of injured dragons.'

'You said a girl was hit,' Sir Raeden said curtly. 'That she managed to survive.'

David's earlier concern returned with a force that overwhelmed his flash of anger. 'Her heart's still beating, but there's something going on. It's almost like she's fighting the charm.'

He saw Sir Raeden and Endrille share a brief look.

Then Endrille turned her head towards the edge of the forest. Except for John and Captain Morton, who remained partially hidden crouched behind the parted hedge, the other members of the group shifted nervously, their expressions clearly conveying their unwillingness to draw upon themselves the wrathful attention of either Sir Raeden or Endrille.

'*Tarmach filiste.*'

At Endrille's softly spoken words, a gentle golden radiance emanated from the section of the forest where the girl lay. The next instant, her body, still wrapped in David's cloak, came floating out from behind the hedge. It glided forward until it came to rest on the ground between Sir Raeden and David.

Sir Raeden swiftly knelt down. In perfect imitation of David's earlier actions, he reached out to gently place his long, slender fingers against the girl's neck. After a moment he removed them and lifted the edge of the cloak. He clasped one of the small, feminine hands in his and whispered a flow of lilting words under his breath. A soft purple light briefly enveloped their connected bodies, then faded.

'Sir Raeden, what is it?'

Endrille's question broke the tense silence. Sir Raeden turned his head to look at her.

'The child is indeed alive,' he said in a voice devoid of all emotion. 'Her body is attempting to fend off the effects of the charm, although the effort is draining her. She has, at most, only a couple of minutes left before her heart gives out completely.'

The silence that fell lasted only a couple of seconds.

'Well, do something! Help her!'

'Steady on, David. Give him a chance.'

David spared John only a brief look, then turned his concerned gaze back on Endrille and Sir Raeden.

'You have to do something,' he commanded fiercely, his voice trembling in spite of his efforts to control it. 'There has to be something you can do!'

'*Never* take that arrogant tone with me again,' Sir Raeden said, his eyes as hard as agates, and as glittering, 'or you'll soon discover any punishments I have handed out in the past will seem like a pleasurable chore compared to what I will give you.'

David clenched his fists. A muscle twitched in his jaw. Then John was resting a comforting hand on his shoulder and murmuring, 'Calm down. I'm sure they'll do all they can.'

'Lady Endrille,' Sir Raeden's voice was once again impeccably smooth as he spoke to the dragon behind him, 'there is only one thing which may prove of any assistance, and I must ask your permission to obtain it.'

David saw his own bewilderment reflected in the faces of everyone else gathered nearby. He gazed at Endrille to see whether she had understood the enigmatic request. To his surprise, he saw not only comprehension in the dragon's large brown eyes, but also great sorrow.

'Permission is so granted, Sir Raeden,' Endrille replied heavily. 'It is given freely, and under no duress.'

Sir Raeden did not waste another moment. Swiftly rising to his feet, he reached Endrille in a few quick strides. From under his cloak he withdrew a small vial. He waited as she slowly lowered her head. Then, in one swift movement, she pierced the scales of her right foreleg with her sharp teeth. Several ruby coloured droplets escaped, only to be caught immediately inside the vial Sir Raeden had ready.

Understanding of Endrille's strange reaction to Sir Raeden's request suddenly swept through David. He grimaced in horror at the possible consequences which could arise from what Sir Raeden was about to do.

His body tense with apprehension, he watched, transfixed, as Sir Raeden speedily returned to the girl's body. He grimaced when the knight simultaneously performed the counter to Glaciocaptus with a flash of pale rose light and tilted the vial to the girl's frozen lips, allowing the small amount of red liquid inside to fall into her mouth.

The reaction was instantaneous.

A piercing scream tore from the girl's throat. Her back arched off the ground. Her limbs flailed spasmodically in a series of frantic movements.

Sir Raeden immediately cast aside the vial and held her down.

David winced as another shrill scream pierced the air. Tearing his gaze away from where it had been locked on the tortured form, he beseeched Endrille, 'Surely there's something you can do to relieve the pain she's feeling? She's in agony!'

The dragon sighed. Her eyes filled with sorrowful compassion, she looked down at him and replied gently, 'My dear child, were it within my power to prevent this innocent's torment do you not believe I would have already acted? Unfortunately, should I choose to interfere now, such an act would only irrevocably seal the girl's death.'

She gazed back at the girl's body, which was now writhing under Sir Raeden's strong grip.

'If her mind and heart are strong enough, she will survive, and mercifully only retain a vague memory of the pain currently possessing her. However, should she not be strong enough …'

David felt John's hand tighten on his shoulder when the dragon fell silent. He knew they were both finishing Endrille's speech inside their heads: *Should her mind and body not be strong enough then she will die, and the issue of any pain she may feel will no longer exist.*

A harsh, gasping breath broke the terrible heaviness surrounding the group.

David's eyes immediately focused once again on the girl's white face as her body abruptly stilled. Then, her long, dark eyelashes flickered. He watched as they slowly slid open.

There was a sharp intake of breath from Endrille. His own lay captured inside his chest. Two bewildered eyes stared up at him, their hue the brilliant gold of a clear sunrise.

~Chapter 4~

SUFFERING

Pain.

Unbearable, searing pain was racing through every nerve in her body.

A thousand white-hot needles were being forced through her skin.

Blood-red fire flooded her veins, a blazing trail burning the darkness enveloping her mind and soul.

How long had it been?

Two minutes, or two hours?

One year, or a century?

Am I alive, or dead?

A hundred thousand thoughts and memories spun through her mind. The whirlpool of words and colourful images obliterated the inky blackness, sending her into a kaleidoscopic daze.

A sudden chill in her blood extinguished the fire.

The shock forced the breath from her lungs in a harsh gasp.

Her body froze into stillness.

Awareness crept back into her awakening consciousness. With that return came the memory of the galloping horsemen.

The cries of triumph. The blinding flash of light. And, most vivid of all, the overwhelming pain.

Strangely, the freezing cold which had permeated her entire being was missing.

A soft warmth gently surrounded her in a protective cocoon.

Confusion tinged with apprehension clouded her mind.

She slowly forced her eyes open.

Three human faces were looking down at her: the pale, concerned countenances of two boys, and the impassive mask of a rather stern man.

Then, her exhausted gaze landed on the anxious but unmistakably reptilian features of what could only be described as a dragon.

'All right. Now I know the bread was mouldy,' Rhiannon mumbled groggily, and promptly descended into unconsciousness once more.

Chapter 5

OF CASTLES AND
DRAGONS

I s tha' a star on 'er face?'

'Alice, don't be so loud! And how did you lot get in here?'

'The door was open. Anyway, we only wanted to look at her 'cause ...'

'... you and David wouldn't tell us anything, and ...'

'... we just wanted to know what someone looked like after they'd drunk blood straight from a dragon. We thought maybe she'd have wings or something exciting like that.'

Drifting back to consciousness, Rhiannon ignored the stiff ache in her body to listen to the numerous voices surrounding her. She frowned when their words finally penetrated the dark fog clouding her mind.

Wonderful, she thought dismally, I haven't the faintest clue where I am, I just heard three different people speak in the same voice and they were saying something about me growing wings!

She shifted uncomfortably and was contemplating opening her eyes when a small, hard body suddenly landed beside her.

'Hey, get off the bed, you cork-brained idiot,' a pleasant masculine voice called from somewhere off to the right.

Rhiannon felt the form beside her move away with all the speed of a reluctant snail.

'I was just seeing if she was awake yet,' a boy's voice grumbled.

'Honestly, Daniel, I would've thought you'd have more sense! Usually it's Edward who doesn't think before he acts.'

'Hey, I resent that, David,' a voice identical to Daniel's interrupted. 'Especially since we all know Robert is the one who gets us into trouble all the time.'

'I do not!'

'Do too!'

'Do not!'

'Do —'

'Oh, shut up, all three of you,' the voice belonging to David demanded exasperatedly. 'You shouldn't even be in here, and your mum's waiting for you out the front. So get out, and take Alice with you.'

Rhiannon mentally cringed at the loud groans and protests that immediately filled the air.

'But what about John?'

'Why doesn't he have to come home? He's not even on duty!'

'Why can't Alice go by herself?'

'I don't wanna go. I wanna 'tay here!'

'Come on, you lot, move it,' John's voice instructed them firmly. 'And Edward, a Chief Robesman is never really off duty once they're given the position. We may get holidays, but our Lord's interests supersede these if a situation calls for it. Although, on this occasion, I'm staying because David asked me to as his friend, and Dad said I could. Now, get going, unless you want Mum to really ring a fine peal over your heads. She's already pretty mad at you for releasing a bagful of frogs in the kitchens.'

'But we didn't release them, John! Honest.'

Rhiannon could not be sure if it was Daniel, Edward or Robert protesting.

'We only put them in the sink so they wouldn't get all dry and horrible. It wasn't our fault they didn't want to be there and jumped out.'

'Well, you can try that explanation with Mum, but I don't think it'll work,' John replied calmly. 'Now, for the last time, take yourselves off before I pitch you out headfirst.'

'Fine,' three disgruntled voices mumbled unhappily. 'Come on, Alice.'

Rhiannon listened in growing bemusement as the three boys dragged an obviously still reluctant Alice from the room.

'Little monsters,' John remarked with brotherly affection.

'You can say that again!' David replied, before asking quietly, 'So, how is she?'

'I'm not sure, I thought I saw her move before, but I can't say for certain. It could've just been from Daniel jumping on the bed. By the way, what did Wyvern have to say about her? He was here this morning, wasn't he?'

David snorted. 'Yes, he was here again, and more annoying than ever. He came to examine her with Apollinaris. They said her body's been healing itself, and that's why she was able to survive the effects of the charm for so long.'

'Healing itself?' John's startled tone indicated he had not expected that answer. 'But that's impossible. I've never even heard of such a talent existing.'

'Neither had I, but according to Father when I asked him, there was a mage centuries ago who could do it.'

'Do you think it might have something to do with her eyes?' John asked unexpectedly. 'I mean gold eyes like hers aren't exactly normal. And even Endrille reacted oddly to them. Well, that, and the strange mark she has near her left eye.'

'I know.' David released a small chuckle as he said wonderingly,

'I don't think I've ever seen her speechless before that moment when she saw them.'

'Has there been any word from the parties sent out to check the forest? Do they know who she is?'

'I've heard they found some footprints belonging to her. They couldn't find a trace of anyone else being there, and no one has made a report of a child going missing.' David paused, then said slowly, 'I think they know something.'

'Who?'

'My father, Endrille and Wyvern. They've all been acting rather strangely for the last few months, in fact, ever since we got back from the visit to Graynor in July and my father spent the morning going over the Book of Prophecy. And what's really odd is that no one has been sent out to make further inquiries about her. I would've thought they'd at least try to locate her family, or whoever was supposed to be looking after her.'

Feeling the two boys coming closer to the bed, Rhiannon tried to remain motionless. However, all thoughts of keeping still vanished in an instant when a warm hand suddenly landed on her forehead. She jerked away and her eyes flew open just in time to see a thick royal blue rug as she rolled off the side of the bed and crashed heavily on the floor.

She ignored the pain shooting through her arm, where it had twisted awkwardly beneath her, and leapt unsteadily to her feet. Her gaze hastily took in the tastefully decorated room, then focused on the two startled boys standing across from her, the four-poster bed draped in shimmering ocean-blue silk between them like an expensively decorated no-man's-land on a battlefield.

For a moment, the room was shrouded in silence as Rhiannon warily examined the boys. The one with gold hair and wearing a blue high-collared tunic with white breeches looked about her own age, perhaps a year or two older. He was certainly taller than she was and possessed an unusual degree of poise compared to all the other boys she knew. A gold signet ring adorned the forefinger of his right hand. The other boy was about the same height, but older, the slight red fuzziness on his jawline proclaiming him to be nearly an adult.

She uneasily noted that both had swords attached to their belts.

On the opposite side of the bed, David and John had identical expressions of bemusement on their faces. In silence they considered Rhiannon's tense form, which was now clothed in a lengthy pink nightdress, its silky shine announcing the quality of the material with every reflection of light. Her hair was a tangle of ringlets cascading past her shoulders to below her waist, and her eyes searched them closely from a face pale with anxiety.

After a long pause, the awkward silence was broken when Rhiannon said uncertainly, 'You're the two boys from the forest, aren't you?'

David and John nodded.

'Yes, that was us,' replied David, brushing a stray golden lock of hair off his cheek. 'I'm David O'Faenart, and this is John Tremaine.'

John smiled reassuringly at her. 'What's your name?' he asked.

Rhiannon hesitated a moment, then said quietly, 'Rhiannon. Rhiannon McBride.'

'Well, Rhiannon, I hope you don't make a habit of pulling stupid stunts like you did in Shaimar Forest four days ago,' David commented bluntly. 'Of all the brainless things to do, that would have to be the dumbest.'

'David!'

The shocked outburst, and a rather sudden thump to his shoulder by a very familiar fist, had David turning to face John.

'Well, she shouldn't have been hiding in those bushes,' he said tersely. 'If she had come out when she heard the group coming, then that clodpole wouldn't have had a chance to hurt her. And besides, who in their right mind actually runs around in the snow in nothing but a piece of thin material?'

Rhiannon's pale face was instantly suffused with an angry red flush. Her nervousness disappearing in a second, she retorted furiously, 'For your information, *David O'Faenart*, I was about to come out when that thing hit me! And let me tell you, if I'd had a choice I wouldn't have chosen to be in some freezing cold forest in a land inhabited by rude, inconsiderate, self-righteous prigs who like to blame everyone but themselves because one of their friends happens to like attacking anything that moves!'

'Friend!' David's incredulous tone was quickly replaced by disgust as he declared vehemently, 'That idiot is no friend of mine, just some guard my father stuck me with.'

'Well, if your father is the one who chose "that idiot" to guard you, why do you think you're entitled to blame anyone who has the misfortune to be attacked by him?' Rhiannon cried angrily.

'I don't think that, you little twit! And I wasn't blaming you for what happened!'

'It certainly sounded like you were!' Rhiannon fired back.

'I think it's time to cry pax and calm down,' John said, stepping forward to intervene. 'Rhiannon, I'm sure David didn't mean to imply that what happened was your fault; and, David, I'm certain the last thing your mother wants to hear is you yelling at a guest who has just woken up after nearly being killed.'

'Killed!'

Rhiannon's shocked exclamation rang through the room. In an instant, all traces of her anger evaporated.

'W-What do you mean "killed"?' she demanded, her face draining of all colour.

David and John shared a look. Then, John said quietly, 'Exton used Glaciocaptus on you.'

Rhiannon stared at him blankly. 'Glacio-whatsit?'

'Glaciocaptus,' said David.

Rhiannon frowned. 'And what is that exactly?'

David and John looked at her short height and undeveloped body.

'I suppose you aren't old enough to have heard about it yet,' John said, and began to explain. 'Glaciocaptus is a Grade 7 Level 10 charm …'

'Charm? As in magic?' Rhiannon interrupted sceptically.

'Yes, well in as much as any technique a magi performs using the gift bestowed upon them in a proper manner can be called magic.'

'And this charm was used by your guard?' Rhiannon glanced at David who nodded.

'He's a mage,' he said, as though that should explain everything.

'Right. Mage. It all makes sense now,' Rhiannon said facetiously. 'And he used a charm that almost killed me.'

'Yes. You see, Rhiannon, the Glaciocaptus charm was designed for dragon anatomy, and while it isn't dangerous against dragons, if used on a mammal it's fatal. Well, normally it is.'

Rhiannon stood immobile as though carved from stone, while her mind sought to halt the flood of thoughts now spinning in her head. Finally, latching on to the tail end of one thought as it flew past, she said stiltedly through suddenly dry lips, 'Dragons? Charms against dragons? I was hit by a *charm* designed for use against *dragons* while in the middle of nowhere and ankle-deep in snow, and apparently I almost *died?*'

Evidently unsure of whether a verbal reply was required of them, both David and John simply nodded.

'Right. Uh huh. Perfect.' Nodding her head slowly, Rhiannon turned around and walked towards the doorway. 'I think I need some air,' she said blankly, then stepped through the opening.

'Hey!' David leapt forward to race after his guest when John grabbed his arm. Twisting around to stare at him, he demanded, 'What're you doing? We can't just let her go out there by herself!'

'It's not as though she can come to any harm here. I think the best thing we can do for now is to leave her alone for a while.'

David frowned at the empty doorway for a moment, then reluctantly agreed.

'Fine, I won't go. However, send a message to all the guards that although she's to be carefully watched, they're not to make her aware of their presence unless they need to help her. I don't want Wyvern blaming me if she suddenly has a relapse, collapses on the stairs and knocks herself out.'

Rhiannon walked swiftly through the labyrinth of brightly lit hallways and staircases, scarcely aware of the fine paintings and rich tapestries mounted on the smooth stone walls.

She paid no heed to the exquisitely designed, precisely placed furniture in the wide corridors, or the glittering array of bejewelled artefacts scattered artistically atop strategically placed tables and shelves. She ignored the pools of rainbows cast upon cool, white, marble floors and luxuriously thick carpets with beautiful, ornate designs.

There were furtive movements near elaborate doorways, but she dismissed these without a second glance.

Her mind in turmoil, she turned the corner of a particularly grand hallway filled with ornate columns and gilded statues to be confronted by an elegant, sweeping staircase of polished stone with a central scarlet carpet running its length.

She descended it without the slightest pause. Then crossing a spacious entrance hall, she made for the magnificent doorway.

The set of double-layered oak doors, embellished with an intricate floral design inset with precious stones, almost reached the high ceiling.

Rhiannon did not even blink when the twin doors suddenly swung outwards, pulled open by invisible hands at her approach.

She stepped across the threshold and absently noted the chill wind sweeping past her.

Her conversation with David and John repeating itself inside her head, she crossed a wide terrace and descended a flight of icy steps into a spacious courtyard.

Nearly killed. Dragon anatomy. Magical charms!

Rhiannon snorted and came to an abrupt stop.

'I'm an idiot!' she muttered to herself. 'As if they were actually telling the truth about what happened. I mean, come on! Dragons and magic aren't real! This is probably just some great, big, elaborate hoax! In fact, there's probably a camera on me right now!'

She glared up at the dark sky overhead.

'I'M NOT FOOLED, YOU KNOW!' she shouted. 'I KNOW YOU'RE OUT THERE SOMEWHERE! I DON'T BELIEVE THIS FOR A SECOND!'

'You are correct in that I am here, but as for not believing, I am afraid there is nothing I can do if you refuse to acknowledge the truth revealed by your own eyes.'

Rhiannon stumbled backwards with a startled yelp. In wide-eyed haste, she retreated from the vast form that had just landed in front of her.

A dragon. A dragon longer than Brakenhurst's tennis court and with a shoulder standing height as tall as the giraffe she had seen at Taronga Zoo on a class trip to Sydney. A dragon that was gazing down at her with an odd mixture of amusement and affection. A dragon that spoke. A dragon that had rather long and sharp teeth!

One bite from those and I'm dead! The less-than-pleasant thought repeated itself in Rhiannon's mind as she continued to back away.

Those claws look sharp too!

Her eyes never leaving the creature in front of her, she stuttered, 'How ... you ... what ...?'

Oh, that sounded intelligent, her inner voice snarked. Try again, McBride!

'Y-You're real!'

Rhiannon's inner voice retreated in disgust.

The dragon smiled gently. 'Of course I'm real. My name is Endrille, and there is no reason to be afraid.'

Another cautious step backwards. A brief pause. 'You mean, you're not going to eat me?'

A laugh, loud and merry, escaped Endrille. 'Dragons do not obtain nourishment by consuming either meat or vegetation. Our lives are sustained by the heat of the sun and the air we breathe.'

Rhiannon still regarded her sharp teeth and claws warily. 'You don't want to rip me to pieces?'

'I mean you no harm, and nor does any other being within these castle walls.'

Rhiannon choked.

'Castle!'

Swallowing the sudden lump rising in her throat, she turned her head and finally took in her surroundings.

A palatial edifice made of stone towered above her, its height illuminated by the golden light pouring from the many rows of arch windows along its length and in several tall towers. Low stone walls engraved with runes guarded the extensive courtyard and the formal flower gardens, whose paths shimmered with a strange glow, while farther away in the gathering darkness, she could see an array of intricately designed buildings. There, nearly half the length of a soccer field away in the middle of the wide courtyard and carved out of white marble, was a large fountain. Lit by an inner light, the pale stone gleamed in the evening twilight. Its centrepiece contained five different stone dragons guarding a sixth, which bore a slight resemblance to Endrille, and mounted on its back were the figures of a youth and a young girl.

'H-How did I get here?' Rhiannon transferred her gaze away from the fountain and back to the living and breathing dragon in front of her. 'And more to the point, where exactly is here?'

'To answer your second question, you are in the land of Álnair, in Valieoth Castle, home of its sovereignty, near the city of Cendillis. Now, as to how you came to be here, you were brought to the palace by myself and Sir Raeden Wyvern after you were struck down by a charm cast by an impetuous and less than intelligent guard.'

'Is that the one who almost killed me?' Rhiannon asked, her wariness slightly lessened by the dragon's calm and gentle manner.

'Yes, it is,' Endrille replied, her voice clearly showing her surprise. 'How did you know that?'

'There were two boys in the room where I woke up. They told me some things.' Rhiannon's eyes suddenly blazed as she remembered the encounter, her anger burning away even more of her earlier fear. 'One of them was extremely rude to me! He made it sound like it was all *my* fault I got attacked in the first place!'

Endrille gave a small chuckle. 'That would have to be David. Stars above, but that boy certainly knows how to make a great first impression. However, I am sure he did not mean to imply that he blamed you.'

Rhiannon gave an indignant sniff, her arms crossing defensively. 'That's what the other one said. But until he apologises, I don't intend to listen to another word he has to say.'

'I suppose I can understand your reluctance. He has been rather difficult these past few days,' Endrille said. 'Although, some allowance must be made for him. Finding your body in the forest and believing you to be dead disturbed him a great deal.

'And now, small one, tell me what you are doing standing out here ankle-deep in snow, in nothing but a nightgown, with no shoes on your feet.'

Startled, Rhiannon glanced down and realised for the first time why she was feeling so cold.

'My sandals are gone!' she exclaimed in surprise.

'Yes, I had noticed,' came Endrille's wry response.

'And this isn't my uniform!' Rhiannon clutched a handful of the silky material adorning her body, gazing at it intently. 'I've certainly never worn anything like this in my life!'

Before Endrille had a chance to respond, the sounds of an argument drifted out through the opening doors of the palace, the voices carrying in the quiet evening.

'It's not *my* fault she left! All I said was ...'

'I did not request a verbatim account of your conversation with the girl, nor do I seek to participate in the pointless exercise of engaging you in a verbal confrontation, which would only serve to lessen my already depleted patience, and increase my desire to use your tongue in one of my experiments.'

Rhiannon was surprised when Endrille, instead of displaying any concern at overhearing such a threat, merely laughed quietly and remarked, 'Sir Raeden is certainly cheerful this evening.'

'But, Sir, John was there too! He can tell you exactly what was said! All I did was try and point out to her that it was stupid to wander about in the snow in nothing more than a thin scrap of material, and ...'

'Did it ever occur to your pampered and overly sheltered brain, *Your Royal Highness*, that perhaps the girl had no other garments to wear?'

The question was asked in a tone so scathing that it came as no surprise to either Rhiannon or Endrille when no answer was forthcoming. Rhiannon was, however, startled by the appellation used to address David.

'I thought not,' the baritone voice continued, 'and I do not want to hear another word from you until we find ...'

'RHIANNON!'

The exclamation rang out in the open courtyard. Gazing at David as he hurried down the steps towards her, Rhiannon was astonished to see him grinning widely. No one in her memory had ever been so happy to see her.

'You're all right! And I see you've met Endrille. It didn't shock you too much, did it? Most people when they see her for the first time do tend to feel a bit overwhelmed, I guess it's because being the only ancient dragon left, she is larger than any of the other dragons you've seen.' David turned to look at the furious man behind him. 'See, I told you she was fine!' he said triumphantly.

'That remains to be seen,' came the sharp reply.

Rhiannon transferred her gaze to the tall figure advancing furiously into the courtyard. His dark burgundy cloak was swirling behind him like enraged storm clouds, and she was bemused to realise his icy glare was not directed at either herself or David, but at Endrille!

'With all due respect, Lady Endrille,' he stated with severe formality, his dark eyebrows drawn together in a glowering frown above his strong nose, 'I hardly expected such careless behaviour from you. The child is barely recovered from an almost fatal attack, and yet you allow her to remain outside in these conditions without first ensuring she has adequate protection against the weather.'

As he came to a halt directly in front of her, Rhiannon watched in disbelief as the man she vaguely recalled seeing near the forest loosened the silver clasp of his cloak from around his neck. Then, with a sweeping gesture, he had the garment off his shoulders and around hers before she could offer even a token protest.

The welcome warmth from the woollen cloak began to seep into her chilled skin, and the scent of sandalwood enveloped her like a cloud. She was further startled when she was swept up into the air and held several feet above the ground by a pair of strong arms.

'What're you doing?'

Rhiannon grasped frantically at Sir Raeden's deep green tunic, struggling to straighten her body from the unfamiliar position.

'By Ryegoth's tail, girl! Calm yourself. I am not likely to drop you, unless you insist on behaving in the manner of a deranged eel.' Tightening his hold around her, Sir Raeden then returned his attention to Endrille. 'Now she is awake, King Stephen has ordered that the hearing to determine her future commence tomorrow morning at 9 o'clock. He felt it necessary to expedite the process given what we know, and her young age.'

'I suppose that makes sense,' David said thoughtfully. 'She can't be more than eleven or twelve.'

Squeaking in outrage, Rhiannon twisted awkwardly in Sir Raeden's arms to glare at him.

'I'll have you know I'm turning fourteen next August, and I can look after myself!'

'That's enough,' Sir Raeden said sharply. He curtailed any further argument by turning about and returning up the path to the palace door, with a warning to David to follow him. 'And if I hear so much as a whispered protest passing your lips, I will have you doing a full training session at dawn every day for a month. Lady Endrille, I will be out shortly to discuss tomorrow's hearing with you.'

Rhiannon glanced over Sir Raeden's shoulder to see Endrille nod solemnly. 'I will be here, Sir Raeden, and my apologies for keeping the child outside.'

The only indication that Sir Raeden heard this was a curt inclination of the head. Then he proceeded through the open door into the warm interior of the palace.

Chapter 6

A DANGEROUS INTEREST

He was going to be late!

The dark-haired man hurriedly dimmed the lights of his office, threw off his official brown robes to put on his fur-lined cloak and strode for the door.

He's not going to be pleased, especially when I tell him it's not ready. Maybe I should send that old goat Plancy in my place.

'Did you hear? The girl they found in the forest is awake.'

The awed voice brought the man to a halt. Intently, he listened to the gossiping voices out in the corridor.

'Do you think it's true? About her surviving the Glaciocaptus?'

'I doubt it. But we'll find out tomorrow. The king's ordered a hearing to take place tomorrow morning.'

The man bit back a virulent oath.

That means I'll have to be here. Still … surviving the Glaciocaptus? If that is true, the girl could be of interest to Him.

The man smiled unpleasantly.

And to me.

~*Chapter 7*~

STORIES IN
THE NIGHT

For Rhiannon, the journey back to her bedchamber was far different from when she had left it. Without having to navigate the long hallways and winding staircases herself, she had the opportunity to better observe their splendour as she was carried through them.

There were gilt-edged furnishings polished to perfection; resplendent marble floors beneath magnificent chandeliers suspended from ornately carved ceilings; and in the entrance hall was a gargantuan Christmas tree between the double staircase bedecked in garlands of flowers and ribbons.

A great number of guards stood at attention throughout the many corridors. Dressed in fine uniforms of white tunics, black breeches, high leather boots and red or dark grey cloaks, they were all armed with swords. Some even had fearsome looking dogs at their sides.

'You need not fear them,' Sir Raeden informed her. 'They are well trained and never attack until ordered to do so.'

'Oh, I'm not afraid of dogs,' she promptly assured him.

And a good thing too, she thought. The dogs all looked like the old Irish Wolfhound the Dashmont's neighbour used to own, only much bigger.

Several twisting corridors later they reached another hallway filled with people in beautiful raiment. The crowd paused in their animated conversations to greet David and Sir Raeden as they passed through.

'Why didn't I see any of them before?' Rhiannon asked David after they left the throng behind.

'They've been having their evening meal. It's where John and I were before we noticed his siblings had disappeared.'

Rhiannon stared at him. 'You mean, someone had to prepare meals for all those people to eat at the same time? That'd take forever!'

'Not really. Hestor the Chief Steward makes sure the cooks have plenty of help. He also oversees all the other staff in the palace. He was the one who appointed one of the maids and House Faeries to look after you while you were sleeping.'

'House Faeries?'

'Yes, there's quite a number of them working here,' David replied. 'My father asked some of the older ones if they wanted to retire, but they said they'd become addlepated with nothing to do. So now there's hundreds of them flying about the place during the day. And at night there's even more out and about when they go to the vegetable garden and orchard to harvest their own food. This is the entrance to the South Wing where your bedchamber is located, so you won't be able to see them from your balcony, but it's quite a sight if you get a chance from the turret on the Main Tower. From there on a clear day you can also see past Cendillis and the farmlands along the western coastline to the town of Belnight, and if you turn to the north you'll see the tallest tower at Ryegoth Academy behind Shaimar Forest, along with the Del Enger Mountains.'

The names all meant nothing to Rhiannon, but she listened as David went on to give a running commentary on the rooms they passed. His earlier flash of anger had apparently burnt itself out, revealing a friendly and rather amiable personality.

Sir Raeden, on the other hand, did not say a word. Preserving a stern silence, he effortlessly carried her through the lengthy hallways and up several staircases, his long stride forcing David to frequently quicken his pace to keep up.

'This is the top level of the Upper South Wing,' David revealed after they finished ascending yet another staircase.

Rhiannon looked up to see a raised dais and stone console inside a small alcove in the wall opposite them.

Sir Raeden turned to the left and headed down the lengthy hallway. Looking over his shoulder, she saw another hallway, equally as long, going in the other direction. Both were beautifully furnished, with tables and chairs placed at calculated intervals between the doorways on either side, and large paintings on the walls. The thick red carpet running down the centre of the marble floor muffled her companion's footsteps, making the prince's voice the only sound to break the elegant silence as he continued his commentary on each room.

The walk took several minutes before they came close to the end of the hallway. Then David announced, 'And here we are, back at your bedchamber.'

Rhiannon looked at the arched doorway. Gold scrollwork, patterened in a series of Celtic knots, decorated the thick stone frame. The intricate design was also engraved in the solid oak door.

David turned and pushed the door's sturdy metal handle.

Sir Raeden walked across the threshold and through the antechamber into the main apartment.

Rhiannon's eyes widened as she beheld it properly for the first time.

Illuminated by the soft light of a small chandelier hung from the high, mural-covered ceiling, every inch of the room radiated elegance, from the sweeping silver-blue curtains covering most of the farthest wall, to the gossamer drapes on the four-poster bed and the beautiful, handcrafted dressing table in the corner. A cheerful fire burned in a large stone hearth, while on the opposite wall an open door led into a luxurious bathroom with a lavish sunken bath. A tall wardrobe towered over the other furnishings in the room, including a fine writing desk containing a pile of parchment, an inkwell and a quill.

Annabelle's room is a poky little cell compared to this, she thought.

Sir Raeden bent down to lower her to the ground with awkward gentleness.

'You may have one of the servants return the cloak later, Miss McBride. For now, I will leave you in the hands of Aleda, whom you will obey implicitly,' he informed her after straightening back up to his full height.

Rhiannon nodded, wondering who Aleda could be.

Sir Raeden answered her unspoken question by turning around and saying clearly, 'Aleda.'

A tiny, shining ball of light began to shimmer in the middle of the chamber, and the delicate aroma of moist earth and fresh grass suffused the space around it.

Then, a small figure appeared.

Although almost humanoid in appearance, it was clear the creature was not human. Standing at just over two feet tall, with glowing fair skin, pointed ears and green hair streaming past its shoulders, and wearing a flowing golden dress, the figure raised its wide brown eyes and smiled.

'Yes, Sir Raeden.'

The melodic voice carried on the air like the sweetest carillon bell.

'Aleda, a warm bath needs to be prepared for Miss McBride, then she is to have a light meal before taking the sleeping draught I will send up for her. She is also required to attend the hearing tomorrow morning at 9 o'clock. Please ensure she is prepared and escorted to the Praeterium in sufficient time. Is that understood?'

Aleda nodded, her feet rising a few inches off the ground. 'Certainly, Sir Raeden, I will ensure everything is as you order,' she said cheerfully.

'Thank you.' Sir Raeden bestowed a final nod in Rhiannon's direction with a polite, 'Good evening,' before striding to the door.

David, who had been idly fiddling with one of the crystal bottles on the dressing table, smiled at her and prepared to leave as well, when an auburn-haired form abruptly stepped through the doorway and collided heavily into Sir Raeden's side.

'OW!'

'Confounded boy! Get your foot off mine this instant!'

John leapt backward only to fall forward once again as he banged into the doorframe.

Watching as the hapless John fumbled against Sir Raeden for a second time while clutching his aching head, David was startled to hear muffled laughter coming from behind him. He turned to find the source of the sound and stared in amazement to find Rhiannon laughing quietly into her hand, her eyes dancing with mirth. Beside her, Aleda's tiny face bore the same expression of amusement.

'I'm so sorry, Sir, I didn't know you were in here.' John's apologetic voice recalled David's attention to his predicament. Turning back, he saw Sir Raeden glaring fiercely at the penitent Chief Robesman.

'Perhaps if you refrained from entering a room in the manner reminiscent of an intoxicated troll, you would not find it difficult to prevent yourself from assailing any person unfortunate enough to be in your vicinity.'

Sir Raeden shot a baleful glare at both boys, straightened his rumpled tunic, then pivoted on his heel while saying sharply over his shoulder, 'You are both expected to be in attendance at the hearing tomorrow morning at 9 o'clock. No exceptions will be made. Tardiness will not be tolerated.' As he stepped through the doorway, he added smoothly, 'And Aleda, should these two miscreants decide to linger, you have full leave to force them out by any means necessary.'

And with that, Sir Raeden disappeared from sight.

For a moment, no one in the room spoke. Then, a little voice said, 'Your eyes are very pretty. They shine like the brightest sunbeam.'

Aleda was hovering in front of a bemused Rhiannon and gazing into her eyes with fascinated awe.

'Um, excuse me, but what are you?'

Aleda flew back several inches and peered at her curiously.

'You have never seen a faery before?' she asked incredulously.

Rhiannon shook her head, the action causing Aleda to gape at her in disbelief, while distinct sounds of surprise came from David and John.

'But how is that possible? My race can be found in any city or small town! And we're not exactly shy of strangers.'

'Now that I will definitely confirm,' David commented drily. 'Some can be the most brazen creatures. John, do you remember the one who tried to flirt with you in Rëalta Lake that time? And you were only nine.'

'Pfft.' Aleda waved a dismissive hand. 'Water Faeries! They never know how to behave, unlike we House Faeries.'

'Oh, really?' David stepped forward. Raising an eyebrow, he asked innocently, 'And who helped the terrible trio infiltrate the kitchen earlier today and release a barrage of frogs?'

An interesting shade of red spread across Aleda's cheeks.

'That was – I was only – they only wanted to watch them play in the water,' she tried to explain.

'All right, enough!' Rhiannon's exasperated voice rang through the room. 'Dragons! Charms! Faeries releasing armies of frogs in a kitchen! Would someone just tell me where I am in a way that makes sense? You say I'm in a palace, but all I've seen are a bunch of rooms and one courtyard, which could easily have been put together inside a very convincing facility used to manipulate me into believing I wasn't kidnapped and brought here for some twisted form of entertainment. Even the dragon and the front of this building could've been an illusion!'

An uncomfortable silence descended.

David and John stared at her, both of them stunned into silence.

Aleda appeared similarly afflicted, but then she flew across the room to grasp the edge of one of the silver-blue curtains.

'It might be best for you to see the truth for yourself,' she said softly, and with a swift tug she pulled the curtain aside, revealing a large, arched doorway leading out to an open balcony.

Aleda opened one of the glass doors and beckoned Rhiannon forward. 'Come, child, and see.'

Rhiannon gathered the luminous folds of Sir Raeden's cloak about her, then cautiously followed the faery. She paused, a warm tingle running through her body as she stepped through the doorway.

'There's something here, I can feel it. What is it?' she asked nervously.

'It will not harm you. It is merely an old enchantment barrier Endrille, Queen of the Ancient Dragons created around the castle,' Aleda explained.

Rhiannon tentatively stepped forward again, then slowly made her way over the chilly stone floor to the edge of the balcony.

The distinctive scent of saltwater perfumed the air.

Placing her hands on the balustrade, she inhaled sharply at the sight that met her eyes. Far below her and spread out beneath the night sky like a giant, shimmering blanket was the ocean. Its surface reflected the brilliant white radiance of the moon and stars overhead, while its soft murmuring waves rolled gently towards an unseen shore.

'It's the Dairíon Ocean,' Aleda informed her.

Rhiannon turned her head and saw the faint outline of the coast, the jagged edges of land stretching into the gathering darkness. Returning her gaze to the ocean, she leant forward. The faintest strains of music drifted on the night air. The tune was beautiful yet melancholy.

She closed her eyes as singing began to blend with the music. The voices were rich and fair, and sung in a strange language, but their lingering melody filled the darkness with a haunting sadness that she could feel deep within her heart.

'What do the lyrics mean?' she asked.

'It is hard to translate them into one of our languages,' David's voice answered quietly from behind her. 'But I will try if you like?'

Rhiannon nodded.

A brief pause fell, then David started speaking again, his clear, soft voice lending his words a poignant quality:

> *Glorious and radiant,*
> *belov'd by all within the sea,*
> *the mighty monarch's daughter*
> *was the fairest ever seen.*
>
> *With skin of shining pearl*
> *and hair of purest starlight,*
> *this jewel of grace and beauty*
> *would soon fade beyond our sight.*

The night was dark and cruel,
when the treachery was committed,
a message was sent to the fair one,
tho' the truth was carefully omitted.

"Your dearest now lies slain,"
the grim message did say,
"in the dread tumult of battle,
he fell this fateful day."

Our glittering star of the sea,
heart-broken by words of violence,
gave in to grief and sorrow,
and faded into silence.

Her dearest love Orthorion
upon hearing of this news,
broke down and wept in anguish,
before making the deception true.

"Who is guilty of this crime,"
wept the stars within the sky.
'Who dared to destroy
the ocean's crowning joy?"

The answer when it came
made them cry out in dismay,
For it was her own dear sister
who betrayed her trust that day.

Through the sins of vanity and spite,
and an envy of her light,
the mighty monarch's daughter
was destroyed that winter night.

But if you look to the heavens,
to this day it can be seen,
the shining northern star
that guides the ships at sea.

This star it did appear,
that very night we are told,
the moment the light faded
from the lovely Elvanor.

David's voice fell silent as the last lingering note of the song floated across the water. Rhiannon surreptitiously wiped at her eyes and sniffed.

'That's so sad,' she whispered.

'It is one of the oldest of the merfolk's ballads,' Aleda said. 'They sing it every year in winter to remember their lost princess. It happened over three thousand years ago, and yet they still remember it as though it were only yesterday.'

Startled, Rhiannon turned to look at Aleda's solemn expression. 'Merfolk?' she exclaimed. 'You mean they-ey … a-achoo!'

The loud sneeze from her charge had Aleda instantly abandoning the conversation, and Rhiannon found herself being hustled back inside her bedroom by the distraught faery.

'Oh, this is my fault!' Aleda cried in distress, hastily closing the glass door and sliding the curtain back into place. 'And me in charge of looking after you! I shouldn't have let you stay outside so long. Sir Raeden will be very angry with me. Oh dear, oh dear! Boys, out of the room this instant. Oh!' An expression of deep mortification spread across Aleda's face. Apologetically, she turned to face David. 'I beg your pardon, Your Royal Highness. I did not mean to sound so rude. I …'

'That's quite all right, Aleda,' David interrupted, waving her apology aside, 'you know I'm not like Aunt Phoebe. Besides, how could I be angry at the one who always helps get me out of trouble?'

He gave the relieved faery another smile and walked towards the door, only to come to an abrupt halt. He glanced awkwardly at Rhiannon's pale face, then ruefully ran a hand through his hair.

Slowly, he returned to stand in front of her.

She looked up and blinked in shock. Underneath his dark, finely arched eyebrows and set between long sooty lashes, his eyes were a rich violet, like freshly watered lavender bathed in sunlight.

Rhiannon had never before seen such a beautiful shade.

'I'm very sorry for how I behaved earlier,' David said with a stilted air of nervous sincerity. 'I know I was a right prat in the way I spoke to you. There's no excuse for it so I won't make any for myself, except to say I was still rattled by the fact you were almost killed by that sapskull, and … well …'

He paused and rubbed the back of his neck.

'I guess I just wanted to let you know I don't blame you for what happened,' he finished, 'and if I really did imply it, then I truly am sorry.'

Rhiannon felt a strange warmth begin to grow inside her. She had never been the recipient of such an honest apology before, and David looked so contrite she could not help but smile.

'It's all right, Dav— I mean, Your Royal Highness. I didn't make things any better by shouting at you. Waking up in a strange place isn't exactly something I'm used to.'

'It's just David,' he said, returning her smile. 'I can't stand all that formal pomp and ceremony. Aleda only does it when she forgets, or if she wants to annoy me. And John does it occasionally when he feels I'm being too insufferable. I'm sure you'll soon find a time to call me it as well. I can be quite haughty when I want to be.'

'That is definitely true,' John agreed. 'He can be a regular peacock sometimes.'

'Only sometimes? I must be improving. You once told me I acted like one most of the time,' David quipped, and turned his attention to the House Faery who was pointedly hovering near the door. 'You're not very subtle, Aleda. All right, we'll go now, so don't throw us out. And don't worry about finding an escort to take Rhiannon to the Praeterium in the morning. John and I will do it. That way, we can explain a few more things to her before the hearing starts.'

'Hang on!' Rhiannon said. 'Everyone keeps talking about a hearing. What's it for? It sounds like they'll be putting me on trial or something.'

'On trial?' David repeated incredulously. 'Why would they be putting you on trial? The hearing is to determine what should happen to you because of our concern for your welfare. You were found alone in the forest, during winter, and wearing nothing but a very short tunic and sandals. You didn't even have a warm cloak with you. I'm surprised your parents let you go out like that!'

'My parents went missing years ago,' Rhiannon said quietly.

'Oh.' David bit his lip. 'Sorry.'

An awkward silence fell and was only broken when John said gently, 'Rhiannon, I think the most important thing right now is for you to have something to eat and then get some sleep. Everything will be sorted out tomorrow.'

David voiced his agreement, adding, 'John and I will stay with you for the whole thing, and remember, you're not in trouble, so don't worry.'

Rhiannon kept her reservations to herself and gave both boys a grateful smile. 'I'll try not to,' she said. 'Goodnight and thank you.'

David stepped out of the room with a friendly 'goodnight'. He disappeared around the corner, only for his head to suddenly tilt back round the doorway. He had a teasing smirk on his face and his eyes sparkled with humour. 'Come along, John! No lingering, remember? We've got ourselves a game of King's Table to play,' he said, referring to a strategy board game, 'and I *am* going to beat you this time. Besides, what would your mother have to say if she heard you were loitering in a lady's bedchamber?'

John muttered good-naturedly about insufferable royal brats, then said his own goodnight and walked out the door. From inside the room, Rhiannon and Aleda heard him say, 'One day I'm going to swap your tooth powder for ground-up stink beetles! And I lay claim to the army attackers! You can be the king and his defenders.'

'But I was going to be the enemy!'

'You were the enemy last time. Anyway, it's more suitable for you to play the part of the king, *Your Royal Highness*.'

A sudden thud echoed back to the bedchamber followed by a pained, 'OW!'

Aleda closed the door as the sound of friendly arguing and scuffles drifted farther away. Spinning around, she took one look at Rhiannon's exhausted face and declared, 'Right, straight in the bath with you, Miss McBride, and then into bed.' She clapped her hands once and pointed commandingly in the direction of the bathroom. 'In you go, and there'll be some lovely chicken and vegetable soup when you finish.'

Rhiannon obediently walked to the bathroom door. She paused when she reached its threshold. Looking back at the hovering faery, she said with a small smile, 'By the way, I do prefer Rhiannon.'

An answering grin appeared on Aleda's face. 'It is an honour and a privilege to serve you, Rhiannon. Now, shoo! Sir Raeden will have my head if you come down sick.'

Rhiannon went into the bathroom without another word and closed the door.

She came out a while later accompanied by a billow of steam. Her body was beautifully warmed by the hot water and dressed in a fresh nightgown. She stumbled tiredly towards the large bed.

'That's the loveliest bathroom I've ever seen,' she mumbled through a yawn as she crawled under the coverlet. She took a moment to appreciate the soft warmth that immediately enveloped her. 'All those gold taps, and the bath is simply enormous! You could fit a dozen people in there!'

Aleda smiled happily and pulled the blankets up to cover her properly. 'You certainly look much better now,' she said, before performing a quick movement with her hand.

A delicate silver tray instantly appeared on Rhiannon's lap.

Her stomach growled in hunger when she smelt the delicious aroma rising out of the bowl. Embarrassed, she placed a hand over her stomach. 'Sorry,' she murmured. 'It's just …'

'No need to apologise for that, child,' Aleda interrupted her pleasantly. 'There's nothing wrong with your stomach declaring it is hungry. In my two hundred years I've heard many sounds, the least offensive of which would have to be a stomach growling.'

Rhiannon choked on the spoonful of soup she had just placed in her mouth. Her eyes watering, she gaped at the faery in front of her.

'Two hundred years!' she exclaimed, politeness forgotten in her shock. 'But, you look so young! You can't be that old!'

A tinkling laugh passed Aleda's lips. Slowly, she sank down onto the bed covers and settled in comfortably. 'Faeries live for a very long time, Rhiannon. Our age can reach into thousands of years. I am still considered a child by many of my people, including my family. The worst is my brother, Isidore. To him I am still the same, helpless little faery child he had to guide in her first flights and rescue on numerous occasions when my curiosity got the best of me.'

'It must be nice having an older brother,' Rhiannon said wistfully, recalling John's affectionate forbearance with his own brothers and sister.

'It certainly has its moments,' Aleda agreed honestly. 'The heavens protect anyone foolish enough to attempt anything against one of Isidore's siblings.'

'How old is your brother?' Rhiannon asked, taking another mouthful of soup.

'Why, let me see now.' Aleda thought for a moment. 'Why, he'll be nine hundred and ninety-eight next spring. Oh dear. I dread to think what he'll be like when he reaches a thousand!' Casting her eyes heavenward, she sighed. 'Once they reach a thousand, most faeries become very pedantic about how things should be done. They forever go on about how things were done in their day and complain about "these flighty younglings".'

Rhiannon's head spun at the thought of any creature living for such a length of time. Then, recalling David's earlier revelations about the House Faeries, she asked, 'Is it true there's hundreds of faeries here in the palace?'

Aleda nodded. 'Once a faery has come here to work, we rarely ever leave again, and those who do only ever go back to the traditional home of our kin in the Del Enger Mountains.'

'So you live here?'

'Yes. We have special quarters designed specifically for us.'

'What sort of work do you all do?'

Aleda shrugged. 'Unlike the men and women of your race who are assigned particular chores by the position they are given, we do whatever needs doing,' she said. 'We particularly attend to cleaning and polishing the high ceilings and windows, for it is much easier for us to do it.'

'Well, I hope you get extra pay for doing that,' Rhiannon said with a small laugh.

'Pay!' Aleda exclaimed in shock. 'We do not ask for monetary rewards for what we do. We have no need of it. We offer our services freely to those who will accept them. If payment it can be called, those who work in the palace are invited to take what food they need from the crops grown in the fields and the trees in the orchards. There are others who work in farmhouses and dwellings in the cities who do the same.'

'So, you get room and board,' Rhiannon summed up.

Her words brought a slight frown to Aleda's face.

'I am not familiar with that phrase,' the faery said.

'Basically, it means you get a place to stay and food in return for doing work.'

'Oh.' Aleda thought it over for a moment, then smiled. 'I like it,' she declared. 'Although it is not quite right, especially for those who work here in the palace. If we become too old to move, or are sick, we may remain. The House of Valieoth has always been kind to our race, just as they are generous to all those who serve them.'

Rhiannon stirred her cooling soup. The glimmer of an idea was beginning to form inside her mind. She still had no idea how she had come to be in this strange place, but certainly (all weird happenings aside!) the people were a lot nicer than those back in Brakenhurst. If she could persuade them to let her stay, she was sure there was something she could do to earn a living – so long as people her age could be employed! Perhaps they might even have a charm that could help her discover what had happened to her parents.

'Do the human servants in the palace get paid?' she asked.

'Of course. For many it is the way they support their families. There are some, like John, who do not receive payment, although any expenses they incur due to performing their duties are paid from the castle treasury.'

'Why doesn't John get paid?'

'He is Chief Robesman to the Prince Royal,' Aleda said, as though this explained everything.

'I'm sorry, but I don't know what that is. My education hasn't been big on describing the different employment opportunities available in a castle,' Rhiannon explained quite truthfully.

Aleda looked suitably astonished. 'Your teachers must be very lax,' she said. 'The position of Robesman has existed since the time of the first High King of Álnair, and several are always appointed to each king and prince royal. Traditionally, the Robesmen's main duties were to accompany their lord whenever he left the castle grounds; perform the duties of an aide; hold his garments when he was bathing; and assist him in changing his raiment every day. The last two duties are now only required on their coronation or wedding day – which is extremely fortunate, for David is at that age where he would not hesitate to kick anyone who tried to help him get dressed!'

Rhiannon giggled at the thought of a half-dressed and scowling David kicking a strangely servile John away as he tried to tie a belt around his waist.

'So, I guess the Chief Robesman is the best out of all of them?' she said.

'In a way,' Aleda replied. 'The Robesmen are those who have proved their loyalty to the king and prince royal. On a prince's fifth birthday, twenty boys from among those he knows are chosen to be his main companions for the next several years. They may be the same age, or older. Derrick Fasani, one of those chosen for David, is his elder by six years. Then, once the prince turns fourteen, the five who have proved to be the most trustworthy will be appointed his Robesmen. The one who has shown the greatest devotion to the prince is given the title of Chief Robesman.

'Of course, friendship is bound to arise, along with a certain informality of manner between them. You saw how John teases David quite openly. But every boy assigned as a Robesman is taught not to take advantage of their position, and to never forget they are to be first and foremost an aide, not a friend. It can be difficult, especially if their lord chooses to put his life in danger and orders them not to interfere. John has an exceptionally hard time with David. That boy attracts trouble like pollen-rich flowers attract bees, and he never permits John to go first if he decides to try something dangerous. When he was eight, he decided he wanted to ride two horses at once. Do you know how that's done?'

Rhiannon shook her head, her attention captured by the story.

'The rider stands atop a pair of horses, with one foot on each mount. It is extremely difficult and quite dangerous. David is an exceptionally gifted rider,' Aleda observed with pride, 'and he was skilled enough to maintain his balance when he took them around the arena. Then he wanted to take them over one of the practice jumps. In the middle of the jump he lost his balance and fell. He broke his left arm and was knocked unconscious. Poor John was watching, and everyone who heard him scream David's name didn't waste any time in getting to the arena – especially the senior guard who was supposed to be with them, and who could've stopped David from doing anything too reckless. He'd been talking with the grooms in the stables and Sir Raeden, who arrived before he did, demoted him on the spot. David remained unconscious for two days. Everyone tried to get John to go home, but he absolutely refused. He insisted it was his responsibility to remain by David's side. Even after David awoke, he remained in the palace until David was completely healed.'

'If he's always like that then I'm not surprised he was appointed Chief Robesman,' Rhiannon said.

Aleda nodded. 'He does not take his duties lightly. Besides, David won his loyalty when he risked his own life to save him the year before.'

'What happened?'

'He got an enraged bull to chase after him. He was visiting John's family with his father, and after they'd indulged their love of climbing trees, the boys walked across a field that was normally kept free of livestock; only this time it wasn't. Unfortunately, they didn't see the horned bull until it was charging towards them. The fence wasn't too far away, but John had sprained his ankle climbing down a tree. David knew the bull would reach them before they could get over the fence, so he told John to keep going and took off at a run in the other direction. Of course, the bull chased after him. If it had managed to catch him, he would've been killed or severely hurt. Thankfully, he's such a resourceful boy. He made straight for the wide stream that runs through the field. He swam across to the other side and left the snorting bull behind him. Ever since that day, John rarely lets a day pass during the holidays when he doesn't come to see David.'

'Why doesn't he live in the palace?' Rhiannon asked. 'I would've thought it would make more sense for him to do that than to have to travel.'

'While he is young, David does not require a Robesman to be in full attendance, so all his Robesmen are free to go home for the night during the month they are rostered to attend upon him. When he is older this will change. He shall always have two in attendance, and accommodation will be provided here in the palace during the months they're on duty.'

'Are rooms provided for all the other servants as well?' Rhiannon said with studied casualness.

'Of course, although there are some who choose to live in the surrounding farms and in Cendillis. They come on the days they are rostered, then return home after their workday.'

Rhiannon, determined not to appear too eager, waited a moment before saying, 'I guess there are a few females working here as well.'

'Indeed there are,' Aleda said, bobbing her head enthusiastically. 'There are the Ladies of the Girdle who wait upon Queen Maiwen, and then all the ones who are paid for their services, like those on the cleaning staff or in the kitchens. There are also the ones who teach in the school, the librarians, healers, apothecaries. There are many positions available for them.' The faery paused, then looked at Rhiannon inquisitively. 'Would you be interested in working here after you finish your schooling?'

'Possibly, but I might not be here. I'm not even entirely sure where I'll be this time tomorrow night,' Rhiannon answered, feeling dismayed that it appeared she would have to leave the palace. Despite his flare of temper, David had been very nice to her (he'd also apologised!) and she would miss not being able to speak with him.

Although even if I was able to work here, it wouldn't mean I'd get to talk to him, she thought. He's a prince! I'm sure there's probably some rule against junior servants being in the same room as him.

She finished the last of the soup, then smothered a large yawn with her hand.

'I'm sorry, Aleda, but I do feel very tired now,' she said, brushing a hand over her eyes.

In a flash, the faery was rising above the bed and making the tray disappear with a flick of her wrist. 'Never mind, we can always talk another time. Now, while you were in the bathroom Sir Raeden sent up the sleeping draught you're to take.' She pointed to a small, blue bottle on the table beside the bed. 'Make sure you drink every drop.'

Rhiannon picked up the glass bottle. She warily unscrewed the lid and took a cautious sniff of its contents.

'Doesn't smell too bad. It's a bit like lemon and chamomile.'

She gave the bottle another suspicious glance, then shrugged. Lifting the bottle to her lips, she swallowed the entire contents in one gulp.

A warm, comforting feeling instantly spread throughout her body. She dropped her suddenly heavy arm back onto the bed and relaxed against the soft feather pillows as her eyes started to close.

A tiny hand passed tenderly over her forehead and as her mind began to drift into unconsciousness, she heard Aleda's soft voice say, 'May your dreams bring you rest, dear child, and may the Blessed Light always shine upon you.'

Chapter 8

A Clandestine Meeting

Y ou're late.'

The chilling voice made the new arrival to the dark moor in the High Wolds hurriedly dismount from his horse. Bowing with obsequious servility, and already regretting his decision not to send Plancy in his stead, he rushed to offer an apology but was cut off.

'Spare me your inane prattling. Where is the potion?'

His hands twisting anxiously, the man shrank into himself. 'It … It's not ready.'

The heavily cloaked figure stepped out of the shadow of a large rock. The dreadful scar on his aged right cheek was a gruesome, red mess in the silver moonlight.

'Why?'

The man flinched at the low, menacing hiss. 'I … I need more ingredients.' Reaching beneath his fur-lined cloak with fumbling fingers, he extracted a small scroll. It was snatched from his hand and opened.

'Three more dragon hearts. The blood of a phoenix. The Dragonstar of ten magi.'

The scroll was incinerated in a flash of blue flame.

'They will be at the laboratory by tomorrow morning. When shall the potion be ready?'

'These things can't be rushed. It's going to take time to ... AH!'

The stream of crimson light encircling the man hurled him against the rock.

'Such are the excuses of idlers and the apathetic. Our master has been imprisoned for far too long and his freedom is paramount. Now, I will ask again: when shall the potion be ready?'

'M ... Mórfran, it's complicated. There are tests I'll need to do.'

'Then you shall immediately commence doing them after I arrive at the laboratory in the morning.'

'I won't ... I won't be there. I have to be back at the castle in the morning. There's to be a hearing for some beggar girl found in the forest.'

'Why would a hearing for such a person be held on a day when all official business is postponed?'

The man shrugged nervously. 'I don't know. The story is she's a lost brat who was hit by Glaciocaptus and survived.'

'That should be impossible.' An ominous note of interest appeared in Mórfran's voice. 'Still, if true, she may be worth studying. Very well. Attend the hearing. Find out about her. I can always arrange her disappearance if our master believes she may be of some use.'

He turned away, his cloak billowing behind him like the wings of a vulture.

'I shall expect better news on the potion when next we meet. Do not disappoint me.'

Then he stepped back into the shadows and vanished.

The man did not waste a moment. He remounted in haste and urged his horse through the moors, as though chased by death itself.

~Chapter 9~

A GUARDIAN FOR
RHIANNON

At the polite but firm knock on her chamber door, Rhiannon hurriedly swallowed the last bite of her breakfast. Nervously, she adjusted her long gown of yellow silk. Then she crossed the antechamber and opened the door.

Lord, love a duck! she thought, her eyes widening at the sight of David.

In his high-collared tunic of deep blue, long white breeches, pristine leather boots and white cloak secured by a gold chain, he made an absolutely striking figure. Beside him, John's appearance was more subdued but no less imposing in a brown tunic and emerald-green cloak. Both had their sword attached to their belt.

'Are you all right?'

Rhiannon blinked at David's concerned query, then shook her head to clear it. 'I'm fine,' she replied. 'Just a little anxious.'

'There's no need to be. Remember, we'll be with you throughout the hearing.'

'And you'd best get her to it right now,' came Aleda's stern voice from the main bedchamber. 'It's eight forty already.'

'Don't worry, we'll go straight there,' David assured her, and six minutes later Rhiannon thought it was fortunate that they had, for she had no desire to be late to the hearing and the distance to the Praeterium was by no means a short stroll. David and John led her down the lengthy hallway from her chambers to the staircase opposite the stone dais. Then they descended three flights of stairs to the massive set of wooden doors which were now in front of her.

The two sentries on duty promptly opened them and stood aside.

'Here we are,' said David, and gestured for her to enter.

Rhiannon slowly moved forward, then crossed over the threshold into the Praeterium.

The room was immense, certainly a lot bigger than the indoor soccer field in Brakenhurst! Tall circular pillars near fresco-covered walls supported the high ceiling, their smooth surface emitting a soft radiance that lit the entire space.

At the very head of the Praeterium was a magnificent mural depicting a wide variety of dragons, merfolk, griffins, dryads, nymphs and faeries, along with a great number of men and women in ceremonial robes. Three high-backed chairs of equal height, of a delicate, glistening silver, stood before it on a high dais. In front of the chairs was a long stone table, heavily engraved with ancient writing.

The middle of the room was cleared of all furniture except for a single chair. Made from black marble, it was set into the ground in the centre of the empty space.

'This way,' urged David, walking up the aisle made by the rows of intricately carved stone benches at the back of the room.

After deciding the best place for her to sit would be in the front row, David placed Rhiannon between himself and John.

Rhiannon shifted on the hard bench to adjust the hem of her gown, then took another look at the head of the room.

'He looks quite fierce,' she said.

'Who?' asked David.

She pointed at the magnificent statue placed near the dais. 'The dragon.'

David smiled. 'Ah, that's Fjenador. Surely you've read about him?'

Rhiannon shook her head. 'Dragons don't really get a mention at my school,' she said carefully.

John looked at her in shock and David inhaled so sharply he choked on empty air.

'Jumping toadstools!' he exclaimed, amid gasps for breath. 'What do you mean they don't get mentioned? Learning about dragons is compulsory!' He shook his head in disbelief.

'All your teachers need to be sacked!' he muttered. Then, in a calmer voice, he explained, 'Fjenador was one of the wisest dragons who ever lived. Not of the ancient line of course. Endrille is the only one of them left, but he was a pretty powerful dragon nonetheless. Some believe it was because his egg was hatched by Endrille after his parents were crushed in the massive landslide in the Del Enger Mountains in 1028. He disappeared about five hundred years ago, and no one has ever been able to find out what happened to him.'

'Couldn't he just have died?' Rhiannon asked. 'I mean, dying is a normal part of life.'

Clearly horrified once again at her lack of general knowledge, David and John simply stared in astonishment. Then, in a serious tone, John said, 'There's nothing normal about a powerful dragon dying.'

'An average dragon can certainly grow old and fade after many centuries,' said David. 'But the only way a truly powerful dragon will die is if they're killed by a physical wound, or by having their energy completely drained.'

'So Fjenador couldn't have just died,' John concluded. 'That's why, even to this day, everyone wonders what became of him. If he was killed, then it must have been something extremely powerful to take him out. I think in terms of power he was second only to Endrille.'

'What's the difference between the two anyway?' Rhiannon asked curiously. 'Between ancient and non-ancient dragons, I mean.'

'Well, the ancients are the elite, if you like, of the dragon races,' David began. 'They possess the full knowledge of the dragon lines, along with incredible power and wisdom. And although their numbers were few, they were universally respected by the other dragons for their leadership and courage.'

'You see, Rhiannon,' John interrupted, 'dragons are like reptiles in that their young are born from an egg. However, while the other dragons can lay up to four eggs every three hundred years, the ancients are only capable of laying one, maybe two eggs, every two thousand years.'

Rhiannon's mouth dropped open in disbelief. 'Did you say two *thousand* years?'

John and David nodded simultaneously.

'Wow.' Rhiannon slowly processed the information before she asked, 'So how old is Endrille?'

'No one knows for sure,' David replied. 'And if you try and ask her, she gets all evasive and speaks in riddles you can't understand, like how time can be measured in many ways by different species.'

John snorted. 'Delia thinks it's because she doesn't want anyone to know how old she is,' he said.

Rhiannon frowned. 'Who's Delia?'

'Delia is John's older sister, Cordelia,' David said with a laugh.

'Although most of the time, I think he would deny that fact if he could.'

John grinned. He went to reply when the doors behind them were thrown open.

Rhiannon, David and John turned around on the bench to gaze at the crowd of people standing there, particularly at the three resplendently robed figures who stood at the front.

Rhiannon stared particularly at the tall man in the middle. His whole being exuded an authoritative presence and noble grace, and a magnificent gold crown adorned his fair head. He wore a long silver-blue robe interspersed with shimmering flecks of red which assumed a purple aura in the light, and at his side there hung a sword whose hilt and sheath were more splendid than David's. A plain gold band encircled his left ring finger, and, like David, on his right forefinger a signet ring glinted under the bright light of the room.

No mistake about it, she thought, that's David's father all right.

Sharing his son's golden hair, strong, slender hands and straight nose, King Stephen stood well over six feet and walked with a confident stride. His high cheekbones were clearly defined under his fair skin, and the laugh lines in the corners of his eyes declared him to also share David's natural good humour.

Rhiannon watched as he made his way up the aisle, his entourage following him at a respectful distance. She saw the impassive expression on his face relax when he saw his son seated beside her.

Then he drew to a halt next to their bench. His voice richly laced with paternal affection, he observed, 'It is certainly an unusual occurrence to see you here early, my son. Are you ill?'

David smiled. 'I do feel rather poorly. I could always go back to bed and come back later, Father.'

King Stephen shook his head in amusement and briefly laid a hand on his son's head.

'Incorrigible boy,' he murmured. Then he looked at his son's companions and Rhiannon saw that, unlike David, his eyes were the clear green of the first leaves of spring.

'Good morning, John,' the king said warmly, 'and this must be our new guest.'

Rhiannon stood up hesitantly, unsure of how she was expected to greet the monarch before her.

'It's an honour to meet you, Your Majesty,' she said politely.

King Stephen smiled and graciously inclined his head. 'I bid you welcome to Valieoth Castle, Rhiannon.'

She stared at him in surprise.

'News travels quickly, my dear. David discovered your name and told Sir Raeden, who then informed Endrille and myself. I believe you have now made the acquaintance of them both.'

'Yes, Your Majesty, I have.'

'Excuse my interruption, Sire,' a respectful voice said, 'but we must commence with the preparations if we are to start on time.'

King Stephen politely acknowledged the man's comment, then returned his attention to Rhiannon. 'I trust you will not find the hearing too overwhelming,' he said kindly. 'And I look forward to speaking to you again once it is finished.'

He bestowed a gentle smile on her, then looked at this son.

There was a distinct twinkle in his eyes when he said, 'David, please try to refrain from creating havoc this time around. I think some of the members are still recovering from the last occasion when you were in attendance.' Transferring his attention to John, he added, 'Although I suppose I should be thankful the terrible trio are not here. I am sure the room would not survive it.'

Rhiannon saw a hint of mirth in John's expression even as he answered in all seriousness, 'I am sure they would be flattered to hear that, Sire. I believe their main mission in life is to wreak havoc wherever they find themselves.'

'Then I had best warn my wife,' King Stephen replied thoughtfully. 'I believe they will be joining the castle school next September. We certainly cannot afford to have Valieoth Castle razed to the ground.'

With a final smile, he stepped away and continued to the front of the room, leaving a confused Rhiannon and two chuckling boys behind him.

'What was that about?' Rhiannon asked in bewilderment.

'What was what about?' David replied.

Rhiannon retook her seat, then pointed to where King Stephen was now seating himself on the middle silver chair. 'What did he mean about you causing trouble and some other people destroying the castle?'

This time it was John who answered her.

'Well, to answer the second question, he was talking about my brothers, Daniel, Edward and Robert. They're triplets who somehow manage to create trouble wherever they go. Demolishing a building that has been standing since before 490AD would be no difficulty for them.'

'As for your first question,' David said with a slight grin, 'the last time I was here I brought along a young snaffler I found.'

Rhiannon frowned. 'Snaffler?'

'They're little creatures with brown fur, slanted eyes, a short bushy tail and a very inquisitive nose. They have a bad habit of taking anything that catches their fancy – even if a person happens to be wearing it. Anyway, I found this tiny one outside my room one morning before I had to come here, so I hid him inside my tunic pocket and brought him along. Halfway through the meeting I realised he'd disappeared. Next thing I know everyone's in an uproar because the sneaky little thing had managed to take the royal seal on the table up there without any of them even being aware of it.'

Rhiannon giggled in amusement. 'Did they find it?'

'Oh, they found it all right,' David snorted. 'While they were all running about trying to find it, the little idiot came back to me and hid himself, and the seal, in my pocket. Of course, when I informed everyone of that they all thought I'd planned the whole thing. I wasn't allowed back for a while. Like that was some awful punishment,' he scoffed. 'These things are usually so boring! Actually, I'll wager the only reason I'm here today is because John and I were the ones who found you, and they may want to ask us some questions. Either that, or they thought you might like having us here for moral support.'

'What exactly is this room for anyway?' Rhiannon asked curiously. 'It seems pretty important.'

'It's the meeting room of the Pelatarrof,' John answered.

She gave him a blank look.

'They're the official court, any serious legal matters are heard before them,' he explained. 'It's also used by the High Council for their meetings.'

'So what do the different colours mean?' Rhiannon asked, pointing at the mixture of green and brown robes.

'The ones in the dark green are chancellors, a higher rank than the ones in the brown who are councillors,' John replied.

Rhiannon looked towards the front of the room. 'And the three silver chairs?'

'Those are for the Trínondras, the three people who have the final decision regarding anything discussed or heard in this room, whether it's to do with the Pelatarrof or the High Council,' David replied. 'As Endrille appointed my family's line as ruler, the reigning monarch is automatically one of the three, and he represents the race of dragons. The second is taken from one of the noble families who will represent the race of men. At the moment it's Lord Anton Mowbray, the man with the grey beard standing next to Father. He's a bit of a grouch, but fair. The third is someone from an untitled family who will ensure the rights of all other creatures will be protected.'

'And which one is he?'

David pointed to the formidable figure standing on his father's other side. With his wild red hair and imposing build, the man would not have looked out of place brandishing a broadsword on a Scottish moor.

'That one, Caiden Alcober. And don't worry, he looks frightening, but he's the best of fellows. Loves a lark as much as we do. It takes a lot to get him riled, but when he does most people duck for cover.'

And I'd be one of them, Rhiannon silently reflected, thinking anyone who managed to make the redheaded giant angry in the first place was either very brave or extremely foolish.

'Since your father's the king, does that mean he outranks the others when they have to make decisions?' she asked.

David shook his head. 'Not in here. All three have equal status in this room and must never use their position outside of it to influence a member of the High Council.'

'What happens if they can't all agree to something? Does the majority decide?'

This time it was John who answered. 'No. If they can't agree, then the Trínondras must rest the decision with Endrille. As last of the ancients, it is she alone who must decide any unresolved disputes or questions.'

Rhiannon shifted uneasily on the bench. 'So what happens with me during this hearing? What do I have to do?'

David patted her reassuringly on the shoulder.

'It's nothing too bad really,' he said encouragingly. He pointed at the black marble chair in the middle of the room. 'They'll ask you to sit over there and then one of the councillors, who's also one of the Pelatarrof's officials, will ask you a few questions about what happened, where you come from, stuff like that.'

'But,' John interjected, 'since you're under sixteen, before they can ask you any questions, an independent guardian has to be chosen to help represent and support you during the hearing. They'll also ensure you aren't bullied during it. You can name any adult you like. If you can't decide on who you want, then they'll assign someone to you.'

'Can it be any adult?' Rhiannon asked.

'Yes, so long as they're Álnairian and have never been found guilty of any serious crime,' John replied.

'I know you said your parents went missing,' David said, his voice gentle with compassion. 'So is there someone else you'd like to name? They can be one of your teachers, or even just a neighbour who has looked after you in the past.' David glanced about the gradually filling room before returning his gaze to Rhiannon's face. 'We do have ways of getting people here quickly if you wanted someone from wherever you live to be here.'

The doors slamming shut, followed by a sudden hush in the room, prevented the truth from leaving Rhiannon's lips.

She looked over her shoulder to see the imposing figure of Sir Raeden striding to the front of the room. The man's long black cloak edged with golden thread swept imperiously along the stone floor. She also noticed, with gathering puzzlement, that those who stepped aside to allow him to pass gave him a look of either fearful loathing or grudging admiration.

'Why did everyone go quiet when he came in?' she whispered in David's ear.

He looked at Sir Raeden who was now walking around the table to hand a bundle of papers to King Stephen.

'He's responsible for securing the room once everyone is

inside,' he replied in equally low tones. 'Once the doors are closed it's the signal for the proceedings to start.'

Rhiannon glanced around and saw everyone was now finding themselves a seat on the stone pews. The only ones who did not were Sir Raeden, Lord Anton and Caiden Alcober. The remaining members of the Trínondras took their place on the two vacant chairs beside King Stephen, while Sir Raeden went and stood beside the statue of Fjenador.

Rhiannon focused her attention on the man standing beside the dragon's statue. She glimpsed an intricately designed gold chain clasped around the high collar of his dark tunic with a seven-pointed silver star suspended from it. She gently nudged David and discreetly pointed in Sir Raeden's direction.

'What's that around his neck?' she asked quietly.

David bent his head towards her own. 'It's the collar worn by those awarded the title of Supreme Royal Protector. It's the highest honour that can be bestowed on any knight, and it's very rarely handed out. I think Wyvern was the first person in over ninety years to actually get it. He was certainly the youngest to ever receive it.'

'How old was he?'

'Twenty-one.'

Any further conversation was curtailed as an official adorned in grey robes moved to the head of the room and began speaking.

'By virtue of their oath and allegiance, all members and parties to these proceedings are bound by the following …'

While she was at first inclined to be intrigued by the novelty of the events taking place, Rhiannon found her interest in the recitation by the low, monotone voice quickly disappearing. Her eyes began to drift closed as the long-winded list of rules and terms of protocol seemed to go on forever.

The dull voice finally descended into welcome silence.

Then a booming voice rang out, startling her to rigid attention.

'The Pelatarrof calls upon the child, Rhiannon McBride, to come forward.'

'That's the High Chancellor, Lord Sharbel,' David muttered under his breath.

He pointed at an impressive bearded figure dressed in vivid scarlet robes adorned by a golden chain of office who was standing before the dais.

'You'd better get up there quickly. Make sure you curtsy when you reach him, and whatever you do, don't speak until he asks you a question.'

Rhiannon's body trembled as she rose to her feet.

Calling upon every ounce of courage she possessed, she made her way to the front of the room and came to a halt before Lord Sharbel.

She panicked for a moment when she realised she had never curtsied in her life. Praying silently that she would not make a fool of herself, she sank down awkwardly.

A few muffled comments and laughs came from behind her.

She raised her chin defiantly. As she straightened to her full height again, she assumed the impassive mask she had perfected while living with her foster parents.

'Please state your full name, child.'

Lord Sharbel's booming voice had softened considerably.

She looked up to see him regarding her with a benevolent smile. Taking a deep breath, she stated calmly, 'Rhiannon Marie McBride.'

'And do you have an independent guardian whom you wish to name?'

She felt the sense of panic rising within her once again. She ruthlessly pushed it down and closed her eyes. Sorting through the maelstrom of thoughts racing through her mind, she focused on the two facts which stood out clearly.

Number one: she was in an unfamiliar world where she knew nothing of their laws.

Number two: of those she had met so far in this world, there was only one person whom she thought would be capable of standing up to a room full of powerful and influential people should the need arise.

Rhiannon made her decision.

She opened her eyes, and in a clear voice declared firmly, 'Yes, I do. I wish to name as my independent guardian Sir Raeden Wyvern.'

Chapter 10

An Unpleasant
Interrogation

Pandemonium erupted throughout the Praeterium.

Chancellors and councillors leapt to their feet.

Voices rose in outcry and protest. Rhiannon could hear parts of the more strenuous objections soaring above the din.

'Preposterous notion! The child's obviously bewitched!'

'The very thought is outrageous!'

'He's hardly the sort to interest himself in her welfare!'

'Entrust a man of *his* family history with an innocent child?'

'It must not be allowed! The idea is ludicrous!'

Dazed at the level of disturbance she had managed to create with so few words, Rhiannon had only a brief moment to witness a strange expression fleetingly cross Sir Raeden's face before it once again transformed into a stony mask of indifference.

A tug on her elbow had her turning around to be confronted with twin looks of disbelief and horror from David and John.

Rhiannon silently obeyed their wordless prompting to follow them.

The arguments continued behind her as she went.

David and John led her over to a small alcove hidden behind one of the pillars. She entered after them and was stunned when they simultaneously turned around, demanding, 'Are you completely pixilated?'

'What?' Rhiannon stared at them in confusion.

David made a gesture with his hands. 'That, out there!' he exclaimed in exasperation. 'What was that? Are you completely out of your mind? Why would you choose that miserable prat?'

Rhiannon frowned. 'He did help me when I was hurt,' she said reasonably. 'Aleda told me all about it this morning while I was eating my breakfast. Besides, he looks really intimidating.'

'We certainly know that,' John declared with a crooked smile. 'But why that would make you choose him …'

'Don't you see?' Rhiannon huffed impatiently. 'You said whomever I choose has to ensure I'm not bullied when they question me. I thought if I picked someone really intimidating then I wouldn't have to worry about anyone taking advantage of the fact that I don't know how things are done in here.'

David and John looked at each other. They managed to maintain their serious expressions for only another few seconds. Then, they both started laughing.

'All right, fine,' David gasped between chuckles. 'You win. I still say you're absolutely and completely barmy, but I am yet to meet anyone who can actually manage to intimidate Wyvern.'

'And it's not like it'll be a permanent guardianship anyway,' John added. 'It'll just be for as long as the hearing lasts.'

'And you can thank heaven for that,' David informed her with a smile. He slowly made his way past her to the alcove's entrance. 'Imagine having him for a real guardian! It's bad enough having him as Commander of the Guard.'

He slipped back into the room, leaving Rhiannon and John to follow him.

The commotion in the Praeterium, far from decreasing in volume, had escalated to the point that not even the High Chancellor's resonating voice could be identified.

'I'll bet this is giving the SilverScribe a rather difficult time,' David commented in amusement.

'What's that?'

David pointed across the room to a scroll suspended in mid-air near the dais. She could see silver writing appearing on it at a blistering rate.

'That's the SilverScribe. It takes down every single word spoken in this room once any official matter is discussed, including the names of those speaking. When everything is over, it disappears and gets stored in the archives.'

'You mean it's been writing down everything I've been saying? Even if I whispered it?' Rhiannon asked nervously.

David grinned and nodded. 'Down to every last syllable,' he said.

Rhiannon groaned in mortification and ducked her head, her long hair falling forward to obscure her face.

'Hey, what's wrong?'

'You all right? It's really not that bad, you know. Hardly anyone ever reads those things anyway. Too boring most of the time.'

Rhiannon peeked between strands of her hair to see John and David looking at her in concern.

'Are you sure most people don't read them?'

'Positive.' John pointed towards David. 'After all, if everyone read them, I don't think he would've survived beyond his first meeting!'

David gave him a slight shove.

A clap of thunder exploded in the air around them.

The room, which had only a second ago sounded like a battlefield, fell into a startled silence.

'If you are through behaving in the manner of ill-bred and

ignorant savages, might I suggest you compose yourselves, and strive to remember in whose presence you are currently standing.'

The caustic voice was all the more deadly for not being raised. Its chilling tone caused more than one member to hasten back to their place on the benches without another word passing their lips.

David, Rhiannon and John all looked towards the source of the familiar voice: Sir Raeden. The man's implacable form stood in front of the statue of Fjenador as he glared at the people in front of him.

'This idiocy has gone on long enough, and I certainly do not intend to waste any more of my valuable time pandering to the whims of fools and idle spectators,' Sir Raeden informed the room curtly. 'The child has named me as her independent guardian, and I accept the appointment for the duration of these proceedings. So desist with this insufferable behaviour immediately.'

Lord Sharbel, having obviously decided to seize this opportunity to make himself heard again, declared pompously, 'As no valid objection can be made against the appointment of Sir Raeden Wyvern as the child's guardian, this hearing will now continue. All members and parties will return to their places. Sir Raeden, bring the child, if you please.'

Everyone, including David and John, moved back to their seats.

Rhiannon could not help feeling a twinge of fear at what was to come when Sir Raeden, his black cloak swirling about his polished dark boots, walked purposefully across the room and paused in front of her. Lifting her eyes to meet his inscrutable gaze, she obediently complied with his short, 'Follow me.'

Sir Raeden remained forbiddingly silent as he led her over to the black marble chair in the middle of the room. It was only as they reached it that he spoke, and then only briefly.

'This chair has been charmed so that you can only reply truthfully to any question. You may not move from it until instructed. Is that understood?'

Rhiannon shot a furtive glare at David and John. They had neglected to inform her of that fact! 'Yes, Sir,' she said respectfully, 'but, what happens if they ask something I don't want to answer?'

'I shall, of course, intervene should any inappropriate question be asked,' he replied brusquely. 'However, should the question be relevant, despite your reluctance, you will answer. You will have no choice.'

Rhiannon gave a resigned nod and stepped closer to the chair. She hesitated for only a second when she felt a strange tingle travel down her spine upon touching it. Then she slowly clambered up onto the cool marble, her feet lifting until they dangled some inches above the ground.

Satisfied that she was settled, Sir Raeden moved to stand beside the chair. A heavy scowl had settled back on his face, and his arms were folded forbiddingly across his chest.

'Councillor Plancy,' the High Chancellor called in his rumbling voice, 'you may now question the child.'

Rhiannon heard shuffling footsteps behind her. She turned around and immediately felt a shiver of apprehension pass over her body. The thin, reedy looking man who was slowly approaching appeared quite harmless, and yet she could not shake the sense of unease that was quickly overwhelming her.

Councillor Plancy looked the picture of aging respectability. His elegant dark-brown robes were carefully tailored to fit his thin frame, and his greying hair was well groomed. His eyes, however, were filled with an inner darkness she instantly distrusted and when he spoke, her skin prickled with warning at his oily voice.

'Miss McBride, please inform us how you came to be in the forest where you were discovered.'

'I don't know,' Rhiannon replied, the truth automatically coming out of her mouth. 'I was walking back to school to return my foster sister's library book and then I was standing in the forest.'

Councillor Plancy frowned at this information. He stared at

her, momentarily nonplussed. 'So you just appeared there. Is that what you are saying?'

'Yes.'

When it appeared he would pursue the subject of her mysterious appearance, King Stephen commented mildly, 'I believe the child has no further insight to give as to how she came to be in the forest. May I suggest moving along to another subject?'

Councillor Plancy gave him a low bow. 'Certainly, Your Majesty,' he said smoothly, and returned his attention to Rhiannon. 'As you cannot tell us how you came to be in the forest,' he said with the barest hint of a sneer, 'perhaps you could inform us as to why you were there?'

'How can I answer that when I don't even know *how* I got there?'

'There is a small disgruntled faction among the people on the island of Malpars who seek a segregation of government from the mainland of Álnair,' he said without any inflection in his voice. Then, 'Were you sent by them?' he demanded abruptly. 'A spy in a child's body. Are you one of the tuagust?'

Rhiannon glared him.

'No, I'm not,' she said curtly. 'And I certainly don't appreciate being accused of spying. If all you're going to do is make crazy accusations, then I can tell you right now this is going to take a very long time.'

'The lass is right, Councillor,' Caiden Alcober interjected. 'It's quite obvious she doesn't know how she came to be there or why. Why don't you try asking some questions to which she *will* know the answer?'

Clearly disgruntled, Councillor Plancy shot a sour look at Rhiannon.

'Are you an Álnairian?' he said harshly.

'No.'

He failed to conceal the flash of triumph in his face as he

declared, 'So you *are* a spy!' He drew himself up to his full height. 'The faction has forsworn their oath to the House of Valieoth and do not consider themselves Álnairian. Confess, Miss McBride, you are nothing but an infiltrator sent to gain access to Valieoth Castle in the hopes of obtaining sensitive information pertaining to our security.'

Twin flares of crimson fire flooded Rhiannon's cheeks.

'I already told you,' she began furiously, and then her voice disappeared. More accurately, her voice was absorbed by a small shimmer of light that appeared in front of her mouth.

She turned to the man standing beside her.

Sir Raeden lowered his hand, the movement causing the light to flicker and then extinguish in a tiny flash.

'I believe my charge has already confirmed she is neither a spy nor a threat,' Sir Raeden remarked coldly. 'She is also not under suspicion of committing any crime, so you will desist with that line of questioning immediately.'

'Miss McBride.'

Lord Anton's impatient voice cut through the icy stalemate which had arisen between Sir Raeden and Councillor Plancy.

'Ignoring, for the moment, the question of your place of origin, tell us in your own words what happened to you once you found yourself in Shaimar Forest.'

'Well, it was very cold,' Rhiannon replied, 'so I went looking for somewhere to get warm. I had just reached the edge of the forest when I heard a yell, so I ducked behind a hedge.'

'And why did you do that?' Councillor Plancy demanded. 'Why would any innocent person have to hide?'

Rhiannon stared at him as though he had grown a second head.

'Innocent people get persecuted all the time,' she retorted, 'and since I had no idea of where I was, or who had yelled, I didn't think it smart to expose myself to someone who could very well be mentally unhinged.'

'That certainly sounds like Officer Exton.'

David's dry comment elicited a round of quiet chuckles from the members in the room.

Rhiannon glanced up at King Stephen to see him quickly covering his mouth with one hand to hide his own smile.

'Prince David, if you have something to add perhaps you would like to come forward,' Caiden Alcober suggested with a small grin.

David waved nonchalantly. 'No, not really. I just felt I should support Rhiannon's statement by confirming that the person she heard yelling is indeed mentally unhinged. So she was quite right to be wary of him.'

Councillor Plancy's face reddened with anger as laughter once again spread through the room. He glared at David's smiling face before returning his attention to Rhiannon.

'So, you hid behind the hedge,' he sneered. 'And then what happened?'

Rhiannon exhaled slowly. She mentioned the stag's brief appearance followed by her falling against the hedge, which led to her being hit by Officer Exton's charm.

All sounds of levity disappeared from the room.

'And then all I felt was pain. Excruciating pain. It felt like my whole body was on fire,' Rhiannon concluded. 'Then suddenly it was gone, and I remember waking up briefly before I passed out again.'

When she finished speaking, an appalled hush lay over her audience.

A dark, intent look crossed Councillor Plancy's face.

Finally, the heavy silence was broken by Lord Anton.

'The accounts of Captain Morton and the other witnesses at the time confirm these events as they relate to the misuse of the Glaciocaptus Charm by Officer Exton. However, as this hearing is in relation to the child's living arrangements, I would suggest the issue of the whereabouts of the child's family and place of residence be resolved.'

Both King Stephen and Caiden Alcober nodded. 'Agreed.'

'I don't know where my parents are,' Rhiannon informed the room quietly. 'My mother and father disappeared when I was two years old. Since that happened, I've been living in the house owned by my foster parents, Gregory and Patricia Dashmont.'

'And where is this house?' Lord Anton asked.

'In a town called Brakenhurst, in Australia.'

Dead silence greeted this revelation.

Puzzled by the unexpected lack of response, Rhiannon peered curiously at her guardian. Sir Raeden's face was coolly impassive, but a strange expression flashed in his keen eyes as he stared down at her.

Rhiannon shifted uncomfortably before saying in a hesitant voice, 'Sir, what's wrong?'

He did not get a chance to answer. The other occupants of the room broke their silence in a tide of hissed whispers and exclamations of disbelief.

'She's from Vetus svet!'

'She came through the foramens.'

'What's to be done with her?'

'No good can come of this!'

'The Lady Endrille must be told.'

'What makes you think she doesn't already know? I heard they didn't bother sending anyone out to make inquiries about her!'

The whispered arguments were steadily increasing in volume.

Rhiannon shrank back into her chair, her nervousness heightened by the raised voices gathering behind her.

'SILENCE!'

The High Chancellor's deep voice rang through the room.

All conversations broke off abruptly and one by one, each person turned to stare at Lord Sharbel's stern countenance.

'Would the members take note this is an official meeting, and not a social gathering at Fagan's Flagon.'

The rebuke echoed around the Praeterium.

Rhiannon twisted around in her chair to cast a quick glance at David and John. They both sent reassuring smiles in her direction. Summoning a weak grin in reply, she hastily returned her attention to the dais in time to hear King Stephen addressing Lord Anton and Caiden Alcober.

'It is not unprecedented for a person to be permitted to remain in Álnair and undertake studies should they request it. However, a full lineage report should be performed prior to any final decision being made.'

Both men nodded solemnly.

'Yes, we cannot afford another incident such as what happened with Fendrel,' Lord Anton added forcefully.

An oppressive chill spread through the assembly at the mention of the name. Rhiannon had only a moment to ponder why, when King Stephen slowly rose to his feet and addressed the Pelatarrof.

'I believe while we discuss this issue further, Miss McBride should be escorted to Professor Egelbert in order that he may conduct the lineage report.' King Stephen then turned to Rhiannon and added kindly, 'Once we have received the results of the report we will send for you, but before you leave would you please answer this question. Do you wish to remain here in Álnair?'

She replied without hesitation. 'I do. I don't have any money, but I'd be willing to work if I'm allowed to get a job.'

King Stephen smiled at her and nodded. 'Very well,' he said. 'Sir Raeden, as the child's independent guardian for these proceedings you must remain here. Although that does mean I shall have to find someone else to accompany Miss McBride.' He cast his eyes around the Praeterium.

Rhiannon saw his lips twitch with ill-concealed mirth as they rested on someone behind her. Turning around to discover who

94

had evoked such a reaction, she bit her lip to contain her laughter when she saw David staring up at his father with an expression of intense pleading on his face.

With a shake of his head, King Stephen acquiesced ruefully.

'All right, David. I know better than to try and keep you here much longer. You and John may accompany Miss McBride to Professor Egelbert. However,' he finished sternly, 'you will conduct yourselves appropriately when in his office, and do not touch any strange items, creatures or experiments you may happen to see. We certainly do not want a repeat of what occurred last week.'

David nodded eagerly and stood up with almost indecent haste.

'We promise, Father,' he assured his parent, then approached the chair where Rhiannon remained seated. 'Come on, Rhiannon.'

She again looked to Sir Raeden, unsure if she had been given permission to leave. He inclined his head slightly.

'You may leave, Miss McBride,' he informed her. He then turned an icy glare on David and John who now stood near him. 'I trust I do not have to mention what will happen to either of you should I discover you neglected your duty to my charge once you left this room?'

They both swallowed and shook their heads. 'No, Sir.'

Rhiannon looked towards King Stephen and received a small nod of dismissal. Rising to her feet, she performed a rather awkward curtsy in his direction, then turned to follow David and John out of the room.

A prickling sensation on her neck made her look back.

Councillor Plancy. The man was staring at her with cold, assessing eyes. They made her feel like a specimen in a jar.

Repressing a shudder, she looked away and hurried out of the room.

~Chapter 11~

A Threatening Presence

It was true! The girl had survived a Glaciocaptus Charm!

The man longed to pick up a quill and start a list of all the different potions and spells he could test on her.

Mórfran had said he could arrange her disappearance. I wonder how long that will take. If they permit her to stay, I may be able to convince one of these fools to suggest she be placed in the care of one of our people. The Grimsbys will do, or the Kotwards. Respectable enough without raising too many questions. Can't get Plancy to suggest it. That young one over there, what's his name? Att-something. Attwater? He'll do. As gullible as they come.

Then another possibility occurred to him.

If she has to go back to Vetus svet, that'll make things easier. She's stated publicly she wants to stay. Being forced to go back could cause her to do something desperate.

A smirk appeared on his face.

A tragic accident befalls her, but no body will be found.

He patted the item tucked away beneath his official brown robes.

I'll do it today if the opportunity presents itself.

Chapter 12

A DARK HISTORY

D o either of you want to tell me what that was all about?'
Out in the long hallway, David and John paused at
Rhiannon's question.

'What what was about?' John asked, puzzled.

Rhiannon rolled her eyes in exasperation. 'The interrogation
by Mister Paranoid in there. I've never met him before, so why
does he dislike me so much?'

David shrugged dismissively. 'I wouldn't worry too much.
He doesn't really like anyone. Besides, he's always been a nasty,
suspicious worm.'

'Well, why did everyone react so strongly when I said I came
from Australia?'

'Australia is in Vetus svet.' David paused, then added ruefully,
'Which of course doesn't mean a thing to you, does it. Come on.'

He walked farther up the hallway until he passed a large gold
statue of a griffon placed atop a wide marble pedestal. Then he
turned and opened a small door on the right. He gestured for her
to enter.

She stepped through the doorway and came to an abrupt halt,
scarcely believing what she was seeing.

A colourful multitude of flowers, surrounded by walls of stone and brightly lit by sunlight overhead, grew across a wide expanse of ground. The mingled scents of fresh grass and blossoms lingered on the air, and from behind a tall elm tree came the soft trickling of a fountain.

Rhiannon dragged her eyes away from the tranquil scene to stare at David in astonishment.

'How's this possible? There's snow everywhere else and yet this looks like a summer garden. And it's enormous! How can it possibly be this big?'

David smiled and pointed up to where a ceiling should have been. 'Protective and dimension-altering enchantment,' he said. 'It keeps the rain and snow out while letting the sun through and allows the room to exist outside of the normal sphere of space, which is why it's so large. Whenever my mother wants some peace and quiet, she always comes here. When it was first created, they named it the Room of Tranquillity.'

'I can see why,' Rhiannon murmured appreciatively, returning her gaze to the garden.

'I thought it might be easier to explain in here before we take you to Professor Egelbert,' David explained. 'Father didn't say anything about going straight there, and we've got some time before we'll be missed, considering how long some of those windbags can talk. We'll just use the transonus system to get to the main gate, otherwise it'd take us at least an hour if we walked.'

'Transonus system?'

David shook his head. 'Sorry, you wouldn't have the faintest idea what that is, would you. It's a network of stone daises built at different locations within a large area that can transport a person from one place to another in the space of a couple of seconds. The castle's network includes a dais on each level in every wing and tower of the palace, plus several positioned throughout the grounds and at each watch-post in the defensive walls. The one closest to your bedchamber is down the hallway from it and opposite the staircase.'

Rhiannon frowned. 'If it transports people so quickly, why don't we use it to get to the professor? Doesn't he have one?'

'He does, but his laboratory isn't within the castle grounds. For security reasons, no dais beyond the outer curtain wall can be linked into our system. Also, to activate each dais you need to have the proper authorisation, so I'm afraid you'll have to hold on to my arm when we use them.'

'I'm sure I can handle a minor thing like that after everything else I've been through,' Rhiannon said wryly.

She sat down on the warm grass and waited until both David and John had seated themselves before asking, 'So what's Vetus svet?'

David settled into a more comfortable position, then began to explain.

'Vetus svet translated from Drakaron, the ancient dragon tongue, means "old world", and it's where the race of Men originated. For thousands of years the different clans there lived peaceably alongside the dragons, who would often visit from their own realm.'

'Their own realm?' Rhiannon interrupted. 'You mean here?'

David nodded. 'Álnair, which means "Of Light", is where the dragons were created, so it's their realm. There were enchanted pathways between the two worlds that allowed the dragons to travel between here and Vetus svet whenever they chose. Circles made of standing stone in both worlds marked the places where the links were strongest.'

'Could people use the pathways too?'

'Yes, the dragons were happy to have them visit here. They were eager to share their world and knowledge with any who asked.'

'So what happened?'

David released a heavy sigh. 'The Time of Persecution,' he replied softly. 'It was an era when man's arrogance and greed overshadowed his love and loyalty. In the late half of the fifth century, many clans in the race of Men began to fear the dragons and the power they possessed. The clans sought to exterminate them. A world that had once treated dragons as beings to be respected, began hunting them down with fanatical hatred. Many dragons were lost through acts of betrayal, while others were simply slaughtered after being captured.'

'But, how?' Rhiannon struggled to ask through her horrified dismay. 'Endrille's so ... I mean, aren't dragons really ...'

'Other dragons aren't as powerful or as large as Endrille,' said John. 'In fact, some are actually quite small by comparison. The ancients are also the only dragons capable of producing fire. However, size and power are irrelevant when an attack is from one you trust. Plus, the Glaciocaptus Charm, the one that hit you, was originally intended to be cast by a group of magi to immobilise injured dragons so their wounds could be treated if they couldn't do it themselves. A few magi were hurt when a dragon reacted to a treatment by unexpectedly swinging out their tail or wing in pain, so the magi worked with the dragons to discover a way to immobilise them, which made the betrayal even worse.'

'The group would ambush the dragon, cast the charm and then kill it while it lay helpless.' David's eyes flashed angrily. 'The miserable cowards didn't have the courage to try and fight them fairly.'

Rhiannon felt sick. In her mind she could see images of the unfortunate dragons, their majestic forms brought down in humiliation and ignominiously murdered.

'Wh ...' she broke off as her voice cracked. Swallowing the lump in her throat, she asked hoarsely, 'What did they do? The dragons, I mean.'

'The only thing they could do,' John replied. 'They left.'

David pulled at the grass, then held up his hand. 'If they had wanted to, the ancients could have easily obliterated each of the clans as easily as I snapped this blade of grass. However, killing a sentient being when there is another option available is an abomination to all dragons, so they chose instead to leave Vetus svet and close the pathways between the two worlds.'

'So how did some of you end up here? I mean, why bring some of the same creatures who've just been trying to kill you into your own world?'

'There were some clans across Vetus svet that remained loyal, so Endrille and the other ancients permitted them to come here,' said John. 'Out of all the clans and their families, David's ancestors, who were from a country I believe you now call Ireland, were the greatest defenders of the dragons. Without their intervention, many more would have been killed. So when they arrived here, Endrille installed the head of the clan as High King. She also gave their House the name of Valieoth, which translated from Drakaron means "One Who Protects". The line has remained unbroken since that time, and all Álnair recognises the authority given to them by Endrille. Well, except for that small group on Malpars. They keep trying to convince other people there to join their movement, but the majority agree that creating a separate government would be an act against Endrille, and they've refused. As for the tuagust, they mostly keep to themselves and are harmless enough. They're shapeshifters, but fortunately they only use their ability to alter their appearance as a defence mechanism against curious visitors to the island.'

'So did everyone who was still loyal to the dragons come here before the pathways closed?' Rhiannon asked.

David shook his head. 'No, not all of them. Some clans from across Vetus svet chose to remain behind with a few dragons to try and restore the peace between the two races. The strongest support remained in the eastern part of Asia and the kingdom we've been told is now called Japan. I understand they still consider dragons as beings to be respected.'

Rhiannon nodded. 'I've read that every year the Dragon Dance is the highlight in their New Year celebrations.'

'It's the same here,' John said with a smile. 'Each of the clans who came had their own customs and celebrations, and that was a particular favourite of Endrille's. Every year it's performed all across Álnair.'

Even as she smiled at his comment, another question arose in Rhiannon's mind. 'If the pathways are closed, then how did I get through?' she asked. 'And how do you know about places like Australia?'

'The pathways weren't completely closed,' David explained. 'The power required to fully close off the pathways would've been immense. As it was, it took the combined energy of the surviving ancient dragons to partially close them. And as to how you got here, when they put up the barrier between the two worlds there was an unexpected side effect. At random moments in time, several small tunnels called foramens appear and briefly connect the worlds once again. If you happen to be in exactly the right place when that happens, either here or there, you'll find yourself caught and transported to the other side before you can move.'

Comprehension filled Rhiannon's mind, along with an overwhelming sense of hope. 'I'm not the first person to come through these tunnels, am I?'

'No, you're not,' David answered. 'And you certainly won't be the last. The foramens ...'

'Then do you know if two people came through about ten years ago?' Rhiannon interrupted him. 'Their names are Patrick and Claire McBride.'

'Your missing parents.'

David's soft words were a statement, not a question. He looked down at her and sighed.

'I'm so sorry, Rhiannon, but the last person reported to come through was over eighty years ago. If anyone did come through about the time your parents went missing, they would've been identified by now.'

A shadow seemed to fall over Rhiannon's eyes. The beautiful garden suddenly lost its brightness.

'But I wouldn't despair of finding them,' David said hastily, his eyes on her face. 'Even though you're from Vetus svet, there could be a way to find out where they are. I'll ask my father, and I'm sure Endrille will help.'

His obvious dismay at having upset her with his previous answer, along with his sincere offer to help, had Rhiannon sending him a warm look of gratitude.

'Thank you,' she said. Then steeling herself against the possibility, she added, 'And if there isn't a way, I'll always appreciate the fact you cared enough to try and …'

A sudden feeling of constriction in her throat caused her to break off.

She gave a small sniff and coughed.

Then, in an effort to divert attention from her lapse in emotional control, she asked, 'These foramens, do they only happen in particular locations?'

David shook his head, tactfully accepting her desire to leave the topic of her parents for the moment.

'They happen everywhere, and they've taken people from all kinds of places. That's where we get most of our information about Vetus svet,' he explained. 'Whenever someone comes through, the Trinondras asks them all sorts of questions.'

'Like what?'

'Oh, things ranging from changes in fashion to new inventions,' John answered.

'Some of the things are ignored if they don't meet with Endrille's approval,' David said. 'She certainly doesn't agree with new weapons being developed like the ones in Vetus svet, or with making things that will damage our land and waterways. Also, the clothing of so many of the people who came through the foramens was so ridiculous they were disregarded. However, some of them were sensible,' he gestured towards his fine leather boots, 'so we adopted them, after making a few modifications.'

'With the foramens are you able to tell where they'll appear?'

David shook his head. 'They do happen quite frequently, but we can't predict when or where they'll occur – well, King Brian and his people can ...'

'Who's he?' Rhiannon interrupted.

'Have you ever heard of leprechauns?'

'Of course I have.'

'Well, King Brian is Lord of the leprechauns.'

'But I thought they were only a myth, something the people in Ireland made up.'

'Certainly out of all the places in Vetus svet, the country of Ireland is the place the leprechauns love the most,' David said with a smile. 'King Brian told me that whenever they go through the foramens, they always make sure they go visit their favourite home away from home. Something to do with keeping their legend alive, he said.'

'Can I meet him?' Rhiannon asked eagerly.

'Eventually, although we're never quite sure where he'll show up,' David admitted. 'He and his people like chasing the foramens and then going through them for fun.'

Rhiannon blinked. 'Fun?' she repeated in disbelief. 'It was completely discombobulating.'

'That's what they like about it,' John grinned.

'Anyway, the people who come through from Vetus svet usually choose to stay here,' David said, 'although there have been some who wanted to return. When that happens, special arrangements have to be made with Endrille and the Trínondras.'

'So it's possible to return?'

David nodded. 'Yes, it's possible.'

'And what happens to the people from here who get sent to Vetus svet?'

'That's where King Brian comes in,' John answered. 'He kind of acts like a retriever since he and his people are able to track the foramens. When they find the person who got taken, they wait for the next foramen to appear and then come back.'

'I suppose there must be quite a few people out there who are grateful to them,' Rhiannon said with a smile. 'I can only imagine what some of them must think when they see a car or train for the first time, let alone trying to explain to people where they come from.'

Suddenly, she frowned.

'Trying to explain,' she repeated slowly. 'Wait a minute! If you've been here since some time in the fifth century, then how on earth do you know English? Didn't they all speak Latin or something like that before the pathways were closed?'

'Actually, there were several forms of Latin,' said David, 'along with the other languages being used by different clans spread across Vetus svet. My ancestors at the time mainly spoke Gaelic. After the pathways closed, the clans who came here all spoke various languages, with an early form of English being the most common. Endrille knew all the ancient dialects so she helped the clans develop the English one here. That way, they could all understand one another, and when someone came through the foramens she was usually able to understand them. The majority who came usually spoke some form of English or Latin, and Endrille thought it wise for us to learn the new styles so we'd always be able to communicate with someone when they arrived.'

'But your English is perfect,' Rhiannon said, 'how did that happen?'

'Sir Reuel Rashbold, Professor of Languages,' David and John said in unison.

'He came here in 1892,' David continued. 'He was caught in a foramen while on his way to deliver a lecture at a university. He ended up right in the middle of Cendillis. He was an expert in a lot of the old languages, so he didn't have any trouble speaking to anyone, and he wrote many textbooks in the four years he stayed here, which are still used in the schools and at the Academy. Before he came, the English being spoken went something like, "Hast thou heard'st the mystick tale that pleas'd of yore." Afterwards, it all changed to what it is now.'

'Then I'm exceedingly grateful to him,' Rhiannon said with a smile, 'because I wouldn't have been able to understand you as much as I do if he hadn't come here. So do you only speak English now?'

'No.' This time it was John who answered. 'Everyone in Álnair is required to learn at least some Drakaron, plus the other basic languages, Latin and Gaelic. There's also the specialised ones Sir Reuel Rashbold wrote books about that people can learn. He knew another forty-three different languages from Vetus svet so there's a fair few of them. I can speak the basic languages, but he,' John pointed at David, 'he's also fluent in all the other ones, plus all those from here, such as Mórskarin, the language used by the merfolk, the various Elvish dialects of the Faeries, Leprechauns and other magic folk, as well as Old Álnairian. As a Prince Royal, he's expected to know several languages, but he set a whole new standard when he learnt every single one we have here. He even had Endrille teach him several other languages from Vetus svet, including some that were no longer being used there when the pathways were closed.'

'It helps that I find it extremely easy to learn them,' David said with a self-deprecating shrug. 'Otherwise I would've just done the basics. With my extra duties as Prince Royal I don't always have a lot of spare study time.'

Rhiannon was staring at both of them, her mouth agape.

'You both speak several languages?' she exclaimed. 'I can only speak one, with a few words of Italian, but that's only because I studied music for a little while.'

'Don't worry,' John reassured her. 'The most common language now is Sir Reuel's English, so you won't have any trouble speaking to people. In fact, when you said something about bread being mouldy before you fell unconscious near the forest, we all thought you were Álnairian. The other languages we have here are mainly only used now by people working in one of the academic fields, or when someone comes through the foramens.'

'What would've happened if I didn't speak any of them?'

'Firstly, it would've be a clear indication that you weren't Álnairian,' said John. 'And I guess we'd have just gone back to using sign language, or asked Endrille if she could understand you. It hasn't happened in over four hundred years. A young boy came through who could only speak his own language that no one recognised. They asked Endrille to speak to him, but when he saw her, he kept saying, "Ná'áshǫ'iitsoh!" and backed away. Endrille said the word he used for dragon is from a dialect of an ancient tribe who dwelt in a land her race called Ranos-kí-arda, which you now call America. When she couldn't calm him down, Endrille put him in an enchanted sleep and had King Brian take him back in the next foramen.'

'Then I'm certainly glad you could understand me!' Rhiannon said fervently. 'I definitely wouldn't have wanted to be sent back without finding out if I had a chance of staying here. When will I know if I can?'

'Once the lineage report is received by the Trínondras,' David said.

'Why do they need one of them anyway? What does it do?'

'It allows them to trace your family history all the way back to when the dragons left Vetus svet,' David informed her. 'It will show whether you have any distant relatives alive here in Álnair, and also confirm whether you're a descendant of one of the clans that were hunting the dragons.'

'But what has that got to do with m – '

Rhiannon's voice broke off as she recalled what Lord Anton had said in the Praeterium: 'We cannot afford another incident such as what happened with Fendrel.'

'That happened before, didn't it?' Rhiannon gazed at her companions with horror as the realisation struck her. 'Someone who was from one of those clans came through and caused trouble.'

'Yes, someone came through,' David said in a low voice. 'And we're lucky some dragon races weren't wiped from existence due to his actions.'

'But wait a minute,' Rhiannon exclaimed. 'What happened to the other ancients? I mean, you've said Endrille is the only one of them who's here. If they all came through, what happened to the rest? Did that Fendrel do something to them?'

A terrible sadness appeared on David's face.

'What happened to the ancients didn't have anything to do with him,' he said. 'Unfortunately, when they were closing the pathways it drained their energies completely. What they did forced them to sacrifice their very essence and they all faded. Endrille was only spared because Ryegoth, the leader of the ancients and her life-mate, ordered her not to join the others when the time came. He wanted to ensure if something went wrong, one of them would survive to be custodian of Álnair.'

Appalled, Rhiannon stared at David. 'You mean the ancient line was all but wiped out because they wanted to protect the other dragons from the people who were hunting them?'

David nodded.

A hollow ache filled Rhiannon's heart. 'How could Endrille possibly forgive us, let alone want to help any of us after that?'

'That's just the way she is,' John replied quietly. 'The way all dragons are. To them, hatred is something that twists and deforms you beyond all recognition, so they don't allow themselves to give in to the feeling. They believe that to be capable of love one must also learn to forgive.'

'Of course, that doesn't mean they will simply ignore anyone that poses a real threat,' David said.

'The man who came through, Fendrel, he was the worst threat to ever exist here,' John stated harshly.

'Who was he?'

David once again took over the storytelling.

'In the sixth century, two boys were brought here. One of them was Fendrel. The other was called Merlin.'

'Merlin!'

At Rhiannon's startled exclamation, David and John stared at her in surprise.

'So you've heard of him?'

Rhiannon rolled her eyes at John's question.

'Who hasn't heard of Merlin? He's only one of the greatest legends where I come from. King Arthur, Camelot, Excalibur. You can't mention one of those names without Merlin being brought up as well.'

'I've often wondered if they still talked about him,' David remarked absently. 'He was the greatest mage to ever train at Ryegoth Academy and they certainly missed him here when he decided to return to Vetus svet. Anyway, to start at the beginning, he came through the foramens with Fendrel, and according to Endrille and the records of those who met them, they were as close as brothers. Where one went the other followed. For years the two of them studied together, then they went on to research and invent new potions and elixirs as a partnership. And when

Morgana, the lady Fendrel liked, married Merlin, they remained friends.

'But then they fell out over an experiment. Fendrel wanted to invent a potion that would give the drinker physical immortality. Merlin believed no one had the right to meddle in such things, so after a few months of arguments they went their separate ways. Merlin continued doing his own research and teaching apprentices when he could, but Fendrel moved to Graynor, a city southeast of here. He secretly began to gather a group of followers who thought as he did, that immortality of the body was something we should have by right and that dragons were only beasts to be used. He managed to turn even the closest of family members against one another, and friends against their neighbours.

'However, in public he spoke strongly about the importance of unity, and managed to convince a lot of people that his experiments were safe, that they would prove beneficial to everyone. He certainly did invent some potions which proved useful and that gained him a lot of support for his other experiments.

'After a few years he began a campaign to have himself elected as a member of the High Council. He travelled to all the larger cities, and even the smaller, more remote villages, hoping to get a wider support base. With every group, his promises changed: riches beyond imagining; tremendous power; freedom from loneliness, fear and rejection; and above all love and acceptance.

'But once he'd achieved his goal, the groups who had believed in his words soon discovered any promises he made were soon forgotten. What they received instead were betrayal, pillage, murder and atrocities beyond measure. His experiments, which many at first had hailed to be fantastic and miraculous, became more depraved and evil with every passing year.'

David's voice suddenly broke off.

Rhiannon saw the muscles in his throat flex and tighten, and a haunted look creep into his eyes. She immediately knew that whatever came next must have been truly horrifying to evoke such a response after so many centuries had passed.

David took a deep breath, then revealed in a quiet voice, 'It was only after one of his closest followers was caught illegally testing an unapproved potion on a group of children, and was questioned by the Pelatarrof, they discovered that Fendrel, or Sados as he had taken to calling himself, had also been hunting down dragons to harvest their body parts and conduct experiments on them. He'd been targeting the younger ones, and those who preferred to live higher up in the mountains by themselves.

'He ... He had a laboratory underneath Mount Perdus where he'd been carrying out his more dangerous experiments, and that's where he'd imprisoned the dragons and people he wanted to keep alive. The records of the things he did ...'

David fell silent again, shaking his head as though to clear an unpleasant image from his mind.

John's hands were fisted in his lap.

Reaching out, Rhiannon laid a gentle hand on David's arm.

'You don't have to say it,' she said quietly. 'I think I can imagine what the records would say.'

'I don't think you could,' he replied, 'in fact, I don't think anyone could possibly grasp the level of depravity to which he sank.'

Rhiannon waited a moment before saying hesitantly, 'What happened after they discovered what he'd been doing?'

'The longest and bloodiest war that ever darkened this world,' David replied shortly. 'By the time his real agenda of taking control of Álnair and enslaving the dragon races was discovered, Fendrel had already amassed himself quite a large following. They called themselves the Myrkroth. Some chose to follow him in order to satisfy their own lust for power, under the delusion he would share whatever power he won with them. Others were the mutated remains of who they used to be before he used them in his experiments.

'He also created all manner of foul beasts through forbidden sorcery. He broke many natural laws and misused his mage abilities to make them. The creatures were made from the blackest and most evil of magic, holding nothing but malice in their hearts. Whenever one was discovered, death was to be its only fate.

'After Fendrel sacked the city of Glenwing, the war finally ended in a major battle between Finbar Forest and the Forbidden Mountains. The area used to be renowned for its beautiful hills and waterways, but it's nothing but a wasteland now. Fendrel and his forces were beaten, thanks largely to both Merlin and Endrille, and after the battle my ancestor, King Fíachra the First, declared it be named The Fell of Fíachra's Woe. He held himself responsible for what happened as he hadn't seen Fendrel's true intent until it was too late.'

'So Fendrel was killed?'

'No. Like the coward he truly was he tried to escape his defeat by fleeing, but Merlin caught up with him. Together, Merlin and Endrille sealed him and all his followers, well, those members of the Myrkroth who could be identified at that time,' David corrected himself, 'in a place of exile. Each of them was marked by Endrille to prevent them ever passing through the barrier enchantment she and Merlin erected around the northern point of Álnair, which lies beyond the Forbidden Mountains. They called it Mérosorc, and the worst criminals are still sent there. Once inside the barrier they can never get out, and if they're a mage they'll find it impossible to use magic.'

'It can't have been easy for those who survived to know Fendrel was still alive,' Rhiannon reflected. 'I'll bet they were relieved when he died.'

No immediate reply came from either David or John.

An awful sense of foreboding took hold of Rhiannon.

'He *is* dead, isn't he?'

David's reply was not comforting.

'No one knows for certain. He was never seen again once he entered Mérosorc. After all this time it'd be natural to assume he is, but those experiments on immortality he was doing? He was performing some on himself. Also, over the passing centuries the guards have arrested several members of new generations of Myrkroth descended from Fendrel's original followers. All of them claimed Fendrel would return one day.'

'Do you think he could?'

A heavy sigh escaped David.

'I don't know,' he admitted. 'It would seem impossible, and yet you're living proof that the impossible can happen.'

The garden was silent as Rhiannon absorbed David's disturbing revelation. Then, she asked, 'Why didn't Endrille and Merlin just send Fendrel back to Vetus svet?' Her tone was one of pure bewilderment. 'I mean, you said they can do that, so why wouldn't they use it to get rid of someone like that rather than keep him here in this world?'

'They couldn't take the risk that he might use his powers against people who would have no way of defending themselves against a mage,' John explained. 'At least kept here in exile they could ensure he was contained.'

I suppose that makes sense, Rhiannon thought. But still …

'Surely they could've suppressed his power or something? You know, taken it away and left him a non-mage.'

Her words elicited looks of horror from David and John.

'Strip someone of their gift! That's one of the worst crimes that could possibly be committed,' David exclaimed. 'You would be tearing out a piece of their soul.'

Rhiannon hastily apologised. 'Sorry, I just thought that with everything else you can do here, making a mage's ability dormant would be easy.'

'It doesn't quite work like that,' John informed her. 'Once awakened, a mage's ability cannot be repressed.'

'I see.' Rhiannon frowned. 'So how does the ability get awakened inside someone?'

'Well, that …'

'… is something we'll have to tell you later,' David interrupted. He glanced at his beautifully crafted wristwatch. 'We'd better go and get you to Professor Egelbert. I didn't mean for us to stay here this long.'

Rhiannon stood up, then pointed at his watch. 'I take it you know about those things from other travellers from Vetus svet?'

He nodded. 'One of the people who came through was a watchmaker from Germany. He showed the clockmakers and some of the faeries here how to make them. The faeries turned out to be better watchmakers, I guess because they're more familiar with using smaller hands.'

David snorted at his own joke. John and Rhiannon just groaned.

'Aleda's grandfather made mine,' David continued. 'Brilliant craftsmanship, don't you think?'

Rhiannon peered at it.

'Definitely,' she agreed. 'Did you know they now make them so they can be worn underwater?'

David stilled, his hand poised above the door handle. 'Really? Without using a preservation charm? I wonder how they do that.'

John lightly shoved David aside with a muttered, 'Here he goes again,' and opened the door himself. Turning to Rhiannon, he informed her with a long-suffering expression, 'Ever since I've known him, he's had some strange obsession with taking watches apart to see how he could improve them. I still blame him for my watch going missing when I was ten, even though he swears he saw a mermaid steal it when we snuck down to the beach for a swim.'

They exited the room and made it halfway down the hallway when David's voice called out eagerly, 'John, do you think Professor Egelbert would know anything about waterproofing watches?'

Chapter 13

OF DRAGONSTARS AND
BLOODLINES

Rhiannon thought she had met some strange people in her life, but Professor Egelbert beat them all in terms of eccentricity.

The man reminded her of an absent-minded Santa Claus pottering around in a science lab, surrounded by numerous concoctions and strange looking artefacts. He had a habit of breaking off mid-sentence to mumble under his breath, before smiling and remarking absently, 'Well, I never! Imagine that!'

His laboratory was inside a spacious manor house less than a mile from the castle's outer wall, isolated enough from the nearby city of Cendillis that his experiments did not pose a threat to the safety of any of the inhabitants.

The lineage report did not take long. Once they informed him of the Pelatarrof's request, it was a simple matter of having her stand still while Professor Egelbert placed his hand on her head and muttered some words under his breath. A scroll appeared a moment later in his hand, which he then handed to a House Faery with the warning to get it straight to King Stephen. After the faery disappeared, David and John encouraged the professor to give a demonstration of his newest invention – a ring that would allow the wearer to pass through solid objects.

It did not take long for them to convince the professor to let them try it out for themselves.

Rhiannon giggled, recalling David's stunned face when John had run straight through him. Then she shivered, remembering the cold, tingling sensation that had consumed her when David had done it to her. It had felt like an icy cloud inside her.

Now they were returning from the professor's laboratory, and she was sidestepping a puddle on the road. She readjusted the heavy woollen cloak David had procured for her, then glanced up.

Speechless, she stopped and stared in astonishment.

Her abrupt stillness had David and John turning to look at her. 'What's wrong?'

In response to David's query, she said in an awed tone, 'I've never seen it properly before.'

When they both continued to look puzzled, she pointed in front of her and declared, 'I knew I was in a palace, but I hadn't really seen it from the outside. I never realised it was so huge!'

Understanding finally dawned on their faces and in perfect synchronisation, they followed the direction of her finger to look up at the towering height of Valieoth Castle.

Set against a brilliant blue sky, with the golden rays of the morning sun turning the aged stones to a gleaming white, the whole length of the palace's upper level stood proud and majestic along the raised coastline behind the great outer wall. Its tall square towers and elaborate turrets stretched up towards the heavens, while the shimmering ocean provided an illusion of infinite space across the horizon.

'The outer wall is fifteen miles across,' David said, drawing her attention to the smooth stone structure which spanned one side of the cliffed coastline to the other in a wide curve. 'The outer wall and the inner walls were built during the war against Fendrel to provide a final line of defence for those seeking refuge in the palace. There's a similar wall around the oldest section of Cendillis.'

Long and impressively high with an array of battlements, the impenetrable appearance of the wall was reinforced by the solid doors of immense size that barricaded the front entrance, and which were flanked by two heavily guarded towers. Above the doors the sharp bottom tips of a portcullis could be seen – the thick, metal grating that when lowered would turn the doors into an impregnable barrier. Inside the outer wall, the tall towers of two other walls spanned from its east side to its west, creating three separate wards.

'How tall is it?' Rhiannon asked. 'That central tower of the palace looks gigantic!'

'It's nearly three hundred feet from the ground,' said David.

Rhiannon felt dizzy just thinking about it.

Then the gentle wave of two banners at the tower's peak caught her attention. The distance made it impossible for her to see the designs, although the bright colours of both were clearly visible.

'What are the two banners for?'

'They're the royal standard of the House of Valieoth and the realm of Álnair.'

'What do they look like?'

'The one with the emerald-green background has a white wreath with a seven-pointed star inside it. That's the one for Álnair. The one with the blue background is for Valieoth. It has a gold depiction of a dragon and his rider above a ring of twelve stars encircling a crown.'

'You actually ride dragons here?' she asked in amazement.

'Sure do,' David replied with a grin. 'Why? You want to try it?'

'Don't be stupid,' John said before she could answer. 'Why would she want to do something like that?'

David gave a casual shrug. 'Just because you don't like flying doesn't mean everyone else has to hate it.'

Rhiannon frowned. 'Why don't you like flying?' she asked John. 'Is it really dangerous?'

'Hardly,' David snorted. 'He just doesn't like heights.'

'With good reason,' John defended himself. 'All that empty space between you and the ground! I'd sooner go face to face with an enraged bull. The only time you'll get me in the air is when I have no other choice.'

'Well, either way I'd like to try it,' Rhiannon stated firmly. 'I think it'd be rather exciting.'

John closed his eyes. 'I'm surrounded by half-wits!' he groaned.

'Oh, come on, John,' David replied bracingly, 'the wind in your face, nothing but open space around you ...'

'The ground hundreds of feet below me,' John retorted. 'No, thank you. I prefer to remain safely on terra firma where I know the greatest distance I'll ever be off the ground is on the back of my horse.'

'I'm sorry you have so little faith in my race's ability to keep you safe while in the air, John Tremaine.'

The amused voice had all three of them spinning around in shock to see Endrille landing in the snow with a warm smile on her face.

'Uh, L-Lady Endrille,' John stammered, his face reddening with embarrassment. 'I d-didn't mean to imply – that is, I only meant ...'

Endrille chuckled and shook her head. 'Be at ease, dear child,' she said kindly, 'I know of your fear, and it was unpardonable of me to seek a moment's jest at your expense. I know you trust me and the rest of my race implicitly.'

'Oh, well, that's good then.' John smiled in relief, then stepped back as David moved closer to the dragon.

'Endrille, has anyone told you? Rhiannon's actually from Vetus svet! She wants to stay here, and we've just taken her to have a lineage report done, but just in case something shows up on it, would you permit her to be your rider for a short flight?'

There was a moment's silence as Endrille considered David's request.

She cast an enigmatic look at Rhiannon.

Then, 'Very well,' she replied.

'Really?'

At Rhiannon's gleeful squeal, David and John flinched.

'This is brilliant! Thank you so much. Seriously, this is the best thing to ever happen to me. I can't believe I'm about to fly on an actual dragon!'

John dropped his head into his hand and moaned. 'I can't believe anyone would be this eager to go tearing through the skies,' he said. 'Honestly, am I the only one with any sense of self-preservation?'

'Looks like it, old man,' David said, clapping him on the back. Then turning away from John, he said, 'Now, Rhiannon, the first thing you have to know is ...'

He broke off abruptly, frowned and looked blankly at the vacant space in front of him. Then he turned around and stared at the sight of Rhiannon already climbing onto Endrille's back under the dragon's watchful guidance.

Rhiannon settled herself comfortably astride Endrille's lower neck, her hands and legs warmed by the soft heat emanating from the dragon's fiery red mane. 'All right, Endrille, I'm ready,' she announced.

'Oi, hang on,' David protested, 'she hasn't even had basic instructions yet.'

'Do not concern yourself, David,' Endrille informed him calmly, 'I have a feeling this child will not require much instruction when it comes to flying.'

With that, Endrille unfurled her powerful wings with a flourish.

In a grand, sweeping movement, she lifted off the ground, the magnificent display of grace and incredible strength eliciting a delighted scream of excitement from her rider.

Instinctively sitting up straighter, Rhiannon used her leg muscles to secure her balance.

She closed her eyes for a moment, enjoying the sensation of the cool wind rushing against her face and whipping her hair out behind her in a bright, chestnut stream. Grinning broadly, she reopened her eyes and gazed down, her gasp of awe stolen away by the wind as she had her first glimpse of the world from a dragon's viewpoint.

It was truly a wondrous sight.

The radiant splendour of Valieoth Castle lay sprawled out below her, its vast grounds going on for miles. A wide stone road began at the main gate and continued in a straight path through two inner walls until it reached the edge of the palace's North Courtyard.

In the Lower Ward, a great assembly of guards clad in cloaks of dark grey and red marched their horses in front of two enormous buildings near the eastern and western walls. In the Middle Ward, a woodland coated in snow lay on each side of the road.

The Upper Ward was immense. The magnificent palace stretched out like a three-tiered rectangular cake with its four sides enclosing an open quadrangle, and its inhabitants scurried through the snow-covered gardens and lavish courtyards like a colourful array of ants. There were extensive outbuildings and orchards, along with two massive stables linked to a large arena crafted from heavy stone. On the palace's southern side was a labyrinth of stairs leading down a sheer cliff to a shallow lagoon, the clear, blue water a stark contrast to the golden sand where the graceful forms of several merfolk were resting in the warm sunlight. Separating the lagoon from the ocean was a series of narrow shoals between the clawed pinchers of headland. A small watchtower surmounted each sharp point.

'It's beautiful,' Rhiannon murmured.

'It is indeed.'

'What's that area outside the castle wall? The one with the little hut at the gate.'

'It's a deer park overseen by Keeper Sujan.'

Before Rhiannon had time to ask another question, Endrille dipped and dived.

In a flash of panic, Rhiannon tightened the grip of her legs. Then she relaxed her tense muscles until she was once again applying only a light, but firm pressure to the dragon's neck.

Endrille gave a nod of approval.

'Very good, child. Always remember to never get so distracted as to risk falling due to a weak hold or incorrect balancing.'

'I'll remember,' Rhiannon said. 'Mind you, if they decide to send me back to Vetus svet after this, I may not get another chance to go flying on a dragon.'

'Do you truly wish to remain here in Álnair?'

'More than anything.'

Endrille was silent for a moment. Then she said, 'It is within my power to offer you a chance to obtain something which would make it impossible for you to be sent back.'

'But the lineage report. If there's an issue with it then it wouldn't be right if I force them to let me stay.'

'Dear child, by those words you have proven your integrity to me, and I place more value on that than on who your antecedents may be. As the supreme custodian of Álnair, my authority surpasses that of the Pelatarrof and should you be willing, I shall attempt to bestow upon you the ultimate symbol of my trust in you.'

Rhiannon thought it over, then nodded. 'All right. What do I need to do?'

'Nothing, except ensure you maintain a firm grip on me.'

'I will, and can we go a bit faster? Please?'

Endrille shook her head in rueful dismay. 'I can see you are going to be just like David when it comes to flying,' she said on a resigned sigh.

'What do you mean?' Rhiannon asked, puzzled.

'The first time he was on my back he was six years old,' Endrille informed her, 'and the only thing he kept saying was, "go faster!"'

Rhiannon grinned impishly. 'I can just hear him saying that. And I bet he was a cheeky little monster too.'

'He certainly had his moments,' Endrille agreed, then continued in a serious tone, 'now, when a dragon is travelling swiftly always remember to maintain your focus and do not, at any time, ever attempt to stand up.'

Rhiannon frowned. 'Why would I try and do something crazy like that?'

'You would be surprised how many people have tried it,' Endrille informed her drily.

'Let me guess, David was one of them.'

'The second time he went flying,' Endrille confirmed. 'He's lucky Sir Raeden was accompanying us that day on Arastar and managed to catch him when he fell.'

'Who's Arastar?'

'The most experienced battle dragon in the castle's forces. Now, are you ready?'

'Most definitely,' Rhiannon replied eagerly.

'Then, here we go!'

Scenery flashed past below them as Endrille soared through the sky, the snow-covered fields and scattered stone cottages morphing into a labyrinth of houses on cobblestone streets, bustling crowds and rumbling carriages drawn by fine horses. Within the protective barrier of a great defensive wall around the oldest section of the settlement, the roads widened and the buildings increased in splendour.

'The city of Cendillis,' Endrille called out and slowed down to enable her rider to get a good look at it.

Rhiannon smiled at the sight of all the beautiful Christmas decorations lining the streets and eagerly took in every stone building: from the great houses and colonnaded shop fronts to the steepled roofs of modest churches and the white dome of a great basilica.

'The Basilica of Saint John,' said Endrille. 'Many of those who came to Álnair from Vetus svet were followers of the Blessed Light's son.'

'The Blessed Light?'

'The being who created us and our world. We do not know Him as your people do, but it was He who forged the link between Álnair and Vetus svet and said the pathways would be ours to govern.' Endrille circled above the impressive basilica. 'The people of Vetus svet had built many such buildings throughout their world so when they came here, they constructed one in each new city. A bishop resides in each one and he instructs the men who choose to serve the people as priests.'

After one last pass over the grand edifice, Endrille continued onwards.

At the coastline in a great harbour, Rhiannon saw a fleet of majestic ships moored at the docks with their sails furled. Dozens of smaller fishing vessels bobbed in the open ocean.

Eventually, the city streets became open farmland and in one paddock stood a large circle of standing stones. Some were broken, their shattered remains embedded in the ground inside the circle.

'Is that where one of the pathways used to be?'

'It is. When they were closed, the power used to make that one tore into the stones and destroyed some of them. Their fragments were left to lie where they fell.'

Next came a wide expanse of forest. The city of trees stood in proud defiance against the elements, their great boughs refusing to bend beneath the weight of the heavy coverlet of snow laid upon them.

'Shaimar Forest,' Endrille called out. 'And as we go onwards, you'll see Rëalta Lake which is on the other side, right next to Ryegoth Academy. Already you should be able to see the tops of its towers, with the Del Enger Mountains behind them.'

Rhiannon looked into the distance and could indeed make out the academy's stone turrets glistening in the sunlight. Behind them, their imposing snow-clad peaks dominating the horizon, lay the Del Enger Mountains.

'I can see them!'

At Rhiannon's exclamation of delight, Endrille glanced back at her with an indulgent smile.

'I take it you now believe this is all real?' she enquired with a laugh.

'I do,' Rhiannon cried joyfully. 'But it's so … I can't … there just aren't any words to describe how I feel! My whole life has changed so quickly, but I've never been happier.'

However, her feelings of bliss lasted only a moment.

Her nerve-endings began to tingle.

A throbbing pulse echoed inside her head.

A warmth encompassed her chest.

She looked down at herself to see an iridescent brilliance spreading over her limbs, her chest, up her neck. Soon it was in front of her face.

Struggling to maintain her balance, Rhiannon tightened her grip on Endrille's mane.

'Something's wrong,' she gasped, and saw the startled look the dragon gave her.

'It should not have happened this quickly,' Endrille murmured in surprise.

'What?' Rhiannon's fear increased. 'What's happening?'

'Your ability to accept my symbol of trust is being confirmed.'

Endrille turned about and hastened back towards Valieoth Castle.

'Do not be frightened,' she said reassuringly, 'you will not be harmed by what is occurring.'

Her senses befuddled, Rhiannon focused solely on maintaining her balance as Endrille sped through the skies.

She felt a *whoosh* of air, then Endrille was landing with swift grace.

'Is she all right?'

'What's happened?'

The concerned questions went unanswered.

'Boys, assist her to the ground.'

Endrille's stern tone had David and John hurriedly moving forward to quickly remove Rhiannon from the dragon's back.

They placed her gently on the snow, then stepped away.

Rhiannon stared up at Endrille as the dragon lowered her head and said softly, 'Rhiannon McBride, accept this offering, freely given, and a symbol of our trust in you. May you always prove worthy of this gift, and may you never succumb to the temptation to abuse it.'

A single sparkling teardrop fell from Endrille's eye and landed on Rhiannon's chest. Against her bare flesh it felt warm and soft, like a bead of honey fallen from a spoon.

She saw David's eyes widen before he cast a stunned glance in Endrille's direction.

'You made the offer to her,' he said in astonishment.

'I did.'

'But … only those of the House of Valieoth have ever been permitted to receive the Dragonstar from you. All others must receive it from other dragons.'

'That is certainly the practice I put in place,' Endrille agreed placidly.

A brilliant burst of light curtailed any further arguments.

Rhiannon looked down to see the shimmering radiance enveloping her body retract towards her chest. It formed into a small luminous glow that hovered over her heart. As she watched the gentle brightness begin to take form, streams of incandescent light solidified and twisted around her neck before surrounding the teardrop Endrille had shed. The fragile liquid hardened, attaining the flawless purity of a diamond.

A moment passed.

The light faded.

Rhiannon slowly sat up, her hand reaching up to grasp the pendant now resting against her chest.

She gazed down at the delicate mixture of interwoven silver metal and the clear, twinkling stone shaped into a star. After a moment, she lifted her head and stared at the three in front of her.

'Does someone want to tell me what just happened?'

'I guess you could say you just received the seal of approval for becoming a mage,' David replied.

Rhiannon stared at him dumbfounded. 'What?'

'Usually, when you're six years old, they put you on a dragon,' John informed her. 'The dragon then takes you for a flight and if you have inside you the ability to use the gift, then the dragon can fully awaken it if you consent.'

'What do you mean "fully awaken"?'

'Everyone is conceived with the gift inside of them,' said David, 'but it's either dormant or partially active. If it's partially active, then some special abilities will manifest themselves.'

'What about where I come from?' Her hand still clutching the pendant around her neck, Rhiannon turned her attention to Endrille. 'Would everyone there also have the gift inside of them?'

Endrille inclined her head. 'The people in Vetus svet certainly would have it,' she replied, 'but it would never be fully awakened. A dragon is required to completely activate the power inside a potential mage, and since any dragon who survived the Time of Persecution has either remained in hiding or died, the people would have no way of unlocking that part of themselves.'

'But they would have access to some of it?'

'You, yourself, Rhiannon, have displayed certain abilities that would not be possible in someone who was not a future mage,' Endrille pointed out, 'although I will admit the healing of oneself is an extremely rare talent.'

'So, what other abilities can show?'

'The more common ones are unusual displays of physical strength, heightened empathetic abilities ...'

'What about summoning or speaking to the dead?' Rhiannon interrupted. 'Back in Vetus svet, there are always disagreements about those who say they can talk to peoples' dead relatives.'

She then noticed the appalled expressions on her companions' faces.

Her expression severe, Endrille said, 'Whether you are a mage or not, no one possesses the skill which allows them to call on the dead or converse with them on demand. And although there are some people who have the gift of neushallough,' at Rhiannon's blank look at the unfamiliar word, Endrille explained, 'it is the ability to see certain events that have happened or will happen. Although some possess this talent, it does not enable them to initiate contact with the dead. Once a person's soul has left their mortal body, then their involvement with the physical world is finished, and an attempt to force contact with them would not only be foolish but exceedingly dangerous.'

'But what if the dead tried to talk to someone among the living?' Rhiannon asked.

'Should the dead ever wish to talk to someone, then I am sure they would be quite capable of speaking directly to that person without resorting to using another person's voice to speak for them,' Endrille replied. 'However, having said that, I would be wary of any and all spirits who attempted to converse with the living. Unless you know with absolute certainty they are who they claim to be, then I would not trust them, for there are many dangerous beings that can impersonate the dead.'

Rhiannon glanced down at the shimmering pendant adorning her chest and traced the delicate design with her finger. 'So, what does this do?' she asked.

'The Dragonstar contains a fragment of the energy of the dragon who provided a part of themselves in the form of a teardrop, which helps focus and stabilise your power,' Endrille informed her. 'And, while you live, it may only be removed by you, the mage for whom it was made.'

'So people can tell you're a mage just by seeing that you're wearing one of these?' Rhiannon asked, holding up the pendant.

'The Dragonstar will become incorporeal shortly after it is first bestowed,' Endrille explained. 'It will only return to a solid state if you decide to remove it, or in the event of your death.'

'Then how do people know who's a mage and who isn't?'

'Well, if you start causing strange things to happen, like making objects float in the air, that's one way of letting people know,' David pointed out.

Endrille gave him a swift, reproving look, then returned her gaze to Rhiannon.

'A list of all awakened magi is kept in the archives at Valieoth Castle,' she said. 'The instant a Dragonstar is created, the name of the mage is recorded, along with a description of their Dragonstar.'

Rhiannon frowned and looked again at her own. 'Don't they all look the same?'

'I certainly wouldn't wear one looking like that, even when it's invisible!' David scoffed. He placed a hand on his chest and appeared to grasp thin air before raising his arm to pull something off from around his neck. A white glow surrounded his palm as his hand came back into view. The next instant, his Dragonstar became visible.

He helped Rhiannon to her feet, then placed his Dragonstar in her hand.

Looking at it, she immediately noticed that although it was also in the form of a star, the silver metal was heavier, and the stone shone with an inner blue radiance.

'It's beautiful,' she murmured.

'I'm not really supposed to let you hold it,' David told her, casting a wary glance in Endrille's direction. 'Even though a Dragonstar can't be used by anyone but the mage for whom it was intended, it's dangerous to let someone else handle it. Without it, you lose your ability to control your power. Also, it's to avoid the other person trying to tamper with it.'

Rhiannon snorted in amusement. 'Somehow I doubt you need worry about that with me. I wouldn't know how to do it,' she said. Realising how that may have sounded, she hurriedly added, 'Not that I would if I did.'

'If I had thought for a moment you were the type to even attempt it, I would never have let you see it, let alone touch it,' David replied, placing a reassuring hand on her shoulder.

Surprised but gratified by his show of trust, Rhiannon smiled. After taking one last look at his Dragonstar, she handed it back to him.

There was a brief shimmer of light as David replaced it around his neck, and then it vanished.

'Is your one like his?' Rhiannon asked John.

'No two Dragonstars are ever the same,' he said, imitating David's actions and revealing his own.

Instead of silver, John's was a burnished copper, while the stone was a stunning shade of jade.

Rhiannon tentatively reached out to touch it. 'Do you mind if I …?'

'Not at all, go ahead.' John placed his Dragonstar in her hand. 'If you didn't do anything to David's (more's the pity) I guess I don't have to worry about mine.'

Ignoring the friendly banter which erupted between the two boys, Rhiannon gently examined the Dragonstar. After a moment she glanced up at Endrille with a puzzled frown.

'It feels different from mine and David's,' she said.

'That is because both yours and David's were made from a part of me. John's contains a fragment gifted by Thandyl.'

After examining the Dragonstar a moment longer, Rhiannon handed it back to John. 'So what happens now?'

'Well, you certainly won't be returning to Vetus svet,' said David. 'You'll get to attend lessons with us after the Christmas holidays.'

Blinking away the hot sting of tears, Rhiannon asked, 'You mean, I'll be able to stay here at the palace?'

'For as long as you like,' David smiled. 'I'll even insist upon it.'

Rhiannon hurled herself forward, throwing her arms around David's startled form with a cry of delight. 'Oh, thank you. Thank you, a million times over!' With her face buried in David's tunic, her words came out muffled.

Disconcerted at being the recipient of such an emotional embrace, David awkwardly patted her on the back. 'Steady on, Rhiannon. Anyone would think I just offered you the throne. Which you can't have by the way,' he added lightly, 'my parents wouldn't approve.'

'Who needs a throne!' Rhiannon smiled and released him. She looked at each of them in turn, desperate to convey her gratitude. 'You've given me something so much better – a place I can call home.' Then, feeling a gentle warmth seep into her chest, she gazed down to see a silvery white light, like the fairest moonbeam in a clear sky, surrounding the Dragonstar. The light remained there for a moment, the Dragonstar became transparent, then both it and the light disappeared.

'That's brilliant.' Rhiannon touched the area near her heart. 'It's like it's there, but at the same time it's not.'

'Bit like David's mind,' John muttered.

'At least we know I have one!' David retorted, clipping him on the shoulder with a shove. He then cast a glance at his watch and sighed. 'I guess we'd better head back in and let the old windbags know what's happened.'

'I believe that would be the best thing to do,' Endrille agreed, tactfully overlooking the less-than-polite reference to the members of the Pelatarrof. 'However, before you depart, Rhiannon, I would have a final few words with you.'

David and John moved back a few paces, leaving Rhiannon alone with the dragon.

Endrille turned around and lowered herself until her silver underbelly was lying flat on the snow. When Rhiannon came and stood near her head, she said, 'Being an awakened mage, you have been gifted with certain abilities and powers. These must always be wielded with humility and right judgement. They are to be used primarily to serve others, never yourself. Outside the field of battle, you must not use them to inflict death on another, although they may be used in self-defence. Also, they should never be used to deprive another of their free will.

'As a mage, you must be cautious and avoid the temptation to use your gift as a solution to every task or problem. It is not a tool to be exploited for the sake of making life easier. Be judicious in your use of it, and do not fall prey to the notion that receiving it makes you greater than those who have not. In receiving this gift, you have been given the responsibility of using it to protect and serve those who may have need of it. You shall learn how to fight, and how to provide healing for this purpose. But one rule is paramount above all others: use your gift to aid life, not control it. One mage who ignored this rule was Fendrel. Have you been informed of him?'

Rhiannon nodded.

'Rather than treating with respect his ability to influence nature, he abused it. He created new forms of life through sorcery and the deaths of not only his fellow men, but a host of other creatures. Therefore, I urge you to treat your gift with the greatest care and guard yourself against arrogance and pride in its power – for such emotions have corrupted some of the wisest among your race.'

Rhiannon swallowed. 'I'll be careful.'

Endrille accepted this with a small nod, then her stern expression relaxed. 'Now that I have issued my warning, I shall wish you every success in your studies, Rhiannon.'

'Thank you. And even if I hadn't received a Dragonstar, going for a flight with you was the most fun I've ever had,' Rhiannon smiled. Then she gestured for Endrille to lower her head.

The last of the ancient dragons obeyed, enabling Rhiannon to brush a gentle kiss against her jaw.

'I really am grateful,' Rhiannon whispered. 'And I'll try to never do anything to make you regret giving me a Dragonstar.'

Then she pulled back and as David and John approached, she gave Endrille another smile.

'All done?' David asked.

'Our conversation is concluded,' Endrille said.

'Then we'd best get going before they start sending out search parties.'

Bidding Endrille a fond goodbye, David, Rhiannon and John turned to head back to the castle.

They did not notice Endrille's keen glance focus on Rhiannon as she walked away, nor did they hear when she said softly, 'I could never regret bestowing a Dragonstar upon you, daughter of Mórell.'

David, Rhiannon and John were confronted by a scene of excited pandemonium upon arriving back at the Praeterium. The members of the Pelatarrof, who had been seated in dignified silence when they left, were now standing in chattering clusters about the room, their voices raised in animated discussions, hand gestures accompanying and punctuating every word.

David looked at the brown-robed figure beside him. 'You must've been relieved when they selected you to come find us, Paul. The noise alone would drive anyone mad.'

Councillor Paul Attwater hastily smothered the laugh that slipped through his lips. 'Indeed, Your Royal Highness,' he replied. 'It was a singular honour which could not have befallen a more grateful recipient.'

'Were they this bad when you left?'

The councillor directed a brief, analysing glance at the scene in front of him, then declared succinctly, 'Worse.'

John gave a low whistle. 'That lineage report must've contained something pretty impressive to cause this amount of racket,' he said.

'It certainly did at that,' came the obscure reply.

David frowned, having caught the strange look Paul sent Rhiannon. He immediately put an end to the discussion by politely thanking the man and ushering Rhiannon into the room.

The loud groups were too distracted to notice the reappearance of the girl who was the cause of their excitement. David managed to lead Rhiannon and John unimpeded to the dais where his father stood in a more subdued discussion with Sir Raeden.

King Stephen greeted their approach with a nod and signalled for Lord Sharbel to bring the discussions in the room to an end.

This was done swiftly and once the last member had retaken their seat, King Stephen announced, 'Given the results of the child's lineage report, I do not believe any further discussion is necessary to determine whether the child should be permitted to remain in Álnair.'

Instantly prepared to do battle on behalf of Rhiannon, David stepped forward and protested vehemently, 'But, Father, we can't send her back to Vetus svet!'

'David ...'

'Father, you simply can't,' David continued, paying no heed to his parent's attempt to interrupt him. 'She needs to stay here because ...'

'David ...'

'... because she received the Dragonstar!' David finished triumphantly.

'David, we're n – what?' His expression mirroring the stunned looks on the faces of the room's other occupants, King Stephen stared at his son in astonishment.

'Rhiannon received the Dragonstar,' David said again, his smile victorious, 'so she can't go back to Vetus svet.'

King Stephen ignored the incredulous exclamations sounding throughout the room and turned his attention to Rhiannon. His surprised expression was replaced by a look of pure amusement.

'I do not need to ask the name of the dragon who decided to bestow a Dragonstar upon you before your lineage report was received,' he commented with a smile. 'Even though she did not tell me the name, Lady Endrille assured me there could be no objection to the person who would show on your lineage report should you express a desire to stay here.'

David frowned at his father's vague speech. 'Father, what did the report say?' he asked.

'David, had you been less hasty in assuming we intended to send Miss McBride back to Vetus svet, I would have been able to inform you there was no possibility of our returning her there unless she requested it.'

'Oh. Well, good,' David said, looking embarrassed that his impassioned intervention on Rhiannon's behalf had not been required after all. 'But you still haven't said who she is.'

King Stephen gave a warm smile. Then, reaching forward, he placed a gentle hand on Rhiannon's shoulder and announced, 'She is Rhiannon Marie McBride, only daughter of Mórell's line.'

David and John stared at him open-mouthed. Rhiannon merely looked puzzled.

'Who's Mórell?'

A familiar voice answered her.

'Mórell was the last daughter born to the ruling family of the O'Faenart clan before the Time of Persecution,' Sir Raeden informed her. 'When the pathways were closed, she chose to remain in Vetus svet with her husband, Níall. Since that time no daughter has been born to the Royal House of Valieoth.'

'You're joking.' Upon seeing Sir Raeden's forbidding scowl, Rhiannon hastily added, 'Sorry, of course you aren't. But seriously, you mean I'm descended from the daughter of a Celtic chieftain?'

'That is the general definition of one who is said to be of a person's line,' Sir Raeden remarked drily.

Rhiannon emitted an awe-struck, 'Strewth,' promptly followed by a worried, 'so what will happen to me now?'

'As daughter to Mórell's line you are entitled to reside within Valieoth Castle,' King Stephen reassured her. 'However, as you are now to be a permanent resident of Álnair we must address the issue of your guardianship.'

Rhiannon shifted uneasily. Her previous experiences with the Dashmonts flooded her mind. She certainly did not want to go to another couple like them!

'Since I'll be staying here, wouldn't that make you my guardian?' she asked.

King Stephen shook his head. 'For their own safety and wellbeing, all those who are of the royal line must be under the protection of their own parents or individual guardians.'

'What about the O'Sullivans, or the Lohengrins? Surely they would be the best ones suited for taking the guardianship of such an important child?'

The owner of the pompous voice, an arrogant looking gentleman in fine green robes, was instantly answered by a scoffing, 'And I'm sure the child's health and happiness would be their first concern, right after they ensured they fulfilled all their social engagements.'

'Well said, Chancellor Borelli.' Nodding her head in agreement, the silver-haired woman seated on the front pew brushed an invisible speck of dust off her brown robes as she declared, 'Vain socialites make notoriously bad parents, and this child needs the guidance that only a sensible husband and wife can provide.'

'Regard must be given to her status,' another voice interjected haughtily. 'We can't let her guardian be any common person in the city.'

'An' what be wrong with bein' one o' the common folk?' demanded Caiden Alcober, his accent thickened in his indignation.

The arguments continued to escalate around her, and Rhiannon spared a thought for the SilverScribe swiftly taking down every word being said. She wondered if it would soon spontaneously combust.

'ENOUGH!'

The deafening roar from Lord Sharbel had all arguments ceasing instantly.

'If you are quite finished behaving like quarrelsome children, I would remind you all these are still official proceedings, and to conduct yourselves with all due decorum.'

Lord Sharbel's acerbic tone and icy glare had many of the members flushing with embarrassment.

'Thank you, Lord Sharbel.'

His voice once again drawing everyone's attention to himself, King Stephen calmly gazed at the members before he continued. 'Sir Raeden has confirmed with the Trínondras that he is agreeable for his current appointment of Independent Guardian, which was only to last for the duration of this hearing, to be amended. Therefore, we, the Trínondras, decree that Sir Raeden Wyvern be appointed the official permanent guardian of Rhiannon Marie McBride.'

The discontented muttering, which had begun at the first mention of Sir Raeden's name, instantly disappeared.

'The Trínondras always makes the final decision.'

John's quiet reminder near Rhiannon's ear was followed by David's unflattering remark on the Trínondras' lack of intelligence.

~*Chapter 14*~

BITTER TIDINGS

The hearing had been adjourned, and the members of the Pelatarrof were slowly exiting the Praeterium when King Stephen called Rhiannon's name.

Followed by the curious eyes of David and John, she made her way over to where the monarch stood at the foot of the dais. He was holding a scroll in his hand.

She could not help but notice the change in his expression. Immediately following the end of the hearing, when he had first descended the dais to congratulate her on receiving a Dragonstar, his countenance had been friendly. Now it was grave.

An uneasy feeling began to grow inside her.

'Yes, Your Majesty,' she said, and was surprised when the king reached out and placed a gentle hand on her shoulder.

'Please, come with me,' he said.

He led her away from the main area to a small antechamber.

The room was furnished with several comfortable chairs placed before a cosy fire burning in a small hearth. Several deeply filled bookshelves lined the walls. In one corner of the room stood a large desk, and behind it she had a magnificent view of the ocean through the tall arched window that almost reached the finely decorated ceiling.

Rhiannon looked over her shoulder towards the door to see Sir Raeden just outside it, with David and John behind him. She turned back to King Stephen, then frowned when he gestured towards one of the chairs.

'Pray be seated, Rhiannon.'

Totally confused, and with the sense of dread mounting, she obediently sat down.

A brief pause fell.

King Stephen hesitated, then lowered himself into the chair beside hers. He did not speak for a moment, and his green eyes stared grimly into the bright flames of the fire.

At length he broke the silence when he inhaled deeply and said quietly, 'Rhiannon, there was more information on the lineage report I did not disclose to the members during the hearing. I did not deem it appropriate to speak of it openly until I had first informed you of it; for you see, it is in relation to your parents.'

Rhiannon snapped forward at these words, her attention fully caught.

'My dear child, there is no easy way to say this, but it must be said.' King Stephen lifted the scroll in his hand as he spoke. 'The lineage report not only reveals the names of your family, but also bears a mark next to their name if they are deceased. Your parents' names both have that mark. I am sorry, Rhiannon.'

Shock and disbelief held her immobile.

In her mind, a voice was screaming out in denial.

A peculiar numbness entered her heart.

For how long she sat there staring blankly at King Stephen she would never know. All sound around her had become distorted, the fading voices out in the Praeterium nothing but muffled noise. It was not until the burning log in the fire shifted, the movement causing a shower of sparks to fly up the chimney with a loud crackling hiss, that coherent thought pierced the haze enveloping her mind.

'May I …?' Rhiannon's hoarse croak broke off. She cleared her throat before trying again. 'May I see it?'

King Stephen handed the report to her without a word.

Her hand was strangely steady as she unfurled the scroll to read the contents inside.

The firm grey parchment was covered in black cursive script. But the beautiful lettering in no way alleviated the grief their words inflicted upon her heart.

Patrick Ewan McBride   *Claire Emmaline McBride (Prewett)*

Rhiannon looked at the names of her parents. Then at the names of her grandparents:

Hugh Rory McBride   *Kathleen Mary McBride (O'Hara)*

Richard Sherman Prewett   *Charlotte Anne Prewett (Romald)*

All were marked as deceased.

The seed of hope of one day being reunited with her parents, which she had nurtured from the day she found the newspaper article in Brakenhurst Library, shrivelled up and died.

A gasping sob escaped her.

The scroll fell to the carpet.

Then Rhiannon buried her face in her hands and wept.

She was aware of a consoling hand being placed on her head, and soft voices murmuring briefly before they fell silent.

Words burst from her lips between harsh sobs. Angry, disappointed, sorrowful words that came from deep inside her.

What she said, she did not know. The dam had burst and a lifetime of hurt and neglect came pouring out in a torrent of disjointed sentences.

Nothing penetrated the shroud of sorrow until a pair of warm, maternal arms encircled her.

She was drawn into a comforting embrace that held the faintest scent of apple blossoms.

She breathed in the delicate fragrance and let her head rest against the woman's shoulder.

Gradually her sobs began to lessen, the pain in her heart eased by the soothing words being whispered near her ear by a gentle voice.

Rhiannon gave a sniff, then pulled back to see who held her. She found herself staring into the face of the most beautiful woman she had ever seen.

The woman's fair complexion was framed by a cloud of hair as black as a starless night, and her wide eyes with their long, curling lashes were a deep shade of violet that Rhiannon instantly recognised. She did not need to see the delicate circlet adorning the woman's head, or the exquisite gown of lavender silk, to identify her as David's mother, Queen Maiwen.

Rhiannon ducked her head behind a curtain of hair, suddenly aware of the sight she must present with her tear-streaked face.

'Come, my dear, surely my appearance is not that frightening.'

Queen Maiwen's light comment was followed by her slowly reaching out and placing a fine handkerchief in Rhiannon's hand.

Rhiannon quickly wiped away the tears staining her cheeks and looked up again.

'I'm sorry,' she tried to say, only to find her apology quietly interrupted.

'There is no need to apologise,' Queen Maiwen said, moving from her kneeling position on the floor to the chair previously occupied by her husband. 'You have every right to grieve for your parents.'

The kindness in the woman's voice had fresh tears welling up in Rhiannon's eyes. Determined not to become a human watering-pot again, she blinked them away, saying, 'I feel like such a fool for crying so much, but it's just I thought I'd be able to find them. Ever since I found the old newspaper article three weeks ago, I've been hoping one day I would. That I'd discover they'd been in an accident and were in a coma all this time, and no one knew who they were until they woke up. Or they'd lost their memories, and I'd run into them one day in the street and they'd see me and suddenly remember everything. Then, when I came here, and found out about other people coming through, I thought maybe they'd be here. David said they couldn't be, but he was going to ask his father and Endrille about a way to find them. I was so sure I'd be able to see them again.'

She paused, then gave a derisive snort. 'Not that I can even remember them,' she said. 'If I hadn't found the article, I wouldn't even know what they looked like. I was two years old when they vanished, and the first couple of foster homes I was placed in weren't given any photos, or if they did get them, they certainly didn't show them to me. By the time I ended up with the Dashmonts and asked if there was one I could have, I was told there were none to be found. "Lost in the system," my social worker told me. I don't even know why I'm so upset! They've been missing for years so it's not like I even knew them!'

'That does not mean they were not important to you; that you did not yearn for the day when you would find them,' Queen Maiwen observed gently. 'Every child must surely long to know their parents, to know they are loved and wanted by their mother and father. You have probably spent many years thinking about them, wondering what their favourite things were, if they were like you. You have built a relationship with them in here,' she laid a hand against her breast, 'and it is inside your heart that you grieve, not up here.' She pointed to her forehead. 'The mind will tell us that life will continue, that death is but a natural occurrence, a brief parting until we shall meet our loved ones after we too take our last breath; but the heart aches for what it no longer has at the moment, and no logic in the world will soothe that pain. Only time can do that.'

Rhiannon sniffed and quickly wiped her nose. 'I don't think I've ever cried so much in my life,' she muttered.

Queen Maiwen smiled.

'When I was your age, I don't think a week went by without me dissolving into tears over some small misfortune. The troubles you have been dealing with certainly do not fall into that category. I think you were quite overdue for a healthy bout of tears,' she remarked with motherly candour.

Rhiannon gave her a watery smile. 'I'll try not to do it too much. I wouldn't want to do an Alice and flood the palace.'

The Queen's finely arched eyebrows lifted in apparent surprise. 'This Alice would appear to be quite a prolific crier to achieve such a feat.'

A startled laugh escaped Rhiannon at her words. 'Oh, she isn't a real person. She's a character in a book I read who cries so much when she grows to an enormous height that a flood of tears fills the room.'

'Undoubtedly a most foolish girl then,' Queen Maiwen declared, 'for she should have thought of all the cleaning she would have to do to get rid of the water damage.'

This time it was a laugh of genuine humour that passed Rhiannon's lips. She looked at the queen and saw a twinkle in her violet eyes which belied the prosaic tone of her voice.

'You did not believe she was real at all, did you?' Rhiannon said.

Queen Maiwen laughed and shook her head. 'I must confess I did not,' she admitted.

Rhiannon fell silent for a moment. Then she said hesitantly, 'It doesn't feel right to be laughing so soon after finding out about my parents. I always thought when you found out someone in your family died it meant being sad all the time for a while.'

Queen Maiwen leant forward to clasp one of Rhiannon's hands in her own.

'Do not feel guilty for laughing,' she told her. 'It is perfectly all right to have a light-hearted moment, even in the greatest times of sadness. In fact, one minute of happiness during a time of sorrow can help strengthen you and give you the motivation to get through another day.'

She gave a small huff of amusement.

'I still find myself smiling whenever I recall a scene from the day after my own father died,' she continued. 'It happened when David was seven years old. My son loved spending time with his grandfather, and he was almost inconsolable when we told him. As you can imagine, I was dreading the prospect of trying to comfort him while also grieving myself. The next morning, I went to his bedchamber only to find it empty. I looked for him in all the places I knew he went when he was upset, but I couldn't find him. It was as I was walking through the East Courtyard that I heard a burst of laughter. I followed the sound down several pathways, and then I found my son. He was chasing one of the wolfhound puppies through the garden. They were both soaking wet and covered in soap bubbles. It was his laughter I'd heard, and he looked as merry as I'd ever seen him. As I watched him, I forgot about my grief and found myself enjoying the simple pleasure of seeing my son laughing so joyously. So do not think it wrong to have a moment of happiness during times of sorrow, Rhiannon. Life continues, and those who must be parted from us by death would not want us to chain ourselves to a single emotion that drains all joy from our lives.'

'I suppose they wouldn't,' Rhiannon agreed.

'Just take each day as it comes, and if you ever want to talk about anything, please do come and find me.'

Rhiannon felt another shard of grief ease in her heart at the queen's kind offer. 'Thank you,' she said sincerely. 'And thank you for staying with me.'

Queen Maiwen waved her gratitude aside.

'It would be a poor thing if I could not offer solace to a soul in need of it,' she said. 'And hearing you laugh at my sad attempt at wit is ample reward for my endeavours. It was lovely to see you smile. I had been told you have a beautiful one, and I can see my son did not exaggerate.'

Rhiannon felt herself blush at the compliment, and at the name of the one who had said it first. She saw a curiously intent look come into the queen's eyes and the beginnings of a smile curl her lips, before she rose gracefully to her feet, saying, 'Come, my dear. You have had an extremely tiring morning and require some rest. Besides, I am sure David and John are anxiously waiting to see that you are all right.'

At the reminder of the male witnesses to her bout of weeping, Rhiannon turned around in her chair to discover she and Queen Maiwen were the only occupants of the room, and the door was discreetly closed.

'My husband and Sir Raeden felt you might feel more comfortable if only I remained in here,' Queen Maiwen explained. 'They will be waiting out in the Praeterium.'

Rhiannon nodded, then looked down at the scroll that still lay where it had fallen on the carpet. Inside it was contained the only link she had to her family, her identity. A list of names going back centuries. It would not have seemed like much to many other people who had the good fortune to at least know their parents, but for her it was proof she was not an abandoned, unwanted child. Knowing that her parents had not willingly left her alone made their absence easier to bear. It was also a symbol of the acceptance she had found here in Álnair.

She picked it up and held it tightly in her hand. She would

mourn her parents, but she would also heed Queen Maiwen's advice, and take each day as it came.

Rhiannon stood up determinedly.

She would make a new life for herself here among the people of Álnair, who had shown more genuine interest in her wellbeing in a few days than the Dashmonts and Annabelle had done in almost a decade.

Walking towards the door, she felt a surge of new hope rise up inside of her. She was now a mage, and she would make every effort not to waste the opportunity given to her. She would make her parents proud, and Endrille would never have reason to regret gifting her a Dragonstar.

After leaving the antechamber, Rhiannon was greeted by David's concerned voice enquiring if she was all right, a friendly smile from John, a benevolent one from King Stephen and Sir Raeden's silent examination of her face.

'I'm fine now,' she assured them. 'Her Majesty was most kind.'

Queen Maiwen accepted the compliment with a small inclination of her head, then turned to Sir Raeden.

'Have you decided where she is to live?' she asked him. 'I shall need to make the proper arrangements if she is to remain in the palace.'

'With Your Majesties' permission, I would have her continue to reside here,' replied Sir Raeden, glancing from her to King Stephen. 'Given the nature of my duties, and her status, I do not believe it prudent, nor indeed appropriate, to settle her in another abode at this time.'

While both sovereigns instantly granted their permission, Rhiannon saw David staring at Sir Raeden in surprise. She wondered if he had expected her guardian to command she be removed to an isolated tower somewhere, like the princess in a child's fairy tale. If he had, she couldn't understand why. Certainly, from what she had seen, Sir Raeden did not spare most people from the sharp edge of his tongue, but he didn't seem particularly evil.

'Rhiannon.'

Queen Maiwen recalled her attention, saying she would stay in the same bedchamber.

'Sir Raeden's rooms are close to it, and you shall be given full access to the transonus system,' the queen informed her, then looked at David. 'I am sure we may safely leave it to you to arrange the authorisation,' she said.

David nodded. 'I can do it now if you don't need Rhiannon for anything else.' He looked from his parents to Sir Raeden. All three of them shook their heads.

And so it was that Rhiannon soon found herself standing on the transonus dais nearest to the Praeterium. Tucked away in a discreet alcove, it had three steps leading up to the platform and a thick stone console at its edge.

David moved in front of the console, then pointed at the thirteen rows of runes engraved along its surface.

'Each rune represents the location of a dais on the system,' he explained. 'There are three rows for each wing, representing the three sections. The upper section is always the top row. The thirteenth row is for all the daises outside in the castle grounds. The order of the wings is north, east, south, then west.' He pointed to a rune halfway on the seventh row. 'That's probably the most important one for you to learn first. It's the one for the second level of the Upper South Wing where your rooms are.'

Rhiannon looked at the confusing number of runes in dismay. 'Is there a diagram of them all that I can study?' she asked, and was relieved to hear there was.

'I'll make sure you get a copy,' said David. Then he told her to place a hand anywhere on the console. 'And don't remove it until I say so,' he added.

Rhiannon reached out and laid her right hand on the smooth, cool stone of the console. Then she watched as David did the same.

The stone beneath her hand grew warm, and the faint light emanating from it gave her pale flesh the appearance of translucent marble.

Without speaking a word, David moved his hand to cover a single rune positioned in the top left corner. He pressed down.

The entire dais lit up.

Rhiannon felt a wave of energy flow through her.

Then the light faded, the tingling sensation disappeared and David told her she could remove her hand.

'Now you can go wherever you like, whenever you like,' he said.

Rhiannon looked to where John was waiting in the hallway. 'Can you do that too?'

'All Robesmen are given full access,' he said, 'along with certain people living or working inside the palace. Anyone else can only go to a dais they've been cleared to use.'

Rhiannon glanced down at the console and asked David, 'And all that's needed is to press the rune where you want to go?'

He nodded, but a beautiful peal of chimes cut off whatever he was going to say. A look of eager delight spread across his face and he announced with boyish enthusiasm, 'That's the summons for lunch, and thank goodness because I'm famished!'

They swiftly covered the distance between the Praeterium and the King's Dining Hall thanks to the transonus system. Rhiannon was soon seated between David and John, enjoying a sumptuous feast of roast meat, delicately flavoured vegetables and fresh bread in the richly decorated hall.

Lit by thousands of lights gathered into five enormous chandeliers, the entire room was a hive of cheerful conversation. The long table was draped in a fine red cloth and covered with a glittering array of gilded plates, shining silver cutlery and exquisite goblets of sparkling crystal.

King Stephen sat in a great chair at one end of the table, with David on his right and Sir Raeden on his left, while Queen Maiwen sat at the opposite end with Lord Sharbel on one side of her and an elegantly dressed woman on the other.

'That's Lady Agnes Fasani, my mother's First Lady of the Girdle,' David said, his words almost drowned out by the chattering voices of the large gathering at the table. 'Her son Derrick is one of my Robesmen. And don't let her appearance mislead you. She may look like a perfectly refined lady, but she's an absolute gorgon when it comes to protecting my mother. A month ago, an attempt was made to abduct them on their way back from visiting my aunt. Lady Agnes took on four of the group herself and injured them so badly, the guards had to fetch a healer for them before they could be moved.'

Rhiannon studied the strong features of Lady Agnes, and thought they held all the feline grace of a tigress.

I wonder if she snarls like one when she fights, she wondered, and was struggling to hold back a nervous giggle when a sudden lull in the conversation at the middle of the table drew her attention.

Several people were rising from their seats to make room for a late arrival.

Rhiannon leant back to look past John's taller form, curious to see who it was.

The cold, dark gaze of Councillor Plancy met hers.

Rhiannon shivered. There was something else behind the man's unpleasant sneer. Something purely malevolent. It clung about him like an insidious toxin. She had felt an inkling of it during the hearing, but it was much stronger now.

Her appetite disappeared, the small amount she had already eaten turning to lead in her stomach. She wanted to get away from those eyes. From the darkness she could sense behind them. She felt unclean. Tainted.

'Is something wrong?'

Rhiannon jumped. She turned to see David staring at her, the solicitous tone in his voice matching the look on his face.

Not knowing how she could explain her reaction to Councillor Plancy's presence without sounding crazy, she pushed her plate away with a quiet, 'I just don't feel very hungry.'

She saw his violet eyes narrow slightly, as though suspecting she wasn't being entirely truthful. 'You look pale,' he said.

'I always look pale.'

He looked down. 'Your hand's trembling.'

Rhiannon took it off the table. 'I must be tired,' she said.

David frowned, then looked down the table. She could see the moment he saw Councillor Plancy. His lips tightened and his eyes darkened to the deep violet of storm clouds before a violent squall.

'I see,' he muttered. Turning back to her, he said, 'It was him, wasn't it?'

Not wanting to tell an actual lie, Rhiannon nodded. 'He looked me in the eyes, and now I just want get as far away from him as possible. He makes my skin crawl.'

'All right,' said David, and to her surprise he turned to his father and asked that he be excused, along with her and John. King Stephen quirked an eyebrow but gave his consent.

Rhiannon stood up in relief, then followed David towards a set of ornate doors made of wood and glass.

'Don't worry about having to see a lot of Plancy,' he told her in a low voice, his words reaching her beneath the din behind them. 'He only ever comes to the palace when he needs to attend official meetings or hearings, and even then he doesn't normally join us in here for meals. There's another one the councillors and staff use, but for today and tomorrow all meals are being served in the King's Dining Hall as quite a few of the staff aren't here.'

The revelation left Rhiannon feeling much better. In a place the size of the palace, she was confident there would be little chance of accidentally encountering the creepy councillor.

She stepped through the doorway after David and felt the brisk chill of the outside envelop her body. Standing on a wide balcony, she looked up and gave a small exclamation of pleasure.

The view was breathtaking!

At the bottom of a sweeping flight of stone steps, a mantle of snow lay upon the vast courtyard and formal gardens. In the distance a small woodland grew, and beyond where the land curved upwards in a natural wall of craggy rocks, the deep blue of the ocean reflected the clear sky above.

'This is the West Terrace,' said David. 'That path there leads to the stables and the quarters of the Royal Guard, along with the castle school.' He pointed at a cleared walkway heading north, then at another. 'And that one leads around to the South Terrace.'

Rhiannon took a brief look to the right and saw the frontage of the two stables she had seen while riding Endrille. Beyond them were two other impressively sized buildings.

'Why are there two stables?' she asked.

'There are over eight thousand horses housed in them,' was David's startling reply.

'Eight *thousand!*' she repeated in disbelief.

'Well, there are a lot of people who live or work here,' David pointed out. 'The Imperial Stables, the building closest to the palace, is mainly for the mounts belonging to my family and our aides, the Royal Guard and visitors. There's also a section on the ground level where all the coaches and carriages are kept. The Small Stables is where the mounts belonging to the palace and stable staff and the castle guards are housed. I'd take you to have a look at them right now, but with this wind you'd freeze before we even left the courtyard.' He gestured to another set of doors farther up the terrace to the north. 'How about we show you the Hall of Time?'

John groaned. 'David, I doubt she'll want to look at a collection of old clocks.'

'No, it's all right,' Rhiannon hurriedly interjected. 'I don't mind.'

'You will once he starts rambling on about suspension springs, dragon hands and astrolabes,' said John.

Rhiannon thought of how David had forgone the rest of his lunch to get her away from Councillor Plancy. She decided that even if it turned out to be the most tedious place she could imagine, she wouldn't complain.

To her surprise, Rhiannon enjoyed the Hall of Time. The great room was filled with clocks of all shapes and sizes showcasing the history of timekeeping in Álnair. Some were enchanted, while others were not. Ranging from ancient sundials to astronomical and pendulum clocks, the size of the collection was staggering. But what made the experience particularly fun was David's enthusiasm. The Prince of Álnair behaved like a little boy in a toy store, spouting off a fount of information about each clock, and eagerly showing her how each one worked. Before she knew it, two hours had passed and David's stomach was beginning to growl like a ravenous lion.

'I think I'll just go get something from the kitchens,' he said. 'Did you want to come?' he asked her.

Rhiannon shook her head. 'Actually, I feel like having a rest,' she admitted.

'That's not surprising,' said John. 'You've been through a lot in the last couple of days, and the hearing this morning wasn't exactly pleasant.'

David led them out of the hall to a long passageway. 'There's a transonus dais down here,' he said, and pointed it out. 'You can do your first solo trip. Do you remember the rune I showed you for the second level of the Upper South Wing?'

Rhiannon recalled the strange symbol shaped like an upside-down square fish and nodded.

'Just press that one. And let Aleda know if you're hungry later. She'll get something sent up to you.'

When they arrived at the dais, David and John waited while she ascended the steps and turned towards the console. It was then she realised the upside-down square fish appeared several times down the thirteen rows, with only minor variations on each one.

'Three rows each wing,' she muttered.

'That's right,' confirmed David. 'And it'll be halfway on the middle row.'

Rhiannon reached out, intending to count the rows up from the bottom. Unfortunately, she pressed her finger a fraction too hard against the rune on the last row.

A blue light lit up the symbol.

Oops. Not good.

Rhiannon looked up. 'What if I ...'

A brilliant flash of white light.

'... press the wrong one?' she finished, her words now addressed to several grooms and horses in a wide enclosed courtyard.

''ere now, ye'll not be goin' out wearin' only that,' a gruff voice declared.

Rhiannon turned to see an old man cast a disapproving glare at her gown and slippers. His solid bear-like frame clad in a neat but dusty tunic, he looked strong enough to lift one of the horses by himself.

'Bloomin' pig-widgeon visitors,' he grumbled into his bushy beard, then shook his finger at her. 'Hen-witted that'd be, what with the wind smellin' o' more snow. Now, off ye go, an' don't let me catch you out 'ere again dressed like that. Even His Royal

Highness has more sense than to go ridin' without a cloak in this weather, an' he's pulled some addlepated stunts.'

'But I wasn't going to go riding,' Rhiannon protested. 'I came here by mistake.'

'Yer a little old t' be pressin' the wrong rune,' the man declared, and a spark of suspicion appeared in his eyes. 'What be yer business at the palace?'

'I live there.'

A snort of disbelief escaped the man. 'Ye'll need t' do better than that. I been servin' 'ere since long before ye were born, an' I know every soul who sleeps within these castle walls.'

'It's true.' Rhiannon warily eyed the man, who looked ready to tie her up like a thief. 'I arrived in Álnair a few days ago, and my guardian Sir Raeden got permission for me to stay here.'

The suspicion died, but the weatherworn face remained unsmiling. 'Well now, so ye'd be Rhiannon McBride.'

'Yes, Sir.'

'There be no need t' be callin' me "sir",' was the man's crotchety response. 'Flavian's me name, an' I be the head groom o' the stables.' He shot her another glare. 'An' if'n ye ever takes out one o' these horses, ye'd best bring 'em back unharmed.'

Not sure what she had done to earn his displeasure, Rhiannon nodded. 'I promise I won't ever hurt a single horse in here,' she said.

A chorus of soft whinnying cries echoed around the enclosure.

Rhiannon looked around to see all the horses in sight staring at her. Then a palomino mare, who had been waiting in docile patience beside one of the grooms, trotted towards the dais where she stood.

The change which came over Flavian was startling. His whole grouchy demeanour morphed into one of gentle tenderness as he addressed the mare.

'Ah, Kateri, ye lovely one! In one of yer playful moods?'

The mare pranced around him, her sights clearly set on reaching Rhiannon.

Never having been near a horse in her life, Rhiannon cautiously approached the edge of the dais. Raising her hand, she stretched it towards Kateri's head.

''ere, be careful.' Flavian's voice had changed again, his tone stern with warning. 'She be one o' Prince David's horses, an' she don't like strangers touchin' her.'

Rhiannon began to pull her hand back, an apology on her lips. But then there was a soft snort of greeting. With no sign of wariness, Kateri stepped closer and nudged Rhiannon's shoulder with her head.

A wide smile broke out across Rhiannon's face. 'Hello there,' she murmured, and ran her hand down the mare's smooth mane. 'You're a pretty one, aren't you?'

Kateri tossed her head and nodded.

'And clever too, no doubt.'

Another nod, this time followed by an affectionate bump to Rhiannon's side.

'Well, in all me born days.'

The stunned utterance had Rhiannon looking up to see the head groom staring at her in shock.

'Ye be the only other person aside from the prince she done that to.' A grudging look of respect appeared in Flavian's eyes. 'If ye can get a horse t' trust yer that quickly, I suppose ye'll not be interested in hurtin' 'em. Unlike some,' he added darkly, and looked in the direction of one of the stalls. 'If I gets me hands on that Plancy fella, I'll take a whip to him, jus' like he done t' poor Ravel. That be the last time I ever lets that dastard borrow a mount from these stables.'

At the mention of Plancy, Rhiannon shuddered. 'Was Ravel badly hurt?' she asked.

Flavian's eyes glittered dangerously. 'Cut right through the skin, he were, in several places. It'll take weeks for the wounds t' heal, even with this.' He held up a jar of slimy green paste in his hand, then cast a fulminous glare in the direction of the palace. 'Should've known by how he raced out o' 'ere this morning that he'd harmed the poor creature.'

Rhiannon stepped down off the dais. 'Are you going to put that on Ravel now?' she asked, pointing at the jar.

'Aye, if he'll let me near him,' was the terse reply. 'Been shakin' and kickin' whenever we go near his stall.'

Without another word, he turned and walked away.

The groom who'd come over to fetch Kateri watched his retreating back and said quietly, 'He's been upset about the whole thing all day, so don't be too offended by his manner, Miss Rhiannon. He ain't normally so tetchy.'

A loud, snorting roar came from Ravel's stall followed by the splintering crash of hoofs against wood. Beside her, Rhiannon saw Kateri shift nervously.

'It's all right, don't be scared,' she whispered, and felt the mare nuzzle her arm.

A second crash sounded. Then a third.

'Poor ol' Flavian. He keeps tryin' to calm him without using a charm but Ravel's well an' truly spooked.' The groom shook his head regretfully, then led Kateri away.

Rhiannon hesitated only a moment before slowly approaching Ravel's stall. Flavian was standing outside it, attempting to soothe the frightened horse inside by speaking in low, soft tones, but all to no avail.

She peered through the open-topped door to see a magnificent stallion give his feed trough a hard kick. The poor animal was terrified and, judging by the reopened wounds on his grey rump, in a lot of pain.

She ignored Flavian's low order for her to step back. Instead, she rested her arms on the lower door and began to speak in the same friendly tone she'd used when greeting animals in Vetus svet.

She spoke for several minutes. Ravel snorted and reared a few more times before his trembling subsided completely. Then, as docile as a newborn lamb, he walked over to the door and pressed his great nostrils against her hand.

Rhiannon gave him a gentle pat before looking up at Flavian.

The head groom looked absolutely dumbfounded. There was a brief pause. Then, 'If ye've a mind to stay, ye can keep him calm while I apply the poultice.'

Rhiannon hid a smile and nodded. It would appear the dour old man's grumbled words were the closest he would get to asking for help.

'But yer t' stay on this side o' the door,' Flavian decreed. 'I got no desire t' be at the end o' one of Sir Raeden's reprimands 'cause ye got yer little feet crushed under a misplaced hoof.'

Quite some time later, Rhiannon was seriously contemplating asking a horse to step on her feet – if only to confirm they were still attached to her body!

After the poultice had been applied to the stallion's wounds, a calmer but still grouchy Flavian had offered to show her around both stables. Not wishing to offend him, she'd accepted. Unfortunately, the thin soles of her slippers offered little support, and her feet had passed the point of aching and were now numb.

'An' in there be the Imperial Coach.' Flavian gestured at a solid wooden door that was securely shut and bolted. 'It's only brought out for coronations an' royal weddin's – not that we'll be seein' another one o' them afore I'm lyin' cold in the catacombs,' he predicted grumpily, and mumbled on, 'An' over 'ere is the main tack room.'

Rhiannon concealed a frustrated groan. She wanted to sit down.

'It's used to store …'

'Many different things,' another voice said, 'but Rhiannon will have to see them another time. It's almost time for dinner.'

Rhiannon didn't think she'd ever heard more beautiful words. Almost giddy with delighted relief, she turned and greeted her deliverer. 'David! How did you know I was here?'

'Word got around the palace about a strange girl helping Flavian with an injured horse. The description matched you, so we came.'

She looked behind him and saw John waiting a short distance away.

'You'll need to change,' David continued. 'I don't see the need myself, but some of the people at dinner might object to you smelling like a stable.'

Flavian grumbled something under his breath. Rhiannon didn't hear it, but David clearly did. He laughed, replying with evident affection, 'I know, you old bear, but not everyone likes horses as much as we do.'

Soon after that, they took their leave of the cantankerous old man. He dismissed Rhiannon's attempts to thank him for the tour with a growled 'hmpf', then strode off towards the stalls.

'Don't mind him,' David said as they set off with John for the transonus dais. 'He's been working here at the castle since before my father was born, and the only thing he cares about are the horses. He knows everything you could possibly need to know about them, plus a whole lot more that you don't.'

Rhiannon nodded wearily. 'He spent a lot of time talking about them while we walked.'

The fatigue in her voice had both David and John gazing at her in concern.

'You look completely done in,' said John. 'How long have you been out here?'

The truth of pressing the wrong rune came out.

'You've been here all this time!' exclaimed David. 'No wonder you're looking peaky. Do you feel up to coming down for dinner?'

Rhiannon hesitated, recalling who else might be in the Dining Hall.

As though reading her mind, David added, 'You don't have to worry about Plancy being there. He's already left the palace to return home.' He frowned. 'Which, come to think of it, is really odd. I've heard he never misses an opportunity to dine here when he has to visit.'

'Then I'm grateful to whatever it is that made him decide to skip dinner this time,' Rhiannon sighed. 'And I'm sure I'll be fine once I sit down. But if you see me dozing off at the table, you will stop me from ending up in my meal, won't you?'

Mercifully, Rhiannon didn't fall asleep in her creamed potatoes and lamb stew. But she did crawl into bed early that night and let her head fall back onto the soft pillow.

Images of the day's events drifted through her mind and with them came an echo of the emotions she had felt. From fear and anger, to joy and sorrow, she had run the gamut of emotions several times. Now, she just felt tired.

She gave a loud yawn and squirmed into a more comfortable position in the bed. Burrowing her head deeper into her pillow's soothing warmth, she hoped blissful slumber would not be long in coming. After having escorted her to her room, David and John had promised to wake her early in the morning once John's family arrived. Apparently, they wanted to ensure she enjoyed her first Christmas morning in Álnair.

I just hope they don't wake me up too early, Rhiannon thought, otherwise I might ask Sir Raeden about moving into a secluded tower myself!

Chapter 15

OF MYSTERIOUS GIFTS
AND ALLOWANCES

Christmas morning in Álnair was unlike anything Rhiannon had ever experienced. She awoke at sunrise to the sight of Aleda trying, and failing, to prevent David and John from entering her room, their arms laden with gifts. It came as no surprise to her when one present from David turned out to be a wristwatch.

She inspected the pile of presents near her desk from various citizens in Álnair and was shocked when David told her she could expect a similar number each year.

'Mórell was the last female born to our House and she was an exceedingly gifted mage. Having a daughter of her bloodline arrive is seen as a sign of good fortune,' he said.

'So Endrille told me yesterday when I saw her near the stables,' Rhiannon replied. A reminscient smile lit her face. 'She also said how she recognised me as Mórell's descendant.'

'Oh?' David looked intrigued. 'I'd like to know that too.'

'It was these.' Rhiannon pointed at her eyes and small birth-mark. 'Endrille said she never thought to see Mórell's eyes looking up at her again. Apparently, the gold shade was unique to Mórell, and my birthmark is something only the females in the O'Faenart Clan possess.' A small sigh escaped her lips. 'When Endrille told me, it was the first time I've ever felt like I truly belonged somewhere.'

David reached out and gently grasped her shoulder. 'You're a welcome addition here at the castle,' he assured her, 'and there can be no doubt that this is where you belong. Now, you'd best find something to wear down to breakfast. If you don't get there early enough all the best dishes will be gone, especially with his brothers' – he pointed at John – 'practically inhaling the food every time they open their mouths.'

John accepted this charge against his siblings with perfect equanimity. 'At least they've finally learnt chewing it makes the food easier to digest,' he remarked.

After her visitors had departed so she could change, Rhiannon went to her wardrobe and found it had been filled with a colourful array of garments and footwear. There was everything she could possibly need, from several fur-lined cloaks and fine gowns, to warm boots and slippers.

'Sir Raeden ordered them yesterday and had them rushed here from Cendillis after you went to bed,' a gleeful Aleda informed her. 'He said you shouldn't have to wear borrowed clothing on Christmas Day.'

Rhiannon stared at the collection, stunned by her guardian's thoughtfulness.

'Are you sure they're all for me?' she asked.

'Sir Raeden wouldn't have any use for them, and it was his name on the delivery,' was Aleda's response.

Resolved to thank her guardian at the first opportunity, Rhiannon dressed in a gown of heavy blue velvet, sprayed on some of the vanilla honey fragrance from John's family and set off through the brightly decorated hallways towards the King's Dining Hall.

It was such a relief not having to cook a huge meal all by herself, as she'd always had to do at the Dashmonts.

Breakfast was a merry affair. The long table groaned under the weight of scrumptious dishes, including crisp bacon and eggs cooked in every way imaginable, warm porridge with honey, cinnamon toast and fresh fruit served in warm custard. Everyone greeted Rhiannon with a cheerful 'Happy Christmas' as the House Faeries flew overhead, singing joyously. Formality was forgotten, and conversation rang out loudly among all the guests.

Included in the gathering was all of John's family, with the exception of his sister Cordelia who was spending the holidays with friends in Graynor. His brothers were identical triplets with mischievous blue eyes and thick black hair like their mother, Lady Isabella. Alice, his little sister of four years, proved to be an adorable chatterbox with gorgeous bright-red curls and green eyes. His father, Sir Julian Tremaine, was a jovial man who looked like an older version of his son. He was an old friend of King Stephen from when they had attended Ryegoth's Academy together, and Rhiannon discovered he had once been a knight in the Royal Guard.

'Had a fine time of it until that unfortunate skirmish with a wounded griffon a few years back,' Sir Julian told her, and patted his right leg. 'Left me with a permanent limp and a mighty fine scar. Still, can't complain. The griffon was good enough not to take my whole leg off, and the poor creature ended up dying of his wounds not long afterwards. Besides, with my Isabella being an accomplished apothecary,' he nodded at the tall, willowy woman at his side, 'I've got a steady supply of pain relief whenever I need it.'

'Which you resist taking like a fractious child,' Lady Isabella revealed with wifely candour.

'Of course I would,' stated Sir Julian with a grin, 'it tastes awful!'

As the crowd laughed appreciatively, Rhiannon reflected it was not only his looks John had inherited from his father but his sense of humour as well.

Time passed quickly, or so it seemed to Rhiannon. She was thoroughly enjoying the first stress-free Christmas of her life, and David was making every effort to ensure she felt included in the festivities – a marked difference from the Dashmonts who had only ever seemed to remember her presence when another snack had to be brought out.

A brief meeting after breakfast with Sir Raeden allowed her to thank him for his generous gift, and she felt an overwhelming desire to hug him when he gave her appearance an approving nod. She restrained herself, of course, unsure if he would welcome such an affectionate gesture.

A light lunch of warm vegetable soup, fresh bread with melted butter, and spiced apples warmed her chilled body after a vigorous snowball fight in the East Garden. Then, in the afternoon, she curled up on the sofa in front of the fire in the small games room, while a little group led by David and John played a rousing match of quoits.

During one match, when David and John were fully focused on beating each other, she saw a boy about her own age furtively enter the room. He cast a quick glance at the noisy group, then came and sat down beside her with a smile. However, unlike David's smile, this one left her feeling like something slimy had slithered down the back of her dress.

'So you're her,' were his first words. 'The daughter of Mórell's line.'

'My name's Rhiannon.'

The boy's expression twisted into a caricature of friendliness. 'Marcus Donahue,' he said by way of introducing himself with a haughty bow. 'I hear you'll be attending the castle school when the new term starts.'

'That's right,' replied Rhiannon, unsure where he was going with the conversation.

'Well, given your bloodline it'll be important for you to make the right friends, and my cousin will certainly mislead you there.' He shot a disdainful glance in David's direction. 'He associates with all the common riff-raff who attend, even a tailor's son! You don't want to be fostering any connections like that.' He returned his attention to her, the oily smile back on his face. 'All of Cendillis is talking about you, and it won't be long before everyone in Álnair knows your name. You'll need someone like me to help you avoid the flotsam of society. I'd introduce you to only the best families, and you'd soon be the most sought-after girl in Álnair.'

Realisation struck Rhiannon and a feeling of contempt flooded through her. Marcus was as shallow and despicable as all the sycophants who had always flocked around Annabelle, hoping to trade off her popularity for their own benefit.

Her voice when she spoke made no secret of her disgust. 'If you're an example of the type of person I'd meet from these "best families", then I'll happily choose the tailor's son over every single one of you.'

All traces of ingratiating affability vanished from Marcus' face. He stood up, an unpleasant sneer on his lips. 'Fine, I wouldn't have wanted to put up with your frumpy looks anyway. The only thing attractive about you is your ancestry.' He looked her over as if she was an oddity in a circus. 'And even that wouldn't have made being near you tolerable for long.'

Though long accustomed to receiving taunts over her rather plain appearance, Rhiannon still felt the stinging bite of his insult. She clenched her fist and went to stand up, only to feel a firm hand grasp her shoulder.

'Marcus, unless you want to find out what a broken jaw feels like, you'll get out of here before I forget what day it is and knock you senseless.'

The grim note in David's voice made his words more than an idle threat.

Rhiannon looked behind her to see him glaring at his cousin, his eyes devoid of all warmth. A spark of incredulous wonder flared to life inside her heart. For the first time in her memory, someone had challenged a bully on her behalf!

'You won't do anything to me in here,' Marcus blustered, his gaze flickering uneasily towards the silent group watching them.

'I warned you,' said David, and stepped around the sofa.

Marcus fled.

'He's gutless without his cronies to back him up.'

'Pretentious little toad. David should've just hit him.'

The comments from the group continued in a similar vein as David focused his attention on Rhiannon. The icy glint in his eyes melted, leaving them warm and friendly again.

'I heard what you said to him,' he told her. 'You couldn't have chosen a better way to insult him than to say you'd prefer Simon's company over his. And don't pay any attention to what he said. I think you look very nice.'

The sincerity of his words was a balm to Rhiannon's wounded pride, and she felt prettier each time she recalled them in the Great Hall that evening for the Christmas Ball.

Arrayed in a marvellous floor-length creation of garnet-red velvet and gold fleece, Rhiannon stepped into the Great Hall and immediately immersed herself in the enchanting atmosphere.

The wide, open space was aglow with light, and cheerful decorations adorned every tall marble pillar. Across the high ceiling, the colourful mural depicting several dragons flying through a blue sky seemed to come alive. On a raised dais at the far west end of the hall, two gold thrones encrusted with jewels were sheltered by the gilded figure of a dragon with its wings outstretched. Their magnificence was enhanced by the light streaming through the long, full-length window behind them, the golden orb of the sun slowly sinking below the shimmering ocean in a blaze of colour that filled the horizon.

Soon, a dizzying number of guests filled the Hall, and she was relieved when David and John shielded her from the more inquisitive ones.

The feast itself, held in the adjoining Banquet Hall, was an enticing, delicious assortment of magnificent dishes with the most delightful, mouth-watering scents. She savoured every bite of the roast meats, vegetables and honey lemon pudding.

Then they returned to the Great Hall where David's parents led their guests in the first dance.

Rhiannon swayed in time to the lively music. Her feet, clad in slippers of gold silk and white leather, were eager to dance to the lilting sounds of harps, fiddles and flutes provided by a group of faeries.

She watched the dancers swirl past and smiled. This was so much better than having to listen to Annabelle play the piano while she served fruit cake and turkey sandwiches to guests who ignored her.

Then her eyes widened in astonishment. Amid the glittering jewels and colourful array of tunics, cloaks and dresses, Sir Raeden was dancing.

Her guardian's extremely tall form performed all the movements with precise grace. His partner was a short, pleasantly plump, dark-haired woman wearing a gown of cheerful yellow brocade. As she watched, the lady moved in the wrong direction and missed her step. However, despite her lack of coordination, the woman was glowing with mirth and good cheer.

Rhiannon turned to David. 'Who's the lady dancing with Sir Raeden?' she asked.

'Professor Egelbert's daughter, Carina. Not the brightest lady,' David added quietly, although his tone was not unkind. 'She'll often go to fetch something for her father and return with a completely random item. Once, she went to get him a new quill and returned with a dozen curtain rods instead. She doesn't tend to get invited to dance a lot because she forgets the steps. In fact, it's only when Sir Raeden attends these balls that she gets asked. I don't know what he does, but after he's danced with her, she's never short of a partner for the rest of the night.'

Rhiannon looked again at the dancing couple as the music came to a rousing conclusion. She saw Sir Raeden carefully avoid having his feet trodden on by Carina, bestow a brief warning glare at one of the other male guests (who immediately hurried forward to meet the pair and offer his arm to Carina) and then take himself off to sit at one of the long tables at the side of the room. Clearly, he had no interest in dancing again.

'He's helping her,' she murmured as the next dance commenced. 'Once he dances with her it'd be rude if the others didn't.'

'Sorry, what was that?' David asked.

'Oh, nothing.'

As the dance picked up momentum, Rhiannon cast another look towards Sir Raeden. To her surprise she saw him accepting a scroll from one of the Royal Guard.

Evidently, even during a celebration he was never off duty.

She watched as he read the contents of the report, then stood up. His expression remained inscrutable, and yet there was an urgency to his steps as he left the Great Hall.

'He's been investigating some incidents for my father,' said David when she mentioned her guardian's abrupt departure. 'He's most likely just been given a lead on them.'

'Will he be back?'

'Once he's got all the information he needs.'

And sure enough, not an hour later, Rhiannon saw her guardian step across the threshold of the main doors to the Great Hall and make his way towards King Stephen.

The two men spoke briefly, then the king laid a hand on Sir Raeden's arm. He said something and was answered by a simple nod. Another short conversation followed, then both men returned to mingling with the crowd.

To Rhiannon, nothing in the exchange between the two men seemed to portend a catastrophe and so, without a second thought, she put it out of her mind and focused on enjoying the rest of the evening.

The night hours passed and in the gaiety and pleasant atmosphere of the party, Rhiannon had no difficulty forgetting everything but the joy of the moment.

David and John took it upon themselves to teach her the steps of the most intricate and fast-paced dances, which mostly ended with the three of them half collapsed on the floor in a tangle of limbs and weak from laughter.

Finally, when the palace bells were chiming the midnight hour, Rhiannon entered her bedchamber, momentarily blinded by a wide yawn. Then, despite her tiredness, she danced her way to the wardrobe where she abandoned her slippers after a graceful pirouette.

Her thoughts now focused on getting some sleep as soon as possible, she approached her bed where Aleda had laid out her nightgown. To her surprise she discovered a small gift placed upon it.

The wrapping was elegant in its simplicity and was bare of any decorative ornaments. The card bore no inscription other than her name and the words:

The time has come for the Jewel of Mórell
to be returned to its rightful owner. May its pure light
always protect you and vanquish all darkness.

Rhiannon's tiredness gave way to curiosity. She slowly picked up the gift, briefly examined it with her hands, then gently removed the wrapping.

It was a delicate silver filigree box.

She opened the lid and peered inside.

A shaken gasp escaped her lips. She sank down on her bed and stared at the object in her hand.

Nestled in blue velvet, and the same size as a quail egg, a jewel shone with an inner radiance that would pierce the darkest night. Through the clear transparency of the stone, she could see dancing rays of light, their movements giving the stone the appearance of being alive.

Cautiously removing the jewel from the box, she clasped it in her hand. A gentle warmth spread throughout her body as the stone's light increased. For a moment, the room was illuminated in a white glow. Then, it slowly faded away.

Replacing the jewel inside the box, Rhiannon considered it for a moment before closing the lid with quiet finality. She set the box inside the dressing table drawer, resolving to ask David and John if they knew anything about it, then prepared herself for bed.

'The old story says that Mórell came to Álnair and together with Ryegoth, crafted a magnificent jewel during the Time of Persecution to assist her in healing the dragons.' David looked down at Rhiannon from where he was perched atop the tallest ladder in Moberly's Book Emporium – the finest bookstore in Cendillis. 'It could apparently cleanse and purify any wound inflicted on them. They made it using the clear water of Rëalta Lake when the light of a thousand stars and the silver moon were cast upon its surface. Then, before the pathways were closed, Mórell gave it to Endrille. There's even a few tales about Merlin using it while he was here.'

Rhiannon frowned. 'Why didn't Mórell keep it with her?' she asked, picking up a discarded book from the floor and absentmindedly placing it on top of the ever-growing pile on the table.

'She probably thought it was too dangerous to have something like it in Vetus svet,' said John, catching another book liberated from the shelf by David and dropped down to him.

'Definitely a wise woman,' commented David. He extracted another book, then hastily replaced it on the shelf with a grimace of disgust. 'The magic in it would be incredibly strong. Make sure you look after it, Rhiannon.' He continued his search along the shelf. Then, with a victorious cry, he withdrew a small book and tossed it down to John.

'Finally, that's the last one,' David said in relief. 'I can't believe Wyvern actually insisted on you learning to do this for yourself.'

'He probably just wants me to get familiar with shopping for my own things. I certainly don't expect to have everything done for me.' Rhiannon glanced around at the impressive array of books. 'Besides, it's all been rather interesting, and you didn't have to come.'

'Don't be such a goose,' David retorted. 'We certainly couldn't let Wyvern bring you. That wouldn't have been pleasant for you at all. Actually, I'm surprised he even agreed to let us take his place.'

He quickly descended the ladder, then wiped imaginary dust from his hands before replacing his sword belt around his waist.

'Is there ever a time when you don't have that thing on you?' Rhiannon asked, pointing at the sword.

'Rarely,' David replied. 'I don't need to have it on me if I'm in my private quarters or attending a ball at the palace. But I definitely never leave the castle grounds without it. John would nag at me like an old crow if I ever did.'

'Better me than Wyvern,' John riposted.

David shuddered at the thought. 'That's true,' he conceded.

'But, why do you need to have one if John's got his?' Rhiannon asked.

'"The Wise first ensure their own invulnerability,"' David quoted. 'To rely upon someone else to protect you is to place not only yourself, but them in danger. Should an attack happen, they would constantly have their focus divided. So, by carrying my own sword, I can lessen the risk of my Robesman being injured. Also, the scabbard bears my family's crest.' He turned so Rhiannon could see it emblazoned on the top of the dark sheath: a gold crown encircled by twelve stars on a blue banner. 'Only the head of the House of Valieoth and his heir are permitted to use this insignia. It's also engraved on our signet rings as proof of our lineage and title if we ever need to declare it.'

'That would be helpful, so long as the other person recognises it,' Rhiannon pointed out.

'If they're from Álnair they would,' said John. 'There's an official photograph of the crest placed in the main foyer of every school approved by the king.'

'Photograph?' Rhiannon asked in surprise.

David and John both frowned at her expression.

'Yes, surely you still have them in Vetus svet?' said David.

'We do, it was just strange hearing you have them too.'

'Why? According to King Brian we were taking them for nearly two hundred years before the first person in Vetus svet thought to do it.' David grimaced. 'Mind you, originally they were called a "foscribo". I think "photograph" sounds much better. There should be a book here that has an example of one in it. I believe ours were quite different from the ones in Vetus svet.'

David skimmed over a few of the leather-bound books, then pulled one out. 'Here we go,' he said, and flipped it open.

Rhiannon looked down and saw, under the name 'Entrose', a perfect, three-dimensional, coloured photograph of a strange plant with a red stem, small white flowers shaped like bells and prickly green leaves. She felt as if she could pick a flower off the plant right out of the book.

'That's incredible!' she exclaimed. 'The photos in Vetus svet are nothing like this. Family portraits must be pretty popular.'

'Not really.' David returned the book to the shelf. 'A lot of people don't like to be photographed, even though it was supposed to be an easier way to have a portrait done. Some families will get a photograph taken on a special occasion, but mostly, people use them to take images for textbooks. They used to be quite different to look at, the image was a bit flatter, but then Professor Egelbert came up with a new way to take the photograph. I think it was about ten or eleven years ago.'

'We could find you some books that explain how it's done,' John offered.

'I don't think I'd have time to even read one page,' was Rhiannon's reply as she glanced at the last book which had joined the pile on the table.

Potions, Poisons & Antidotes, by Artemis Mugwort.

She transferred her gaze to the rest of the pile. 'Do I have to read all of these before starting lessons?' she asked faintly.

David snorted. 'Of course not. I doubt anyone has ever read them all cover to cover. I mean, five minutes of reading *Álnair: A Geographical Guide* and you'll be cured of insomnia forever.'

'Most students either skim read or just browse through them,' John said. 'Occasionally you'll get assigned a book that is actually interesting, but mostly they're pretty boring.'

'Besides, most of these are just to help you catch up to where you need to be for when school restarts,' David explained.

'But I've already missed a whole year and a half according to Sir Raeden,' Rhiannon pointed out worriedly. 'How am I supposed to get all that covered in two weeks – even with Sir Raeden saying he'll make sure I'm ready?'

'Firstly, if Wyvern says he'll get you ready, then he will. The man can be a harsh instructor, but he does know what information is important for you to have, and what isn't. Secondly, the first year of study is mainly only theory and pretty basic theory at that. Quite frankly, I don't know how my brothers are going to handle it,' John finished with an amused chuckle.

'So, what subjects do you have to do each year?'

Ticking each one off on his fingers, David listed them. 'Dragons: Society & Culture; Arithmetic; Languages; Defence: Magi, Weaponry & Physical; History; and Magical Application & Control – although, that one is strictly magi only, and, reluctant though I am to admit it, Wyvern is probably the only person who can get you to the level you need to be in such a short time.'

'I guess that's not so bad,' Rhiannon said in relief. 'That's only six subjects. What about the others?'

'After the first year you do two years where you also have to study Natural Science and Philosophy, Astronomy, Creatures and Beasts, Herblore, and Geography. For the last two years you get to choose which subjects you want to continue doing and drop the rest. After that, you can choose to do further study at Ryegoth Academy.'

'So basically, for the next two weeks I should do nothing but study,' Rhiannon reflected gloomily. 'I suppose it's fortunate I tend to remember things quite well after I've read them.'

'Don't stress too much about it all,' John said with a smile. 'David and I will be able to help you, and we'll make sure we only cover things we've already done in class.'

'We certainly won't make you read ahead,' David agreed. 'And unlike the Academy, where each grade is taught separately, the castle school has us all mixed in together. There's only forty-five students at the moment and the teachers felt that the older ones could help the juniors.'

'Forty-five students?' Rhiannon said in astonishment. 'I would've thought there'd be more with Cendillis so close.'

'There's a few schools here so the castle one is mainly for those living in the palace, and any boy originally appointed to me as a companion. Some of the guards and employees who live outside the grounds also choose to send their children there.'

Rhiannon looked at John. With the reddish shadow on his shaved cheeks, he looked more like a mature adult than a student. 'Do you still attend the school?'

John nodded. 'I'm in my last official year. But I won't be going on to the Academy. Not yet, anyway.'

'John, I told you I don't mind if you go.' David turned to Rhiannon, explaining, 'He wants to wait until I'm going so he doesn't fail in his duties as Chief Robesman. I've tried to tell him he's being ridiculous, that I'd still have two Robesmen at the school so he doesn't have to delay going, but he won't listen to me.'

'I've sworn an oath, and I intend to keep it,' John said calmly.

'Which means he's even going to put himself through the torture of a further two years at the castle school.'

At Rhiannon's incredulous expression, David nodded, adding, 'Ridiculous, isn't it.'

Rhiannon turned to look at John. 'Can't you do private study instead of basically repeating the same grade a few times?'

'That's what I'll be doing. While the others do their own grade, I'll be getting a head start for when I go to the Academy.'

David shook his head.

'You are definitely mad,' he declared. Then having checked the time, he said, 'Now, since we're all done here, where would you like to go next? We still have to get you measured for the robes to cover your other clothes when we do the experiments in Natural Science, along with the other things my mother put on the list. But first, we could get some lunch.'

Rhiannon stared at him in disbelief. 'Lunch? But you only ate an hour ago!'

David shrugged. 'Doesn't mean I can't be hungry now.'

'You ate half a chicken by yourself! And it wasn't exactly a small one either!'

'Climbing that ladder must've given me an appetite.'

'How about we take care of paying for these first, and then continue this outside?' John tactfully suggested, picking up the nearest pile of books.

'Good plan,' David agreed. 'The sooner we pay, the sooner we eat.' Gathering up the remaining pile of books in his arms, he turned to follow John to the counter, leaving an empty-handed Rhiannon to follow him.

'But I still don't know how I'm going to pay for all this,' Rhiannon protested. 'I don't have any money.'

'Actually, you do,' David informed her, placing the books beside the pile John had sat on the counter. 'Wyvern's quite plump in the pocket, and as your guardian he's responsible for paying for your things.'

'That doesn't seem fair.' Rhiannon frowned. 'He didn't ask to be my guardian, so why should he have to pay for anything? And what does him being a bit plump in the pocket have to do with it?'

David and John laughed.

'I guess you may not use that expression anymore in Vetus svet,' David said. 'It means he's quite wealthy.'

'Oh.' Rhiannon was silent for a moment. 'It still doesn't seem fair,' she said, and resolved to speak to her guardian about doing something to earn an allowance so she could buy her own things. She did not want to be anyone's charity case.

'Anyway,' she continued, 'since he's not here with me, I still don't know how I'm going to pay for all of these.' Gesturing at the stack of books, she gave a small grimace. 'Also, I can't say I'm looking forward to having to carry them around with me while we finish buying everything.'

'Pfft.' David brushed this concern away with a wave of his hand. 'We'll have them delivered to you. As for the payment, you'll just need to sign your name on the authorisation card Mr Moberly will give you. He'll send that to Wyvern. The amounts will either be in gold, silver or bronze coins, with gold being the most valuable of course. One gold coin is equal to fifty of the silver or a hundred of the bronze.' He looked around the busy store, drumming his fingers impatiently on the counter. 'I only hope it doesn't take the old fellow too long to tally these all up. I'm starving!'

Thankfully, for the sake of David's stomach, Oscar Moberly (a tall, thin old man wearing wire-rimmed spectacles) returned quickly to serve them. When they were outside, they decided that feeding David took precedence over any further school purchases.

After he had finished consuming his meal, the size of which left Rhiannon feeling nauseated, David led the way to Amelia's Apparel & Haberdashery Boutique. He halted just outside the store and pointed inside.

'You can get most of your clothes in there. Just give Madame Dubois the list my mother gave you, and she'll take your measurements to make up what you need. We'll wait out here.'

All Rhiannon had ever worn in the past had been Annabelle's hand-me-downs, and the new pyjamas she'd received at Christmas. She had never been clothes shopping in her life. The prospect of being left alone with someone who might laugh at her ignorance was daunting. She turned to face David, prepared to insist he and John come with her. That was when she noticed the faint tinge of red working its way up his neck. Turning to look at John, she noticed that he too seemed to share David's sense of male embarrassment. With an inward sigh, and taking pity on their discomfort, she stifled her own feelings of dismay and smiled.

'If you're sure you want to wait here, that's fine with me,' she said valiantly, 'I shouldn't be too long.'

Then, she marched up the steps into the brightly lit store, choosing to ignore David's murmured, 'Four gold coins say she'll be more than thirty minutes,' and John's scoffing reply of, 'A female in a clothes shop? Of course she'll be more than thirty minutes. Delia's minimum record still stands at one hour and forty-three minutes – and that was just for a pair of gloves!'

Six hours after she had entered Amelia's Apparel & Haberdashery Boutique, Rhiannon arrived back at the palace in a state of complete exhaustion. Getting measured for her clothes had taken up a considerable time, and then David and John had decided to add a bit of sightseeing to the outing.

I must be crazy! Rhiannon thought as she followed Aleda down the long passageway in the Upper South Wing towards her guardian's private chambers. Now, when all I want to do is fall onto my bed and sleep, I'm choosing to speak to Sir Raeden about money.

After turning into a wider hallway, the green-haired faery stopped outside a wide archway. Rhiannon looked through it to see an empty open space with a large door in each of the three walls.

'That leads to his office,' Aleda said, pointing to the door on the right. 'And that one,' she continued, indicating the door on the left, 'leads to his laboratory. You should never go in there without his permission.'

Rhiannon looked at the middle door. 'So, through that one is his bedchamber?'

Aleda nodded. 'It is, but it has an antechamber where you may speak with him if he's inside.'

'"He" is standing behind you,' said a very distinctive voice.

Rhiannon jumped and spun around to see her guardian looking down at her.

'And if you wish to speak to me, pray do so quickly.'

Seeing that he was wearing his official uniform, Rhiannon started to step away, saying, 'It's all right. I can come back another time.'

'You are here now,' Sir Raeden said laconically.

Aleda chose this moment to tell him, 'She was most anxious to see you, Sir Raeden. She would not even wait to put off her cloak after returning from Cendillis.'

'As I can see.' Clearly deciding not to waste any time on debating the best time for a discussion, Sir Raeden stepped past them and walked towards the middle door. 'Thank you for showing her the way, Aleda. You may go. Come with me, Rhiannon.'

She hesitated only long enough to say a quick word of thanks to Aleda, then followed her guardian through the doorway.

The room she entered was large and beautifully decorated. A long table littered with books stood in the middle of it, and in front of a small hearth were two comfortable chairs with matching footstools and a thick woollen rug. Through another doorway across the room, she caught a glimpse of an immense four-poster bed covered in drapes and a matching coverlet of dark turquoise.

Returning her attention to Sir Raeden, she saw he had moved away from the main door and was now sitting on a low bench, which reduced his towering height to a less imposing level.

'I gather, given the urgency with which you sought me out, that what you have to say is rather important,' he said.

Rhiannon nodded, feeling nervous. Sir Raeden was still quite intimidating, even when he was sitting down and not scowling.

'It is,' she answered, 'at least, to me it is. You see, I hadn't even thought of money until we went to pay for the books, then David told me you were going to be paying for my things. You shouldn't have to spend your own money on me when you never even asked to be my guardian. So, I wanted to speak with you before all the bills from today arrived.'

Sir Raeden quirked one eyebrow in mild curiosity. 'To what purpose?'

'To stop you paying them.'

'That would hardly be fair to those who expect payment for their goods and services.'

Rhiannon made a small sound of annoyance. 'I don't mean they shouldn't be paid! That would be dishonest.'

'I am relieved you realise that fact,' Sir Raeden said imperturbably. 'With what money, then, do you propose to pay them?'

'My own.'

'I was not aware you had possession of financial assets in Álnair.'

Rhiannon gave her guardian a frustrated look. 'You know I don't.'

'Then from where do you intend to obtain this wealth?'

'I'll work for it.'

'I see. You wish to be reliant upon no one.'

Sir Raeden stood up and straightened to his full height.

'While I applaud your sense of independence, it is a nonsensical stance to take at this moment,' he said evenly. 'Your time and energy need to be focused on nothing but preparing yourself for school. You may have requested my appointment as your guardian for the duration of the hearing, but I was not obliged to accept it. Nor, may I add, was I coerced into giving my consent to being assigned as your permanent guardian. I undertook the position in full knowledge of my obligations to you, therefore any expenditure I do on your behalf is to fulfil those responsibilities, and not to satisfy an inclination to bestow charity upon you.'

At his last words, Rhiannon felt a betraying blush rise in her cheeks. How had he known that was what she was thinking!

'But it still doesn't feel right,' she felt the need to protest.

Sir Raeden gazed at her in silence for a moment. She saw the sharp, measuring look in his eyes, and wondered what he was thinking.

She did not have to wait long to find out.

'Were you required to pay for your own clothes and school materials in Vetus svet?' he asked.

'No,' she answered truthfully.

'Then in what way is this arrangement different?'

Rhiannon shifted uncomfortably and looked down at her feet. Sometimes she had felt that all the chores she had been told to do at the Dashmonts was their way of having her repay them for anything they did.

'I shouldn't get things for nothing,' she finally admitted. 'I should do something to earn them, like I did before.'

'Rhiannon, look at me.'

At her guardian's stern command, Rhiannon lifted her head.

'The provision of clothes and basic necessities is not a luxury to be earnt by any child,' Sir Raeden said, 'they are things which should be given without any condition attached to them. Certainly, a child should be encouraged to perform small tasks to assist those who care for them; however, this should be done to learn discipline and responsibility, not to instil a sense of having to give restitution in return for their care. Therefore, until you come of age, I shall pay these expenses, and you will not seek to repay me in any fashion for doing so. Now, should you wish to earn an allowance, then I am prepared to offer you an appropriate sum each week, and in return you will perform some minor chores in my laboratory for two hours on Saturdays. Is that agreeable to you?'

Rhiannon nodded. 'Yes, Sir,' she said.

'Excellent.' Sir Raeden walked towards the door as he spoke. 'Tomorrow is Sunday, so we shall agree your allowance will be paid every week starting from today. I will set up the arrangements with the castle's treasurer so you may have any accounts sent here to be paid. Lord Grenwa will see that you receive regular balance reports.'

Sir Raeden paused next to the door and turned to give her a severe look.

'Should I learn you have been using this allowance to purchase *any* school materials, or apparel, then it will cease, and the bills for all the items you order shall have to come to me for approval and payment. With your desire to be dependent upon no one, I am sure this would not be at all to your liking.'

'No, Sir,' she said fervently. 'I promise I'll just use the money to buy gifts and other sorts of things.'

Sir Raeden gave a curt nod. 'Then we have reached an understanding,' he said, and held the door open for her.

She walked past him, then cast an enquiring look at the door leading to his laboratory. 'Do you want me to do some chores now?' she asked, ignoring her tired body's immediate protest.

A fleeting hint of humour seemed to flash through Sir Raeden's eyes, the spark of amusement turning them a deep sapphire blue.

'You are nothing if not persistent,' he remarked. 'For these two weeks you will not do any chores. You will instead focus on completing the reading homework that will be set for you and attending the lessons I will provide. Believe me,' he added, upon seeing a protest begin to form on Rhiannon's face, 'after two weeks of intense study, you will feel you have earnt every gold coin of your allowance.'

Chapter 16

EVIL AT WORK

The man tilted the bottle in his hand and let the required amount of phoenix blood drip into the large cauldron. Mórfran would not hesitate to punish him if he wasted a single drop.

It was so pleasant not having seen him for over two weeks. If only it had been two years!

'How long until *this* test is completed?'

The man did not turn around, wishing to avoid looking at that horrible scarred face.

'A few hours,' he answered briefly.

A pause. Then, 'Tell me about the beggar girl. Who was she?'

With all the delicate caution expected of one handling an expensive and rare item, the man replaced the bottle of phoenix blood on the bench, then stirred the potion.

'A newcomer from Vetus svet. She's of the line of Mórell.'

'Go on,' said the cold voice.

'She did survive the Glaciocaptus, and she's to remain in Álnair as the ward of Sir Raeden Wyvern.'

A bark of laughter filled with malicious amusement filled the laboratory.

'How is young Wyvern?' Mórfran enquired with false solicitude. 'Is he still as precocious as ever?'

'He's dangerous. The disappearance of a few dragons concerns him, but it will not take him long to realise who is behind the deaths of the owners of these Dragonstars, should he ever learn of them.'

'Are you saying he will recognise my work?'

Mórfran sounded disturbingly pleased at the prospect.

The man repressed a shudder.

'He has personally witnessed your style of execution once before. It is not likely he would forget.'

The man picked up a bloodstained Dragonstar from the pile on the bench. He wiped it clean, then placed it in the bubbling cauldron.

There was a loud *crack*.

The potion turned a deathly shade of white, streaked with crimson veins.

'He's also being extremely vigilant in his watch over this girl,' the man continued. 'Already, he has received permission for her to live at the castle, and she is frequently in company with the royal brat and his Chief Robesman. It will not be easy to get near her.'

'There will be time enough for planning her capture once our master is free,' Mórfran stated. 'For now, nothing takes precedence over perfecting that potion.' He stepped closer to the man, his voice lowering to a menacing pitch. 'And what news can you give me of when that will be?'

The man swallowed and his hand trembled where it gripped the stirring rod.

'I ... I'll have a working potion by the end of the week.'

A burning sensation wrapped around his neck. The air became hotter.

'Be sure that you do,' advised Mórfran with chilling indifference to the pain he was inflicting. 'My patience is not inexhaustible.'

The heat intensified briefly, then vanished.

The man collapsed against the bench, flinching when the laboratory door slammed behind his visitor.

Just once couldn't Mórfran come when that misbegotten old goat Plancy is here instead of me?

Chapter 17

A Challenge
is Accepted

The days leading up to the start of the school term passed in a blur for Rhiannon. The strict timetable Sir Raeden had set allowed for some periods of recreation, but mostly her days were spent reading textbooks and learning how to use her power. Sir Raeden had explained that charms were the result of a magi focusing their power and giving it intent. There was one, the Liborean Charm, which was used to release someone from restraints that caused her a bit of trouble. She ended up being tied to a chair for ten minutes before she managed to get the pronunciation correct.

David and John also took her on a tour of the castle school.

It was the most ornate school she had ever seen.

Built as one large building near the second inner wall, it was constructed of grey stone with arched windows on every side, and a tall belltower at the front. Inside, the classroom was a wide-open space on the ground floor. Bright silver lamps suspended from the ceiling illuminated it, while a great hearth at the back ensured the occupants of the room would not freeze during winter. A long blackboard ran the length of the south wall, and rows of removable desks were placed in uniform lines before it. In the foyer, beside a transonus dais, was an elegant spiral staircase leading to the laboratories and toilets on the second level. Nearby but outside was an extensive training area which was currently covered in snow.

When she enquired about additional study resources, she learnt all the students were permitted to use the palace library. Also available for their lessons in Natural Science and Herblore were the extensive greenhouses and the herb and vegetable gardens. She quickly made use of all three places, finding the array of herbs in the garden and the ancient collection of scrolls and books in the library fascinating.

Sir Raeden also instructed her each day in weaponry and physical defence, while David and John supervised her riding lessons on both horse and dragon.

She winced when she thought of how her body had ached after her first horseback ride.

She was still tender as she stood panting for breath in the outside training area of the school.

Monday the twelfth of January had arrived.

The first day of the new school term.

And the first lesson was Defence. She'd been asked to put her hastily learnt sword-fighting skills up against David's more experienced ones and she was failing miserably.

The other students around her were similarly engaged, all displaying various degrees of skill. She noticed that Eamon Bowler and Izana Sato, two of David's other Robesmen who also attended the school, were among the better fighters. Izana was particularly brilliant, and his mature face betrayed no emotion as he fought John.

A terse, familiar voice telling her to keep up her guard had Rhiannon sticking out her tongue at David when he smirked.

However, she obeyed Sir Raeden's command and fixed her stance, then raised the long wooden sword in her hand.

It had been the biggest surprise for her to discover that the Commander of the Guard and her newly appointed guardian was also the school's Defence instructor. David had gloomily confirmed this information to be correct after Aleda mentioned it one evening, adding it was all due to his father having requested Sir Raeden take the position upon David commencing his first year.

'He said he wanted someone there whom he trusted, and who'd make sure I wouldn't take any unnecessary risks,' David told her. 'For some reason he thought Wyvern was the best choice.'

Rhiannon stole a quick glance at the tall man watching them from a raised dais. She thought King Stephen had good reason to believe that Sir Raeden was the best choice. One glacial look from those blue eyes would be enough to freeze the blood in any normal person and make them think twice before disobeying one of his orders.

'Halt.'

Sir Raeden's voice rang out through the open grounds.

All the students' voices and the clash of wooden swords immediately ceased and their movements stilled.

'Clearly, the majority of you have not bothered to practise during the past three weeks.'

Sir Raeden descended from the dais, stalked towards the group of students and picked out the worst offenders.

'Campeth, your footwork is disgraceful. In a real fight you would have been killed five times over. Truscott, you keep leaving yourself open. Donar, it is a sword, not a baton to be waved about in that foolish manner. Hardinge, if you concentrated more on your form instead of daydreaming you might actually manage to deflect an attack. Donahue, focus on your opponent, not on keeping your boots clean.'

David's cousin flushed angrily when several girls looked at him and sniggered.

Sir Raeden then returned his attention to the entire class.

'While Álnair is a peaceful land, there are still dangers lurking within its cities, mountains and forests. Unscrupulous people exist – those who have chosen to follow a path of hate and destruction and who may one day threaten you or those whom you love. There are wild beasts that may attack you. You are instructed in this form of defence to help you survive. Those of you who are magi are probably thinking you can use your mage abilities in any situation, and therefore do not consider this skill to be of any benefit. If that is the case, then your stupidity may one day get you killed. There will be times when being a mage will be of no use to you. You could find yourself facing a beast that is invulnerable to whatever charm you cast upon it. There could be an enchantment barrier suppressing all forms of magic. When that happens, you will be on the same level as those who are not magi; in fact, you will be more vulnerable as you will have to rely solely on your own physical and mental capabilities – something you would not be accustomed to doing.'

Without warning, Sir Raeden spun and knocked the sword from the hand of the student closest to him. Falling back with a startled cry, the boy Rhiannon recognised as Rolfe Zemit cringed when Sir Raeden picked up the sword and pointed it at him.

'Another lesson to remember: you yourself are the weapon. Anything else is just an extension of yourself and can be discarded or lost. If you place too much reliance on your blade, staff or bow you are again creating a weakness that an enemy can exploit. If this happens, then …' with a controlled thrust, Sir Raeden had the tip of the sword against Rolfe's chest, 'when you're disarmed the fight is already over.'

Rolfe gulped and stared down at the sword's blunt point gently pressing against his chest. He looked back up into Sir Raeden's cool eyes. 'Y-yes, Sir,' he stammered. 'I-I'll try not to let it h-happen again.'

'You will do more than try, Mr Zemit,' Sir Raeden corrected him. 'You will not let it happen again.'

'N-no, Sir, I mean, yes, Sir.'

Sir Raeden returned the sword to Rolfe's shaking hand, then walked back to the dais.

'You all will now spend the next fifteen minutes going over the proper technique to deflect a frontal thrust,' he announced curtly. 'Afterwards, the magi among you will spend the remaining twenty minutes practising their Cosaint Charm, while the rest of you will use these balls donated by Professor Egelbert,' he pointed to a basket filled with a colourful assortment of balls, 'to test the strength of their protection charms. Any balls that make it through the charm will leave a mark where they hit your target. These balls are incapable of inflicting any serious form of injury – so do not hesitate to put the full force of your strength behind them.'

A few of the non-magi boys grinned at this, and Rhiannon knew there would be some inventive attacks taking place very shortly.

John obviously shared her opinion. 'Keep an eye out for Felix,' he muttered to David. 'He may not be able to hurt you with those balls, but he'll certainly try to trip you up.'

'Don't worry,' David replied. 'He's not likely to try anything too dangerous with Wyvern watching, and I can take care of myself.'

Thirty minutes later, Rhiannon realised David had spoken the truth.

Felix Costanzo repeatedly attempted to separate David from the rest of the magi students. His intent appeared to be to manoeuvre him off the snow-covered ground to the icy, slippery path behind them.

However, all his efforts were in vain.

David continued to cast a perfect protection charm with a quiet *'cosain'*, while dodging the other students who leapt away from the incoming balls when they failed to properly cast their own charms.

By the time Sir Raeden called another halt to the lesson, Felix was glaring at David, who merely smiled.

'Why did he only go after you?' Rhiannon asked after Sir Raeden had dismissed them and they were entering the schoolroom for their next class. 'It's almost as if he really dislikes you.'

David shrugged. 'He's been like that ever since I can remember. His father is a distant relative on my mother's side. He and my cousin always begrudged the fact that my ancestor was appointed High King by Endrille, and that one day I'll be the ruler of Álnair. I can't really understand it about Marcus. Uncle Oliver, his father, is my mother's younger brother, and he and his wife Lucia have always been nice to me.'

'So I take it they'll be at your birthday party tomorrow night?'

Rhiannon's question startled David, who stopped and looked at her in surprise.

'Who told you it was my birthday tomorrow?'

John raised his hand. 'I did,' he said. 'When we were in Cendillis doing Rhiannon's school shopping. You got distracted by that new watch in Kaufmann's store, and I mentioned your birthday was coming up. Of course, I then had to admit mine's the 25th of May.' He directed a playful wink in Rhiannon's direction. 'Nice presents are always appreciated.'

'Just tell him your presence is his present,' David suggested with a grin, then said, 'I know my mother will want to know your birth date so she can organise a special ball for you. Come on,' he urged when she hesitated, 'don't be shy about it.'

'It's August 14th,' Rhiannon said reluctantly. Her birthdays had never been anything special. Annabelle usually had an eisteddfod or concert to go to, which meant a party was always out of the question – even if she had had someone to invite.

'I always wanted my birthday to fall during the holidays,' John admitted, then stepped to the side with a cheerful, 'sorry, Leila,' upon noticing the girl behind him attempting to get past.

Leila gave him a warm smile, her round, white face faintly pink, before she carefully manoeuvred herself around him and made for her seat in the middle row.

'Getting back to my question,' Rhiannon said, turning to David again. 'Will Marcus and Felix be at your party?'

'Most likely,' he replied. 'My dear mother likes to encourage family unity on all these occasions, and to make things worse, this year it won't be a ball so we'll probably have to talk to them. But I live in hope they'll get caught in a foramen and be taken away to Vetus svet.'

Unfortunately, David's hopes in relation to his relatives disappearing were dashed the following night when they entered the Great Hall. Thanks to the intervention of John's brothers, however, Marcus and Felix were kept occupied by the persistent attentions of gossipy old ladies with a predilection for lecturing anyone under the age of sixty-five.

Upon being introduced to Marcus' parents, Rhiannon was not quite sure what to make of them. Both were extremely pleasant to her; however, Councillor Oliver Donahue's easy charm soon became cloying. She much preferred the quiet sobriety of Queen Maiwen's older brother Lord Timothy Donahue and his wife Lady Adriana, and the rigid politeness of her younger sister Phoebe.

She then met David's only surviving grandparent.

Lady Norita Donahue, who had travelled to attend the party from her home in the small village of Pyron on the Ardara Road, was a silver-haired replica of her eldest daughter. She welcomed Rhiannon to Álnair with sincere warmth, then expressed the hope she would enjoy the festivities.

As the party events unfolded, Rhiannon was sure she would enjoy them.

In some ways, the party was similar to Annabelle Dashmont's sixteenth birthday the year before, albeit on a much larger scale. A group of faeries with their harps and fiddles were unobtrusively playing a medley of cheerful music to the chattering harmony of several dozen voices engaged in animated conversation. The vast array of tables set up around the Great Hall groaned under the weight of all the delicious food and drink placed upon them.

But there, the similarities ended.

At David's party she wasn't ignored by the guests, and David didn't keep telling her to go away like Annabelle had done. In fact, he made sure she was introduced to everyone, including his other Robesmen who had come down from Ryegoth Academy to attend the celebration. Lord Derrick Fasani, a tall, stoic man of twenty-one, and Gareth Harulf, who seemed like an indolent man of nineteen until you noticed his alert posture and keen eyes, both welcomed her with the polite reserve of well-trained bodyguards. Rhiannon wasn't sure whether she met with their approval or not.

Eamon and Izana were also attending, and it was from the more extroverted Eamon that she learnt more about the other Robesmen.

'Izana is the smartest of all of us,' he told her when David was caught up talking with Caiden Alcober. 'He'll only be seventeen in November, which is why he's in Grade Four and not Five with John, but he seems older a lot of the time. He can hold his own against most of the professors in a debate, and he's an excellent swordsman. Quite a skilled mage too. He doesn't like to talk about himself, and doesn't make friends easily, so don't get offended if he seems standoffish. His mother, Lady Hikari, is one of the queen's closest friends, and his father, Lord Daiki ...' he pointed at a dark-haired, athletic man dressed in ivory-green garments, 'is a chancellor of the Pelatarrof and the Chief Robesman to King Stephen.

'Derrick's the eldest, but hardly the most cheerful. I've never even seen him smile! Sometimes I think he doesn't have any emotions at all. He's a pretty good mage, and a brilliant duellist. He inherited his title after his father died suddenly when he was twelve. From what I've heard, Lord Rinaldo just keeled over at his desk one day, and right in front of him! I tried asking him about it once, but he told me quite bluntly never to bring the subject up with him again.

'Gareth's not so bad once he feels certain you won't pose a threat to David. He's the only non-mage among us, but he's probably the best all-round fighter. He's mastered all the weapons and in a fight, I've only seen Sir Raeden and David succeed in defeating him. Actually, no. Izana's done it a few times as well. The man over there with the eyepatch is Lord Madoc, his father. His wife was the last High Chancellor before Lord Sharbel. A few years ago, they were attacked near Shadow Pass in the Del Enger Mountains. He lost an eye during the fight and Lady Siana was taken. Sir Madoc has led numerous search parties to look for her, but she's never been found. Oh, and just a friendly word of advice: don't go thinking you're in love with Gareth like all the other girls tend to do. As long as I've known him, he's only ever been interested in improving his fighting skills. There's some talk about him liking a girl at the Academy, but I'll believe that when I see it!'

When he finally took a breath, Rhiannon asked, 'And what about you?'

'Not much to say really. I'm the youngest child of the humble Captain Fergus Bowler and his wife Mildred, with the unfortunate luck to have four very bossy older sisters. I'm a few months younger than David, and I'm not as clever as the others. I'm all right with a sword but put a bow and arrow in my hand, and I'll hit the target every time at five hundred paces.'

194

Rhiannon also soon discovered he was adept at disappearing without a trace. When King Stephen called for the cake to be brought in, she briefly looked away from the young Robesman then turned back – only to find he had vanished. She could only assume the reason for his abrupt departure was the clearly frustrated young woman who was standing nearby, enquiring if she'd seen where her brother had gone.

'Bridget's quite nice, but she does have a habit of nagging poor Eamon about his appearance,' David explained when he rejoined her. 'Either his hair's too short or too long, or his tunic doesn't match his shirt.'

'No wonder he took off,' she said, then looked up as the birthday cake was carried in.

It was an elegant creation of dark chocolate with two rows of candles set in the icing.

Rhiannon frowned when she counted them. John had told her in Cendillis that David was turning fifteen, but there were sixteen candles on the cake.

'I am fifteen today,' David confirmed when she quietly pointed this out to him. 'Placing an extra candle on the cake is an old tradition here in Álnair. It represents the wish that the light of life will remain with the person for another year, and they remove it before blowing out the others. They then give the still burning candle to the person who will use it to light the Hope Lanterns that are released once the cake is cut. The lanterns have to be released over a body of water, so here in the palace it's done on the South Terrace since it overlooks the ocean.'

A discreet cough from his mother drew David's attention to the main table where the cake had now been placed. He gave Rhiannon an apologetic look, then walked forwards to stand in front of it. Removing one candle, he took a deep breath and blew out the others in one go. As applause broke out among the guests, he handed the lit candle to Hestor, the castle's Chief Steward, who placed it inside a small crystal holder. Then taking up a fine silver knife, he went to cut the cake.

'Be careful not to cut the bottom,' Rhiannon called out, enjoying the unique opportunity of being able to tease someone with the line.

David paused, the tip of the knife just touching the chocolate icing. He looked up in bewilderment. 'Why can't I cut it?' he asked.

Rhiannon realised everyone else was also staring quizzically at her. A fiery blush spread across her cheeks as realisation struck.

'Oh, sorry,' she said. 'It's just a tradition where I come from. Forget I said anything.'

David raised the knife away from the cake. 'Now, I really am curious. What's the tradition?'

She fidgeted as everyone continued to look at her. 'It's really silly,' she tried to say, only to have David shake his head.

'Come on, Rhiannon,' he said, 'you've got everyone intrigued. Why can't I cut the bottom of the cake?'

She looked around and saw all the faces turned towards her. She also noticed another factor, which heightened her mortification and led her to mumble the explanation.

David frowned. 'I didn't catch a word of that,' he said.

She grimaced, then said in a slightly louder voice, 'If you cut the bottom you have to kiss the person of the opposite sex who's nearest to you, and relatives don't count.'

A brief silence fell. Then the room filled with laughter. Everyone, except for Sir Raeden, Derrick and Izana, lost their composure at the horrified look on David's face as he stared at some of the older women standing near the table.

But then John obviously realised what had made Rhiannon mumble the first time.

'Looks like Rhiannon would be the lucky lady this evening,' he declared.

David's eyes widened and a faint blush appeared in his cheeks.

'I think we may have to adopt this tradition,' Queen Maiwen's amused voice announced clearly, and she urged her son to cut the cake.

David cast a last glance in Rhiannon's direction, then lowered the knife once more.

'Can I kith Pwinth David too?'

The loud demand was accompanied by the appearance of John's younger sister Alice. Her red curls bouncing with every hurried step, she ran to where David was standing.

The Prince of Álnair spared her only the briefest look before returning his attention to his task. And never had a cake been cut with more care.

The knife slowly descended, cutting through the chocolate with ease.

The first slice had to be cut out by David. How would he manage to avoid cutting through the bottom?

He couldn't.

A delicate *chink* broke the expectant silence, causing a round of good-natured cheers and applause. Then, to Alice's more than obvious childish delight, David resignedly bent down and gave her a brotherly kiss on the forehead.

Rhiannon was not sure why she suddenly wished she could jump back in time and prevent herself from ever mentioning the Australian birthday cake tradition.

Then David was moving away to allow the rest of the cake to be cut, and the group of revellers were making their way through the palace to the South Terrace.

Rhiannon watched as the Chief Steward approached the stone balustrade of the wide balcony. A long line of small delicate lanterns hovered in the air above it. Each one was made from a thin, transparent material with a tiny bowl at the bottom.

'May the light of life inside His Royal Highness, Crown Prince David Alexander of Álnair, continue to burn for another year,' the

Chief Steward's words rang out. Then he reached out and placed the lit candle inside the tiny bowl of the first lantern.

A flame sprang to life. The lantern's transparent material turned an ethereal golden white.

Rhiannon had only a moment to think how pretty it looked, when an invisible spark seemed to touch all the other lanterns. One after another they all started to glow.

Her gaze transfixed on the Hope Lanterns, she tilted back her head as they slowly rose towards the sky before drifting out over the Dairíon Ocean.

The crisp winter night air and everything else was forgotten in the quiet beauty of that moment.

Everyone was silent.

The only sound was the gentle rolling of the waves.

Rhiannon was oblivious to everything except the enchanting scene before her.

She did not hear when David and John came to stand next to her.

She did not see the soft, contemplative expression in David's eyes as he observed her innocent delight. Nor the sharp, perceptive glance cast in his direction by Izana.

Then each of the lanterns began to disappear in a burst of twinkling lights, the dazzling array of colours transforming the night sky into a shimmering canvas.

The last lantern disappeared in a brilliant display of red, blue and gold.

'Did you like it?'

Rhiannon turned towards David. 'Like it?' she gasped. 'That was the most beautiful thing I've ever seen!'

'I thought you might enjoy it,' he said with a smile.

Rhiannon was certain it had to be the highlight of the entire evening. However, after they all returned inside to eat the cake and David finished opening a mountain of gifts, she discovered she was wrong.

Her small present to David had been buried at the bottom of the pile and he opened it last.

David took one look at the pocket watch he had admired in Kaufmann's Novelty Giftware and declared it the best present of all.

His obvious sincerity made that moment the brightest one of the evening.

The rest of Rhiannon's first week of lessons was hard. Sir Raeden's assistance had certainly brought her knowledge and skills up to a respectable level; however, there were still areas that needed a lot of improvement.

She found she used too much power doing the simplest enchantment, causing Professor Athena Plessington to dread hearing her name called, especially after Rhiannon melted all the snow in the Upper Ward and caused a minor flood. She mispronounced her words in whatever language Master Hubert Gadshill decided to teach them each day. And she was bewildered when Professor Lavinia Harbuckle asked her the location of a small town or forest in Álnair.

She was therefore relieved when Saturday morning arrived, and David and John insisted she lay aside her books to go outside with them.

She adjusted the cloak around her shoulders, then stepped out of the Entrance Hall and onto the North Terrace.

Inhaling deeply, she breathed out a long sigh of relief.

'Now, that sounds like a typical reaction after a week of lessons,' said David.

'I can honestly say I never thought I'd be so happy to see the end of a school week,' she said. 'I used to loathe weekends, but I'm very grateful for this one.'

'It's certainly been harder on you than the rest of us,' said John, 'what with having to speed-study to catch up.'

'You did well though,' David reassured her, as they started down the flight of steps. 'I even heard Professor Treshart say to my father that you knew more history about Álnair than she expected from someone only recently arrived from Vetus svet. You've certainly impressed her.'

'I only knew so much because Sir Raeden and you two helped me,' she confessed. 'Otherwise, I would've looked like a complete and utter ignoramus whenever she asked me a question.'

'Well, you certainly showed that you're a fast learner,' said David.

'I wouldn't say that,' a voice behind them sneered, 'since she's still hanging around you two.'

David took a deep breath, then turned around slowly. He fixed a glare eerily similar to Sir Raeden's on his dark-haired cousin and Felix Costanzo, who were hovering just behind them.

'Haven't you got anything better to do than follow us around, Marcus?' he demanded.

'Why would he want to be following you?' Felix retorted.

'Or are you so desperate for friends you think anyone near you must actually want to be associated with you?' Marcus scoffed.

'You're the one who spoke to us first,' John pointed out.

'I was just correcting my *dear* cousin's comment,' Marcus said, in a falsely innocent tone. 'After all, anyone who hangs around you two can't be that bright.'

'You're just irritated she beat you in Defence yesterday,' David shot back. 'She's only had a few weeks' training and can already disarm you in a fight.'

'Let it go, David,' Rhiannon said quietly, placing a hand on his arm.

Marcus' face flushed red with anger at the reminder of his humiliation.

'One lucky move doesn't prove anything,' he spat. 'In a real contest of skill, I'd have no problem winning against a mere girl like her.'

'What!' Rhiannon's conciliatory manner disappeared instantly. Her voice heavy with indignation, she rounded on the target of her ire. 'I may be a girl, but that doesn't mean I can't defeat an arrogant little twit like you,' she said furiously.

'Prove it.' His supercilious attitude quickly returning, Marcus had a taunting edge to his voice as he said, 'I challenge you to a proper high-speed race.'

'I'd be careful if I were you, Marcus,' warned David. 'She may be from Vetus svet and a girl, but she's already surpassed the skills of most people who've been riding dragons for several years.'

'Oh yeah? Well, I bet you twenty gold pieces she can't even make it past the finish line!'

'Fifty says she'll leave your arrogant face trailing in the dust,' David retorted.

'No fear of that,' Marcus stated arrogantly. 'The dragon I got my Dragonstar from said I was the most talented rider he'd ever had on his back. In fact, I saw him outside the castle walls when I arrived with my father. I'm sure he'd love to be my dragon in this race. While I go and speak to him, you'd better see who you can manage to find in the next hour for her.'

Marcus' triumphant glance towards Rhiannon made it clear he did not think it likely she would find any dragon suitable in that short time.

'The race will start at the main gate in an hour,' Felix announced with a smug smile. 'If you're not there, we'll know you were too cowardly to show your face.'

'We'll be there,' Rhiannon replied, her eyes narrowed.

Marcus and Felix strode away, their bodies exuding an air of self-satisfaction and superiority.

'Are you sure you want to do this, Rhiannon?' asked John. 'We know you've been out a few times on Endrille but being in a race is completely different from normal flying.'

Rhiannon straightened her shoulders determinedly. 'I'm sure,' she said. 'If he'd said anything else, I wouldn't have cared that much, but to sneer at me just because I'm a girl …'

She clenched her fists as her voice trailed off.

'I always knew he was an idiot,' David observed thoughtfully. 'As far as I'm concerned, females are the scariest beings ever created, and you insult one at your peril.'

Rhiannon cuffed him on the shoulder. 'I seem to recall you insulting me after I first woke up here,' she reminded him.

'Temporary insanity,' he said firmly. 'And now we'd better find you a decent dragon for this race.'

'Why can't we ask Endrille?' she asked.

'Ancient dragons aren't permitted to participate in races,' David informed her. 'Even though they wouldn't be doing it deliberately, their magic would allow them to unfairly increase their speed and power, putting all other dragon breeds at a disadvantage.'

'How about one of the battle dragons?' John suggested. 'Most of them are Parvus, so we know they'll have the speed and agility required for a race.'

David nodded. 'Good choice, and after we fetch the bridle from the armoury, I think I know just the one we can ask.'

Rhiannon leant over and placed her hands on her knees, breathless from racing down the labyrinth of steps which led to the pristine sands of the lagoon.

They had rushed to find the dragon David had in mind, and their quest had led them here: the sandy beach where a dragon of modest size lay gazing out at the ocean. He was certainly much smaller than Endrille (she guessed he was only about sixteen feet long), and yet he possessed an air of no less distinction than the ancient dragon.

As David called a greeting in Drakaron, she looked at the distinctive shiny grey scales and light-blue markings across the dragon's back. From the readings she had done, she knew she was gazing upon a prime example of the cave-dwelling Parvus Dragons.

The dragon stood up on its four muscular legs, and Rhiannon blinked when she realised his shoulder standing height could only be about seven or eight feet. There was a gentle warmth radiating from him, and the pleasant scent permeating the air around him made her think of a cool, dry evening after a day of scorching heat.

'Rhiannon, I'd like you to meet Arastar.' David turned back to the dragon who was now looking upon them with an indulgent glint in his otherwise stern eyes. 'Arastar, this is Rhiannon McBride, only daughter of Mórell's line.'

The dragon bowed his head while Rhiannon stared up at him in surprise.

'You're the one Endrille told me about,' she exclaimed. 'She said you're the best battle dragon in the castle's forces.'

'My queen does me great honour with such words,' Arastar said, his voice a deep, rumbling sound that reverberated through the air around him.

Rhiannon noted he did not refute the title Endrille had bestowed on him. Clearly, he had no time for false modesty.

'Queen Endrille has also spoken to me of you, little one,' Arastar continued. 'I welcome you to Álnair and trust you will be happy with us.'

'Before you two get carried away with your conversation,' David said, swiftly interrupting any more pleasantries being exchanged, 'we've got something urgent we need to speak to you about, Arastar. I know you only returned last night, but we really need you to help us out. My cousin Marcus has challenged Rhiannon to a high-speed race. You're the only dragon I can think of who would be able to look after her and help her win at the same time.'

Alarmingly, the dragon straightened to his full height and glared at David.

'You would ask that I, Arastar, a battle dragon of the most unblemished reputation, participate in such a trivial matter?' he demanded wrathfully.

David, Rhiannon and John all stepped back in shock.

'We're sorry,' Rhiannon began uncertainly, but the dragon's next words stopped her cold.

'I would have been insulted had you not asked,' Arastar said more calmly, and she breathed a sigh of relief upon seeing the shadow of a smile in his eyes.

'So, you will help me?' she asked hopefully.

'It would be an honour to assist the only daughter of Mórell's line,' Arastar replied gravely, but she also perceived a new excitement shining in his eyes, an almost playful spark, as if the prospect of competition had lit some long-dormant youthful fire in his dragon heart. And when he next spoke, her suspicions over his willingness to assist her only increased.

'It has been many years since I last tasted the thrill of a simple race. Would you believe that in my youth some two centuries ago, I was the fastest among the Parvus in all of Álnair?'

He unfurled his wings in a burst of movement and whooshed them down.

The sudden action sent the sand swirling into the air behind him in a white, hazy torrent.

Rhiannon, who had leapt backwards in fright at his swift demonstration, relaxed and even laughed.

The happy sound brought a look of pleased humour to Arastar's face.

'You have the heart of a good rider,' he chuckled. 'It's important to possess the ability to recover quickly from sudden shocks, especially if you're going to participate in a race.'

His manner so reminded Rhiannon of a kindly old grandfather that she had to sternly suppress the impulse to run up and hug him around his long neck.

'Well, young David, you had best put that bridle on me,' Arastar said, and crouched down.

David quickly placed the bridle on him and fastened it with expert efficiency. Then he glanced at his watch. 'We'd best get to the main gate. We've only got four minutes left.'

'Climb on,' Arastar instructed, then huffed out an impatient breath when only Rhiannon stepped forward. 'Unless you two boys have suddenly sprouted wings in the time I've been gone, you'd best get on as well, or you'll never make it to the starting point on time.'

'You can't carry all three of us,' David protested.

'I have carried two fully-grown men dressed in battle armour on my back and flown two hundred miles without any difficulty,' Arastar declared. 'The three of you will not be a problem.'

David accepted his reassurance without further argument and hurriedly followed after Rhiannon, who was already settled comfortably on Arastar's back with the reins in her hands. However, John's reluctance at having to fly was plain. His face was pale as he slowly took his place behind David.

Arastar rose swiftly into the air, the weight of three humans on his back not hindering his smooth ascent in the slightest.

'I think I'm going to be sick,' John muttered.

'Just close your eyes and try not to think about it,' David suggested.

John did not answer. He merely groaned miserably.

'I see Master Tremaine has not overcome his dislike of flying,' Arastar called.

'Not even a little,' David replied.

'It is then indeed fortunate your cousin did not issue the challenge to him,' Arastar observed with a deep chuckle, his powerful wings moving with efficient grace to take them quickly over the castle's south walls and towers.

Rhiannon, her hands maintaining their firm grip on the reins, listened to the conversation. However, her attention was focused more on adjusting to the different sensation of riding a much smaller dragon than Endrille, and enjoying the closer view of Valieoth Castle from the outside.

Beneath her, Arastar's sleeker build allowed her legs to rest at an easier angle, and his size permitted them to fly closer to the palace than Endrille's more majestic one.

As they flew over the long inner courtyard of the palace, she looked down and saw several people walking across the snow-covered ground. Some were even seated on the edge of the circular fountain set in the middle of the open space. She suspected they were taking the opportunity to enjoy the heat of the winter sunlight that was gradually dispelling the early morning frost.

Arastar passed the two standards set atop the Main Tower, his wings creating a fierce gust of wind that sent them fluttering in his wake. Then he set a fast pace towards the Main Gate. Soon they were approaching the designated starting point for the race.

'John, we're almost there,' Rhiannon called. She looked back to check on him only to see his mass of auburn curls spilling over David's shoulder as he hid his face.

'In fact, we've arrived,' David announced.

There was a slight impact as Arastar gently landed, followed by an exclamation of relief from John. With a heartfelt sigh, he slid off Arastar and bent over. He took a few deep breaths, then raised his head.

'Are you all right?' asked Rhiannon.

'I'm fine now,' he said with a shaky smile. 'Just … David, don't ever ask me to do that again.'

'I'll certainly try not to,' David promised, then in stark contrast to John's more ungainly descent, he dismounted with casual grace.

'When may we expect your cousin to show?' Arastar enquired.

David shrugged. 'Knowing his propensity for dramatics, he'll probably show up five seconds before the hour is up.'

'And do you know who your cousin is choosing to assist him in this race?'

'Why do you need to know that?' said Rhiannon.

'Know thy enemy,' Arastar replied solemnly, 'or in this case it is more a case of know thy rival.'

'He mentioned asking the dragon who gave him his Dragonstar.'

Arastar snorted at David's answer. 'Baegolz,' he said.

'You know him?'

'Indeed.' Arastar looked at Rhiannon. 'I am saddened to say he is one of the most arrogant among all the dragon races. He believes he should only be touched by humans of noble blood.'

The chattering of voices put an end to any further discussion.

The four of them all turned to face the main gate. Out of its wide opening came Felix Costanzo, leading most of the other students from the castle school towards them.

'Just what are they doing here?' David demanded.

'They're witnesses,' Felix informed him with a smirk. 'We wouldn't want to hide the knowledge of Marcus' victory now, would we?'

Before anyone could reply to this arrogant assumption there was a strong gust of wind.

Then, like a winged, long-necked stegosaurus falling out of the sky, the vast, green-scaled body of a Gora Dragon landed with a *plomp*. Its thick, serpentine tail, which could easily smash holes into the sides of the mountain dragon's lair, sent up a spray of snow as it connected with the ground.

Marcus and Baegolz had arrived.

Rhiannon glanced at her watch.

Just as David had predicted, Marcus had arrived exactly five seconds before the hour was up.

Chapter 18

MARCUS VS RHIANNON

The tense atmosphere that had fallen was finally broken by Arastar.

'The standard rules will apply,' he announced with a warning glare at Marcus. 'No charm is to be used against any other participant in the race, and any deviation from the set course will result in immediate disqualification.'

Marcus nonchalantly waved one hand. 'I don't need to cheat to win against her – as you'll all soon see,' he declared. 'Now, let's get on with it.'

'The starting point will be there.' Felix pointed to an area just beyond the main gate where an ancient oak tree stood. 'You'll both start on this side of the tree and then fly over Cendillis and Shaimar Forest until you reach Ryegoth Academy. Once you've circled around Ryegoth's tallest tower, you'll return over Rëalta Lake and follow the Deora River until it reaches the Dairíon Ocean. From there, you'll turn and come back here, sticking to the coastline until you reach the castle. The first ones over the castle and back past the tree will be the winners.'

'That's over ninety miles all up!' cried Rolfe Zemit from the crowd of students.

Felix smirked. 'It takes less than an hour to complete if you're skilled enough.' He shot a condescending look at Rhiannon. 'It's not too late to withdraw.'

'Forget it,' she bit out.

He shrugged. 'Then this should be amusing,' he jeered, and turned away.

'Good luck and take care. We do want you back in one piece,' John said.

Rhiannon gave a small smile at his words.

'Thanks, and don't worry about me, I'll be fine,' she said. 'I'm sure Arastar will make sure of that.'

'He will,' David said confidently. 'And don't worry if you can't remember the exact route. Arastar knows these parts extremely well and he'll make certain you go the right way.'

'You have my word that I will,' Arastar promised.

David took a step closer to Arastar's side and stripped off his gloves. He reached up, placing them in Rhiannon's hands.

'Wear them over yours,' he instructed. 'At the speed you'll be travelling, the wind will be like ice, and we don't have time to get you a proper pair of race gloves. And you'd best take my cloak as well. The one you're wearing isn't enough for a long-distance flight. Make sure you turn the collar up, so it protects your face as much as possible.' Then clasping one of her hands in his for a moment, he murmured, 'Take care, Rhiannon, and whatever you do, keep an eye on Marcus. I wouldn't put it past him to try some underhanded trick against you.'

Rhiannon shot a quick look at her boastful opponent and nodded.

'I'll be careful,' she promised.

'Your Royal Highness?'

David released her hand with a final reassuring squeeze, then turned to face Baegolz.

'As the highest-ranking person in this gathering, you must

appoint the official for the race,' Baegolz said. He looked pained as he gazed at the casually dressed assembly before him. 'I sincerely trust you will choose someone whose noble blood will make them worthy of such a position.'

Rhiannon saw David stiffen at the blatant insult to his fellow students who were of less distinguished birth.

'Anyone, whatever their social status, is worthy of the position, provided they are honest and fair in their judgement,' he snapped. He turned to look at the crowd and quickly made his decision.

'Simon Truscott.'

The gangly, redheaded son of one of the palace tailors stepped forward.

'You want me to do it?' he asked in an awed voice.

'Your judgement will be unbiased when declaring the winner, since neither Marcus nor I can claim you as one of our close friends,' David explained.

Simon almost ran to the oak tree in his eagerness to accept the position.

'I promise I'll be fair,' he shouted back to them. 'Just wait until me ma hears about this! Contestants, take your positions.'

'You sure you don't want to switch your bet, cousin?' Marcus taunted as Baegolz moved towards the starting point. 'It's not too late to change your mind and realise I'm the better choice.'

Rhiannon looked down to see David's hands clench into fists.

'How did I ever end up having that conceited little prat for a relative,' he muttered, glaring at his cousin's back.

'Just ignore him,' John advised quietly.

Rhiannon turned her head away and urged Arastar forward, grimly resolved to wipe the arrogant smirk off Marcus' face.

Both dragons took their positions at the starting point. The small crowd of students watched them in excitement, their voices calling out a mixture of advice, encouragement and wagers.

Rhiannon heard Leila Hardinge, a Third-Grade student and the daughter of the castle's Chief Herbalist, calling out enthusiastically for her to 'show that pompous muckworm what a girl can do!'

However, it became clear most of the other students were supporting Marcus' chance at winning.

She saw Simon grin. Clearly, he was enjoying his moment of importance.

'Now, do both Riders swear they have not been coerced into this race and are entering it of their own free will?' he called.

'Yes,' she answered, and heard Marcus echo her reply.

'Do you acknowledge that the results of this race shall be binding, unless a rematch is required?'

'Yes.'

'Do you swear to hold to the set course and not wander from it?'

'Yes.'

'Then the best of luck to both of you. And remember: any physical or magical attacks against another rider will mean instant disqualification. Are you ready?'

Rhiannon gave a quick nod and grasped the reins around Arastar's neck.

'I am,' she said, her voice sounding muffled behind the collar of David's cloak.

'Just get on with it,' Marcus spat impatiently.

'GO!'

Both Arastar and Baegolz shot forward.

With one powerful backward thrust of their unfurled wings, they launched themselves into the sky.

The cold air blasted against Rhiannon, the chill freezing her skin. Her fingers frantically clutched at the reins.

She looked ahead.

Baegolz and Marcus were in front. The larger dragon's more powerful thrust had put them in the lead.

'Come on,' she muttered.

Arastar swiftly dodged to avoid hitting an eagle.

Rhiannon lost her balance. Gasping, she grasped desperately at the reins. Her frightened eyes locked on the ground far below.

Suddenly, Arastar straightened his body.

'Regain your balance,' he ordered.

Rhiannon hastily obeyed, then held on for dear life as Arastar shot forward with incredible speed.

Marcus and Baegolz had gained a small lead.

Rhiannon clung on when Arastar twisted and dipped, his nimble manoeuvres swiftly closing the gap.

The streets of Cendillis flashed by.

Arastar twisted again, narrowly missing Baegolz's tail.

A burst of speed. A bellow of fury from Marcus. Then Rhiannon and Arastar were in first place.

The wind pushed against Rhiannon's face. Her eyes were narrowed to mere slits against its force.

She ducked her head. The scenery below had changed.

A number of small, dark figures walked over snow-covered fields. They paused and looked up, as the shadows of Arastar and Baegolz shot past. She could hear a few muffled cheers coming from them.

The snowy fields became the dense woodland of Shaimar Forest, the trees a wide sea of green and brown, topped with the white foam of snow.

Then, they were approaching the magnificent towers of Ryegoth Academy.

'When I go around, do not fight against the turn, lean into it, and keep your hold firm.' Arastar gave the instruction without even turning his head or slowing down.

Rhiannon glanced over her shoulder.

Baegolz and Marcus were not far behind them.

'Will Baegolz have to slow down to make the turn?'

A rumble of laughter vibrated through Arastar's body.

'If he has any sense he will. At this speed, his weight and size will go against him on such a tight angle.'

They passed over the impressive size of Ryegoth Academy.

Many students were outside in the vast grounds. They waved in welcome when they flew over.

'Grip hard!' Arastar barked out.

Rhiannon had only a second to obey.

Arastar spread his wings to their fullest extent. With the precision of a prima ballerina performing a triple pirouette, he shot around the tallest tower.

Rhiannon leant forward into the turn, tightening her grip even more.

Arastar abruptly levelled out his body.

Rhiannon felt a slight dizziness come over her. She took a deep breath, then glanced over her shoulder. She saw Baegolz take the turn at the same high speed as Arastar. His weight, combined with his speed, carried him out of the turn.

'Baegolz miscalculated. He's had to slow down,' she cried.

Arastar snorted in disgust. 'He always did have more brawn than brain.'

He sped over the wide shimmering reflection of Rëalta Lake.

Then they were at the opening of Deora River.

The icy wind turned colder as they flew over the long waterway, a bitter chill rising from the freezing water flowing towards the estuary.

Rhiannon shivered under her two woollen cloaks.

'It is not far now,' Arastar reassured her as they approached a large stone bridge. 'That's Haldoron Bridge. It connects the main road from Cendillis and Valieoth Castle with the road to Ryegoth Academy and Ardara. About another five miles and we'll reach the ocean.'

Rhiannon took another look over her shoulder. She blinked. Then looked again.

'Arastar, something's wrong.'

'What is it?'

'I think Marcus is sick, he looks like he's about to fall off Baegolz.'

Arastar scoffed in disbelief, tossing a glance behind him. His speed did not slacken in the slightest.

'A simple amateur's trick to try and get his competitors to slow down, then catch them off guard when they offer assistance.'

'But what if he's not pretending?' Rhiannon asked worriedly, her conscience prodding against her determination to win. 'What if he does fall?'

'Baegolz will catch him.'

'What if he doesn't?'

Rhiannon cast a fleeting look at her rival, who was now slumped even further over Baegolz's neck, and bit her lip. Trick or not, she knew she couldn't ignore the situation.

'We have to check and make sure he's all right.'

'What?'

'I'm sorry, Arastar, but I need you to turn around.'

'Rhiannon ...'

'Please, just do it. If I'm wrong, and this is a trick and we lose, then I'll take full responsibility with whoever was supporting us in the race.'

Arastar shook his head resignedly. 'As my rider I must obey your order – although it goes completely against my better judgement. Hang on tight.'

He gave a short thrust of his wings. Sharply, he circled about and headed back.

'Look to your rider, Baegolz!' he roared.

'Marcus, are you all right?' cried Rhiannon.

Marcus' drooping figure suddenly shot upright. He gave a jeering laugh. Then he and Baegolz flew past, the larger dragon almost knocking Arastar off balance.

'See you at the finish line, dalcop!'

Rhiannon's blood boiled at Marcus' mocking comment.

Arastar growled. He pivoted without warning.

Rhiannon's fingers frantically grasped at the reins.

Arastar descended into a steep dive.

A hurricane blasted against Rhiannon's face.

'What're you doing?' she cried.

Arastar did not answer. He increased his speed until he was shooting towards the approaching estuary.

'Arastar!'

'Do not let go.'

Rhiannon clung desperately to the reins.

The wind tore at her clothes and drove the breath from her lungs. She crouched down until she was almost lying across Arastar's neck.

Baegolz's form was slightly ahead of them, but still flying high in the air.

Rhiannon looked down. Her eyes widened.

'Arastar, you'll crash into the water.'

He ignored her cry and continued to descend.

Then, with a quick twist of his body, he pulled out of the dive and hurtled upwards in a sharp turn. The speed of his descent provided extra force to his upward flight, sending him racing in front of Baegolz's startled face.

'Hey, that's cheating!' Marcus' indignant yell rang out behind them.

They ignored him.

Arastar swiftly flew along the coastline towards the castle.

Rhiannon's heart leapt into her throat when they reached, then passed over, the immense towers and turrets.

The Upper and Middle Wards went by in a flash.

All sound disappeared from around Rhiannon as she focused on the finish line just beyond the main gate.

Only a little bit farther … and then … it was all over.

Rhiannon's heart found its way back into its rightful position. Her lungs resumed working. Her ears opened to David's and John's cries of triumph and congratulations.

Arastar swooped down and landed with a victorious flourish. Then he turned his head and gazed down at her.

'You did well, daughter of Mórell.'

Rhiannon shook her head at his words.

'You were right, Arastar. He was just pulling a trick, and because of me we almost lost. If it hadn't been for your quick thinking he would've won.'

'Do not be ashamed of your actions,' Arastar said gently. 'You acted nobly and with honour. The shame belongs to those who sought to win through trickery.'

David, who had run up with John and Simon in time to hear these words, instantly lost his smile. 'What happened?' he demanded.

Still feeling a fool for how easily she had fallen for the deception, Rhiannon hung her head in embarrassment as Arastar described Marcus' actions.

When Arastar finished explaining, she waited for David to rebuke her for not remembering his warning before the race. To her utter astonishment, he simply held up a hand to help her dismount and said calmly, 'I certainly didn't think he'd be such a prat as to pull a tasteless and dishonest trick like that one. *Your* actions do you credit; his, however, show only a poor and disgraceful lack of integrity that will reflect badly on him.'

Hearing a commotion coming towards them, they looked around to see a fuming Marcus heading in their direction.

'Let the complaining commence,' John muttered darkly.

'I demand a rematch!' Marcus shouted without preamble.

'On what grounds?' Simon asked, folding his arms over his chest.

'They cheated!' Marcus pointed angrily at Rhiannon and Arastar, who both glared back at him.

'Says the one who tried to win by a deceitful stunt,' John scoffed.

'And how exactly did they cheat?' Simon asked.

Floundering to reply to Simon's question, Marcus finally spat, 'They deliberately pulled up out of a dive right in front of us.'

'That's not against the rules,' Simon corrected him. 'In fact, that's one of the most dangerous race manoeuvres there is because of the excessive speed that can build up, so very few riders and dragons attempt it.'

'But ...'

'Rhiannon and Arastar won this race,' Simon said decisively, cutting off Marcus' objection. 'And they won it without cheating or using cheap tricks.'

His face flushing red with anger, Marcus spun away and stormed off. His group of followers scurried after him.

The remaining students wasted no time in offering the winners their congratulations, with Leila's being the most fervent. The gleeful girl was almost dancing with joy, relishing Marcus' defeat.

'I'll get my father to send you some bottles of his best creams and lotions, Rhiannon! It took fifty-two minutes and twenty seconds to wipe the smirk off that toad's face, but you did it!' Leila laughed, giving Rhiannon a quick hug. She bounced backwards and bumped into David as he went to remove the bridle from Arastar's neck. Thankfully, John caught them both before they ended up sprawled in the snow.

'Thanks Leila, but most of the credit goes to Arastar,' Rhiannon said honestly. She looked at the Parvus Dragon, who had now been joined by Baegolz.

'My felicitations on your achievement.' The obvious reluctance in the Gora Dragon's voice robbed his words of any real congratulatory sentiment.

To his credit, Arastar merely bowed his head and answered politely, 'Thank you, Baegolz.'

Ignoring Simon, the mountain dragon gave David and Rhiannon a slight nod, then took off into the air without another word. He did not look back once as he flew away.

'I still don't understand why he has such a prejudice against people who aren't nobly born,' Rhiannon said with a puzzled frown as he disappeared.

'Like humans, each dragon is unique in their personality and character,' Arastar explained. 'Unfortunately, Baegolz suffers from a misguided notion that because one of his ancestors was the friend of a Nordic king back in Vetus svet, this makes him superior to many of his dragon brethren. He believes only those humans of noble blood are important enough to touch him, or even speak to him.'

'I wouldn't worry about it,' David told her with a smile. 'It's not likely you'll come across him that often, and even if you do, I doubt he'd cause you any trouble.'

Returning his smile, she was about to reply when her attention was caught by the sight of someone stalking out of the castle's main gate. The dark cloak was a menacing cloud swirling around his body, and a forbidding glare was focused in their direction.

Sir Raeden!

As he drew nearer, and she saw his ire was also directed at her, Rhiannon had to suppress a sudden desire to impersonate a mole and burrow into the ground. Anything that made her guardian look so cross could not be good.

When everyone else in the group realised who was heading in their direction, they all, with the exception of David and John, apprehensively backed away.

Sir Raeden paid no heed to their fearful reaction. His un-wavering glare was focused solely on his targets: Rhiannon, David and John.

He came to a halt in front of them, his icy-blue eyes now darkened to a tumultuous navy hue. Scowling fiercely, he bit out with chilling calm, 'The three of you get yourselves to my office this instant. As for the rest of you, this foolishness is over. Now, get out of my sight.'

With sympathetic looks at the three left behind to deal with their irate teacher, the others in the group dispersed and hurried away.

'Sir Raeden.' Arastar's voice made Rhiannon, David and John pause on their way towards the castle gate. 'I believe you should know ...'

'I do not wish to hear a word,' Sir Raeden interrupted coldly. 'Lady Endrille will no doubt have something to say to you about your part in this tomfoolery. You can explain yourself to her. These three, however, will explain themselves to me.'

Chapter 19

A BINDING CONTRACT

The ominous tension permeating Sir Raeden's large office was becoming unbearable. The clock on the wall ticked off the seconds with relentless precision. Through the open window, the ocean waves could be heard crashing violently against the rocks in the distance. In a great hearth of stone, several logs crackled as the burning flames engulfed the wood, the fire casting up a shower of sparks that had dark shadows flickering over the long rows of books on the walls.

Since their arrival, apart from a terse command to stand in front of his desk and remain silent, Sir Raeden had not said a word. Seating himself, he picked up a scroll that marred the tidy perfection of his desk by appearing to have been flung down in unusual haste, and proceeded to read its contents. The slight hardening of his jaw was the only indication that instead of receding, his anger was simply being tightly restrained.

Having evidently reached the end of the document, he slowly replaced the scroll on his desk and lifted his head. With a single glacial look at David, Rhiannon and John, he said in a dangerously quiet voice, 'Whose idea was the race?'

Rhiannon swallowed apprehensively. 'Sir, I agreed to do it,' she confessed, 'please don't blame David or John for it.'

'That is not what I asked,' Sir Raeden corrected, his voice still unnervingly soft. 'Who came up with the idea to hold a race where you, a child placed under my guardianship, actually participated?'

A brief pause fell. Then, Rhiannon admitted reluctantly, 'It was Marcus Donahue.'

'I see. And in what manner was the race proposed by Mr Donahue?'

'Well, I guess he, that is to say ...' Rhiannon faltered to a stop, uncertain whether she should admit to the whole truth.

'He challenged her,' David answered truthfully and without hesitation, solving Rhiannon's dilemma. 'He made a comment about her being just a girl and that he could beat her in a real test of skill.'

'And you think that justifies her endangering her life, or risking permanent injury?' Sir Raeden asked almost casually.

'I knew Arastar would look after her and he did,' David said. 'Besides, it was just a race.'

'Just a race,' Sir Raeden repeated, and then again menacingly, 'just – a – race!'

SMACK!

David, Rhiannon and John flinched as Sir Raeden slammed his hand down on the desk, the unexpected move made all the more intimidating when he slowly rose out of his seat and straightened to his full towering height.

'It would have been foolhardy at any other time for her to have done anything so reckless with her limited experience in flying, no matter how much natural ability she may possess,' he said in a cold fury. 'But for you to have permitted this race to take place at this particular time of this year was the most irresponsible act I have ever had the misfortune to witness. Because of your lack of thought, and my ward's actions, she is now bound to participate in the Dragon's Cup.'

'B-But that's impossible!'

David's shocked exclamation, accompanied by John's horrified countenance, sent a chill straight down Rhiannon's spine.

'What's the Dragon's Cup?'

'It most certainly is not impossible,' Sir Raeden retorted sharply, ignoring Rhiannon's hesitant question as he stabbed at the scroll on his desk with one long finger. 'That is the notification given to all those who qualify. Because of her age, it was naturally delivered to me by the castle's postal faery the instant it was issued, to inform me of my ward's contractual obligation now that she had won a qualifying race.'

'But she's only thirteen,' John protested. 'Surely that would disqualify her?'

The anger in Sir Raeden's face did not lessen. 'As you know,' he bit out, 'any underage person who enters a qualifying race is presumed to have obtained the approval and consent of their parents or legal guardians – which, needless to say, is not often. The lack of my consent, unfortunately, is not sufficient grounds to break a contract of this nature. Not even Lady Endrille or King Stephen can intervene.'

'Does someone want to tell me what the Dragon's Cup actually is?'

Rhiannon's exasperated question had the three males in the room turning to stare down at her.

'The Dragon's Cup is a race which is held every thirteen years in mid-July,' Sir Raeden informed her curtly. 'It requires the human rider to have exceptional skill in flying, and the ability to think analytically and strategically to assist them in passing a set of obstacles and traps set up over a course that takes an entire day to complete.'

Rhiannon's forehead creased in a bewildered frown. 'But

I didn't even enter my name for it, so how could I have been accepted?'

'You entered your name the instant you participated in an official race between the First of January and the First of June this year,' Sir Raeden answered with a grim look at David and John. 'Something which these two imbeciles should have realised and prevented from happening.'

'But it was just a race between Marcus and me,' Rhiannon protested.

'It ceased to be a normal race when you fulfilled all the requirements to make it an official one,' Sir Raeden corrected. 'Firstly, you certainly had more than twenty witnesses present. Secondly, the course of the race would have been greater than thirty miles. Thirdly, knowing these two miscreants and Mr Donahue as I do, I have no doubt certain wagers were placed on the possible outcome of the race. Fourthly, you would have sworn you were not participating under any form of coercion and would acknowledge the results of the race to be binding. Lastly, and most importantly, you had present at the race a member of the Valieoth royal family.'

'And I can't pull out?' Rhiannon queried.

Sir Raeden shook his head. 'The agreement is a magical contract that exists between you and the charm the ancient dragons placed upon the actual Dragon's Cup, the trophy which is kept inside the palace and is only taken out on the day of the race. Nothing short of death will break it.' At Rhiannon's wide-eyed look of fear, he explained briefly, 'The ancient dragons take their oaths seriously, and by competing in and winning an official race you have physically sworn that oath and must now abide by it.'

'We're truly sorry, Rhiannon,' David said remorsefully. 'John and I should've realised what was taking place but we didn't think. We'll certainly help you with learning whatever Sir Raeden thinks necessary,' he quickly promised. 'And I know Endrille and Arastar will do everything they can to help as well.'

'We've still got just over five months,' John pointed out.

'That is hardly sufficient time in which to teach you all I would wish,' Sir Raeden told her bluntly. 'I will therefore rearrange your other lessons so the least important ones are removed from your timetable. The hours on the weekends when you would have been doing your chores will also be utilised. We can use all of those periods to work on the areas you need to strengthen. As for the lessons you will miss, you will just have to make up for them during the summer holidays once the race is over.'

Astonished, Rhiannon gazed up at her guardian. 'You mean you'll be teaching me?'

'I can think of no one I would trust more than myself to do it,' he replied shortly.

'Though I hate to admit it,' David interjected, 'he is the best one to train you, considering he won the last race that was held. He also holds the record for being the youngest to have ever done it.'

Rhiannon looked at Sir Raeden in awe.

'I certainly got the best guardian, didn't I,' she observed to no one in particular.

The glance David and John shared clearly communicated that despite Sir Raeden's achievements, they found her opinion debatable. Sir Raeden merely ignored the comment.

'Once I have reorganised your schedule, you will receive your new timetable. Considering the serious nature of these events, I expect you to show the appropriate respect towards the lessons I will be giving you by arriving promptly and doing the work without complaint.' Sir Raeden's warning tone promised the most unpleasant consequences should she fail to heed these instructions.

'Yes, Sir.'

Sir Raeden pointed towards the door.

'You're all dismissed,' he ordered tersely. 'However, I expect you two boys to inform your parents of your actions today. On this occasion, be thankful that as Rhiannon's guardian I am unable to choose your punishment.'

David, John and Rhiannon retreated in haste. The thick wooden door closed behind them with a decisive thud.

'In some ways I wish he could've punished us without our parents finding out what we did,' John remarked dismally. 'Mum's going to be so disappointed, and I hate to think what Dad will say.'

'I know what you mean,' David said with a heavy sigh. 'I'd rather have Mother make me do the most disgusting chore as punishment than give me that look she does when I've done something wrong.'

'Would it help if I told them you didn't encourage me to race against Marcus?' Rhiannon asked in concern.

David shook his head, giving her a rueful smile.

'It's nice of you to offer, but Wyvern is right,' he said. 'We should've remembered about the Dragon's Cup and put a stop to the race – or at least ensured that one of the criteria making it an official race wasn't fulfilled.'

Rhiannon was silent for a moment. Then, in a quiet voice laced with trepidation, she asked, 'Is the race really dangerous?'

'Some of the traps and obstacles can be a bit risky,' David admitted. 'John and I have obviously only ever read about the ones in the past. Although some people have been hurt, sometimes quite badly, no deaths have ever occurred. Also, with Sir Raeden's help, you'll be better prepared than some of the others who'll be entering.'

'Is he really the youngest person ever to have won it?'

John nodded. 'Before him, the youngest person was back in 1809, Arginald Stubbington who was twenty-six.'

'So how young was Sir Raeden?'

'If I remember correctly, one of the books say his birthday is the fifteenth of March.' David's eyebrows creased in concentration. 'So, he'd have been eighteen and a few months.'

'Just think, when you win the race, you'll beat his record,' John said with a grin, clearly in an attempt to lighten their spirits.

'I'll be happy just to finish it,' Rhiannon replied. 'And by the sounds of it I'm going to need all the help I can get to even do that much.'

Later that evening, when the silver moon was high in the night sky, Rhiannon's bedchamber was still aglow with light.

Unable to sleep, she lay reading on her bed. Her textbook, *The Art of Defence,* had seemed like a good choice for distracting her mind.

Golem

Creation of a golem is a very difficult and complex process and should only be attempted by highly skilled magi.

The golem is created entirely from inanimate matter, the most common materials being stone and clay. It is then animated, given life, with an inscription on the forehead of the ancient word 'emet' (meaning 'truth').

Some golems have successfully been animated by use of an 'inscription stone'. This is when the animating inscription is placed on an image of the golem carved into the source material whence it came. However, as the golem is unable to move beyond a distance of eighty feet from the inscription stone, this method of animation is rarely used.

Humanoid in appearance, but lacking all cognitive and emotional ability, a golem is nothing more than an animated statue. It is without conscience, and incapable of reason. If commanded to perform a task, it will carry out the instructions literally. It does not tire or feel pain, nor does it require nourishment. This, of course, makes it a perfect guard for an object to be protected or defended.

Once it has fulfilled its purpose, the golem can be destroyed by damaging the first letter of the inscription of 'emet', thus changing it to 'met' (meaning 'death').

'Rhiannon, are you still awake?'

The soft voice of Queen Maiwen calling her name through her bedchamber door had Rhiannon hastily sitting up.

'Rhiannon?'

'Please come in, Your Majesty,' she called, tossing the book aside and scrambling out from under the coverlet.

Queen Maiwen quietly pushed opened the door, then paused on the threshold. 'Oh, you were already in bed,' she said apologetically. 'I just wished to check on you.'

'It's all right. I really was awake. I couldn't get to sleep.'

'I am not surprised about that. David told me what happened when I returned home just now.'

Hearing the stern note in the woman's voice when she mentioned her son's name, Rhiannon hastily tried to explain.

'It wasn't his fault,' she said, 'Marcus challenged me to the race, and I accepted. David ...'

'Should have exercised a bit of common sense, remembered you have not yet been here a month, and put a stop to it,' Queen Maiwen interrupted her bluntly with a twinge of motherly annoyance in her voice. 'His forgetting about the Dragon's Cup is also inexcusable. He certainly has heard it mentioned several times in the past year.'

Queen Maiwen's shoulders suddenly fell, as though under a heavy weight. Then she walked across the room to sit down on Rhiannon's bed with a sigh.

'I'm sorry for my outburst, Rhiannon,' she said quietly. 'It is just the Dragon's Cup is no place for a young girl to be competing. Especially one so new to Álnair. I would not have had this happen to you for anything, my dear. The race is deliberately designed to test the skill and bravery of the participants, so some of the obstacles can be quite dangerous. And, I could not bear to see you hurt.'

Rhiannon heard the genuine concern in her voice and fought back a desire to cry. Patricia Dashmont had never come to sit with her like this, let alone said anything so maternal.

'Sir Raeden has said he'll help me,' she forced through a throat tight with emotion. 'I just hope I'm clever enough to remember what he teaches me.'

'He is an extremely talented man, and I am sure I can think of none better to instruct you,' Queen Maiwen admitted. 'And if I can be of any assistance, I am more than happy to help.' A small, proud smile appeared on her lips as she added, 'I was the champion duellist at Ryegoth Academy three years in a row in both magi and physical defence.'

Rhiannon stared at the beautiful woman beside her. A hint of amusement appeared on her face.

'I bet the boys loved that,' she said wryly. 'They probably thought they'd have to hold back when they first saw you.'

'The foolish among them certainly did, and then paid dearly for it.'

Her tone was serene, but Rhiannon saw an unmistakable glint of reminiscent satisfaction in the queen's eyes.

'To look at, I certainly was not the most intimidating opponent,' Queen Maiwen continued, 'in fact, I recall one exceptionally insufferable boy referring to me as The Ephemeral, implying I would not last long in the fight. I quickly showed him that there was another way to take that name. I trounced him completely in less than two minutes.'

She paused to smile at Rhiannon's snort of laughter.

'People underestimated me,' she went on, 'and I proved them wrong in their assumptions. My own fears for your safety aside, I believe you perfectly capable of learning everything you're taught to succeed in finishing this race. Do not let the doubts of others, or your own uncertainties, make this race more difficult than it already will be.'

Rhiannon cast her eyes down to stare at her lap. There was a large lump in her throat that was making it difficult to swallow.

'Thank you, Your Majesty,' she whispered, then found herself wrapped in a quick embrace.

'You're an intelligent, brave, young lady,' Queen Maiwen said as she pulled away, 'and the descendant of Mórell, the greatest female mage of the O'Faenart clan. Hold your head up high and be resolute in your purpose. Now, I have delayed you from sleeping long enough, and you shall need plenty of rest to get through the coming months.'

She got up and walked towards the door, then looked back.

'Rhiannon? "Your Majesty" is such a formal title to use in these private conservations. I think Lady Maiwen will do,' she said warmly. 'Goodnight, my dear.'

And then she was gone.

Rhiannon got back under the coverlet and lay down. The visit by the queen had been a surprise, but a pleasant one. She had not made light of the danger involved in the race and yet, her words had eased the tense knot of steel that had been squeezing her stomach.

For the first time since learning she would be participating in the race, she felt that she would survive it.

'How is Rhiannon going to survive this?'

In the study of David's grand apartments at the opposite end of the Upper South Wing, John glanced up from his contemplation of the King's Table board to look at his prince.

'Wyvern will ensure she's prepared,' he said.

David turned away from the window, not looking the least bit reassured. A worried frown creased his forehead, and John could see the dark shadows that had appeared in his eyes after speaking to his mother lingering.

'I know he will, but she's only human. She's going to find the next couple of months horrendous with all the study she'll have to do, not to mention all the training Wyvern's going to be giving her.' David sighed. 'Mother was right, I was negligent and irresponsible. None of this would've happened if I'd stopped the race.'

'David, you can hardly take all the blame,' John pointed out reasonably. 'I was there, and I should've remembered about the Dragon's Cup. Izana certainly would've if he'd been there! I also could've tried harder to prevent the race instead of just asking Rhiannon if she was sure she wanted to do it. Quite honestly, though, she really had the bit between her teeth, and I don't think either of us would've been able to persuade her not to do it.'

A brief glint of admiration flickered in David's eyes.

'She was determined to beat him, wasn't she? I don't think I've ever understood how someone's eyes could flash fire, but hers certainly did when she glared at Marcus. She's quite something when she gets all fired up like that.'

'Definitely eye-catching,' said John, hiding the amused smile that rose to his lips. Despite the many females who had chased after David since he was old enough to be interested in them, he had never given any of them more than a cursory glance. Now, he was noticing how Rhiannon looked when she was angry!

'And with her study and training, we did say we would help her,' John continued. 'I'm sure between us we can prevent her from getting too overwhelmed.'

'I suppose,' David said. 'I just hate to think of her being put under so much pressure when she should be enjoying her first year here. I only hope there's no other surprise waiting for her.'

'I cannot help but be uneasy about this,' King Stephen confessed.

He leant back into the armchair set before the warm fire in Sir Raeden's personal antechamber. His regular nightly meetings to receive the Commander of the Guard's report, coupled with having known him from the time Raeden was a boy of seven, had led to a singular informality between them when out of sight of others.

He took a sip of wine from the fine goblet in his hand, then looked at the man to whom he had entrusted the training of his son and the safety of the only daughter of Mórell's line.

'The girl is very young and after reading some of the reports I have received, it's possible the faction on Malpars may be plotting to cause trouble during the race.'

Sir Raeden shook his head.

'They would not dare to anger Lady Endrille,' he declared. 'I have observed the members of the group. Underneath their bravado they are a spineless, malingering pack of fools who lack any true conviction. The only way they would ever take any form of action against anyone was if they were roused by a highly motivated leader.'

'And what of the "marked darkness"?' King Stephen asked. 'Do we yet know to whom that refers?'

'There are several prisoners on Culhos who bear a mark they placed upon themselves, but none have exhibited any unusual behaviour. There is also the possibility it refers to an exile still living in Mérosorc.' Sir Raeden paused, then said, 'Sire, the second part of the prophecy was not explicitly linked to Rhiannon; in fact, I believe the mention of her arrival in the first part was merely to serve as a sign that the other would soon come to pass. However, I do share your misgivings about these events, particularly as there will be times in the future when Rhiannon will be vulnerable. Therefore, I seek your permission, and that of the Trínondras, to instruct my ward in those charms I deem necessary for her to adequately protect herself should the need arise.'

King Stephen did not hesitate in giving his approval to this proposal.

'I know there is no one better qualified to instruct her,' he said. 'I will speak with Lord Anton and Caiden Alcober in the morning and explain the circumstances to them. I am sure they will not withhold their consent. And let us just hope we are both suffering from excessive paranoia, and the only dangers Rhiannon shall face will be the carefully devised and controlled ones in the race.'

Chapter 20

OF POTIONS
AND PLOTS

Inside the dense woodland of the mountain, a malevolent aura surrounded a small stone building.

His body heavily cloaked, Mórfran moved towards its heavy wooden door with arrogant confidence.

He pushed the door open and stepped into a scene of chaos.

Tall jars containing an assortment of specimens were placed haphazardly upon a long bench.

Scrunched up pieces of paper lay scattered around the room.

Amid the complex paraphernalia atop the tables spread throughout the room, the foul smelling contents of several cauldrons bubbled and hissed.

At one table stood the hunched-over figure of a man. He too was heavily cloaked, and the shadows in the room concealed his face. Suddenly, he picked up a bottle, then threw it against the wall.

The glass exploded in a shower of glinting blue shards.

'This is useless! The potion is not strong enough!' he shouted.

'Another failure? I thought you said it would work this time?'

Mórfran's harsh voice had the intended effect. The other

man nearly jumped out of his skin. Hastily, he turned towards his visitor.

'M … Mórfran! I did not expect you here so soon!'

Mórfran kicked the door closed and strode forward. 'Clearly you did not,' he bit out. 'Now, why have you not completed the potion?'

The man nervously stepped back. 'Nothing's powerful enough,' he rattled off in a panic. 'Even the combined magic in the Dragonstars was too weak to counteract the binding enchantment. I need something with an exceptionally strong magical core, but there isn't one!'

'There is one, you misbegotten fool,' Mórfran snapped. 'Must I do all the thinking for you? What will finally be taken out this year and displayed for all of Álnair to see?'

The other man gaped at him. 'You don't mean … how could I … it's impossible!' he exclaimed in horror.

'It is possible,' Mórfran snarled, 'and you will do it. The Dragon's Cup contains more magic power than a thousand Dragonstars. Your connection to the House of Valieoth should make your taking possession of it easy enough, or you can get your snake of an assistant at the palace to help. I want that potion perfected before the first moon of August rises. And it had better work. He is getting extremely impatient to be released.'

Chapter 21

A GIFT FOR
SIR RAEDEN

The astonishing news of Rhiannon's participation in the Dragon's Cup spread swiftly through the palace. Curious stares followed her wherever she went and while most people wished her luck, there were some who did not, Marcus Donahue being the most notable among them.

'It's hardly worth making a wager on where you'll come in the race,' he taunted outside the school on Monday morning. 'You're sure to come in last. In fact, I doubt you'll even make it past the first challenge.'

'If you're so sure about that then I'll bet you ten gold pieces that she does make it past the first, and all the others,' declared Rolfe Zemit.

'Same here,' chorused a few of the other boys.

Marcus sneered at them. 'I don't gamble with those inferior to me, especially not over someone like her.' He shot Rhiannon a look of utter disdain. 'A dull, untalented girl with no looks to speak of and whose parents probably died to get away from her.'

With a sound like that of a wounded animal, Rhiannon flew at him. Rage made her clumsy, forgetting all she had been taught in the previous few weeks. Her hands lashed out in uncoordinated attacks.

An unmanly squeal escaped her tormentor's lips. They both crashed onto the icy, snow-covered ground in a tangle of flailing limbs.

People were shouting.

Hands were desperately pulling her back.

A sharp pain lanced across her cheek.

Something trickled down her face.

Rhiannon barely registered the gentle warmth encompassing the wound as it healed. Her gaze locked on Marcus' face, on the vindictive glint in his eyes, as she was lifted bodily away from him.

Arms enfolded her from behind, pressing her tightly against a hard torso.

Rhiannon struggled, but the arms were a steel vice about her.

'Easy,' David's voice urged in a soothing tone above her head.

'He said ... my parents didn't ...'

'I know.'

Marcus rose unsteadily to his feet. 'I'm going to ...'

'Do nothing,' interpolated the quiet voice of Izana Sato, 'except go and tidy yourself up before Sir Raeden arrives.'

Marcus glared at the Robesman's composed face. 'She attacked me and I'm going to see she gets punished for it!'

'Will this be before or after you confess your cruel words to her?' Izana turned and Rhiannon saw his eyes carefully examine her cheek. 'Or before or after you confess your own action in striking her across the face and drawing her blood with your ring?' he added. 'You may be sure Sir Raeden will not overlook your behaviour towards his ward. She may be reprimanded for her actions, but you will undoubtedly receive a harsher punishment for instigating the fight.'

'And for not showing proper restraint in defending yourself

against a less experienced opponent,' David stated coldly. 'Her emotions were affecting her skills to the extent you could easily have defended yourself without harming her, but you didn't. So, you can either wait here and let Wyvern see you looking like a damp rag and accept the punishment he'll give you, or do as Izana said and go tidy yourself up before he comes.'

Marcus gave no answer, but with a glare of vehement dislike at his cousin he turned and stalked away, closely followed by Felix and several other students.

'If I loosen my hold, do you promise not to chase after him?'

At David's question, Rhiannon gave a small nod. A moment later she was free and facing him.

'You had best go and clean your face,' David suggested. 'It won't do to have Wyvern seeing you like this. Also,' he looked down at her gown which thanks to the snow, was sodden in patches and clinging to her body. '*Astarai*,' he murmured.

A stream of dull red light flowed from his hand to envelop the wet fabric. Rhiannon felt the glow of heat drying out the material in less than a second.

'Wyvern will arrive soon, so you'd best be quick,' John warned.

Her emotions still making it difficult to control her voice, Rhiannon mutely nodded. She turned away, only to pause when David gently laid his hand on her arm.

'I'm sorry Marcus hurt you, and I don't just mean his cutting your cheek,' he said. 'That poisonous tongue of his can inflict more painful wounds than any physical weapon. Just remember what he said about you and your parents was nothing more than the vile musings of a spiteful mind without an ounce of truth in it.'

A warm spark entered the swirling mess of emotions inside Rhiannon's chest. Tears sprang to her eyes. The tight constriction in her throat eased. She looked at David's earnest expression and a tremulous smile of gratitude quivered on her lips.

'Thank you,' she whispered. Then, before the first tear could fall, she spun away and fled to the girls' bathroom in the school.

It did not take long to wash the blood from her cheek, but tidying her hair was another matter. Marcus had pulled some of it from the careful style Aleda had arranged that morning and the loose tendrils hung in disarray about her face. It was times like this that she really missed the convenience of elastic hairbands. Rhiannon sighed and removed the last pins from her hair. As the mass of ringlets tumbled down her back, she glanced in the mirror to see the reflection of the bathroom door opening.

A wave of apprehension crashed over her upon seeing several girls led by Leila Hardinge enter and look straight at her. The last time a group of girls had sought her out in a school bathroom was in Vetus svet, and that had ended with Rhiannon curled up in pain on the floor with the contents of her school bag in the bin. Leila's friendly behaviour after the race on Saturday was no guarantee she had no cause for alarm. Girls often behaved differently in front of boys than when among themselves.

Warily, Rhiannon turned around, the hairpins clutched in her hand. Feeling trapped, she flicked her eyes towards the door.

'You really should be more careful.'

The ominous words came from Viola Rastell, the tall, freckled redhead standing behind Leila.

Rhiannon stiffened, her body preparing for the attack that in her experience usually followed the seemingly innocuous greeting.

'If you're going to fight someone, you should always do it with a clear head. Getting emotional only makes your form sloppy and your technique miserably ineffective.' Viola shook her head. 'And I was so hoping to see Donahue with a bloody nose. Next time, control your emotions, Rhiannon, and punch the smirk right off that little troll's face.'

Wait. What?

Rhiannon stared from one girl to the other. To her shock, the glares she was expecting to encounter were missing. In their place were only various looks of concern and support.

'Are you all right?' Innogen Calloway, a petite brunette with very fair skin, stepped closer, a worried expression in her wide blue eyes.

'Of course she's not all right,' Leila exclaimed. 'Marcus was always a nasty toad with a barbed tongue, and to say what he did about her parents was viciously cruel.' She turned back to Rhiannon. 'If it wouldn't mean getting you in trouble with Sir Raeden, I'd tell him exactly what that pasty-faced muckworm said to you. When he said it, I wanted to cover him in hogsbane sap, then put stinging nettles in his mouth, then ...'

'Leila, we don't have time for you to daydream about which of your precious plants would inflict the worst pain on him,' Viola interrupted. 'The bell's already been rung, which means Sir Raeden will be here in less than three minutes. And I'm sure if we're not back down in two minutes, Prince David will be here ten seconds later wanting to know what's wrong. He's very worried about you,' she added as an aside to Rhiannon. 'Now come on, let's get you fixed up.'

To Rhiannon's astonishment, she found herself bustled onto a low bench as the group of girls swiftly arranged her hair into a series of tidy braids encircling her head. The experience was so surreal she had to pinch herself to make sure she wasn't dreaming.

Exactly one minute and thirty seconds later, she descended the stairs accompanied by the other girls in time to see Sir Raeden arrive on the transonus dais. He brusquely returned their greeting, then handed Rhiannon a tidily bound scroll.

'Your new schedule,' he informed her. 'I trust you will abide by it without complaint.'

Upon hearing this, Rhiannon immediately knew her preparation for the Dragon's Cup was going to be horrendous.

For Rhiannon, the next few weeks passed at a tremendous speed. Her days were filled with flying sessions with Arastar and working diligently on the subjects listed in the new timetable provided to her by Sir Raeden.

When she first looked over the new schedule, she thought he had made a mistake. Only five of her original twelve classes were on it, with all the other timeslots now taken over by specialised lessons he would be giving her. But, as time passed, she realised that although she was now only studying Defence, Herblore, Languages, Magical Application & Control and Natural Science & Philosophy with the other students, she was actually still learning a few things relating to the other subjects in her lessons with Sir Raeden, particularly Creatures & Beasts.

She arrived at his office one morning in February to discover he had decided to tell her about a creature that dwelt in the Del Enger Mountains.

'Basilisks, which are the largest form of burrowing serpents, can be found hiding throughout the mountains,' he said, 'and you may come across one during the section of the race that occurs inside Mount Solus. They are immense in size but extremely timid creatures that are more likely to retreat in terror than attack upon seeing you. However, if one feels sufficiently threatened, it may be frightened enough to strike. And despite its head being the size of a small pony's, they do not particularly like the smell of human flesh, so you need not be afraid of being eaten by one. They much prefer rats and other small rodents.

'There was a time, before the pathways were closed, when a virulent rumour was set about in Vetus svet that they were capable of killing people who looked into their eyes. A small group had come to visit Álnair, and unfortunately one of their number, a healthy young man, dropped dead upon seeing the size of the serpent they encountered. The group's other members put it about that the serpent had developed the ability to kill with its stare. When the Time of Persecution came, the lie had grown and was perpetuated by those slaying the dragons. They claimed the dragons were amassing an army of basilisks, intending to use them against the clans.

'Of course, their accusation was all moonshine on the water,' he continued. 'The eyes of a basilisk are no more deadly than mine.'

The last comment elicited an internal snigger from Rhiannon.

He could certainly petrify someone with one glare, she thought. He made most of the students cringe with a single lift of his eyebrow, and one of his smirks generally made them wonder how quickly they could tell their friends goodbye.

'Just remain still and wait until it retreats before moving again,' Sir Raeden said, recalling her attention to him.

'Don't worry; not moving when face to face with a basilisk will not be a problem,' she said truthfully. 'What else could I come across?'

Sir Raeden waved dismissively. 'There are several others but being winged creatures, they tend to remain outside the mountain, such as the phoenix.'

'Phoenix!' Rhiannon exclaimed. 'So they actually exist as well?'

'I would not have mentioned the name if they did not,' Sir Raeden said brusquely.

'What are they like?'

Sir Raeden appeared to be on the point of refusing her request, but then he looked down at her face. Whether he could see the honest curiosity in her eyes, or he was just feeling magnanimous, she would never know, but his voice had lost some of its harshness when he next spoke.

'They are very intelligent and have a developed sense of self.

They are quite large, with a wingspan of seven feet, and they are predominantly red and gold in colour. They can fly like normal birds, but can also disappear in a burst of flames, which is why a phoenix feather will protect you from any kind of fire. The feathers are highly sought-after as they enhance the potency of various elixirs. However, they are exceedingly difficult to acquire.'

Rhiannon frowned. 'Why?'

'A phoenix will only ever give a feather to those they feel are worthy of receiving it, therefore, the feathers are extremely rare. It is considered a high honour to receive one.'

Sir Raeden then put an end to the discussion by announcing it was time to work on her mage abilities, specifically the charm to make herself invisible and its countercharm. Rhiannon was not sure what sort of obstacles she would come up against that would require the use of the charm – unless she had to go up against a Tyrannosaurus Rex!

Two hours later, Rhiannon left her guardian's office on legs which felt like jelly. The Aoratos Charm and its counter did not require her to do anything physically strenuous, but the mental effort required to control the charm had made her drowsy. The tonic Sir Raeden had provided to restore her depleted energy levels was also slow in taking effect.

When her foot slipped on a patch of marble floor, her exhausted reflexes were too sluggish to respond promptly.

Rhiannon flung out her arms as she stumbled, then gasped when she felt two strong hands catch hold of her shoulders.

'Thank you,' she said as the same hands maintained their grip until she regained her balance. She looked up and found herself gazing at the ash-blond hair and brown eyes of Izana Sato.

The Robesman stepped back and bowed his head slightly.

'Are you hurt?'

Izana's voice was pitched quite low, and Rhiannon realised in some surprise that his question was the most personal thing he had ever said to her.

'I'm fine, just a bit off-balance,' she replied. 'I had a lesson with Sir Raeden.'

'Then your lack of equilibrium is understandable.'

Rhiannon grimaced. 'It seems to be a common thing these days,' she sighed, and in a burst of tired exasperation declared, 'I just can't seem to control my power properly so I end up releasing too much, and then I get exhausted. I keep practising, but nothing seems to work!'

Izana regarded her briefly, then suggested with no inflection in his voice, 'There is a mixture of herbs that when brewed and consumed can temporarily help regulate the release of magical energy. You can procure it from the apothecary in Cendillis, or from the Chief Herbalist here in the palace.'

Even before he finished speaking, Rhiannon was shaking her head.

'No, thank you. I'd prefer to get it right myself without having to use something like that. If I used the herbs once, I'd probably keep doing it and never learn how to control my power without an aid.'

Izana stared down at her for a moment, examining her intently. Unexpectedly, a glint of approval shone in his eyes and a small hint of a smile breached his reserved expression.

'You do not give up easily when faced with a difficult challenge,' he observed. 'I see now why David admires you.'

Rhiannon felt a flame of colour flood her cheeks.

Izana ignored her embarrassment and gestured towards a nearby chair. 'Come, sit down. I'll teach you the technique my grandfather taught me. Are you comfortable? Good. Now, close your eyes and control your breathing. Each breath should be slow and even. Next, picture in your mind the slow-burning flame of a candle. Each tiny flicker of the fire is the amount of energy you need to release. Too much power, and the flame will be extinguished. Let the energy flow from you, like small wafts of smoke. Now, try the charm Sir Raeden was showing you.'

Rhiannon focused on the mental image of the lighted candle. The flame burned steadily and slowly. Then this was overlapped by the grey miasma Sir Raeden had told her to visualise prior to saying *aoratos*.

Rhiannon whispered the charm.

Izana's eyes widened slightly when her body disappeared. He had expected Sir Raeden to have taught her a simple Grade 2 charm, which he could easily undo if required, not a Grade 10 Level 12 charm that only the ruling family and the most trusted of their guards were taught – and then only with the approval of the Trínondras! He just hoped she knew the countercharm as well.

'Very good,' he said softly, being careful to modulate his voice so as not to break her concentration. 'Now, I want you to say the countercharm after I count to ten. Focus on the flame of the candle in your mind and breathe.'

Rhiannon listened as Izana slowly counted out the numbers. She didn't feel tired or strained like before.

'Ten,' Izana said clearly.

Rhiannon pictured the grey miasma evaporating, and whispered, '*Horatos*.'

Her body reappeared in the flicker of an eye.

'Well done,' Izana said sincerely. 'If you practise all your charms using that technique, they will become easier to do. You can also use it to focus your concentration before a sparring match.'

Rhiannon gave him a grateful smile. 'Thanks, Izana. This'll be a big help.'

The Robesman hesitated for a moment, then offered with aloof kindness, 'If I may be of further assistance to you during your training for the race, I would be happy to provide it. I know you must already have a surfeit of people helping you, but my skill with a blade and my knowledge in various areas are at your disposal.'

'I certainly won't turn down any offer of help,' Rhiannon told him, 'and I am grateful to you for giving up your free time for my benefit.'

'My Lord Prince's peace of mind is important to me,' Izana said with an enigmatic look on his face, 'I only apologise it has taken me so long to volunteer my services to you.'

Rhiannon smiled. 'It hasn't been that long. And even had it been the day before the race, I would still appreciate the offer. Thank you, Izana.'

Izana heard the ring of truth in her voice, and it drew from him something only a select few had been privileged to see on him – a genuine smile.

'I would hold off expressing your gratitude until you have survived your first sparring session with me,' he told her in a rare display of humour. 'I am accounted to be a rather fine swordsman, and I will not coddle you.'

'I don't want or ask to be coddled,' Rhiannon retorted.

'No, that is obvious,' Izana conceded, then added in a soft murmur as he turned away, 'And it's becoming clearer that's one of the reasons why he likes you.'

By the time the chill of winter had slowly faded into the glorious first colours of spring, Rhiannon felt as though she had already participated in a dozen races. Each week brought a new meaning to the word 'exhausted' when she was called upon to use her newly acquired knowledge to defeat a host of challenges devised by Sir Raeden.

David, John and Izana kept their word by helping her when

their own schedules permitted, and on several occasions David and John offered to miss their more tedious lessons to assist her. As was to be expected, on those occasions, Sir Raeden sent them away with an icy glare and a few caustic words.

Her guardian was relentless in his training of her, unwilling to overlook even the smallest error. However, Rhiannon found he could also be very patient, even considerate, when she genuinely struggled to understand or perform what he was trying to teach her. Rather than insulting her when she made a mistake, Sir Raeden would quietly correct her, or slowly show her the move again until she had it right.

After one particularly difficult lesson on counteracting concealing enchantments in Sir Raeden's office, she extracted a small box from the inside pocket of her robes. Nervously, she placed it in front of her guardian as he was gathering the books off his desk.

Sir Raeden cast a brief glance at it, then turned his head to look at her. 'What is this?' he asked.

'It's a ...' Rhiannon paused to clear her throat. Taking a deep breath, she announced, 'It's a gift. For you.'

'A gift?' Sir Raeden frowned and stared down at the box again as though he expected it to suddenly attack him. 'Why are you giving me a gift? If you are seeking to bribe me into allowing you to miss your next class ...'

'Of course not!' Rhiannon huffed indignantly. 'I just wanted to say thank you for all the help you're giving me, and ... well, that is ... it's also, sort of, a birthday present.'

An awkward silence fell when Sir Raeden did not respond to this revelation.

Rhiannon shifted uncomfortably, glancing uncertainly at the gift.

'Look, I didn't mean to offend you or anything,' she said, 'and if you don't want it I'll take it back.'

Reaching out, she went to pick up the box when Sir Raeden's voice stopped her.

'How did you know today is my birthday?'

'David told me.'

'And you actually bought me a gift?' Sir Raeden sounded puzzled over this fact.

'Why wouldn't I?' Rhiannon asked, bewildered in her turn. 'You're my guardian, and you've done nothing but help me since I arrived here. I tried to find something you'd like, but since I haven't known you very long, I've probably guessed wrong, so if you don't want it I can take it back, and ...'

'Thank you.'

The quiet words of gratitude made Rhiannon fall silent.

'It was a very kind thought, and I will not insult you by refusing to accept it.'

A warm smile spread across Rhiannon's face at his words. Then she watched hopefully as Sir Raeden picked up the box and opened the lid.

Sir Raeden's expression betrayed none of his thoughts when he lifted out the clear crystal phial that lay nestled inside the box. He examined its contents closely.

'This is purified entrose,' he said, 'it is almost impossible to procure due to the plant's scarcity, and the fact they can only be found in the Aidan Desert. How did you come by it?'

'I told the apothecary in Cendillis I needed it and he found it for me. He seemed quite eager to do it. But don't worry, I had John's mother with me at the time,' Rhiannon hastily added, 'I knew he couldn't let me have it unless an adult came with me. I read it was used in specialised healing potions, and after David told me you were awarded the Imperial Order of Merit for not only Defence, but for your research in Natural Science and Herblore, I thought you might be able to use it.'

Sir Raeden replaced the phial back in the box.

'You chose well, Rhiannon, it is an extremely useful gift,' he observed quietly. 'Now, you had best get along to your next class.'

'Yes, Sir.'

Rhiannon turned away but had only made it a few steps when her guardian spoke again.

'And, McBride, your pronunciation of the countercharm is to be perfect for next time,' he said sternly.

With an internal groan at the return of his teacher voice, Rhiannon looked back at her guardian. 'And if it's not?' she asked curiously.

His expression one of grim humour, Sir Raeden declared, 'Then I guess you will not be seeing your belongings again after I cast a concealment charm on them.'

Rhiannon sighed. 'I thought it'd be something like that, though I hadn't expected you to forewarn me, Sir.'

Sir Raeden gave a brief smile. 'Consider it a token of my thanks for your gift,' he said. 'Now, off you go.'

Rhiannon did not wait to be told again. She hurried out of the room, determined to have the countercharm of *undolthgare* perfected by the end of the day.

In her initial haste, she forgot to close the door. Quietly retracing her steps, she looked into the room to see Sir Raeden lower his head and place a hand over his left shoulder, as though to ease an old injury. The unexpected vulnerability of the gesture shocked her. Without a word, she swiftly retreated, unwilling to discover what her proud guardian's reaction would be to being observed in a moment of weakness.

~*Chapter 22*~

SWORDFIGHTS AND
CHARMS

hiannon lunged forward, the sword in her hand slashing towards the ground with a sharp hiss.

Sweat dripped down her face in icy rivulets.

Her breath came in deep, harsh gasps that created white puffs of mist in the late-night air.

The large enclosed area of the castle's inner courtyard was bathed in the soft glow of the golden lamps lining the tiered colonnades, and the silver moon was fully risen in the dark sky.

With a grim look of resolution on her face, Rhiannon dismissed the late hour as unimportant.

She retook her stance to begin another set of drills. There were only five days left until the end of March, and she was determined to perfect her technique before the first day of April.

The water fountain in the middle of the courtyard lay silent, and the stillness of night surrounded her as she inhaled deeply.

Her eyes focused on the space in front of her.

The sword in her hand sliced through the air.

She would get this right – even if it meant forgoing sleep for several days.

'Is that the time?'

David's startled exclamation as he looked at his watch broke the silence of his private study in the Upper South Wing. He stood up hurriedly from behind his desk. 'Izana, you should've gone home ages ago!'

His rostered Robesman for the month looked up from the book in his hand. 'I don't mind staying to help you, especially when you've got official work to do for your father, although you shouldn't need my help much longer with preparing those draft reports. You are getting much better at them.'

'Thanks to you.'

'Nonsense. You would've worked it out eventually. I know for a fact you're quite intelligent.'

David smirked. 'Now you sound like my mother.'

'I shall take that as a compliment,' Izana said placidly, and closed his book. 'As tomorrow's Saturday, would you like me to come a bit later in the morning?'

'It's almost midnight! You don't think I'm letting you go home now?' David said in astonishment. 'You're staying here tonight. The guest chambers are always ready, so you can sleep in one of them.'

'David, I'm not an inexperienced rider,' Izana pointed out. 'I'll be fine.'

'Oh, I know you'll be fine. I'm just worried about Regina. I wouldn't want her to sprain a fetlock stumbling in the dark.'

'I might've known it was my horse's welfare that concerned you.'

David grinned. 'Well, she is a lovely mare. But all jokes aside, it's too late for you to set out. One of the House Faeries can take a message to your parents and fetch anything you'll need for tomorrow.'

'Very well,' Izana conceded, then added with a small smile, 'and since I'll already be here, we can get in an early sparring session. It's been a while since we had a proper one.'

'How about we do it now? I'm not feeling very tired and I could use the exercise after sitting at this desk for so long.'

'Not to mention you'd prefer to sleep in,' came Izana's dry response as he opened the door.

'There is that too,' David remarked, and led the way out of his study.

At the main armoury, David and Izana greeted the guards on duty, selected their training swords from the assortment of weapons then went through the doors to the south balcony overlooking the inner courtyard. The guards positioned inside the colonnade stood in mute silence as they walked by them.

Approaching the staircase leading to the open quadrangle below, they paused upon hearing the rhythmic tap of booted feet on solid pavement.

A glance over the stone balustrade revealed a familiar figure clad in tunic, shirt and breeches determinedly moving through a series of drill exercises.

The mass of ringlets on the person's head was unmistakeable. 'Rhiannon.'

David's low voice went unheard by the girl in the courtyard. Izana, however, cast him a sideways glance, then studied him intently.

Feeling his Robesman's scrutiny but choosing to ignore it, David leant on the balustrade, his gaze focused on Rhiannon. Admiration flowed through him as he watched her go through each of the drills, and he smiled upon observing the improvement she had made since her very first lesson.

But then he narrowed his eyes in concern.

'Her form is off slightly. Look at the slant of her shoulders. She's exhausting herself.'

He hurriedly made for the stairs with Izana right behind him.

Rhiannon was so intent on her exercises that she did not hear them coming. Then they were right behind her.

'Rhiannon.'

She spun around with a startled gasp on hearing David's voice. Her sword-wielding hand dropped to her side.

'David! Izana! What're you doing here?'

'The better question is, why are you? It's past midnight, and you look like you've been here for hours.'

'I needed to practise.'

'There's practice, and then there's working yourself into the ground,' David told her. 'You look completely worn out. Tiredness won't help you learn proper form. You need to go to bed.'

'But I have to keep practising,' Rhiannon insisted. 'The race is only a few months away, and I completely failed the test Sir Raeden gave me today.'

'You're pushing yourself too hard. And if you want to do the moves properly, you don't practise them when you're so tired you can't tell when you make a mistake.'

'It's true, Rhiannon,' said Izana. 'If you repeatedly perform a move incorrectly it will become difficult to unlearn it, and when you fight you cannot afford to make mistakes. Also, when you're tired it decreases your reaction time. If you're willing, I will demonstrate. From our sessions, and what I have observed during Defence class, I know how quickly you can move. I want you to try and defeat me in a duel.'

'Izana,' David began, only to have his Robesman cut him off with, 'I won't use my full speed.'

Rhiannon frowned. 'Why not? If you're wanting to make a point, do it properly.'

Izana looked at her, then nodded. 'All right. David will give the signal.'

His expression still one of concern, David reluctantly stepped back. 'Just be careful,' he said.

Rhiannon and Izana wordlessly took their positions, then turned to face David.

Looking up at the colonnade above them, David saw a few curious guards turn around to watch, and on the third balcony the faint outline of a girl with a cloud of dark curls peering down at them from the shadows.

Suspecting who the female observer was and more importantly, who she would be wanting to win, David looked at Izana and gave a slight tilt of his head. Izana glanced briefly at the third balcony and David saw a small smile appear on his lips.

When his Robesman returned his attention to him, David lifted his sword.

Izana and Rhiannon turned to face each other.

David's eyes flickered between the two combatants. He mentally counted to ten. Then, in a swift cutting motion, he brought his sword down and called, 'Begin!'

With the speed of a striking cobra, Izana attacked.

Rhiannon barely managed to deflect his first blow before she was disarmed and the rounded point of Izana's sword was pushed against her shoulder. Her shock clear, she stared up into his stern brown eyes.

'If you were not tired, you would have lasted ten seconds longer,' Izana said quietly. 'In our normal sparring sessions, when I have adjusted my speed to suit your level of experience, you manage to hold your own for over two minutes. At the moment, you would be incapable of surviving more than thirty seconds. Your body is weary, and your instincts are dulled by exhaustion. You achieve nothing by continuing to practise in such a state.'

David walked up and placed a hand on Rhiannon's shoulder.

'There's no shame in admitting your body needs rest,' he said. 'All of us get to that point. Sometimes, continuing to train when fatigue first appears does help increase your stamina, but to push yourself to the point where you're ready to collapse is foolish. It can also damage your health. If you want extra training, just ask me, John or Izana. Or even Wyvern! An hour with us will do you more good than several by yourself.'

Rhiannon looked from him to Izana, her face a stubborn mask.

David, genuinely concerned she would insist on continuing with her late-night activity, gave her shoulder a gentle squeeze. 'Please, Rhiannon. Get some rest.'

There was a brief silence. Then Rhiannon's shoulders slumped, as though the sword in her hand had suddenly gained fifty pounds.

'All right. I'll stop – for now.'

David smiled. Reaching out, he took the sword from her hand. 'If you want to watch Izana and I spar, you can rest on one of the steps over there. Otherwise, we could walk you to your chamber before we start.'

Rhiannon shook her head. 'It's fine. I'll stay and watch. Who knows, I might learn something.'

Once she had sat down, David and Izana got into position. They faced each other on the eastern side of the courtyard, and Rhiannon observed them as they bowed then lifted their swords. Apart from the controlled environment of Defence class, and the slow demonstrations in her private lessons, she had not seen a proper sparring match.

For a long moment, neither David nor Izana moved. They eyed each other carefully, gauging their movements for the slightest twitch.

Then they both attacked.

Rhiannon blinked at their speed.

The wooden swords were a blur as they cracked against each other in a series of lightning blows.

Izana aimed a low swipe at David's feet. David jumped to avoid it, then retaliated with a fierce strike at Izana's back. The blow was parried at the last moment.

Rhiannon's eyes widened as the fight continued. David and Izana were not holding back in their attacks, and their speed was phenomenal. They moved with lithe grace upon the hard pavement, each seeking to gain an advantage over the other.

Rhiannon gasped.

Izana's sword slashed towards David's face. A perfect block and a counterattack put him back on the defensive. A misdirection by the Robesman had them back to trading fast blows.

The fight went on, and Rhiannon could only marvel at the stamina of the combatants. They struck and parried, blocked and attacked. But even after half an hour, no victory could be claimed by either of them.

Then, Rhiannon's heart leapt into her throat.

David lunged forward, directly into the path of Izana's sword. But then he sidestepped and his own sword smacked against Izana's stomach.

The Robesman gasped, all the breath knocked out of him.

A cry of concern came from the girl on the third balcony.

'Hit acknowledged,' Izana wheezed with a bow. 'Well done.'

David bowed in return, his own breathing deep and heavy. 'Now, we're even,' he panted, smiling.

'Until next time.'

Using the back of their hands, they wiped the sweat from their brows. Then they both turned towards Rhiannon as she walked up to them.

'That was incredible!' she exclaimed. 'And now I know how much you've both been holding back when sparring with me. But why didn't you use any charms?'

'Sometimes we have to rely only on our physical skill rather than our mage abilities,' said David.

'As Sir Raeden has mentioned before, you may find yourself in a situation where you can't use magic,' Izana added, 'and if you've become too dependent upon it you'll be at a severe disadvantage. Therefore, it's best to vary the types of sparring sessions so you never become too complacent with just one style.'

'I'd love to see you spar using your mage abilities.'

At Rhiannon's comment, David looked at Izana. 'Are you up for it?'

His Robesman nodded. 'However, we'll put a limit of ten minutes on it.' He pointed to the large clock over the top central archway in the northern colonnades. 'We'll stop at 1 o'clock.'

'Agreed.' David turned to Rhiannon. 'Make sure you stay here and don't move,' he warned her. 'We need to know your location, so we don't accidentally send a charm in your direction.'

'I'll stay right here,' she promised.

Satisfied, David and Izana took up their previous positions. Their swords had been left with Rhiannon, and yet she thought they both looked as formidable as they had before.

She glanced up to see all the guards spread throughout the colonnades looking down to watch the duel between the two magi. The girl on the balcony was clutching the balustrade, her head turned in the direction of the Robesman.

Rhiannon returned her attention to David and Izana. They bowed, then watched each other for a long moment.

A tense silence filled the courtyard.

The tick of the large clock sounded out loudly in the night air.

In the distance, the fair singing voices of the merfolk could be heard.

Then, the standoff was broken.

A flash of brown light shot out of David's raised hand. It hit the golden shield of Izana's Cosaint Charm with a sizzling *crack!*

Rhiannon stared. Neither of them had spoken a single word!

A dizzying array of colours then lit up the courtyard. David and Izana moved between them with the fleet nimbleness of a pair of squirrels. They dodged, weaved and spun amid the bright flashes of light.

Izana sent a beam of cobalt blue towards the fountain.

The pooled water swirled upwards, then hurtled towards David. A wide burst of brilliant golden-red light from him transformed the tidal wave into clouds of steamy mist. Through the haze, a blast of dull orange sent David reeling.

He swiftly sent back a flare of silver sparks.

Izana spun through the air and landed on the pavement with a grating crash. But the Robesman was not defeated. He leapt up, shooting a dark lavender stream towards David.

Ducking the attack, David unexpectedly grinned. He sent a ray of pale gold light in the direction of Izana's shadow. The moment the light hit its target, Izana froze, his hand raised towards David.

For an instant Rhiannon thought the match was over. But then, despite his immobility, Izana sent a blistering shower of vivid green sparks at David. A single spark caught him on the left shoulder as he rolled to the side. Rhiannon saw his arm go limp.

A loud cracking sound was heard. Izana burst from his frozen state in a glittering shower of silver-blue stars.

Both combatants paused. Their eyes locked.

Then they both stepped back and bowed as the clock chimed one.

The ten minutes were up.

David rubbed his left shoulder. 'I'd say that's a draw. *Exsusartus.*' A soft pink glow enveloped his arm. He flexed it a few times and smiled at Izana. 'You almost had me with the Flacartus Charm.'

'You did well to avoid most of it,' Izana complimented him. 'And I didn't know you had learnt Varjocaptus. You performed it perfectly.'

Rhiannon hurried up to them, anxiety causing her heart to race.

'Are you both all right?' she asked.

'We're fine,' David reassured her. 'We were careful not to use anything too powerful.'

Rhiannon stared. From what she had seen, some of the charms had looked capable of inflicting serious damage.

'Cassandra, you need to finish your astronomy homework. Come on.' The stern voice drifted down from the balcony and gazing up, the three saw the girl silently withdraw.

In the courtyard, David went to pick up his discarded sword, calling over his shoulder, 'So, what did you think of the fight?'

'I think my heart stopped several times. I didn't realise you could perform a charm without words.'

'It uses up a lot more energy, so most people don't do it. But it is useful in a fight, as it can give you a slight advantage over your opponent.'

'Along with enabling you to defend yourself if you've been physically incapacitated,' said Izana. 'If I hadn't been able to, then David would've defeated me as soon as I was hit with the Varjocaptus Charm.'

'How does that one work?' Rhiannon asked.

'Your shadow is linked to your body,' Izana explained. 'The charm is designed so that when it hits your shadow, it spreads to your physical body, freezing it instantly. The effects last for three hours, unless you know the counter, Varjolaxus, and can perform it wordlessly.'

'We could teach it to you,' David offered. 'It's a Grade 5, so a bit more advanced than some of the others you're learning, but I'm sure you'd be able to do it.'

Rhiannon thought it over for a moment, then regretfully shook her head. 'Until I'm able to do all the ones Sir Raeden has given me, I don't think I should be trying any extra ones.'

'That's probably a wise decision,' Izana agreed. Then, as a wide yawn escaped her, he suggested it was time they all sought their beds for what remained of the night.

'We'll walk you to your chamber,' David said, collecting her sword from the staircase.

Rhiannon's cheeks flushed. 'You don't have to do that.'

'I know I don't, but I want to.'

A burning heat sparked to life inside Rhiannon's heart. She returned David's warm smile and, offering no further objection, followed him to the armoury to return the swords.

Izana was a silent shadow behind them, but even feeling the weight of his gaze on her back did nothing to dampen Rhiannon's happiness as she and David conversed on the way to her bedchamber.

'The charm Izana used on the water was Eruptusilma,' said David. 'It was designed to help clear away floodwaters, but as you saw, it can be useful against an opponent.'

'How did the water turn into steam?'

'I heated it with Laeflamos. The golden-red light you saw is like a shield of flame, so the water vaporised as soon as the light touched it. Then the first one that hit me was Afflictolapsis.' David rubbed his chest. 'It feels like someone giving you a hard shove right here. And the one that got my shoulder was the Flacartus Charm. It paralyses the limb it hits and can last up to five hours. Even with the countercharm, you still feel as if a bunch of needles is sticking into your skin for a while.'

'What was the one with the silver sparks?'

'Volverso. The spinning in the air leaves a lot of people feeling sick. Of course, Izana wouldn't be one of them! He sent Confanimo at me without much of a problem.'

'What would it have done?'

'Disorientate me. Basically, I would've thought down was up, and up was down. There's no countercharm to reverse it, but the effects wear off after about a minute.'

'So, you really weren't using any dangerous charms?'

David shook his head. 'No. In a duel between magi, the idea is to incapacitate your opponent without causing permanent injury. Really, it's more a battle of wits than anything else. All the charms we used tonight are fairly harmless. The one with the brown light is Inhoudentar. If you get hit with it, you'll feel like you're swamped in tar. And if you don't know the counter, Dissoutentar, you'll be stuck for a few days if no one helps you.

'A useful one to know is the Soporus Charm. It was the one with the yellow light. It'll put your opponent to sleep for several hours. Once the duel is over, you wake them up using Vinaro. Oh, and if you ever see the bright-red one coming for you, get out of the way, or make sure your Cosaint Charm is perfect. It's the Limarus, and it'll make a burning itch spread all over your body that won't go away unless you use the counter, Solavit.'

Rhiannon scratched the back of her neck. 'Sounds nasty,' she said.

'It is, and I suppose if someone were to combine it with Ketevos, you could say it's quite cruel.' At Rhiannon's questioning look, David explained, 'Ketevos was the one with the deep blue light. It magically binds a person until they're released with the Liborean Charm.'

'Now, that one I know!' Rhiannon said.

'But it won't do you any good if you're the one bound by Ketevos,' David warned her. 'The charm not only binds you physically, it also prevents you from using your mage abilities. Once you're caught, you can't do anything until someone else releases you.'

Rhiannon suddenly grinned. 'Then I'm surprised no one's tried to use it to keep you out of trouble.'

Izana's mouth twitched while David openly laughed.

'If it weren't for the fact I'm a prince, they probably would've done it dozens of times,' he admitted, then came to a halt when they reached the arched doorway of Rhiannon's bedchamber. 'Most of the charms we used tonight are ones you'll learn when you go up a grade. Although I'm sure Wyvern will be teaching you some of them for the race. And of course, you can count on us to help you practise them. So don't stay up to all hours of the night trying to learn them by yourself,' he finished with a stern look.

Rhiannon rolled her eyes. 'Yes, Your Royal Highness,' she smirked.

'Oi! None of that!' David exclaimed, trying to sound offended but failing miserably, especially when a laugh escaped him. 'I wasn't being haughty.'

'No, but you did sound awfully like a rigid old uncle.'

'Hey!' yelped David, offended. Then he glared in mild exasperation at his Robesman whose normally reserved expression had cracked and a merry laugh escaped his lips.

'Izana, I think the only time you laugh is when there's a joke at my expense,' he said.

'It does seem that way.'

'Before you two decide to have another sparring match right here, I'll say goodnight,' Rhiannon interrupted.

David and Izana turned back towards her and said their own goodnights.

'And despite the risk of being told I sound like a "rigid old uncle" again, I will say, make sure you go straight to bed, and don't stay up studying,' David added.

'You don't have to worry about that,' Rhiannon said, stepping over the threshold into her chamber. 'I'll probably fall asleep as soon as my head hits the pillow.' She gave David an impish smile. 'So you won't have to sing me a lullaby, dear uncle.'

David sighed. 'John has been a terrible influence on you,' he lamented.

Rhiannon grinned. Then, with a final goodnight, she turned away and closed the door.

Unable to quell the smile on his face, David looked at Izana and felt himself flush under the Robesman's mild look of amusement.

'Oh, shut up,' he said.

'I didn't say anything.'

'No, but you didn't have to. The corners of your eyes crinkle when you're amused.'

'If I'm amused it is for the best of reasons.'

David paused on his way down the hallway. 'And what's that?'

'I now understand why John is not continuously hovering around you two like a mother hen. We know your dislike of dealing with the infatuated attentions of young girls, and we've certainly had to chase off several enamoured females in the past. However, I don't believe we will ever be required to do the same with Rhiannon. She doesn't exhibit the fawning behaviour most other girls do when speaking to you, which certainly has increased my respect for her, and having observed you together it is clear to me you trust her.'

'So you approve of her?'

'It is not my place to approve or disapprove. All that matters is whether you have an objection to her company or not, and it is plainly evident you do not. But,' Izana's tone softened, 'if pressed, as your friend, I would say I approve of her.'

'And coming from you that says a lot,' said David.

'She is rather stubborn at times,' Izana added, 'and her temper, like yours,' he said with a significant look at David, 'has a tendency to get her into trouble – her ending up in this race being a perfect example. Still, I cannot fault her determination to meet a challenge head on, nor her unaffected nature when speaking with the other students in the school.'

'Not to mention being able to put up with Wyvern.' David shook his head. 'The man works her into the ground and I've never heard her complain!'

'In all likelihood she realises what he's putting her through is for her benefit,' Izana replied. 'Besides, I seem to recall you always save your complaints for when you're out of his earshot.'

David snorted.

'Of course I do. If he ever hears me complain he simply makes me train longer until I feel like Rhiannon probably does right now – ready to collapse into bed, fully clothed, and convinced I'll never move again.'

~Chapter 23~

THE PRISONER

The man watched impassively as the prisoner gave another shrill scream. Inside her cell, the woman's emaciated body twisted under the torment being inflicted by the potion he'd given her.

'Administer the tonic.'

The woman beside the man obeyed Mórfran's order.

The prisoner choked on the cool orange liquid, the potion dribbling down her fragile chin.

She swallowed convulsively.

Her screams ceased.

Panting, she lay curled up on the stone floor.

Mórfran turned her over with his foot. 'Now, My Lady. Let's try again. Where is the Dragon's Eye?'

A mute shake of her head was the prisoner's only response.

'You will tell me. Just as you told me of its existence.'

A shuddering sigh of heartbroken grief escaped the prisoner. 'Your torture cannot make a traitor of me again,' she whispered.

The man stepped forward. 'I doubt you can endure another four years of this. You'd be wise to tell us, otherwise you'll receive another dose.'

Hazel eyes devoid of all lustre stared at the bottle of potion in his hand.

'It will do you no good.'

The hoarse words were followed by a wracking cough.

The prisoner drew a shuddering breath, then almost smirked at them. 'The enchantment placed upon the Eye won't let me tell you,' she said.

A tense pause. Then, Mórfran barked, 'Give her another dose.' He turned and stalked for the door. 'Our original plan remains,' his icy voice decreed. 'Obtain the Dragon's Cup and complete that potion.'

~*Chapter 24*~

SUSPICIOUS BEHAVIOUR

I t was a fine Saturday morning and the warmer weather of spring had finally melted the last of the winter snow when Rhiannon, David and John stood outside the castle walls. A short distance away, in a large meadow of vibrant green grass, Endrille, Arastar and Sir Raeden were holding a quiet conference.

It had never been discovered what Endrille had said to Arastar about his part in getting Rhiannon selected for the Dragon's Cup. David and John, however, had little doubt the lecture the two of them had endured from Sir Raeden, combined with the ones from their parents, were mild spring zephyrs rustling a few leaves compared to the thundering summer squall of the ancient dragon's condemnation of the Parvus Dragon's negligence. Certainly, the words she had spoken to the boys had been enough to make them cringe in shame.

'What do you suppose they're saying?'

John's question drew identical shrugs from David and Rhiannon.

'When we met up with you, we'd only just received a note from Sir Raeden telling us to meet them out here,' said Rhiannon.

'Do you think they want to test your skills?' John asked. 'After all, the race is next month.'

'I seriously hope not,' Rhiannon replied tiredly, 'seeing as how Sir Raeden's been testing me every week.'

'You never told us that!'

David's exclamation had Endrille looking over in their direction, then lowering her head to say something to Sir Raeden.

'I didn't want to worry you both,' Rhiannon muttered, as her guardian left the two dragons and made his way towards them.

'Mr Tremaine, unless you have suddenly conquered your fear of heights, I doubt you will enjoy participating in today's planned activity,' were his words of greeting.

John's normally cheerful expression turned into a frown. 'What do you mean, Sir?'

'It has been suggested Rhiannon would benefit from taking a break from studying, and Lady Endrille has offered to take both her and Prince David to Belnight. I will of course follow on Arastar.'

'Oh.' John's face paled. Then his expression hardened. 'I will go,' he said firmly. 'I'm on duty at the moment.'

'John, don't be an idiot,' said David, exasperated. 'I'd never make you come flying unless there was an urgent need for it.'

'And it is not necessary for Mr Tremaine to come, as I will be accompanying you,' Sir Raeden stated.

John looked at him for a moment, then nodded. 'Thank you, Sir,' he said, his expression grave. 'And, in my capacity as Chief Robesman to the Prince Royal, I request that you ensure My Lord's safety at all times.'

Sir Raeden gave him a solemn nod and spoke the words of the Robesmen's pledge each time they came on duty: 'My life shall I place in his service.'

Satisfied, John turned to David and Rhiannon. 'Have fun, you two,' he said. 'Don't get into too much trouble. While you're gone

I'll just pay a visit to Sujan and see if he needs any help with the injured fawn he found yesterday.'

'John, we won't go if you can't co…'

Cutting off David's protest with a small wave, John said, 'We're friends, David, but I'm your Chief Robesman first. I'm not required to accompany you on this occasion, thanks to Sir Raeden's presence, so I'll remain behind. Go with Rhiannon and help her enjoy the day in Belnight. The three of us can always go there another time, and we'll definitely go on horseback. Now, go on, you don't want to keep them waiting.'

Rhiannon and David gave him one last uncertain look, then turned and walked towards Endrille.

'Why do you suppose they chose Belnight?' Rhiannon asked.

'Probably because it's the smallest town closest to here, and they don't want a repeat of what happened in Cendillis,' David answered. 'In a place the size of Belnight, you won't have to worry about groups of people following you around and asking questions about the race.'

Rhiannon grimaced at the reminder of the incident of three weeks before. She had gone to Cendillis for a fitting of the special outfit Sir Raeden commissioned for her and been swamped by a crowd of inquisitive racegoers.

'I can certainly do without experiencing that again,' she admitted truthfully.

'Mind you,' David added with a sudden smirk, 'we could've gone to Cendillis today. With Wyvern along this time I sincerely doubt anyone would've been brave enough to risk making him angry by coming over and pestering you.'

Rhiannon glanced at her guardian's stern expression and sensed David was right. Somehow, it was a very comforting thought.

The small town of Belnight, close to Ryegoth Academy, was not quite the rustic village Rhiannon had been expecting. The main street was lined with a respectable number of shops, each one built to a unique design. A beautiful parkland was clearly the site of many community gatherings, and a large tavern the most popular place on a Saturday.

When they arrived, the townspeople were thrilled to see them. However, after their first enthusiastic greeting, they respectfully retreated with only a few attempting to remain. Upon encountering Sir Raeden's blistering glare, the lingering folk quickly changed their minds, muttered their apologies and hastened away.

While Endrille and Arastar stayed on the outskirts of the town, Rhiannon, Sir Raeden and David gradually made their way through all the open shops. Sir Raeden tended to remain standing just outside each entrance, his towering presence dissuading a number of nervous patrons from following his charges into the buildings.

Upon exiting the apothecary, one of the few places Sir Raeden actually entered, the three heard the town bell strike twelve.

'No wonder I'm hungry,' David commented. 'It's lunchtime.'

'You're always hungry,' Rhiannon pointed out with a smile. 'Sir, will we be having lunch here?'

'That is certainly my intention.' Sir Raeden gazed down at the two of them and instructed, 'You will both order something healthy. I will not have you gorging yourselves on desserts and then complaining all the way home about having an upset stomach.'

A mutinous expression crossed David's face, and a protest was clearly forming on his lips.

Rhiannon immediately gave him a warning kick on the ankle.

'Why'd you do that?' he demanded quietly after Sir Raeden turned away and started walking in the direction of the tavern.

'If you complained, he might've changed his mind and made us fly home straightaway without having lunch.'

David considered her words, then shuddered. 'He certainly is diabolical enough to do something like that,' he said.

When they arrived at the tavern, they were shown to one of the more discreet corners by a harried, but friendly, waitress.

Sir Raeden and Rhiannon gave their orders quickly. David, however, seemed determined to test the lengths of Sir Raeden's patience by taking his time to decide. He finally chose the roast chicken and vegetables.

Their lunch passed amicably. David and Rhiannon held a quiet conversation, discussing the various items they had found in each shop, while Sir Raeden seemed content to consume his meal in silence. It therefore came as no surprise when he was the first to clear his plate.

Instructing them to sit and finish their meals, Sir Raeden stood up, then headed in the direction of the taproom to pay for their lunch.

Rhiannon watched his tall form disappear around a corner, then glanced casually around the room. She froze when her gaze fell on a face she had been striving to forget. Partially hidden in the shadows of the darkest area of the room, the man ensured with his hostile demeanour none of the tavern's happier patrons came near him. A chill ran down her spine and her meal became as appetising as sawdust.

'David, Councillor Plancy is here.'

David turned and looked to where the unpleasant councillor was standing near the old fireplace. She saw David frown, then an expression of surprise crossed his face.

'That's Darvill Crumper.'

'Who?'

'The man speaking to him. He's one of the seven other riders who'll be racing next month. He only just qualified in the last official race. Father told me it was a very close call between him and Edgar Cassell, who was the favourite.'

Rhiannon returned her attention to Councillor Plancy and shuddered. 'I never would've thought he had an interest in racing,' she said, 'or any kind of sport to be honest.'

'He doesn't.' David sounded genuinely puzzled. 'He's never attended any racing events, so why would he be having a rather secretive conversation with one of the riders in the biggest racing event in Álnair?' He glanced at her, a hint of concern in his eyes. 'Do you feel like getting closer to find out? I know being near him makes you uncomfortable.'

Rhiannon grimaced. 'He makes me feel ill. But, for the sake of finding out what he's up to, I'll contain my desire to run in the opposite direction,' she said, then shifted awkwardly when she caught David gazing at her with a strange smile on his face. 'What?'

'Don't ever believe anyone who tells you you're not brave,' he said warmly before continuing in a more prosaic tone, 'in this room, Plancy's sure to spot me as soon as I stand up, and he's bound to recognise you once he sees your face. I suppose we could use the Aoratos Charm to get over there so he doesn't see us coming, but how do we get around Wyvern's order to stay here if he comes back while we're gone?'

Rhiannon frowned and sat in silence for a moment. Then a small smile spread across her face. 'David, how chivalrous are you feeling?' she asked.

Startled, David stared at her, a wariness stealing into his eyes. 'Why do you ask that?'

Rhiannon assumed a blatantly false air of timidity. 'I've no doubt many in this crowd are avid racegoers, and I really don't like my chances of passing through them unnoticed. I'm sure to be surrounded and assaulted by a barrage of questions. I would feel so much safer if you escorted me to the ladies' private room.'

Comprehension dawned on David's face.

'It just so happens my suit of armour was polished this very morning,' he replied with a grin, 'so I guess you could say I'm a regular knight in shining armour. And what a happy coincidence the ladies' room is around the corner, not far from where Plancy is currently standing. Looks like we'll have to walk right by them.'

Sharing a brief smile, they hastily checked to ensure no one was watching their own secluded corner then murmured, '*Aoratos.*'

Faster than a master thief's sleight of hand, their bodies vanished.

'I'm really grateful Wyvern taught you this one,' came David's disembodied voice, 'although I'm surprised he managed to get the approval from the Trínondras. They're usually fairly strict in regulating who can learn it. Now, I think we'd best keep to the walls if we don't want to risk running into anyone.'

'Good thinking.'

Something bumped against Rhiannon's nose.

'OW!'

'Sorry, that was me.' David's apologetic words were accompanied by a tentative tap on Rhiannon's shoulder. 'I was trying to find where you are. We'll need to keep a hold of each other, so we don't stumble over ourselves.'

Rhiannon agreed and covered David's invisible hand with hers. 'I'll let you go first,' she said, 'that way if you stop unexpectedly, and I run into you, it's not likely I'll knock you off your feet.'

David acknowledged the sense in this and soon was leading the way around the room to where Plancy and Darvill Crumper were standing. The two men were talking in the lowest of voices, impossible to hear.

David and Rhiannon crept closer until they were only three feet away.

Neither dared to breathe too deeply as they silently manoeuvred themselves in between the little gap between the unlit fireplace and the ancient stone walls. It was a tight squeeze, but at least they could now hear every word spoken, without having to fear someone might bump into them at any moment.

'These are the terms: half of the money will be transferred to your bank vault today. The rest will be paid when you've won.'

'Fine, but I still don't get why you've chosen me to help you. I'm certainly not one of the top favourites.'

'I need someone who will do whatever it takes to win.'

Plancy's choice of words sent a shaft of foreboding through both his young listeners.

Crumper must have also felt slightly uneasy. There was a tinge of wariness in his voice as he said, 'For someone who's never concerned himself with racing before, you're certainly quite fanatical about seeing me win this thing.'

'Whatever my motives, they are my own affair. You accepted my offer, so the only thing you need concern yourself with is making sure you win. Once you hold the Dragon's Cup in your hands, I'll consider you to have fulfilled your part of the deal.'

Plancy reached out and placed something in Crumper's palm. 'You must ensure you have that on you throughout the entirety of the race, and when you receive the Dragon's Cup,' he directed. 'Do not under any circumstances lose it or damage it.'

No matter how hard they tried, neither Rhiannon nor David could clearly see the item before Crumper slid it into the pouch hanging from his belt.

'Before the race, you will not attempt to contact me,' Plancy continued. 'Nor will you tell anyone that we have met.'

Crumper gestured at the crowded room. 'And what do you suggest we say to all these people?' he asked, a mocking note entering his voice. 'I doubt they will conveniently forget about seeing us together.'

Plancy sent a contemptuous look towards the occupants of the room. He waved off Crumper's concern with a dismissive, 'I have not been in this misbegotten town in over fifty years, and

I doubt the collective intelligence of its people would be capable of recognising anyone of real importance.' With that, he turned and walked away.

'Insufferable old toad,' Crumper muttered, then followed Plancy out of the tavern. His last comment indicated to his listeners it was only the monetary aspect of the deal that would make him carry out his part in it, and not some misguided loyalty to the councillor.

David and Rhiannon slowly moved out of their hiding place.

Then David groaned softly under his breath.

'What is it?'

'Wyvern's back already.'

Sure enough, when Rhiannon gazed in the direction of their table, Sir Raeden was striding towards it. Her guardian's face was a stony mask as he considered the empty seats and their abandoned meals.

'Come on.'

Rhiannon tightened her hold on David's hand and dragged him away from the fireplace. She led him around the corner to the darkened corridor which led to the toilets. Thankfully, from this angle, Sir Raeden would not be able to see them appear out of thin air.

Rhiannon looked around to ensure no one was watching, then quickly whispered, '*Horatos*.'

The next instant she was perfectly visible again.

David quickly followed her example and gazed at her in concern.

'You'll definitely have to look out for Crumper during the race. I can speak to Endrille and my father but given the nature of the race, they can't really put too many safeguards into place.'

Rhiannon shrugged. 'It's not like I'm going to be a threat to him. All I'm concerned about is surviving the thing. I don't really care if I win or not.'

'You may not care, but they obviously do – and that makes them dangerous,' David argued.

'I don't doubt it, but we should probably talk about this later. Right now, I think we should get back before Sir Raeden starts tearing this place apart looking for us.'

David frowned. 'But aren't we using the excuse you had to go in there.'

Rhiannon followed the direction of his finger as it pointed to the ladies' room.

'Yes, so?'

'Well, don't girls usually take forever when they do?'

Seeing the impish twinkle in his eyes, Rhiannon smacked him on the shoulder. 'That's only when they go in there as a group,' she retorted. 'And the ones who do have a thing with giggling about boys and discussing other things, which I'm sure you don't want to know anything about.'

Recalling some snippets of conversation he had accidentally overheard between his female classmates while passing the girls' toilets at the school, David was quite sure he did not want to know either.

'Now, come on, Sir Knight,' Rhiannon said, 'it's time you returned this damsel to her guardian.'

Deliberately adopting a casual pace, the two walked around the corner and headed back to their table.

Sir Raeden was standing with his arms folded across his chest, his lips forming a thin line in a grim face as his eyes immediately fixed upon his two errant charges.

Rhiannon did not give him a chance to voice the rebuke that was no doubt burning on his tongue.

'I'm so sorry, Sir,' she said quickly, 'but I had to, um, you know ...'

She thought her act of girlish embarrassment to be quite convincing as she pointed in the direction of the toilets.

Still, suspicion lingered in Sir Raeden's eyes. 'And this required you both leaving the table?'

'I couldn't let her go through the crowd by herself,' David said. 'After what happened in Cendillis, she was a bit anxious in case people here started behaving like that when they saw her alone.'

'I see. So it was a noble action on your part.'

David's eyes widened in disbelief at Sir Raeden's calm, almost approving words. But then Sir Raeden's next words closed an icy hand around his chest.

'And so, leaving the table had nothing at all to do with the fact Councillor Plancy and Darvill Crumper were standing on the other side of the room, and the both of you wanting to eavesdrop on the conversation?'

David and Rhiannon stared at him in astonishment. Their reaction caused a sardonic glint to appear in Sir Raeden's eyes.

'Did you honestly believe I would be unaware of their presence?'

'I suppose we did,' Rhiannon confessed.

'And you thought satisfying your curiosity as to why they were here was more important than obeying my instructions?'

Rhiannon fidgeted with her cloak and looked down at her feet. 'It wasn't like that, well, not really,' she started to explain.

'It's just as well we did listen,' David interrupted. 'Plancy is paying Crumper to make sure he wins the Dragon's Cup. He told him he wants someone who will do whatever it takes to win.'

'David!'

Returning Rhiannon's glare with a stubborn look, David pointed out, 'My father would've just told Sir Raeden anyway when I told him. At least he might have some ideas on how to keep you safe.'

Sir Raeden cast a withering look in his direction and bit out a mocking 'thank you' in response to David's less-than-overwhelming confidence in his abilities. He then demanded to be informed of the precise words in the conversation between Plancy and Darvill Crumper.

It did not take them long to repeat the very short conversation.

Sir Raeden's attention sharpened when they mentioned the item Plancy had given to Crumper.

'And neither of you was able to see it?' he questioned.

Both shook their heads.

'Plancy just said to make sure Crumper kept it on him throughout the race, and when he got handed the Dragon's Cup.'

'I will certainly discuss this with the king, and appropriate measures will be taken to ensure the safety of all the riders as much as possible,' Sir Raeden informed David. 'Unfortunately, as no specific threat has been made towards any of the riders, and their only objective appears to be to win at all costs (not unusual given the event in question), there is not much else we will be able to do.' Then he fixed both his charges with a stern look. 'However, in the matter of your behaviour, punishment can and will be issued. You both not only disobeyed me, you also attempted to cover that disobedience with a lie. I also suspect you inappropriately employed the use of your mage abilities to conduct your eavesdropping.'

Rhiannon flushed guiltily and David, his conscience pricked by the fact he had used his power to satisfy his own curiosity, confessed, 'We used the Aoratos Charm.'

'A charm which you know is only to be used when there is imminent danger to yourself.' Sir Raeden's severe tone held all the icy chill of a winter wind. 'You may both consider your leisure time tomorrow to be forfeit. Instead, you will write a concise and detailed essay on what you did wrong and an explanation of why it was wrong.'

Rhiannon and David did not attempt to argue against the punishment. They merely nodded, then followed Sir Raeden out of the tavern and back to where Endrille and Arastar were patiently waiting, basking their large forms contentedly in the afternoon sunlight.

'She's not going to be happy about any of this, is she?' Rhiannon said quietly.

David shook his head. 'But she'll be more disappointed in me than you over our using the Aoratos Charm. As for Plancy and Crumper, I think it's safe to say they're not going to be on her favourite humans list anytime soon.'

Chapter 25

THE RIDERS

The weeks following Rhiannon's visit to Belnight were filled with an unrelenting round of tests and defence training with Sir Raeden. Her guardian never seemed to tire of creating new and ever-more-difficult situations for her to overcome. On several occasions he even had her battling not only himself but Queen Maiwen, David, John, Izana and four members of the Royal Guard. The first few times, he did not permit her to use any of her mage abilities, which meant she had to be extra-vigilant and extremely precise in her movements. It was only after she managed to survive one encounter, without being badly bruised, that Sir Raeden then allowed her to start using charms.

Then, the day of the race finally arrived.

Rhiannon stood outside the castle walls in the early morning light, nervously fiddling with the hilt of the sword hanging from her side. The sword, with its lightweight, strong, durable blade, had been specifically designed for her by Sir Raeden, and crafted by the best master swordsmith in Álnair. Her guardian had also been granted permission by King Stephen to have the scabbard marked with the crest of Mórell: a silver cluster of oak leaves and an acorn on a green banner.

Her outfit, the other gift from her guardian, fitted her perfectly, the leather jerkin feeling like a second skin over the tunic, shirt and breeches. Predominantly in forest colours of green and brown, they were matched by dark leather pauldrons protecting her shoulders and upper chest, arm braces, gloves, a belt and boots. A cloak woven from fine grey wool completed her outfit and was fastened about her neck by a silver brooch, shaped to match the oak leaves and acorn of the crest of Mórell.

Thanks to her guardian's efforts, Rhiannon now felt slightly confident that she would make it through the race with most of her limbs intact. Nevertheless, looking at the other riders, she could not help feeling her experience would be surpassed by the seven adults who were confidently chatting to the crowd.

'You know you're more than capable of beating every single one of them.'

A relieved smile spread across Rhiannon's face. She quickly concealed it and turned to look at David with a mock frown.

'And just where have you been? I've been waiting here half an hour for you and John.'

'Unfortunately, I couldn't just sneak out this morning,' he said. 'Father insisted I present myself to him and Mother so they could ensure I was dressed appropriately for the occasion.' He gestured at the shining coronet adorning his head, then at his formal raiment: a long-sleeved tunic of resplendent blue, a flowing white cloak edged with gold, black boots polished to perfection, pristine white breeches and his long sword.

Rhiannon made a show of examining his appearance, even circling him before announcing, 'It's acceptable, I suppose.'

'Acceptable?' David exclaimed indignantly. 'I should jolly well hope it's more than *acceptable,* considering how uncomfortable formal attire is to wear! This coronet alone will weigh a tonne by the end of the day.'

'O how heavy lies the crown on the head of a prince.'

281

John's laughing comment caused both David and Rhiannon to turn and greet him.

'I'll crown you if you're not careful,' David warned.

'The heroine of the day will protect me,' declared John, stepping behind Rhiannon.

'Not likely.' Rhiannon moved to the side and waved her arm theatrically. 'Have at him,' she instructed imperiously.

David took an exaggerated battle stance.

'Pax! I surrender!' John cried.

David grinned and lowered his fists. 'Just as well. I really didn't want to get blood on my new tunic.'

'Miss McBride.'

Rhiannon looked over her shoulder at the young face of Councillor Attwater.

'Yes?'

'They want all the riders to head over to the Royal Pavilion.'

'All right, I'll come now.'

The councillor turned his attention to David. 'You had best go there as well, Your Royal Highness,' he said, 'otherwise you might cause a bit of an upset among the officials if you're absent.'

'I'll be there,' David promised.

Councillor Attwater bowed and walked away.

There was a short, solemn silence.

'I guess we'd better get going,' David said reluctantly.

Rhiannon nodded in agreement and adjusted the cloak around her shoulders. 'Any last words of advice?' she asked.

'Don't worry about how all the other riders are doing,' said John.

'Just look after yourself and try to remember everything Wyvern taught you,' David answered.

Rhiannon grasped the hilt of her sword. Straightening her shoulders, she breathed out slowly. 'Right then. Let's go,' she said.

They walked to the Royal Pavilion in silence.

The crowd frequently cheered Rhiannon's name, but the only acknowledgement she gave was a smile and a brief wave.

Upon reaching their destination, John halted outside.

'This is where I stop,' he said. 'With Sir Raeden and so many of the Royal Guard present, none of David's Robesmen are rostered for official duty, so no special privileges for me today. I'll just head over to where Endrille and the dragons are waiting and have a quick chat.'

'We'll see you later,' Rhiannon and David promised him, then they both walked through the silken drapes of the tent.

They passed the other riders gathered in the middle of the pavilion and made their way to where King Stephen and Queen Maiwen stood, with Lord Daiki Sato and Lady Agnes Fasani beside them.

In formal robes of the most exquisite design, and their crowns shining radiantly upon their heads, both monarchs exuded regal grace and nobility as they greeted Rhiannon with a warm smile.

Then King Stephen turned his attention to the whole group assembled before them.

'Riders, I bid you welcome on this very special day. All of you have proven you possess the necessary skill to participate in this event, and I wish each of you equal good fortune. I know you are anxious to be off, so let us begin the formalities. As tradition demands from the time this race was held in Vetus svet, I ask the previous champion, Sir Raeden Wyvern, to please bring forth the Dragon's Cup.'

At these words, two guards positioned at an opening at the back drew apart two silken drapes to reveal the imposing sight of Sir Raeden. He was arrayed in his full official uniform, the collar of Supreme Royal Protector glinting against his dark tunic. In his hands he held the most beautiful trophy Rhiannon had ever seen.

The Dragon's Cup.

It was an impressive three feet high, but what caught her

attention was the pure crystal embedded in the cup, shimmering as though lit from within by millions of stars, the liquefying movement making the crystal appear alive. Inside the dim confines of the pavilion, it cast a light of white brilliance, like the full moon on a clear night.

'It's magnificent.'

Rhiannon's whispered words were echoed by many others who could scarce draw their gaze away from the trophy.

'Sir Raeden will now lead all riders to where they will be presented to Lady Endrille,' King Stephen said. 'During this race I trust each and every one of you will remember the lesson taught to us by her race: *Eiíos í fíondae na quelduil, san í lakinell o dharlow.*'

'Better to fail with honour than to win by cheating.' David's warm breath stirred the air near Rhiannon's cheek as he murmured the translation into her ear. 'Although I seriously doubt Crumper will remember that.'

Rhiannon glanced over to look at Darvill Crumper. She had little doubt that David was correct. His covetous gaze was fixed on the Dragon's Cup as Sir Raeden and the two front guards made their way to the main entrance.

The other riders fell in behind Sir Raeden and followed him outside through the silken drapes.

Rhiannon went to follow, then felt a gentle hand cover the myriad of braids wrapped around her head. Looking up, she saw King Stephen smile down at her.

'I normally would not single out any particular rider, however, on this occasion, I do wish you the very best of success, my dear.'

'Thank you, Sire.'

'I've been told your progress in both your theory and practical lessons has come along quite brilliantly, so I have every faith in your ability to overcome each trial that has been set. Now, you'd best get along before your guardian realises you're missing and comes looking for you.'

Seeing the twinkle in his eyes, Rhiannon grinned.

'I'd just have to blame you, Your Majesty, then I'd have nothing to worry about.'

'Impertinent imp.' King Stephen turned to his son in light-hearted dismay. 'I can see you have been a bad influence on her.'

'You say that like it's a bad thing,' David retorted with a cheeky smile.

'Oh, go on, both of you.' King Stephen waved a regal hand in dismissal. 'We'll follow behind you.'

'Yes, Father.'

'Good luck, Rhiannon.' Queen Maiwen stepped forward and pulled her into a quick embrace. Upon releasing her, she added, 'And be careful.'

Rhiannon nodded. 'I will.'

Then, she and David exited the Royal Pavilion and hastily caught up with Sir Raeden, who had almost reached the place where Endrille stood waiting. Arastar, and the other seven dragons in the race, were gathered behind her.

The crowd, which had appeared so large before, seemed to have tripled in size, and the noise was now a deafening cacophony of lively music, cheers and chattering voices.

Rhiannon spotted the familiar faces of Izana, Derrick, Gareth and Eamon among the great host of people, and was encouraged by their individual displays of support: a small smile; a brief nod; a raised fist; a loud cheer. The last was echoed by several students from the castle school, including Leila Hardinge, Viola Rastell, Innogen Calloway and Simon Truscott.

The only sour note was catching a glimpse of Marcus and Felix's scowling expressions. She deliberately turned her head away and ignored them.

As the group drew nearer to Endrille, Rhiannon noticed a grand platform beside her. The intricate design and delicate craftsmanship that had gone into creating such a beautiful structure clearly marked it as not having been made by human hands.

Upon reaching the platform, Sir Raeden, now flanked by the two guards, slowly mounted the steps and made his way to the tall stand in the centre.

King Stephen, Queen Maiwen and their chief aides followed them with dignified grace. David, obeying a signal from his father, gave Rhiannon an encouraging smile before accompanying them up the steps.

The noise of the crowd began to diminish and soon a complete hush had fallen.

Sir Raeden placed the Dragon's Cup upon the stand. Then he turned and in a loud voice that easily carried over the now silent crowd, declared, 'This is not just a symbol of victory. The Dragon's Cup, created through the power of the ancient dragons, is our reminder of the friendship, loyalty and love they extended to the race of Men. It also serves as a physical bond between our two races. Each time a rider wins this event, that bond is renewed. Lady Endrille, Your Majesties, it is my privilege to formally introduce to you, and to everyone present, the riders for the Dragon's Cup.

'First we have Gwenneth Billsborough.'

A tall, graceful, blonde woman with a haughty expression moved with feline grace up the steps.

'Jeronim Perrett.'

A cheerful man rushed forward, waving enthusiastically at the crowd. He stumbled on the first step, recovered, and gave another friendly wave.

'Takeo Fukui.'

Rhiannon saw many women in the crowd crane their necks to catch a glimpse of the rider's handsome features as he ascended the steps with quiet dignity.

'Ivo Pembroke.'

The extremely confident young man Rhiannon recognised as

one of the archers in the castle guards strode forward. His wide grin lasted until he reached the platform and was met by Sir Raeden's glare.

'Corin O'Shannessy.'

An athletic young man with dark good looks and a charming smile preened at the roar of approval from the crowd. He took his time mounting the steps, pausing to wave and flirt with his adoring supporters.

'Bjorn Steinberg.'

A slightly older man with an unsmiling and serious demeanour bowed briefly to the crowd. He walked up the steps, then bowed deeply to Lady Endrille and David's parents.

'Darvill Crumper.'

Rhiannon glared at the stocky rider who was in league with Councillor Plancy. The man smirked at the crowd and took his place among the other riders with smug arrogance.

A brief silence fell. Then Sir Raeden spoke again.

'Our last rider is a young lady who participated in an unscheduled official race. She will be turning fourteen next month, making her the youngest person to ever participate in this, or any other official race, in Álnair's history. I present to you, Rhiannon McBride.'

Thunderous applause broke out among the crowd.

Cries of 'good luck' and 'bless you, daughter of Mórell' rang in Rhiannon's ears as she reached the top of the platform. Placing her right arm across her chest, she performed a short bow first to Endrille, then to David's parents, as Sir Raeden had instructed her to do. She took the small nod from her guardian to mean she had done it correctly.

She walked over to take her place, which thankfully was close to David and his parents, then listened as Endrille thanked Sir Raeden and added some general words of encouragement to all the riders.

'This race is not just about who comes first,' Endrille said in conclusion. 'It is a test, not only of your skill, but of your courage. There may come a time when you feel your strength fade, when an obstacle may seem insurmountable and you will want to give up. That is the time when a true champion emerges. I hope you will all discover that inside each of you dwells just such a champion.'

A mighty round of applause spread throughout the crowd in a powerful display of agreement. After several moments, King Stephen stepped forward and raised his hands for silence.

'Clearly, I am not the only one who supports Lady Endrille's words,' he said with a smile once the noise had died down. 'Now, before we send the riders off to join their dragons, I would like to take this opportunity to thank Professor Egelbert and the professors at Ryegoth Academy who have been responsible for designing the trials in this race. I am sure these will prove to be worthy challenges for our riders.'

The crowd showed their approval by bursting into another round of applause.

King Stephen turned towards the riders.

'As you all know, the first part of the race will be a flight to the Del Enger Mountains. On Mount Solus there is an entrance into the mountain. Each of your dragons will leave you at that entrance, then go to the place where you will meet up with them if you are successful in reaching, and passing, the last trial set up in the mountain. Once you have left the mountain, your dragon will inform you of the final part of the race. You now have fifteen minutes before the race commences, so we'd best let you go and make any necessary final preparations.' Looking back at the crowd, he loudly declared, 'Ladies and gentlemen – the eight Dragon Cup Riders!'

The cheers of the crowd drowned out all other sounds as the riders began to leave the platform.

Rhiannon reached the last step before she realised both David and Sir Raeden were immediately behind her.

'Coming to see me off, are you?'

'Seemed like the decent thing to do,' David replied with a smile.

They continued following the other riders to where the dragons were waiting.

'Wait up, you two!'

Rhiannon and David paused at John's yell. Sir Raeden gave each of them a nudge.

'We do not have time to waste on idle dawdling,' he said briefly. 'Mr Tremaine will catch up shortly.'

Sure enough, they had not gone another ten yards before John was at their side sounding winded and straightening his long cloak.

'Trying to get through that crowd was like battling my sister for the bathroom,' he panted.

'Only this time you actually emerged the victor.'

David's comment drew a laugh from Rhiannon and an indignant protest from John.

'I'll have you know I've won a few times,' he said with great dignity.

David's eyebrow went up sceptically. 'Oh really?'

'Well, maybe once or twice,' John amended.

When David's expression remained unconvinced, John finally admitted, 'All right, I've never won against Delia.'

'With your lack of ability to overcome such an obstacle, it is fortunate you are not one of the riders,' Sir Raeden commented drily.

'I wouldn't say that,' John said defensively. 'I doubt anything in the trials could be half as scary as my sister when she first wakes up.'

Dodging to the side to avoid a collision with an overeager admirer of Ivo Pembroke, Rhiannon caught a glimpse of Arastar through the thick crowd.

'There he is!'

She hastened forward and soon reached the side of the Parvus Dragon.

Arastar lowered his head to greet her in his rumbling voice, then said, 'I'm pleased to see you have arranged your hair sensibly.'

Rhiannon touched her hair confined in its complicated braids. 'Sir Raeden told me to make sure Aleda put it up like this so it wouldn't get in the way.'

Arastar cast an approving look in Sir Raeden's direction. 'A wise piece of advice.'

'Have you got everything you need?'

In answer to David's question, Rhiannon patted the hilt of her sword and Arastar's neck. 'I'm sure these two will do me fine.'

'Along with these.' Sir Raeden reached under his cloak and withdrew a small flask and a sheathed dagger. 'It's water,' he said in answer to her curious look. 'You never know when you may need it.'

She took the flask and attached it to her belt. She then nodded at the dagger. 'Why would I need that?' she asked. 'Shouldn't the sword be enough?'

'There are some occasions where a dagger is more practical than a sword,' Sir Raeden said.

Not willing to think about what any of those occasions might be, Rhiannon reluctantly took the dagger and hung its sheath next to the flask. Looking back at her guardian, she shifted awkwardly, and said, 'I do thank you for all the help you've given me. I know if I manage to get through this thing it's only because of everything you've taught me.'

Sir Raeden glared at her. 'Of course you will "get through it",' he retorted. 'I would not have spent my time instructing you if I did not believe you capable of learning everything you would need to know in order to succeed.'

Rhiannon smiled, pleased at her guardian's words. 'You know that's about the nicest thing anyone has ever said to me,' she said.

Sir Raeden scoffed. 'I did not say it for the sake of being *nice*, and I certainly did not say it to give you an inflated opinion of yourself or your abilities. Just remember what you have been taught, listen to your instincts and do not take foolish risks.'

'Yes, Sir.'

'It is almost time to start,' Arastar said, glancing over to where the other riders and their dragons were now all gathering.

Instantly, the nerves Rhiannon thought had disappeared came flooding back.

'Take care of yourself.' John stepped forward and placed a brotherly hand on her shoulder. 'We all know you can do this, and Arastar will certainly be the quickest out of all these dragons so you should get to the mountains first, giving you a bit of a head start.'

Rhiannon took a closer look at the other dragons and thought he was most likely correct. The different breeds were all far larger than Arastar.

John gave her a final encouraging pat on the shoulder, then stepped back so David could take his place.

'Watch out for Crumper,' David said quietly. 'Don't let him near you if you can help it.'

'I won't,' she promised.

David hesitated a moment, then suddenly wrapped his arms around her in a tight hug. Startled, she did not immediately respond, but then she slowly raised her arms and returned the embrace.

'If something happens to you, I'll never forgive myself,' David muttered.

Rhiannon slowly pulled away, a frown appearing on her face. 'Why?'

'I'm the idiot who caused you to be selected for this race. I should've remembered what year it was and made sure at least one criteria wasn't fulfilled so you wouldn't have had to participate in a qualifying race.'

Rhiannon gave him a light punch on the shoulder. 'I don't blame you for what happened,' she said with a small smile. 'It was an honest mistake, and I'll be all right.'

Turning away, she walked over to Arastar and climbed up into the new low saddle on his back. With the saddle's reduced height offering less wind resistance, Rhiannon wondered how much faster the Parvus Dragon would go. Hopefully, not enough to rip her off his back! She gathered the reins into her hands and heard David's quiet, 'Look after her,' to Arastar. The dragon gave a slight nod, then turned about and headed for the starting line.

'I'll see you all later,' she called.

'Good luck!'

She was not surprised to hear only David and John's voices call out after her. She looked over her shoulder and saw Sir Raeden's grim expression. He did not wave to her like David and John were doing, but he did briefly incline his head. This small sign of encouragement was enough for her before she returned her gaze to the front, focusing on the task before her: surviving the next couple of hours and returning to Valieoth Castle in one piece.

Chapter 26

INSIDE THE MOUNTAIN

Rhiannon approached the spread-out line-up of dragons and noticed she was placed between Takeo Fukui and Bjorn Steinberg.

Fukui was riding a beautiful Síuld Dragon, a breed commonly found in forests where its brown scales would help it blend in among the trees.

Steinberg was mounted on a wild-looking Erímos Dragon. The desert breed with its black and yellow scales looked dangerous. It reminded Rhiannon of a tiger snake. She just hoped the dragon did not share the snake's vicious nature.

She looked around at the crowds, noticing that along with the large numbers of people, a host of other creatures had also gathered. There were several dragons along with a multitude of faeries, their brightly coloured hair making their small forms easily recognisable even from a distance. For a moment she also thought she spotted a few short figures jumping about in green and gold jackets with tall green hats on their heads, but when she looked again the figures had disappeared.

DONG! DONG! DONG!

The warning bell rang out, causing the few stragglers in the crowd to hurry into place.

'All the riders and their dragons are ready and in position.'

The loud voice coming from the tall tower at the side of the line sounded out across the open area.

'King Stephen will now send up the starting flare.'

The tall figure of King Stephen stepped out from under the shelter of the tower. He raised his arm.

An expectant hush descended over the crowd.

'Be ready,' Arastar said, his muscles tensing in anticipation.

Rhiannon's hands tightened instinctively.

The leather of her gloves creaked in the silence.

She could hear each breath she took over the blood rushing through her head.

Then, a bright, glowing spark shot out of King Stephen's hand. It travelled straight up, high into the sky. With the force of a hundred fireworks, the spark burst into a shower of colours with an explosive *BOOM!*

Swifter than a flicker of light, Arastar launched into the air, his wings unfurled in an instant. In a flawless display of speed and agility, he shot ahead of the other dragons.

The crowd broke out into a screaming crescendo of applause.

Rhiannon quickly adjusted her grip on the reins. 'You certainly took off quicker than you did in our first race,' she called out.

'I'm not holding back this time.'

She soon realised just how much he had been holding back against Marcus and Baegolz.

He zoomed over the same landmarks of their first race at a phenomenal speed. The magnificent city of Cendillis and the wide expanse of Shaimar Forest were nothing but a blur. The glittering waters of Rëalta Lake and the towers of Ryegoth Academy were gone in a flash.

His speed did not lessen when they reached the faraway

Del Enger Mountains. The thick, white clouds blanketing the hazardous peaks did not even make him falter.

Rhiannon clung to the reins as he swooped and glided, his sharp precision frequently taking them within an inch of disaster.

They streaked around a particularly nasty summit, barely missing the jagged rocks protruding from its side.

'Wouldn't it be easier to fly *above* the clouds, not through them?' Rhiannon gasped.

'Getting above them would cost us time. It's much quicker this way. Besides, the clouds are beginning to thin out.'

Rhiannon noticed that they were.

She looked ahead and could now make out the outline of the mountain peaks, instead of just a white haze.

'There it is!'

Arastar's cry had her eagerly leaning forward to catch her first glimpse of Mount Solus.

The highest peak of the Del Enger Mountains towered above all the others, its stark beauty enhanced by the vivid blue sky and the sun creating mysterious shadows on its sides. At the very pinnacle of the mountain, the entrance was carved from stone and a small ledge in front of it provided the only area where a rider could safely dismount from a dragon – unless they wished to attempt climbing up the steep, rocky slope from the comparably flat terrain a fair distance below.

Arastar barely reduced his speed as he approached the entrance.

Then, with a swift, upward glide, he reached the stone doorway.

His sharp claws clung to the rocky surface of the mountain as Rhiannon swiftly slid down onto the ledge.

'It appears as though O'Shannessy and Pembroke decided on the safer route.'

Rhiannon shot a quick look behind her at Arastar's words.

Some distance away, the two riders and their dragons were descending from above the clouds. Clearly, neither duo had wanted to run the risk of having the larger dragons collide with any hidden obstacles in the obscured mountain range.

'Best be going then,' she said. 'Thanks for getting me here, Arastar. I'll see you later.'

'Good luck, daughter of Mórell. May the spirits of the ancients guide and protect you.'

The dragon's last words seemed to echo in Rhiannon's ears as she hurried through the doorway. After only a few steps, she halted in her tracks at the sight in front of her.

What should have been a small cavern with a pathway down into the depths of the mountain was instead a spacious entry with a smooth floor reflecting the lights from the numerous sconces lining the walls.

'Lovely piece of enchantment isn't it?'

Rhiannon jumped at the sound of the voice.

She darted a look to the only shadowed corner of the room.

A glint of bright blue hair close to the ground caught a stray shaft of light.

She did not have to guess very hard as to which race the speaker might belong.

'You're a faery.'

'Correct.' The masculine tone was matched by the long strides the faery took as he stepped out into the light. His large eyes sharing the same vibrant shade as his hair, he looked up at Rhiannon with a rueful expression. 'I guess I owe my sister a new dress, since you got here first. I thought it would be O'Shannessy.'

'Your sister?'

'Aleda.'

Realisation struck Rhiannon. 'You're Isidore, her older brother.'

'I am.' Rising off the ground, Isidore observed, 'You certainly did well getting here before everyone else, so I'd best explain what happens now. There are eight doors leading out of this room and into a labyrinth of passages. They all lead by separate routes to the way out of the mountain. Each rider has been assigned a door; however, the doors are not visible until I make them so. To make your door visible you must tell me a riddle. If I successfully guess the answer you will need to continue telling them until I cannot. I will then concede you the victory and allow you to proceed.'

'So, it's a test of my wits.'

'Yes.'

'All right.'

Rhiannon stood in silence for a moment.

One side of her mind was madly going through the riddles she had memorised. The other side screamed at her to hurry as the others were sure to catch up very shortly.

Then one of the trickier riddles from *A Treasury of Riddles & Verse* popped into her head. She looked at Isidore and recited it.

> *I fly, but am never caught.*
> *With a fortune I cannot be bought.*
> *I ravage, but also mend.*
> *To the vain, I am no friend.*
> *I conquer, but never fight.*
> *I bring all things to light.*

Isidore frowned and scratched his head.

'Not a faery then. The fighting bit rules us out,' he muttered. 'Not a dragon either. Bird. Insect. A griffon maybe? No, that's not right either.' After a long pause he finally admitted, 'Your first riddle and I can't guess it.'

He raised his hands and gave a short, sharp clap. On the far side of the room, a door became visible.

'There you are, child, and good luck.' Tilting his head to one side, he listened intently before adding, 'Best hurry off. Sounds like the next ones are here. But tell me quickly, what was the answer?'

'Time!' cried Rhiannon, running through the doorway.

'You stupid faery! Of all the obvious answers!'

Isidore's cry of self-disgust echoed behind her. Then the door closed, and all sound from the other side was cut off.

Rhiannon paused to examine the passageway before her.

The walls of rough stone twinkled in the faint glow of lights spaced evenly along the path.

She stepped closer to the wall for a better look.

Embedded in the stone, and scattered like radiant stars across the dark surface, were thousands of precious gems.

'Annabelle certainly would love to get her hands on these!' She tapped a particularly brilliant green gem and was startled when it shifted slightly. 'What on earth?'

She gently placed a finger against the gem. To her surprise, the small amount of pressure dislodged the beautiful jewel. The glittering stone fell into her hand.

Rhiannon stared at the object through narrowed eyes, a tinge of suspicion creeping over her.

'That's not natural,' she muttered. 'Gems don't just come out of stone like that.'

She reached up to push against a large red jewel. Again, the gem shifted, then descended into her open palm.

'Definitely not natural.'

Scanning the long walls, she calculated there would have to be a fortune of precious gems in just one small section alone.

'It's got to be a test of some sort,' she told herself. 'See who's gullible enough to try and take some when we probably don't need any of it.'

She bent down and placed both gems on the ground.

'In any case, I don't have anywhere to put them.'

She straightened back up, took one last look at the glittering array, then turned and continued onwards. She did not turn her head back once to take another look at the tempting display of jewels on either side of her.

She soon walked through another door, then followed a

seemingly endless path through a maze of twists and turns, each one taking her deeper into the heart of the mountain.

At length, she reached a beautifully crafted stone bridge stretched over a deep ravine. On the opposite side was a wide warren of stalagmites, their glistening forms rising from the ground like sentinels to guard the narrow opening behind them.

Rhiannon swiftly crossed the bridge, then halted. She had the oddest feeling of being watched. A prickling sensation going down her neck was her only warning before a flash of light shot towards her from the left.

'*Cosain!*'

The magical shield of golden light flared brightly in front of her, deflecting the attack.

She ducked behind the nearest stalagmite, fortunately a large one, and crouched. Taking a quiet, steadying breath, she listened carefully.

A long moment passed. Then, she heard a faint skittering of loose rocks among the crystallised formations closest to the ravine on her side of the bridge.

Rhiannon peeked out cautiously. Another burst of light sped in her direction. She moved out of the way, but not before she caught a glimpse of the betraying shadow of her unknown assailant.

A jumble of charms passed through her mind. She dismissed using Aoratos. Being invisible wouldn't help her cross the rocky ground soundlessly. Finally, one charm stood out.

Varjocaptus! The charm she had been introduced to when David had used it on Izana. After mastering the list Sir Raeden had given her, she had practised the Grade 5 Level 8 charm, but so far had only managed to freeze her sparring partner for a few minutes before the effects wore off.

She peered out, deflecting a spray of vivid green sparks with the Cosaint Charm, then drew back again.

The shadow was closer. Her opponent would soon reach the

bridge, leaving only the short distance to the large stalagmite between them.

She inhaled slowly, using the technique Izana had taught her. She had to get it right, and not give any warning of what she was about to do.

A small rock lay beside her foot. She picked it up, weighing it in her hand. Casting her eyes to the right, she found a location she might have been able to reach without being seen. She threw the rock towards it. The stone clattered to the ground.

Before the flash of scarlet light had passed the bridge, she shot up. A brilliant ray of pale gold light exploded from her hand. It hurtled towards the slim shadow cast over a row of short stalagmites.

She was already running across the open space before the charm hit its mark.

'*Ketevos!*'

Her binding charm struck and froze the masculine figure just as a loud cracking sound came from her opponent. He had been too late with his countercharm.

She took a few deep breaths. David was right – casting enchantments wordlessly did use up a lot more energy!

When the lightheaded feeling disappeared, she examined the man in the dark-grey cloak. His white tunic with its simple insignia of a silver seven-rayed star marked him as one of the castle guards. He didn't look very old.

'Dear girl, are you going to stand there all day, or finish the race?'

Rhiannon spun around to find the owner of the voice.

Movement near the narrow opening in the mountain wall caught her attention. She watched as a familiar old man stepped forward. He wore the red cloak of a captain and the white tunic embossed with a gold depiction of twelve stars encircling a crown of the Royal Guard.

'Captain Morton!'

'You've passed this challenge, so you're free to continue onward. Just follow the path through the opening. I'll release Laurent once you're gone.'

She voiced her thanks and quickly moved past him.

'Oh, and I've got a wager on you coming in first, so the best of luck to you, Miss McBride.'

She looked back at him with a warm smile. 'Thank you, Captain. I'll try not to disappoint.'

After leaving Captain Morton and the bound Laurent, Rhiannon followed the path through the narrow opening. It led down a twisting staircase to another passage. She walked to the end, turned the corner and found herself confronted by her next obstacle.

There was a wide gap in the path. She peered down it to see a deep, shadowed trench filled with sharp lances pointing towards her.

On the other side of the pit was a narrow ledge in front of a stone wall. There was no door, and the wall was covered in an acrid smelling, yellow liquid that hissed and steamed.

'What am I meant to do here?' she muttered, looking around for anything that might be a clue as to how she was meant to pass the challenge.

There was no device that she could see. Running her hands over the stone walls revealed nothing.

'*Sepono.*'

The charm David had shown her for creating openings in barriers failed to create a hole in any of the walls.

She cast another glance at the hissing yellow liquid. There must be something she was missing.

She stepped to the edge of the gap to examine the far wall more closely.

Yes. There! Behind the swirling liquid, writing was engraved into the stone.

TO PASS THROUGH MY SURFACE IS NOT SO
HARD TO DO, IF THE SPARK THAT ANIMATES
CAN BE FOUND IN YOU.

'"Pass through my surface" sounds promising,' Rhiannon said with a thoughtful frown. She examined the whole wall. 'It means the way to get through is in the wall. Probably a hidden door.'

She reached out her hand, moved it in a circular clockwise motion and said firmly, '*Undolthgare.*'

The counter to the concealment charm, which she had worked so hard to perfect, failed to reveal a single narrow crevice in the wall.

'I know I did it right,' she muttered. 'They've probably got an enchantment barrier up.'

She removed her gloves and tucked them into her belt. Then she extracted a thick hairpin from her braids. She aimed it at the wall and threw it. The pin evaporated the instant it hit the liquid.

Rhiannon gulped.

'Maybe I threw it at the wrong spot. A door has to be there! Why else would it say walking through it isn't hard?' She reread the words, paused, then focused on "the spark that animates".

'I know I've come across that phrase before,' she said. 'The animating spark. Something found inside of us that makes us animated. What can a spark do? It can start something, make it go, make it come alive ...'

Rhiannon slapped herself on the forehead. 'It makes us come alive. The spark gives us life. The flame of life, or, as they call it in philosophy, the soul. You can't pass through the wall unless you're alive and have a soul within you.'

Swallowing, she took another look at the wall. 'At least,

hopefully that's what it means,' she said faintly, 'or my own spark is about to be snuffed out.'

She backed away from the gap, calculating a long enough distance for a decent run-up.

'Just like long jump, only with a more dangerous pit,' she told herself bracingly. She tried to forget how badly she had always done in long jump.

Then, she ran.

The edge of the gap loomed before her as she neared it. One wrong miscalculation in her jump and she would end up pierced by the sharp lances.

Almost there.

Now!

Rhiannon hurled herself across the wide, perilous trench. A wind whistled in her ears, her momentum sending her flying towards the wall. She was getting closer. Closer. Clos ...

'AH!'

Rhiannon screamed.

Her arms frantically reached out towards the ledge.

Her hands caught on rough stone.

She gasped when her body jerked to a halt, then dangled helplessly above the deadly cluster of lances below.

Her heart pounded.

Her breath came in heavy laboured pants.

Rhiannon groaned, the muscles in her arms burning as she slowly began to pull herself up. Wielding a sword and shield in Defence had strengthened her arms, but she was no Amazon!

Finally, she lifted herself up enough to crawl onto the ledge.

She lay on the ground for a moment, breathing heavily. Then, peering over into the pit, she saw the lances had disappeared. The deep space was now half-filled with water. If she had fallen in, she wouldn't have been pierced, merely wet and cold.

Rhiannon's head fell back to the ground with a soft thump.

'It was water all the time! The lances were just an illusion. Top marks for the scare factor, professors!'

She got up and inched towards the wall.

The yellow liquid fizzed and spat when her fingers touched it. But it did not burn her.

She put her whole hand against the wall. Her hand passed through the stone as if it was swirls of mist.

'It feels like David did when he walked through me wearing Professor Egelbert's ring,' she realised. Not wasting another moment, she stepped through the wall and into the passageway on the other side.

Rhiannon followed the stone path through another series of long passages that sent her deeper into the mountain. The labyrinth seemed to go on forever, and it was filled with sharp corners that she navigated with care.

Finally, she arrived at the opening of a long, wide corridor.

She looked down the passage to see a solid door at the end of it.

She walked towards the closed door, perceiving there was no obvious door handle. Not even a keyhole. She searched around the door, trying to locate the opening mechanism, meeting with no success.

She turned her attention to the walls. Using the light from the two torches placed on either side of the door, she ran her hands over the rough surfaces.

There! Something moved!

She pushed against the loose stone, then prised it out of the wall. It made a faint scritching sound as it came away.

Rhiannon peered into the hole. She saw the glint of a metal lever inside.

Without hesitation, she reached in and pulled the lever forward.

An ominous groaning echoed throughout the walls.

The ground began to tremble.

The floor beneath her feet shifted violently, throwing her off balance and against the wall.

She looked around when the floor moved again. With dawning horror, she saw a chasm had opened in the ground – and it was steadily growing larger. Already, the opening was too wide for her to jump across to the other side. From out of the crack, billows of smoke drifted upward.

Rhiannon hurriedly reached into the hole and pushed the lever back to its original position.

The floor continued to move.

She turned her attention back to the walls.

'The real device to open the door has to be here somewhere.'

She retraced her previous actions with meticulous haste, growing desperate when the location of the real device continued to elude her.

With each passing second, the opening in the ground widened even more.

The jerking movement sent her sprawling onto the floor.

A tower of flames shot out of the dark chasm.

Rhiannon scrambled back to her feet, her eyes returning to their frantic search of the walls.

Then her gaze fell on the torches by the door.

The disruption in the airflow created by the widening chasm behind her was causing one of the flames to flicker, the movement casting dancing shadows on the wall. However, the other flame remained unnaturally still, its light strangely unaffected.

Stumbling over to the motionless flame, she swiftly raised her right arm and placed her hand close to the light. Nothing. There was no burning sensation, or even a slight warmth emanating from the fire.

'It's not real.'

Rhiannon put her hand into the flame, praying she would find the way to open the door. Being unable to see down into its head, she could only feel her way around the top of the sconce until her fingers found a small circular device. Without wasting another second, she pressed it down – just as the last few inches of the floor began to give way.

She launched herself through the opening crack when the door began to slide across.

She crashed onto the ground with a painful thud.

Her breaths coming out in panting gasps of relief, she lay on the hard stone until her pounding heart gradually slowed down.

Pushing herself up, she crawled over to the recently opened doorway and found herself, for the third time that day, looking down into a chasm. Only this time, instead of empty space, or lances at the bottom, there was a river of flame.

'Let's just hope there's not a fourth time.'

She rose slowly to her feet and backed away from the edge. She took a moment to readjust her cloak and sword. Then turning around, she continued on her way, sincerely hoping she was getting close to the last obstacle.

After traversing yet another warren of passageways, Rhiannon found herself entering a small chamber. At first glance she could see nothing out of the ordinary; no spikes materialised out of the ground, no grisly beasts came out to greet her. The entire room seemed unremarkable. That was until she noticed the stairs.

Made of fine, polished stone they circled a pillar on the left side of the room. Rhiannon's eyes widened as they followed their path, realising she could not see the ceiling, only what seemed to be an endless flight of stairs into nothing.

'Oh no, there's no way I'm going up there,' she said loudly, and started walking determinedly for the door on the opposite side of the room.

A long, mournful call came down from above. The sound pierced right into her heart, making it ache.

She looked up again but could not see the source of the cry, even when it came a second time. Hesitating briefly, she considered ignoring the desolate sound when she heard it echoing down for the third time.

Then she knew she could not in good conscience leave in its current state whatever poor creature was making that noise.

She made her way to the bottom of the stairs and took the first step up.

'It's not like I was trying to win this race anyway,' she reminded herself.

After that, all she could concentrate on was placing one foot in front of the other. The stairs continued to spiral ever upwards, while the creature's sad cries filled her ears.

Finally, just when she thought she would not be able to walk up another step, the stairs levelled out to form a thin balcony. There, at the stone's edge, was the most beautiful bird she had ever seen.

The bird was as large as an eagle, and its vibrant feathers were of shades of gold and red, its eyes a brilliant sapphire blue and its beak the colour of a rosy dawn.

'You're a phoenix!'

At Rhiannon's exclamation, the bird nodded before gazing at her with beseeching eyes.

'What's wrong?'

The phoenix lifted up one silver foot. There was a black ring wrapped around its leg. The ring was attached to a chain secured to the ground, thus holding the majestic bird prisoner.

Rhiannon stared at them in horror.

'I can't believe they did this to you.' Moving with extreme care, she approached the restrained creature. 'It's all right, I should be able to get that thing off pretty quickly,' she said gently.

The phoenix bowed its head and waited patiently as she reached out and felt the dark metal. A frown marred her brow when she noticed the enchantment lingering on it.

'I certainly won't be cutting through this with the dagger,' she muttered. Looking the firebird in the eye, she said, 'I'm going to have to use a charm to get it off.'

The phoenix nodded its understanding, then remained still as she laid her hand over the metal wrapped around its leg. '*Liborean.*'

A brief glow of green light shone. Then the shackle broke apart, leaving the bird free and unfettered.

Rising into the air with one sweep of its magnificent wings, the phoenix gave a joyful screech. Then, in a single dive, it latched its talons into the pauldrons on Rhiannon's shoulders.

'Wait, what're you doing?'

Her shocked cry had hardly passed her lips when she felt herself being lifted off the stone balcony and flown out over the empty air below.

Her reaction was unadulterated fear. However, this was soon supplanted by relief when her body was not immediately dropped, but rather lowered with smooth grace to the distant ground below at an astonishing speed.

The moment her feet touched the ground, Rhiannon's muscles relaxed.

Its long tail a bright flash of fiery colour, the phoenix flew around her head before gliding down to land next to her legs. The firebird stretched its head around to groom its back feathers, then extracted a particularly fine one. The long golden-red feather glowed like the first rays of the rising sun in the dim, underground light.

The phoenix twisted its head back around to face Rhiannon. With a high trilling croon sounding in its throat, it nudged her thigh with one end of the feather.

'Is that for me?'

When the phoenix nodded, she reached down and took the feather. Sir Raeden's words repeated themselves inside her mind: *A phoenix will only ever give a feather to those they feel are worthy of receiving it. It is considered a high honour to receive one.*

She gave the feather a soft, tender stroke, then tucked it between her tunic and undershirt while bestowing a quiet smile on the phoenix.

'Thank you.'

The phoenix accepted her gratitude with unblinking dignity. It gave one last crooning note before soaring upwards, its body becoming engulfed in flames as it flew ever higher. Then, in a flash of light, it disappeared.

'If only it was that easy for me to get out of here,' Rhiannon sighed, heading towards the door and to whatever came next.

To her surprise, Rhiannon only had to walk down three corridors until she came to another room. She peeked into the large chamber and saw a multitude of grey statues in the form of human soldiers wearing battle armour. They were also carrying an assortment of weapons. Behind them on the opposite side of the room was the doorway leading out the other side.

Rhiannon stepped cautiously into the room, then instantly froze into stillness when every single statue turned its head to look in her direction.

For the space of a few heartbeats she did not move, waiting to see what would happen. As the seconds dragged on and not one statue moved an inch, she took another step forward. In unison, all the statues instantly turned their bodies to face her.

She hastily backed out of the doorway, mentally retracing her steps from the last room with the phoenix to her present location, trying to recall if there might have been an alternative route for her to take.

Unfortunately, no such route came to mind.

Resigning herself to the inevitable, she removed her cloak, drew her sword and slowly re-entered the room. The statues remained in their last position.

She hesitantly took another step. The statues all moved forward and raised their weapons.

Guessing that enchantments would be ineffective against them, Rhiannon nonetheless tried a simple disarming charm.

Not one weapon so much as shifted an inch.

'*Ketevos.*'

The binding charm also failed.

'*Volverso.*'

The charm, which had sent Izana flying in his duel with David, did not even push one of the statues back a step.

Rhiannon frowned. 'Maybe they work on movement,' she muttered, and quickly whispered, '*Aoratos.*'

Her reflection in the shields of the statues vanished. Hoping the invisibility charm would work, she took a small step forward, only to jump back when one statue swung at her with a sword.

'They can still see me. Great. *Horatos.*'

Rhiannon's body reappeared.

'All right, the hard way it is,' she said, eyeing the group of living stone in front of her. 'Sir Raeden always says plan ahead and use whatever is available.'

Being careful not to take another step forward, she considered her options, then struck out at the arm of the nearest statue. The limb broke off, causing the metal shield it held to fall to the ground.

Like ravenous wolves descending upon their prey, the statues leapt forward.

Rhiannon ducked and swept up the shield.

Wielding her sword with all the skill Sir Raeden, Izana and David had worked so tirelessly to perfect, she fought her way towards the second door.

She dodged and weaved between deadly blows, using her shield to deflect the worst assaults.

Unfortunately, no matter what she did, or how many limbs she cut off, the ferocity of the statues' attack did not lessen, and her progress to the other door was minimal. To make matters worse, each time she cut off a statue's limb, another would instantly form.

A sword broke through her guard. A hot, burning pain sliced across her arm.

Retreat and regroup!

Sir Raeden's instruction rang inside her head.

Rhiannon obeyed the call.

Desperately, she fought her way back to the first doorway. The moment she reached it, the statues all halted.

Her breath coming in heavy pants, Rhiannon wiped away the sweat trickling into her eyes and looked down at her arm. Her shirt was torn, and a red stain was spreading across it. She inspected the wound and was relieved to find that, although it stung, it was not deep.

'I sure hope I don't get in trouble for that,' she muttered. 'He'll probably go off his head about it.'

The image of Sir Raeden's displeased face then morphed into David's.

'Actually, make that both of them,' she amended, and looked at the wound again as a soothing heat enveloped it. Her skin was already beginning to seal itself back together.

Rhiannon wiped away the blood trickling down her arm, then turned to consider the room.

'How do I get past a bunch of indestructible statues?'

She keenly surveyed the room, attempting to spot anything that would give her an indication of how to overcome this latest obstacle.

Her gaze passed over a section of the wall on the left side of the room.

Wait! What was that?

Rhiannon looked back, her eyes narrowed in concentration.

The engraved image carved into the smooth surface of a large grey stone was similar to the statues littering the room. However, unlike the statutes, the image's forehead was marked by the word 'emet'.

'Emet. Emet. How do I know that word?'

Rhiannon stared at the image, her mind sorting through her memories.

A page of a book. Animated statues of clay and stone. A visit by Queen Maiwen late at night.

Realisation dawned. The word had been mentioned in the book she had been reading after she won the race against Marcus.

'Golems.'

Rhiannon shifted her attention back to the soldiers of stone.

'They're all golems. But none of them have the animating word on their forehead. Does that mean they're all linked to the one on the wall?'

Rhiannon tightened her grip on the hilt of her sword and pondered this new quandary.

'I'll have to believe it does,' she finally decided. 'Now, the book in Defence said golems were created from stone and clay. To animate them, they must be marked with the word "emet". But, to return them to their original state, the first letter must be destroyed, or at least damaged. The question becomes, what can I use to do that?'

She glanced at the sword in her right hand, contemplated using it, but then reconsidered.

'A bit too cumbersome to make a precise hit on something like that,' she admitted.

She placed her shield on the ground, then drew the dagger Sir Raeden had given to her from its sheath. Simply by looking at it, she knew the blade had been honed to a smooth and deadly sharpness.

'This should do.'

She cast an assessing look at the golems, noting where they were all positioned.

'Misdirecting them first may give me a better chance of making it to the wall,' she murmured, and turning to the right, she took two large but cautious steps forward.

As she had hoped, every golem turned and took a step towards her.

Rhiannon backed away, carefully retreating to the doorway.

'Now, I just have to make it to the wall before they do.'

She focused on the task of quickly calculating the best and most efficient way to perform this feat, ignoring the voice inside her head that told her she would fail. It sounded suspiciously like her foster-sister Annabelle.

She took a deep breath, adjusting her grip on her two weapons.

Then, without giving herself the chance to question the wisdom of what she was about to do, she darted to the left.

Like a terrifying choreographed group of dancers, the golems all around the room turned and launched themselves at her, their weapons glinting menacingly with cold purpose as they attacked.

Rhiannon's heart pounded. She used every tactic and move Sir Raeden had drummed into her to avoid being struck down in her tracks.

Dodging a particularly vicious blow, she struck out fiercely with a swift upward slash.

She did not wait to see the golem's arm regrow.

Barrelling forward, she struck out at the last golem that stood between her and the engraved image, separating the head from its body with one clean swipe of her sword.

She lunged forward, the dagger raised in her other hand.

With a burst of wild energy, she drove the blade into the image's forehead. The sharp point easily penetrated the soft, grey stone, obliterating the first 'e'.

CRASH!

Rhiannon spun around at the noise, then watched in relief as each golem's body broke apart. The cracked pieces of statue fell to the ground in a thundering pile of crumbled stone.

The noise finally abated, and the cloud of dust dissipated.

Rhiannon turned from her silent contemplation of the ruined golems to extract her dagger from the wall. Thankfully, it had survived being stabbed into the stone remarkably well.

Replacing her weapons in their sheaths, she retrieved her cloak and walked in the direction of the now unprotected exit. She rubbed her aching elbow as she drew closer to the doorway, saying optimistically, 'Hopefully that should be the last ...'

Fzzzzzz!

Rhiannon's voice broke off as a wave of fiery heat encircled the room.

In a burst of red flame, a towering ring of fire erupted along each of the walls, including across the doorway that only seconds before had been free of any obstacles.

'You've got to be joking!'

Unsurprisingly, Rhiannon's cry of protest went unanswered, except for the loud crackle of the flames.

'Is there no end to this part of the race?'

Rhiannon warily approached the burning fire spread across the doorway. An intense heat warmed her skin. She looked down at Sir Raeden's other gift to her: the flask of water. Untying it from her belt, she removed the wooden stopper and tossed some water into the flames. The liquid evaporated instantly with a quiet hiss.

'Not a heated illusion then,' she muttered.

She looked down to see the broken torso of one of the golems consumed by the blaze. The once grey stone was now discoloured and blackened.

'Definitely a real fire.'

Rhiannon frowned as she reattached the flask to her belt.

'I could probably try casting a protection charm on myself, but who knows if it would work against an enchanted flame. A dousing charm also wouldn't be of much help. Maybe if I ...'

She abruptly broke off and laughed.

'That's why they chose a phoenix! It was probably in on the whole thing!'

She reached inside her tunic and retrieved the fire-bird's golden-red feather. Holding it up, she watched as the colour morphed to a brilliant crimson.

'"A phoenix feather will protect you from any kind of fire,"' she quoted aloud. Looking up ruefully at the burning flames, she added, 'I just wish it wasn't quite so large.'

Rhiannon slowly approached the fiery blaze, then cautiously stretched out a hand and put it into the fire. The heat was intense and the flames licked over her flesh, but she felt no pain.

'Let's just hope I don't drop the feather,' she observed with a tinge of morbid humour. 'Rhiannon Flambé would not be a good look.' Taking a deep breath, she stepped into the burning inferno.

Hot. Roasting. Lying fully exposed on a hot tin roof in the middle of the most sweltering day in summer. Bathed in lava. None of these could adequately describe the intense heat that engulfed her as she hastily made her way through the thick wall of fire. Her body did not catch alight, but it felt as though it had.

She burst out the other side, getting as far from the flames as she possibly could. In her hand, the phoenix's feather returned to its previous golden-red colour.

'Thank goodness I had that,' she said, 'I really didn't fancy becoming a human torch.'

She tucked the precious feather back under her tunic, then looked around at her new surroundings.

She was in a wide chamber with a high ceiling which was lit by a soft light, like the first glow of the sun at dawn. In the middle of the room, with three steps leading up to it, was a large, square dais carved from ivory stone and surrounded by eight marble pillars. However, the most important feature to Rhiannon was the lack of a second doorway.

'This has to be the last room,' she said optimistically. 'And that looks like a transonus dais.'

She mounted the steps with growing hope. Walking to the middle of the dais, she looked down in time to see a multitude of previously invisible runes begin to glow.

The faint blue light spread throughout the dim room, flooding every crevice with its brilliance.

Then, with a radiant flash of white light, Rhiannon's body vanished, leaving the dais empty of any trace of her.

~Chapter 27~

FOUL PLAY

Rhiannon reappeared in a burst of incandescent light and immediately began to survey her new surroundings. Once the brilliant glow faded, she saw she was standing on an exact replica of the dais in the mountain. This one, however, was facing a vast gathering of tall birch trees which stood like proud sentinels on the edge of a large forest. The mid-afternoon sun in the west created dancing shadows among the trees.

'I see you were successful in passing the trials in the mountain.'

The deep, reassuring voice of Arastar came from behind her. She turned around to look at him and saw the other seven dragons across the wide expanse of ground between the forest and the Del Enger Mountains.

'It was a close call on a few occasions,' she admitted honestly. 'I think anyone would have to be crazy to knowingly sign up for this race.'

'It's not quite over yet,' Arastar reminded her. 'That is Finbar Forest. Inside it is the Pool of Remembrance. You need to find the pool and retrieve some of the water, then return here before we can leave for Valieoth Castle. I would hurry though; several of the other riders have already entered.'

'Have any returned?'

'No.' Arastar appeared to find this fact amusing because a roguish smile spread across his face. 'Although that does not mean they won't soon recall why they are in the forest and come hurrying out.'

Puzzled by these words, Rhiannon descended from the dais and stared into the depths of the forest.

'A word of warning, child,' Arastar called out.

She looked back over her shoulder at him and raised a questioning eyebrow.

'A short distance inside the forest you will find a clearing with several pathways leading from it,' he said. 'The pathways were created by the pixies who inhabit the forest; therefore, you will need to choose carefully which path to follow. Only one actually leads you directly to the Pool of Remembrance.'

'Let me guess: the others all lead you around in circles, completely off-course or add miles to the walk.'

'I see someone has explained the mischievous nature of pixies to you.' Arastar looked up at the sun's position. 'Do not take too long,' he added, 'you don't want to get caught on a pixie pathway when night falls. They have a way of disappearing in the dark.'

Rhiannon promised she would do her best, then strode into the forest. The clean, fresh scent of the trees enveloped her the moment she entered, while the leaves coating the ground rustled with the movements of all manner of small animals. She jumped as a laedary, a strange creature with the appearance of a badger crossed with a rabbit, scurried within inches of her foot. Fortunately, she did not injure it, for laedaries, like badgers, were ruthless when seeking to avenge a wrong done to them.

She soon came across the clearing Arastar had mentioned.

Noticing the rings of smooth delicate stones that covered the ground, she stepped into the circular area. Several paths led away from there deeper into the forest.

'Choosing the right one is going to be almost impossible,' she muttered.

'The path you seek is the least obvious of all.'

The soft, melodious voice floated on the air like the gentle ringing of wind chimes on a summer breeze.

Rhiannon spun around, her eyes warily scanning the surrounding trees.

'Who's there?' she called guardedly, her hand reaching instinctively for the hilt of her sword.

'One who means you no harm,' the serene voice replied. Then the speaker glided out of the trunk of a giant ash tree with barely a whisper of sound and took corporeal form.

Rhiannon's eyes widened in stunned surprise. Mutely, she stared at the tall creature now standing in front of her with its flowing raiment shimmering with every movement.

'Greetings, small one. I am Edranel, a dryad of these woods.' The tree spirit smiled in welcome. Its face shone with a pure radiance, and its shining fair hair danced as though moved by an unfelt wind.

'But I thought dryads only came out at night.'

'Our preference is indeed when the sun has sunk to her rest, and the moon and stars have risen. However, we can venture forth during daylight if we choose.' Edranel considered Rhiannon silently for a moment, then remarked, 'I believe you are the child of whom the old one spoke.'

'The old one? Who's that?'

'A stag of immense age who informed the forest spirits and animals of your kindness to him in the winter when he escaped his pursuers. He described a human female child with golden eyes, a pleasant voice and bearing a strange mark as one who had his trust and favour.'

Rhiannon smiled, recalling the magnificent stag she had encountered shortly before she was hit by Officer Exton's capturing charm. 'I remember him,' she said, 'and I'm honoured he thought so highly of me.'

'He asked that all spirits of the forest provide you with assistance should you ever require it,' Edranel informed her.

She gaped at him in astonishment. 'He did?' she squeaked.

Laughter like soft birdsong passed the lips of the dryad.

'I can see why he liked you,' the spirit remarked. 'It will be a pleasure to assist you.'

The dryad reached out one very pale hand and gently grasped hers, its long fingers engulfing her small ones until they disappeared from view.

'This way, little one, the path you seek is over here.'

Rhiannon felt like a toddler walking beside her very tall father as she obediently accompanied the dryad. It led her off to the far side where the cobblestones formed a narrow path. The trail appeared to lead back to the edge of the forest.

'Do not believe what your eyes tell you,' Edranel advised, 'this path will safely lead you to the Pool of Remembrance. Do not leave it, or you may find your way onto one of the other paths, and many have spent days lost on them. Good luck to you, small one.'

The dryad released her hand and moved away. She watched as the beautiful tree spirit disappeared into the trunk of the large ash tree, leaving no trace that it had ever been out.

'Thank you,' she called, before turning back to the opening in front of her.

Inhaling deeply, she stepped forward and began her trek along the narrow path.

Rhiannon quickly discovered Edranel had been telling the truth. Although it appeared that the path was leading her back to the edge of the forest, it soon became apparent this was not the case. The path twisted and weaved in between the trees in a strange pattern that soon took her deeper into the forest. Keeping her eyes on the path, she was careful not to let her attention stray.

'It can't be too much farther,' she muttered, ducking under another low-hanging branch.

As though to prove her correct, the sounds of playful splashing carried from somewhere off to her left.

She quickened her steps and soon was stepping off the path to gaze at what could only be the Pool of Remembrance. The extensive body of crystal-clear water sparkled in the sunlight, and at its far end she could see a grove of elm trees.

She paused next to a large grey rock to politely greet the lithe figure who was casually sitting on it, the gossamer fabric draped over their form shimmering like rivulets of water cascading down a waterfall.

The feminine looking creature gracefully turned its head, the seductive smile on its lips melting away as it cast its luminous eyes over Rhiannon's girlish features. A pout of disappointment appeared, and indeed the creature almost seemed to be sulking.

'A *female* human! You'll be no fun at all.' Despite the complaining words, the creature's voice held a bewitching quality. 'Why do all my sisters get to ensnare a man and I don't!'

The creature pointed off to the side.

Rhiannon followed its direction to see a very dishevelled Corin O'Shannessy. The rider's cloak was covered in scorch marks and his hair looked badly singed. Beside him sat Ivo Pembroke and Takeo Fukui, both of whom had a phoenix feather tucked inside their tunics. All three men were on the water's edge, staring enraptured at three female figures who were singing and swimming about in the water.

Comprehension dawned on Rhiannon.

'You're water nymphs.'

Now she could understand Arastar's amusement, and also why none of the men had found their way back to the forest entrance.

David and John had told her about the water nymphs, who took delight in bewitching any male who happened upon them. Only a man who was extremely strong-willed, or whose mind was completely focused on some other matter, could ignore the allure of the beguiling creatures' singing. Nevertheless, several irate and frantic wives had discovered that the best way to break the nymph's charm over a man was to give them a sound whack on the back of their head.

Rhiannon smiled up at the dejected nymph. 'I'm sorry I disappointed you,' she said, 'but there are still a couple of other men to come. Maybe you could ensnare one of them.'

The nymph smiled joyously, immediately brightened at this prospect. 'Really? Oh, that is splendid!' she cried.

Taking advantage of the creature's happier mood, Rhiannon respectfully asked, 'Would you mind if I took some of the water from the pool?'

The beautiful creature waved one dainty hand. 'Not at all, my dear,' she said pleasantly. 'Take as much as you like.'

Rhiannon uttered a quick word of thanks and hurried forward.

She removed the flask from her belt, pulled out the stopper and tipped out the contents already inside. Kneeling down, she dipped the flask into the pool. A small amount of water seeped inside it. After a moment she withdrew it and replaced the seal.

Straightening up, she reattached the flask to her belt and turned away from the water's edge to walk back towards the path. She had almost reached it when the sound of heavy footsteps made her look up.

She only had a second to take in the sight of a badly singed Darvill Crumper racing off the path before he knocked into her. Stumbling backwards, she fell and collided heavily against the nymph's rock.

A sharp pain shot through the back of her head.

She winced, then blinked in shock when Crumper paused. He

roughly clasped her bare wrist with one beringed hand and hauled her back to her feet.

'I'm terribly sorry, are you all right?'

Rhiannon stared at him, stunned. Why would he, of all the riders, care if she was all right?

'Oh, glorious delight! Another man!'

The nymph's pleased exclamation forestalled Rhiannon's reply. She cast a brief look at the creature, then took off.

On the path, she raced down the cobblestones. The nymph's flirtatious voice sounded out like a siren's song behind her. Soon, it was accompanied by Crumper's impatient protests.

She took a sharp corner at a run and smashed into a very strong and solid form.

Her arms flailing, she felt herself falling backwards for the second time in less than a minute.

Two hands reached out and grasped her shoulders. She looked up past the broad chest now adorned with a phoenix feather, into the unsmiling face of Bjorn Steinberg.

'Watch yourself, child,' the rider said with gruff kindness, helping her regain her balance. 'We certainly don't want to see you get injured.'

'Thank you.'

'Just be careful,' he muttered, before making a move to go past her.

'Wait!' Rhiannon grasped one of his forearms. 'Since you stopped me from having a bad fall, it's only fair I warn you there are nymphs at the pool.'

A grim smile spread across Steinberg's face.

'Child, you are looking at the most dour and determined bachelor in all of Álnair. Their wiles won't get far with me.'

With a courteous bow, he hurried away and continued down the path.

Rhiannon did not wait to see him disappear.

She turned and ran until she finally reached the clearing where Edranel's large ash tree stood. She hurried past it, calling out a breathless, 'Thanks for your help,' before dashing in among the tall birch trees.

Finally, she burst out of the forest to where Arastar now stood waiting.

She clambered up into the saddle on his back and took hold of the reins.

'Let's go!' she cried.

Arastar lifted off the ground with one powerful thrust of his wings.

Rhiannon glanced back at the forest in time to see the drenched form of Darvill Crumper emerge with a furious bellow.

'That nymph must've dragged him into the water,' she gasped with a laugh.

Arastar shot up and flew over the first of the mountains.

Rhiannon clung to the reins, a sudden wave of dizziness assailing her.

She shrugged it off as a side-effect of changing altitudes too quickly.

'Crumper's not far behind us!' she called out. 'I don't care how fast you have to go, Arastar, but we can't let him win.'

'Understood. The castle lies a hundred miles from here, so hold on tight!'

With a fantastic burst of speed, he raced over the mountains, his body twisting and shooting past obstacles at an incredible rate. The clouds from earlier had cleared, and Rhiannon was able to see Mount Solus in the distance.

She took another look behind her to see how close Crumper was to them.

An even stronger wave of dizziness almost toppled her over.

She fought to regain her balance.

Through her distorted vision she could make out the forms

of Crumper and his dragon chasing after them. They were closer than before.

'Faster, Arastar!' she yelled. 'Faster!'

A third and much stronger sensation of having her head spin engulfed her.

She resisted the inclination to close her eyes.

Terrified she might fall, she began to loop the reins around her hands.

As she was struggling to secure one of the reins, her blurred gaze fell on a fine scratch mark on the inside of her right wrist. The skin around it was slightly inflamed. The image of Crumper's beringed hand tightly gripping her wrist flashed before her eyes.

'That slimy little creep. He's drugged me.'

Her whispered words were muffled by the rushing wind.

A feeling of dread entered her heart.

Tightening her grip on the reins, she shouted, 'FASTER!'

Arastar heard the urgent tone in her voice and obeyed, pushing himself even harder.

The fogginess enveloping Rhiannon's mind and blinding her vision increased with every passing moment. Everything became a befuddling mess of blurred images and disjointed thoughts – except for a single voice that sounded like David's demanding she stay upright and keep a firm hold on the reins.

The first indication Rhiannon had that they were nearing the end of the race was when a chorus of cheers and shouts rang out.

She kept her focus on the back of Arastar's head, clinging grimly to the reins. She did not even turn to see whether Crumper had succeeded in getting closer.

'Come on,' she breathed desperately, 'come on!'

As Arastar dived towards the ground, the angle of his descent increased his speed nauseatingly and her stomach jerked up into her throat.

The wind rushed by, the force pushing against her face, and

the noise blocking all other sound. The sensation of the reins being squeezed tight in her hands was the only thing keeping her grounded. Then, with a deafening roar and his body swooping into a smooth upward glide, Arastar's speed decreased.

Rhiannon's ears were once again free of the muffling noise of the wind.

She heard the clamorous applause and cheers rise up from below her.

She felt Arastar gracefully pivot and slowly fly towards the ground.

Off to the side, blurry figures were racing towards them, their voices calling out happy words of greeting she could not understand.

There was a light *thump.*

Arastar had reached the ground.

She instantly slumped forward, her hands finally loosening their grip on the reins.

Through her daze, she heard the tone in the voices changing, their cheerful, welcoming words transforming into cries of concern.

'She never loosened her grip,' said Arastar. 'The only thing she said was to go faster.'

'There's blood on the sleeve of her shirt!' said David.

Rhiannon felt a pair of strong hands lift her so she was leaning against a chest which held the distinct scent of sandalwood. She slowly tilted her head to watch as a familiar pair of hands started to undo the reins wrapped around hers.

'Sir.' Her voice came out as a low groan, as weak as a newborn kitten's.

'Be silent, child.'

Sir Raeden's rebuke lacked his usual frigid tone as he gently freed her wrists, then gathered her limp form into his arms.

Her eyelids finally surrendered to their desire to close. She felt a swift *whoosh*, then a slight jarring thud that told her Sir Raeden had actually jumped off Arastar's back while holding her.

'Best get her to the Healers Pavilion.' King Stephen's authoritative voice sliced through the noise of the crowd. 'And, Lord Anton, get all the other riders back here at once.'

'Is she all right?'

'What's happened to her?'

David and John's concerned questions went unanswered as Sir Raeden strode through the crowd, his forbidding glare and stern expression dissuading anyone from approaching him.

Inside the Healers Pavilion, the tumultuous sounds of the crowd mercifully faded.

Rhiannon moaned gratefully when Sir Raeden knelt down to lay her on a cot. The smooth material sank under her weight.

'Can she tell us what happened?'

The unknown voice sounded very close to Rhiannon's right ear. She weakly tried to raise her arm to push the speaker away. Her hand had not risen very far before it was caught in a firm grip.

'I do not believe that will be necessary,' Sir Raeden's voice replied.

Rhiannon felt his cool fingers examine the inside of her wrist with professional skill.

'This scratch is too precise and fine to have been made with anything other than a needle.'

A warm waft of air drifted across Rhiannon's skin. She forced her eyes open. Through a narrow slit, she could make out the blurry and strangely humorous sight of her guardian's head bent cautiously over her wrist as he inhaled carefully. Feeling too lethargic to even smile, she closed her eyes again.

A stream of harsh, foreign words suddenly erupted from Sir Raeden's mouth.

'Get me a bottle of purified thranlaire. Quickly!'

Horrified sounds came from David and John.

Something must be dreadfully wrong, Rhiannon thought absently.

'Rhiannon. Look at me, child.'

Dreamily trying to obey her guardian's gentle words, Rhiannon found her body was quite unwilling to comply.

'McBride! Open your eyes!'

Rhiannon mumbled in protest at the more familiar barking tone of Sir Raeden's voice, but reluctantly forced her weary eyelids to open.

She looked up drowsily at the stern face hovering above hers. Distractedly, she thought her guardian's eyes were like the night sky now they had darkened from their normal icy blue to a deep indigo.

'You need to focus on me,' Sir Raeden ordered sharply, 'do not close your eyes. You have a high concentration of somlyne in your system. Even your ability for self-healing cannot save you should it overcome you. If you succumb to it, you will never wake up again.'

'Bu' 'm sleepy.'

'That is the toxin in your blood. Your body has absorbed almost a pure dose of it.'

''e did it.'

'Who?'

''arvill 'umper.'

'He will be dealt with very soon,' Sir Raeden promised, comprehending her slurred utterance. 'But you must stay awake.'

Rhiannon fought to obey, but every part of her body protested the battle. Her body had exhausted itself fighting the effects of the toxin all the way from the forest. It had not even been able to heal the scratch on her wrist!

'Rhiannon!'

Sir Raeden's harsh call barely penetrated the thick fog now clouding her mind.

'Tremaine, go see what's taking that fool of a healer so long.'

'Yes, Sir.'

Rhiannon moaned when an arm slid under her shoulders and lifted her upright. A babble of incomprehensible mutterings fell from her lips.

'Go to her other side and talk to her. Get her to respond.'

Sir Raeden's order was promptly acted upon as David's voice came nearer until it was right beside her.

'Rhiannon, tell me about the phoenix feather. Did you meet a phoenix in the race?'

An image of the firebird drifted through her befuddled mind. 'Pwetty bird.'

'I'll take that as yes,' said David. 'Did you use the feather?'

Memory of the enchanted flames in the golem chamber erupted in her head. 'Fire. Lots o' fire.'

'What else did you see?'

Her head tilted even lower.

'Rhiannon! What else did you see?'

A short, stinging slap landed on her cheek. Rhiannon did not even flinch, the pain barely registering in her mind. Her whole being felt as if it was ablaze with heat. The gentle warmth that normally sealed a wound in her flesh had intensified until it felt like a raging furnace, and it was enveloping her entire body.

'Rhiannon, come on! Fight it!'

David's desperate plea was almost drowned out by John's cry of, 'We've got it!'

'Pour it over her wrist,' Sir Raeden ordered sharply.

'But … but, Sir Raeden,' the unknown voice from earlier objected, 'thranlaire should only be administered in small amounts due to …'

'Give it here!' David's curt words cut off the man's protest.

'Wait! Your Royal Highness! You can't take that! Only fully trained healers are permitted to administer restricted substances. Hey! Let go of me!'

'I cannot permit you to interfere,' came Izana's stern voice. 'And I'd advise you to keep silent.'

'Ensure you pour it over the entire wound,' Sir Raeden instructed.

David immediately complied.

A cool, thick liquid touched the skin on Rhiannon's wrist. A strong, sweet perfume like that of early spring blossoms spread through the pavilion.

'Sir, how long does it take to work?'

'Considering how long the somlyne has been in her system, it may take a few minutes or it may have no effect at all. Her body's ability to heal itself may have helped delay the toxin from spreading as quickly as it normally would, but having a poison in her bloodstream is a lot different than mending a broken bone or fighting off a charm. The effects of the somlyne may already be irreversible.'

Even as Sir Raeden spoke, Rhiannon could feel a cool sensation spread over her wrist, then radiate up her arm and throughout her entire body. Soon, all her nerves were tingling with an icy, chilling sensation. Then the fog that had seeped into her mind mercifully began to dissipate.

Soon the coolness caused by the thranlaire morphed into the familiar gentle warmth of her own body's healing power.

Rhiannon inhaled deeply as the oppressive cloud finally evaporated. She took a moment to appreciate the feeling before she slowly opened her eyes and gazed into a pair of deeply concerned violet ones.

Chapter 28

AN OMINOUS DISCOVERY

Honestly, I'm fine,' Rhiannon said, for what seemed like the thousandth time since she had first opened her eyes to see David looking down at her. 'I'm certainly feeling a lot better than that healer will be once Sir Raeden gets through lecturing him on his "absolute incompetence" and "arrant stupidity" in trying to interfere.'

'What's the name of John's horse?' David repeated his question, ignoring her protests.

'Asaph,' she replied impatiently. 'Yours is called Cináed. You also have a really annoying cousin called Marcus, and you love to take watches apart. See, nothing wrong with my memory or my mind.'

John gave a snort of laughter. 'You do sound like yourself again,' he said with a smile.

'I definitely feel better,' she admitted. 'Whatever it was that Crumper poisoned me with was certainly unpleasant.'

'It's called somlyne,' David said quietly. 'It's made from the flowers on the somlyne plants that grow in the Valley of Dreams. If you inhale the pollen from the actual flower it sends you into a deep sleep, and a diluted form is used as a sedative. But a concentrated version put directly into your bloodstream and not treated in time will put you in an irreversible coma. You got a pure dose of it.'

'You're lucky Sir Raeden recognised the scent left on your skin,' Izana informed her, his eyes solemn. 'If he hadn't known to use thranlaire on it, you would've been beyond help by now.'

'What's thranlaire?'

'It's a herb,' David replied. 'Its healing properties are potent, and it's the only thing known to counteract the effects of somlyne – if used in time.'

'So what will happen to Crumper now?'

'He and Plancy will most likely be paying a rather extended visit to the Isle of Culhos.'

Rhiannon frowned at David's reply. 'Isn't that the island prison where serious offenders are sent?'

John nodded. 'Poisoning someone with somlyne is not a minor crime,' he said.

'But how will they prove Crumper even did it? Or that Plancy was involved? I doubt they'll just take my word for it.'

The sound of the silken drapes at the pavilion entrance being drawn back had its four occupants looking around to see Sir Raeden step through the opening. Queen Maiwen, Lady Agnes and Caiden Alcober were close behind him.

The queen ignored everyone else in the pavilion and went immediately to Rhiannon to engulf her in a hug.

'Dear child, I believe I aged ten years waiting for Sir Raeden to reappear and tell us you were all right,' she said softly, placing a tender kiss on top of Rhiannon's head. 'I do not think I have been so terrified since the day they brought David home unconscious.'

Rhiannon could not say anything in reply. Queen Maiwen was behaving in the same manner she had always dreamed her own mother would if she hadn't disappeared. It was making her heart ache with bittersweet joy.

'And your arm was hurt,' Queen Maiwen continued, reaching out a hand to inspect the damaged and bloodied sleeve. She frowned. 'This tear was made by a sword.'

Rhiannon swallowed and nodded, casting an anxious look at Sir Raeden, David and Izana.

'There was a room full of golems,' she was finally able to reply. 'I had to fight them to get to the last doorway in the mountain. One of them got through my guard. I'm sorry.'

'Dear girl, there's no need to apologise,' Queen Maiwen said. 'To have defeated a number of golems is no small feat. Would you not agree, Sir Raeden?'

Rhiannon looked at her guardian and saw him nod. 'You did well to only receive a single injury,' he told her briefly.

'I'll say,' David announced. 'You're definitely not a novice with a sword anymore, Rhiannon.'

Izana gave her a small smile. 'You worked hard to improve your skills, and you succeeded brilliantly. Well done.'

She gave all four of them a slightly teary grin, then looked at Caiden Alcober, who said, 'Had to see with me own eyes tha' you were all right, lass.'

She gave the Trínondras member a warm smile. 'Thank you, although I certainly wouldn't be without Sir Raeden's help.' She cast a grateful look at her guardian.

Sir Raeden acknowledged this praise with a slight inclination of his head. Then he informed her in a detached voice that her presence was now required outside.

'And you will remain next to me at all times once we have exited this pavilion,' he ordered.

Obediently following his instructions, Rhiannon exited the Healers Pavilion into the late afternoon sunlight and was instantly made aware of the reason for her guardian's direction. Jostling and shoving one another aside, their faces filled with expectant anticipation and curiosity, the crowd gathered near the entrance immediately swarmed closer like a plague of locusts. Their voices rose to a thunderous crescendo as they cheered.

Rhiannon only caught the odd word from the roaring sound. She turned a puzzled face to David who was on her other side with John beside him.

'Why are they congratulating me? Sir Raeden's the one who deserves it.'

David laughed. 'They're congratulating you on becoming the youngest rider to ever win the Dragon's Cup.'

'Y-You mean I won?' she gasped.

'Of course you did!'

'Your riding skills allowed Arastar to fly at his top speed,' came Queen Maiwen's voice from behind them. Izana and Caiden Alcober were on either side of her, with Lady Agnes bringing up the rear, looking like an overprotective tigress as she stared at the crowd with watchful eyes. 'He has informed me on numerous occasions that he regularly has to adjust his speed to accommodate his rider.'

'If you'd been any less skilled, he would've had to go slower,' John said. 'If that had happened, Crumper might've had a chance of beating you.'

Stunned by these revelations, Rhiannon could only look again at the cheering crowd. She wondered if this speechless disbelief was how a competitor felt when they won an Olympic event.

Upon seeing David's other Robesmen in the frontline of the crowd, she gave them a small wave. All of them, even Derrick, looked relieved to see her alive and walking unaided.

She saw Marcus sullenly standing beside his parents. His mother gave her a sweet smile, but his father first stared at her as if she was an exhibit at a freak show before his charming mien reappeared. Thankfully, the movement of the crowd soon obscured the family from her sight.

The small group led by Sir Raeden slowly approached the large platform where the Dragon's Cup shone like a glittering beacon in the afternoon sunlight. All the dragons from the race were watching from the far side of the platform, while the other riders were gathered at the bottom of the steps. The three men whom Rhiannon had left watching the nymphs with adoring faces were now standing with identical expressions of sheepish embarrassment. Bjorn Steinberg was standing next to them, regarding all three with a derisive look of contempt.

Rhiannon gazed up at the group standing on the platform, and gasped.

'What's Councillor Plancy doing up there?'

'Don't fret yerself, lass,' Caiden Alcober said. 'Everythin' is fine.'

'But he ...'

A sharp warning for her to be quiet came from Sir Raeden.

She stared up at her guardian in shock.

'A member of the High Council is always present when the Dragon's Cup is handed to the winner,' Sir Raeden said. 'On this occasion, Councillor Plancy has been selected for that singular honour.'

Sir Raeden's tone clearly conveyed he expected no further comment from her. He continued towards the platform, leaving her with no choice but to follow in bewildered silence.

Queen Maiwen and Lady Agnes parted from the group when they reached the platform, taking their place beside King Stephen and Lord Daiki. The remainder of them continued to where the other riders were standing. Rhiannon noticed that Crumper, far from looking worried that his actions against her would be revealed, only wore a disgruntled expression as he glared at the ground.

A booming voice from the platform drew Rhiannon's attention to the impressive figure of Lord Sharbel. The High Chancellor was standing with raised arms to emphasise his request for everyone to be quiet.

An eager hush descended upon the crowd.

'Thank you, Lord Sharbel.'

All eyes focused on King Stephen's tall form as he stepped forward and spoke.

'The challenges faced by the riders in this race are always designed and selected with the greatest of care, and in the utmost secrecy, by Professor Ambrose Egelbert and the professors at Ryegoth Academy. No one, not even myself or the members of the High Council, are told what the challenges will be. Like you, we have to wait for the details to be revealed in the Champion Rider's interview after the race, although sometimes, even that does not tell us much.'

A ripple of laughter went through the crowd.

Rhiannon looked at David in confusion.

'Sir Raeden's interview is famous for being the shortest ever given,' David said to her in a low voice. 'When asked to describe the tasks he faced, all he said was, "Clearly, they were not insurmountable."'

Rhiannon bit her lip to stifle her laughter. It wasn't difficult to picture a younger version of her guardian saying those exact words in a cold, dismissive manner. Certainly, no one would ever be able to accuse Sir Raeden of being an emotionally verbose winner.

She returned her attention to King Stephen to hear him continue with, 'However, today our riders received an additional challenge that was known only to a select few.'

Thoroughly intrigued by this revelation, the crowd ceased murmuring.

'Each rider was informed by their dragon upon exiting Mount Solus to retrieve a small amount of water from the Pool of Remembrance. For those of you who do not think that is a difficult challenge, you have clearly not met the nymphs who dwell there.'

Rhiannon peered into the crowd. She noticed the men sending sympathetic glances towards the male riders. The women in comparison merely shared looks of feminine disgust.

'Sadly, only three of our riders who reached the pool were successful in completing this last challenge, and we ask that they please present the proof of their achievement.'

Rhiannon removed the flask from her belt and stepped forward.

Bjorn Steinberg and Darvill Crumper did the same.

Obeying a gesture from King Stephen, they made their way onto the platform.

To her relief, Rhiannon noticed David and Sir Raeden following her up the steps.

'Now, King Nuallán, if you would be so kind.'

A bright glow briefly illuminated the space next to King Stephen, heralding the arrival of several small figures with a colourful array of hair colours.

Four of the faeries were carrying a large silver basin, delicately crafted and engraved with strange hieroglyphics.

The other faery, the tallest of them all, stood proudly erect, his ancient eyes set in a face that remained free of any of the normal signs of ageing.

'King Stephen, my people and I are honoured to lend you the Míargstan.'

Without warning, David leapt past Rhiannon and hurled himself at Darvill Crumper. The entire crowd watched in shock as he grappled with the rider. Then he wrestled the flask out of Crumper's hand.

His face now a picture of panicked dismay, Crumper whirled around, only to have his attempt at escape ruthlessly intercepted by Sir Raeden's fist.

'Ketevos!'

A deep blue light issued from Sir Raeden's hand to wrap around the torso of his barely conscious prisoner.

Two castle guards stepped in to take charge of the bound man.

David carried the flask to his father, saying, 'He didn't get a chance to tip any of it out.'

King Stephen accepted the flask, then called out for Lord Anton and Caiden Alcober to join him. The two men walked up the steps as he removed the stopper from Crumper's flask and poured the contents into the Míargstan.

'As our disgraced rider has realised, there was another reason why they were asked to retrieve a sample of water from the Pool of Remembrance,' King Stephen said, handing the empty flask back to David. He nodded to the two other Trínondras members. Together, they bowed their heads and gazed into the shimmering water.

Rhiannon waited for David to return to her side, then asked, 'What is that?'

'It's the Míargstan, the oldest known artefact of the faery people. When water from the Pool of Remembrance is poured into it, the recent memories of the person who drew the water are reflected on its surface. Father told me after the race started that he'd commanded the race officials early this morning to include retrieving some of the water as the last challenge, so if something did happen to one of the riders, then they'd be able to see exactly what happened.'

'A poison ring!'

Caiden Alcober's furious cry echoed across the area.

All three members of the Trínondras turned away from the silvery light emitting from the basin to glare at the bound rider.

'He scratched th' poor lass with th' needle of a poison ring!'

'It wasn't my idea!' Crumper protested weakly. 'He gave me the ring. Told me it'd only make 'er sleep.'

'Who did?'

A movement near the tall stand where the Dragon's Cup was

placed made Rhiannon's head snap to the side just as Crumper revealed, 'Councillor Plancy!'

'NO!'

Pandemonium broke out as Rhiannon dashed forward to prevent the councillor from grabbing the glittering prize. She rammed into the man, feeling a spark of satisfaction when he stumbled backwards.

His elderly body teetering precariously on the edge of the platform, Councillor Plancy's flailing limbs were roughly seized and dragged back to safety by Lord Daiki.

A small object dislodged from the councillor's robes and clattered to the ground. Of dark metal, it depicted the head of a dragon being pierced by a thunderbolt. Rhiannon bent down to retrieve it, only to find herself pulled back with a sudden jerk.

'Don't touch it!'

Sir Raeden's harsh order drew everyone's attention back to the two of them.

'Why? What does it do?'

Instead of answering her question, Sir Raeden shot a burning look at Councillor Plancy and ordered sharply, 'Bring me Crumper's belongings.'

One guard hastily brought them over. Without a word, Sir Raeden reached for a small leather pouch. He undid the fastening, then swiftly tipped out the contents.

Another small metal object, identical to the one dropped by Councillor Plancy, landed at Sir Raeden's feet.

'Talismans of Sados.'

The horrified gasp came from a very pale King Nuallán. The faery stared at the objects as a mouse would a rearing cobra.

'Impossible!'

'They were all destroyed!'

The worried voices drew no response from Sir Raeden. He strode forward and tore the left sleeve from Councillor Plancy's brown robe. Laying the fabric on the ground, he carefully shifted the two talismans with one booted foot until they lay on it. Then folding the material until there was not the slightest chance that anyone could inadvertently touch one of the talismans with their bare flesh, he picked up the ominous parcel.

'Captain Makhluf, take the prisoners to the palace holding cells. Strip them of everything but their undershirt and breeches. They are to receive no visitors, and they are to be kept separate at all times.'

'Yes, Sir.'

The grey-haired captain and several of the castle guards led the disgraced Councillor Plancy and Crumper away, their journey accompanied by the loud, derisive calls of the crowd.

'What do you intend to do, Sir Raeden?' a quiet voice asked.

Sir Raeden turned around to look up at Endrille.

'I will do what needs to be done,' he answered. 'These talismans are designed to transport the holder to a specific location upon activation. Councillor Plancy planned to take the Dragon's Cup for a reason, and I mean to discover what that reason is. It is possible we may be a step closer to discovering the identity of the marked darkness.'

The last of the ancient dragons considered the man in front of her in silence for a moment. Then she nodded. 'I will only tell you to be cautious and to summon me should you need assistance. In the meantime, I will watch over your ward and ensure no further harm comes to her.'

Endrille cast her eyes over the crowd. They seemed to be recovering their earlier high spirits now the drama of mysterious revelations was finished and the culprits apprehended. 'I believe no one will notice if you slip away during the celebrations,' she commented to the knight at her side.

'Then make the announcement,' Sir Raeden said curtly, clearly impatient to be away.

Endrille bestowed a fond smile on him, then threw back her head and released a tremendous roar that set the rocks on the ground shaking.

'Show-off.'

David's comment was said with such affection that Rhiannon knew he meant it as a compliment.

Her voice carrying over the wide open space with ease, Endrille declared, 'The last time this race was won I recall mentioning that age should never be used to judge the level of courage, skill or talent a being may possess – nor the strength of their mind and heart. It is therefore my greatest pleasure to announce that Rhiannon McBride, daughter of the line of Mórell, and the youngest rider to ever qualify, is the Champion Rider and winner of today's Dragon's Cup Race.'

The crowd burst into boisterous applause.

Queen Maiwen stepped forward and carefully placed a laurel wreath on Rhiannon's braided hair.

Then King Stephen lifted up the Dragon's Cup. He came to Rhiannon's side and placed it in her hands.

She grasped the tall trophy, her arms trembling under its weight. She held it up for a brief moment, then hastily lowered it to the ground.

With a rueful smile at David's father and Endrille, she said, 'Although I agree with everything you said about age, Lady Endrille, I have to admit there is a downside to being young.' At their questioning glances, she indicated her own height and sighed, 'Being so short.'

Even Sir Raeden's mouth twitched slightly as everyone else openly laughed.

It was not long, or so it seemed to Rhiannon, before it became apparent that the ugly scene from earlier had been forgotten by the majority of the race's spectators.

King Nuallán and the other faeries disappeared, taking the Míargstan with them, and the large crowd once again became a cheerful, bustling throng. Their happy sounds carried across the grounds, giving the impression the only concern any of those present had was ensuring the evening was not spoilt by any further unpleasantness.

'THEY'VE BEEN STOLEN!'

Then again, maybe not.

Rhiannon saw Gwenneth Billsborough, the only other female rider, storming towards one of the guards through the milling crowd.

'I demand a search be undertaken at once. Someone has stolen my jewels.'

To his credit, the young soldier calmly asked her to describe the missing items.

'They're beautiful gems I found during the race,' the rider ranted. 'Diamonds, rubies, emeralds. I want them found and returned to me at once.'

'Oh, you found some too.'

Corin O'Shannessy.

Rhiannon almost laughed when he came forward and loudly complained, 'Mine went missing too.'

'Well, I never! Don't tell me some of you actually fell for that trick?' Professor Egelbert stepped out from the crowd. He shook his head and surveyed the two riders as though they were the result of a science experiment gone wrong. 'And I told the others that using leprechaun treasure would not pose a worthy challenge. How very disappointing.'

'Leprechaun treasure!'

Professor Egelbert didn't reply to the outraged exclamations of the two riders. He simply turned and walked away, his mind clearly already occupied with more interesting problems as he began to mutter calculations beneath his breath.

'No wonder they can't find them.'

Rhiannon looked at Izana who was standing with David, John and the other Robesmen beside her. 'What do you mean?'

'Leprechauns like to play games with people and their treasure is a perfect example of one of their tricks,' he said. 'They'll let you think you've found yourself a couple of precious stones, but then the gems will vanish and return to the throne room of King Brian.'

'He must've let them borrow some for the race,' said David. 'He would've thought it a great joke.'

'Well, I for one am glad I didn't fall for it,' Rhiannon said.

'Be doubly thankful you did not, for I would not have hesitated in rewarding such stupidity with a most unpleasant punishment.'

Sir Raeden's words had the small group quickly turning around to face him.

He fixed a cold stare on David and John. 'I expect the both of you to assist in watching over her in my absence,' he instructed. 'I do not anticipate being away long. However, you will ensure she begins working on those subjects which have been neglected these past few months.'

'But, Sir!' David protested, braving the icy glare in the man's blue eyes. 'You can't expect her to start studying straightaway! The school year's ended, and she's just won the race. What about the party we're planning?'

Sir Raeden raised one eyebrow. 'If she has made sufficient progress with her studies, she may have an evening off. If not, I'm sure there will be room on the dining table for her books.'

Then he turned his attention to Rhiannon. He looked at her silently for a short moment, an inscrutable expression flickering across his eyes before it vanished.

'Do not let your victory of today give you delusions of your abilities,' he warned. 'Overconfidence has led to more than one idiot taking unnecessary risks and paying heavily for their mistake.'

On that grim note he left them, his dark cloak swirling majestically behind him as he descended the steps and entered the crowd.

Rhiannon watched his tall form move away and admitted to herself she was sorry to see him leave. For all his coldness and harsh manner, her guardian's presence was something she had come to rely upon. Plus, he did have his nicer moments.

'What a curmudgeon! He really knows how to kill the mood,' David muttered.

'Maybe he just needs a hug,' John suggested. As David shot him a disbelieving look, he grinned, and added, 'From a wild bear.'

'I don't think that would work,' David said after a slight pause, 'it might actually scare the bear.'

'He's not that terrible,' Rhiannon said, 'in fact, compared to some people I've known he's positively sweet.'

This, of course, sent David, John and Eamon into paroxysms of laughter. Izana and Gareth smiled, while Derrick stood in stoic silence.

A small smile crossed Rhiannon's face as she watched them. She could not help thinking back to her last day at Brakenhurst High School when she had desperately wanted to be part of one of the merry groups of students. It had taken being transported to another world, being almost killed (numerous times if you counted the golems) and poisoned, but she had received her wish.

She looked again to where Sir Raeden had left. Even though he might bring back news of something horrible brewing, she would not want to be anywhere other than where she was. She finally had people, and numerous other creatures, who genuinely cared about her. She had also, heartbreaking though it was, discovered the reason for her parents' disappearance. Moreover, she had discovered that her abilities were truly not a freakish abnormality but signs that she was a mage.

'Come on, Rhiannon! Stop thinking about Wyvern's orders and relax for a while. The books will still be there in the morning.'

Rhiannon turned back to David with a smile and found she did not even mind the prospect of having to study over the holidays.

After all, what was a little study compared to feeling the happiest she had ever been.

DEAR READER

I'm absolutely thrilled to finally get *Rhiannon McBride and the Dragon's Cup* into your hands. It's been a long time from when I was first inspired to write the story, but thanks to the support and encouragement of many wonderful people, I have at last achieved one of my dearest dreams: to have a book published.

I do hope you enjoyed reading this story, the first instalment in a fantasy trilogy. The adventures of Rhiannon and David will continue in the next book *Rhiannon McBride and the Dragon's Eye*. Magic, danger and mystery will abound, along with a touch of romance. I'm aiming to have it ready for publication in 2023.

If you liked *Rhiannon McBride and the Dragon's Cup,* I would love to hear from you. You can contact me via my website at sarahmmturner.com or via social media. If you would like to be among the first to know the release date for the next book, please also join my Reader's List using the link on my website.

Thank you for taking the time to share in this journey to the magical land of Álnair with me by reading *Rhiannon McBride and the Dragon's Cup!*

My sincerest regards,

ACKNOWLEDGEMENTS

I will always be grateful to God for giving me such an awesome family.

To my dearest mother, June,

you have always encouraged me in all my writing endeavours by patiently reading all my stories and offering advice where it was needed. You're the best mother in the world!

To my late father, George,

you gave me a wondrous gift when you praised each story I wrote in school and taught me that language is a very powerful tool.

To my dear brothers, Luke, Gerard, John Paul and Peter, and my brother-in-law, Matthew,

you prove to me every day that there are still gentlemen in the world, and I appreciate all the support and assistance you have given to me.

To my wise and beloved sister, Mary,

your imagination and priceless knowledge of fantasy came to my aid on more than one occasion. No words can express how much I value your help, love and support.

To my treasured sister, Judith,

you urged me to keep writing, and always reminded me that I

had a gift to be shared. I will always be grateful for your love and encouragement.

To my late grandmother, Monica,

you always urged me to do my best and use my talents wisely. Although you didn't live to see this book completed, I like to think you would have enjoyed it.

And to those two distinguished writers, J.R.R. Tolkien and C.S. Lewis, who inspired in me as a child a deep love of fantasy and beautiful stories, I say thank you, and may your stories continue to entertain generations of children for centuries to come.